BONES
OF THE
BELLATORS

A.M. KAY

BOOK ONE OF THE NYXTERIA

Created with Vellum

To Michael, my happy ending.

*To anyone searching for the light in the
dark and scarred places of themselves.
I'm with you. You are not alone.*

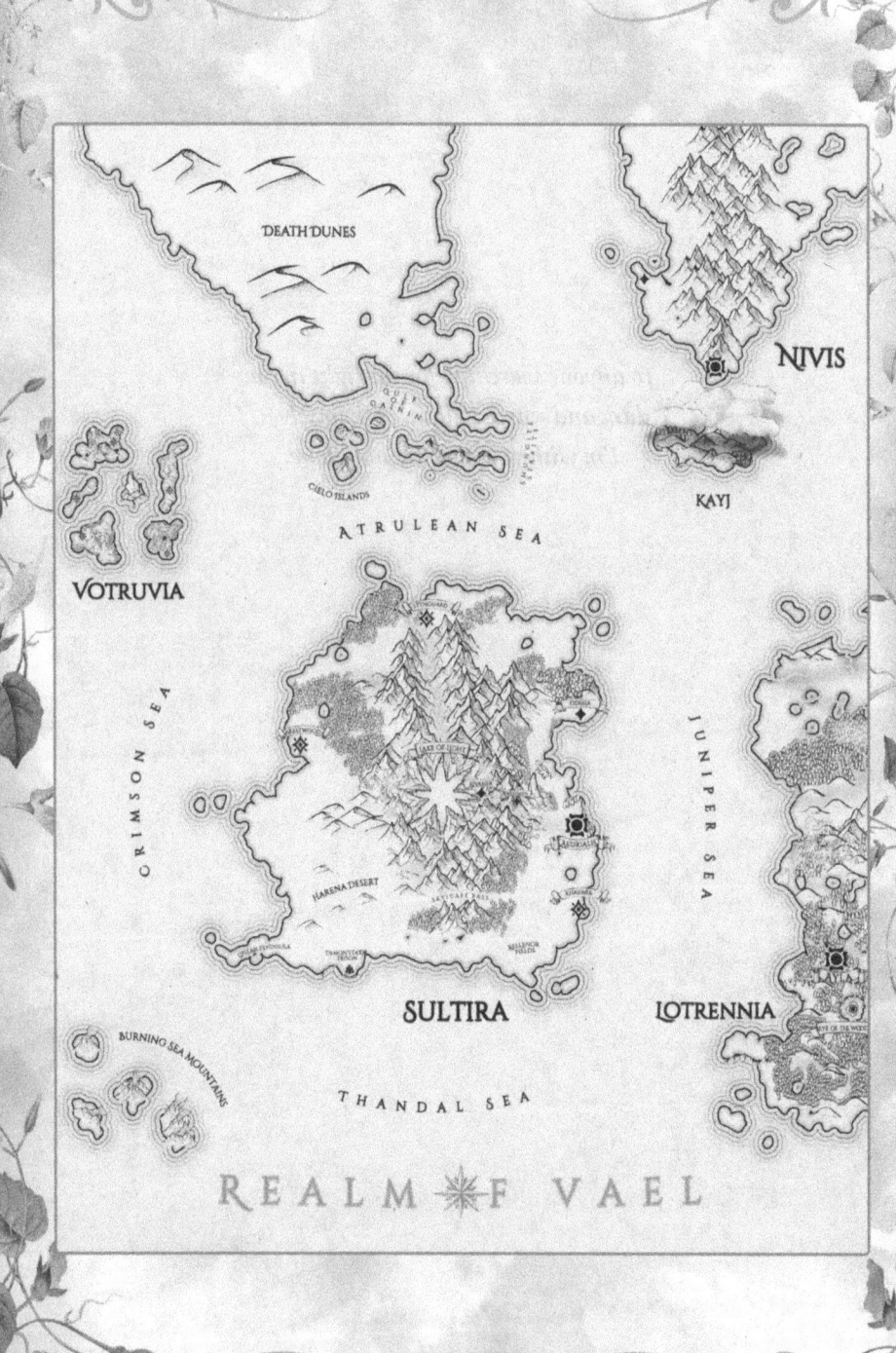

DEATH DUNES

NIVIS

CIELO ISLANDS

KAYJ

ATRULEAN SEA

VOTRUVIA

LAKE OF LIGHT

JUNIPER SEA

HARSNA DESERT

SULTIRA

LOTRENNIA

BURNING SEA MOUNTAINS

THANDAL SEA

REALM ✦ F VAEL

SULTIRA

SULTIRAN CALENDAR

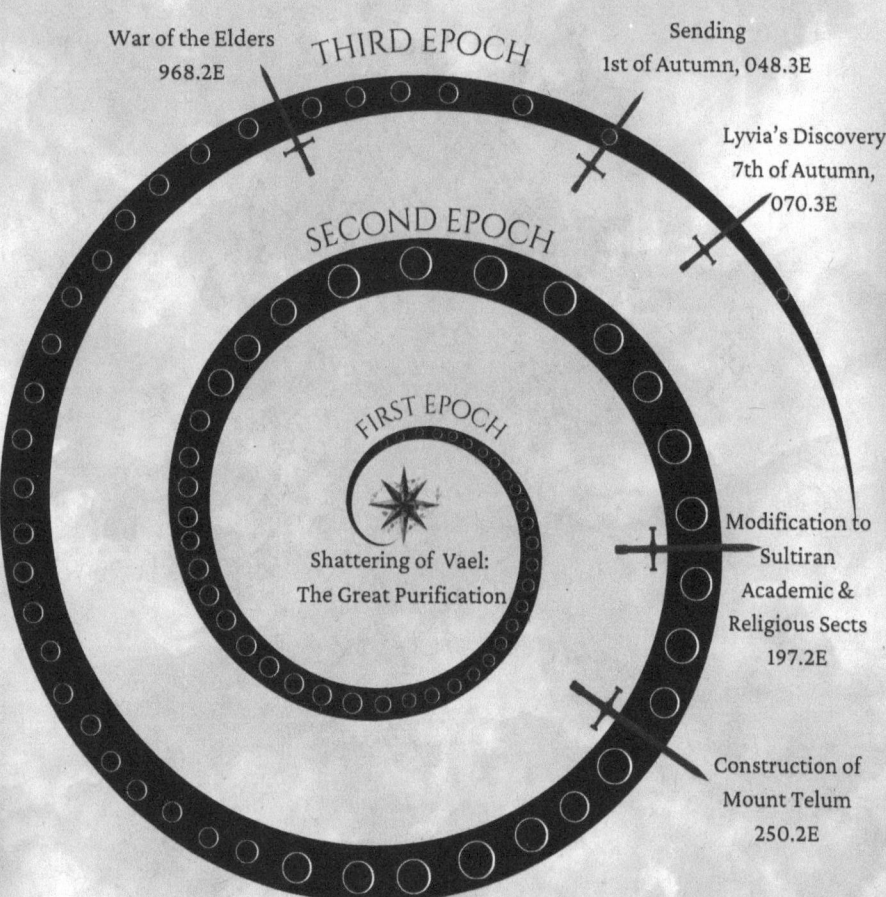

War of the Elders
968.2E

THIRD EPOCH

Sending
1st of Autumn, 048.3E

Lyvia's Discovery
7th of Autumn,
070.3E

SECOND EPOCH

FIRST EPOCH

Shattering of Vael:
The Great Purification

Modification to
Sultiran
Academic &
Religious Sects
197.2E

Construction of
Mount Telum
250.2E

Occurrences of the Twin Eclipse, otherwise known as the Sending, monitored and documented by the Sky Scholar order and marked by the following symbol:

PRONUNCIATION GUIDE

People:

Aeriden: AIR-rih-den
Antares: ant-AIR-eez
Astraeus: as-TRAY-us
Belgar: BELL-gar
Bayne: bane
Calvus: KAL-vuss
Cantor: CAN-tore
Daimos: DAY-mose
Drystan: DRISS-ten
Eira: EYE-rah
Enya: EN-yah
Evony: EH-vunn-ee
Ezrich: EHZ-rick
Galena: gah-LEE-nah
Helmar: HELL-mar
Isla: EYE-lah
Lida: LEE-dah
Lyvia: LIV-ee-yah
Marian: MAR-ee-en
Morwyn: MORE-win
Nerissa: nerr-ISS-ah
Olienna: oh-lee-ENN-ah
Oslo: OZ-low
Pavel: pah-VELL
Ravindra: rah-VIN-druh
Ronan: ROE-nan
Saros: SAHR-ohss
Selvina: sell-VEE-nah
Vander: VAN-der
Vienah: vee-EHN-uh
Vulcan: VULL-can
Willem: WILL-ehm

Animals:

Anchor: ANG-kerr
Aquila: ah-KEY-lah
Tiberius: tie-BEER-ee-uss

Creatures:

Agrippa: ah-GRIH-pah
Ashen: ASH-enn
Caeluma: kie-LOO-mah
Kryax: CRY-axe
Tauruk: tore-OOK

Places:

Aedrialis: ay-dree-AL-iss
Atrulean: ah-TRU-lee-en
Juniper: JOO-ni-per
Kayj: cage
Nivis: NEE-viss
Vael: vail
Votruvia: voe-TRU-vee-ah
Westwyn: WEST-winn
Odessa: oh-DESS-ah
Rivaner: RIV-ann-er
Stynguard: STIN-gard
Sultira: sull-TEER-ah
Telum: tell-OOM
Thandal: THAN-dahl

Deities:

Aelius: AY-lee-us
Ganmira: gan-MEER-ah
Renova: renn-OH-vah
Tynan: TIE-nan

Other:

Bonscaíh: bone-SKY
Driadalis: dree-ah-DA-liss
Evecta: ee-VECK-tah
Marisarma: mah-ree-SARM-ah
Hydra: HY-drah
Impetum: im-PEE-tuhm
Itherian: ith-EER-ee-ann
Lumerian: loom-AIR-ee-ann
Nyxteria: nicks-TAIR-ee-uh
Ridecus: RID-eh-kuss
Sobraena: so-BRAY-nah
Paedor: pay-DOR

A NOTE TO READERS:

Bones of the Bellators is an adult, high fantasy novel intended for mature readers and includes explicit content and certain dark elements that could be triggering for some readers. For a list of content warnings, please turn to the last page of this book.

CHAPTER ONE

The weapon rests above the cage, dormant until the return of
the Hidden Hero's enemy.
— Unmarked Scroll. Private Library, Mount Telum.
Aedrialis.

I *am not afraid of the dark.*

    The words were a chant, a repetitive prayer in my mind as I took steadying breaths of stale, dust-laden air. My heart thumped savagely in my chest as I did my best to survey our surroundings.

    I blinked twice in an attempt to clear the stars that blossomed in my vision upon our fall but was met with darkness. Pitch-black nothing. Rough, undisturbed rock scraped against my palm as I slid my hand over the wall, fingers tracing the lines of ancient, carved script.

    "We should have waited."

    Drystan's fingers trembled as he signed the letters of the

words into my other hand, the two of us now trapped in the dank, cool space we'd fallen into. He was right, of course. But as it often did, curiosity had gotten the best of me when my eyes had snagged on the strange stone archway hewn into the side of the mountain. I would have missed it entirely had it not been for the once-in-a-lifetime storm that blew through the Kingdom of Sultira the week prior, stripping this little section of the Lumerian foothills bare.

Hum, hum, hum.

There it was again.

More of a feeling than a sound. The other reason I'd lead us to this place at the edge of the mountains. I'd always had a knack for finding the excavation sites for the Death Scholars, these ancient places where the ground shifted beneath the rocks and grasses as if singing aged melodies and whispering tales of their hidden past. But this was different. I'd insisted on climbing up to get a better look at the ruins, dragging Drystan through the brush. We'd knelt next to the arch when the ground beneath us gave way, trapping us inside this chamber.

"Lyvia, can you hear me?"

My father's words were frantic and muffled beyond the rock.

"Yes!" I called back, a shaky edge to my voice.

"I'm going for help! Don't move!" he responded. The thunder of his agrippa's hooves vibrated against the stone walls of where we stood, softening into nothing as my father, the kingdom's horse lord, rode back to the capital city of Aedrialis on his massive black war stallion.

"He's going for help," I signed back into Drystan's hand, the words taking painstakingly long to spell, each letter a different symbol.

"Two hours at least," Drystan replied, the tremors in his thin hands growing.

I gripped and steadied them, before signing for the both of us, "We are not afraid of the dark. Nor death. We will get out."

The whoosh of his shuddering sigh blew into my face, and I pulled his hand against the wall, feeling along the snaking carved lines. He released my grip, understanding my meaning. Words lined the wall. Old, but perhaps written in the common tongue. And we were trained to examine ancient things, particularly dead ones.

My friend and fellow Death Scholar apprentice stayed close, his hip against mine as we shuffled blindly down the stone, fingers sliding up and down the wall, working out the letters. I stopped, the script seeming to end, my stomach knotting in a strange mixture of apprehension and anticipation as I processed the words written on the wall.

"*Death Lies Below*," Drys recited them into my hand.

"Fitting," I replied. Though I couldn't see his expression in the blackness of the chamber, amusement bubbled up at the scowl I knew was plastered on his face.

Cool rock met my knee as I knelt. My hands slid along the floor, a smoother, more worked rock than the walls of the chamber. I hissed as I hit something sharp at its edge, pulling my hand back and wrapping it in the sleeve of my sheepskin coat to stanch the blood. Drystan gripped my arm as a section of the floor slowly sank away.

I blindly inched closer to the opening until my booted foot slid over the edge and hit a step. Then another. Drystan's throat made a protesting sound I pretended not to hear as I tugged him down behind me.

A whisper of air reached us as we arrived at the bottom, our steps echoing into black nothingness.

I am not afraid of the dark, I repeated in my head. But damn, would it be nice to have a torch.

Drys grabbed my arm and placed my hand against a large

3

piece of stone jutting out of the wall. He grunted as he tried to pull. A lever?

I reached up and gripped the top with him, heaving, until a grinding, rock on rock groan sounded high above us, and we toppled over each other. Light flooded the chamber. My hand flew to my face, and I blinked my eyes against the blinding glare. They needed a moment to adjust, and I needed a moment to process what lay before us.

High above the massive cavern, a small window opened to the sky. Early autumn sunshine blazed through the little window, hitting the first mirror with its rays. Rows and rows of hanging mirrors lined the edges of the cavern, illuminating the massive space as light bounced between them. The design was so genius, even the midnight light of our two moons would have been enough to brighten the entire space.

An elaborately carved stone mound sat in the center, at least thirty feet in diameter. Two lines of stars cut across it at a diagonal. Depictions of our moons, Ganmira and Renova, arched across the top in transition. Aelius, our sun, sat opposite a strange swirl. Delicate, flowering vines were carved around its edge, snowflakes etched between the leaves.

In its center, a large glittering stalagmite reached high into the air nearly connecting to an identical stalactite hanging down from a sloped section of the ceiling. Between the two, hung an object.

Hum, hum, hum.

Drystan's hurried steps followed as I approached the stone mound. His hand gripped the back of my coat, pulling me back.

"We should wait for Father Marcus and the others," he signed.

The rapid movements of his hand were a relief to both of us now that we had enough light to use them again.

I gritted my teeth knowing he was right. Father Marcus

wouldn't be happy. A pang of guilt twisted in my gut. He'd become more of a grandfather to the two of us than simply our master scholar.

"We have hours in here," I signed back. "You said so yourself. We might as well see what's here."

The light off the mirrors caught on his crystal blue, almond-shaped eyes as they narrowed at me. They were eerily similar to our two moons. *Blessed with blue, your heart is true*, as they said. Blue eyes were lucky, and their bearers were deemed smarter, more loyal, more trustworthy. Given his brilliance and the hue of his irises, I'd no doubt Drys would end up at Stynguard University by the end of the year. Me, on the other hand...

As a lady-in-waiting, I'd be forced to make the Match by twenty-five, my years of freedom now dwindling to three. My father had indulged my scholarly love for the past four years, using his sway with King Saros to allow me to study and attend the historical excavations with the Death Scholars.

Bones are our final storytellers, they would say. How someone lived... How they died... Who they were... Always revealing more than I expected, more than I was ready for.

Of course, I knew I would never wear their black robes. Most formal education for girls ended at age fourteen, in time for their years of "societal preparation." The sole exception was for the women who joined the Life Scholars to become midwives.

But at age eleven, I unexpectedly found myself holding the hand of our lady's maid as she brought her child into the world. I was somewhere between girl and woman myself in that moment, as if I were stuck between a trot and a canter, unsure what was supposed to happen next. Had my mother been living, she might have told me.

I'd looked at my father as the lady's maid cried out and

panic began to take root, but he'd turned his back as he left the room, leaving the women to their work. The contents of my lunch ended up on the floor, pooling with the dark blood and other fluids that poured out of her before the heart-starting cry of a newborn babe pierced the air. I knew then I hadn't the stomach for midwifery, as beautiful as bringing life into the world was.

No, I'd always been drawn to death.

I shook my head, clearing my thoughts and the impending dread that always accompanied the anticipation of my future. I turned back and climbed the mound, walking up its sloped center to get a better look at what sat between the two rock formations.

The humming quieted as I approached, and I sucked in a quick breath, marveling at the object slowly rotating between the rock formations. Drystan's shadow darkened the object for a moment as he approached, craning his neck and pinching his black brows as he examined the floating gray, diamond-shaped rock.

Floating.

The word rolled over my mind as I leaned closer, noting the tips of the stone didn't quite touch the stalactite and stalagmite. Instead, a steady stream of air flowed down from the stalactite and up from the stalagmite at the exact force and the perfect angle to keep it suspended in mid-air.

Drys pulled his spectacles from his coat and leaned in closer. I stood, arms crossed, and began to circle the formations, marveling at the impossibility of it all.

I reached a hand forward, the compulsion to pull the stone diamond from the formations strong and illogical. Drystan's copper hand gripped my arm as my fingers clasped around the diamond stone. He shot me a look. I tugged anyway, but the stone didn't budge, somehow locked into place in a cage of air that floated over my olive skin. Drys blew out the breath he'd been holding as I pulled my arm out of his grasp, scowling at him. I reached again with both hands.

The instant they touched the stone, air stole through the room like a tide. Black strands of hair ripped through my braid and flickered over my vision as I pulled the object free.

"*Lyvia*," Drystan warned, his hand movements as stern as any tone of voice. I pointedly ignored him and walked back to the entrance of the chamber where I slunk against the wall.

I tucked my feet beneath my knees as I sat, ever grateful for the riding leggings I donned in place of the traditional travel dress of Sultiran court as I examined the eight sides of the diamond.

An octahedron, I realized.

The eight triangular panes of the stone were further broken into nine smaller triangles, each one etched with an elaborate design.

"These look like fragments of bones," I signed to Drystan, setting it momentarily in my lap.

He sat across from me and adjusted his spectacles. "A mandible here." He pointed to two small squares that appeared as if they should somehow connect.

"And canines, perhaps?" I responded.

I twisted the top half of the stone, the slide of rock on rock surprisingly smooth. I twisted again, this time moving the side of the diamond. My lips tugged up in genuine delight and surprise as I realized what I was holding.

"It's a puzzle."

———⟡———

AN HOUR LATER, six of the eight faces of the octahedron had been rearranged, three of them depicting skulls of various animals. Some type of canine, a peculiar, horned predator and bird of prey made up three of the faces. The other three seemed to be a collection of connecting stars, constellations depicting what appeared to be the same creatures. But as I got closer and closer to completing the last two sides, I undoubtedly reversed the work I'd done on the others, the body parts refusing to align in a way that made sense. I heaved a sigh, frustrated with the damn thing before setting it down.

Drystan continued his anxious trek around the mound at the center of the cavern. I made to join him, and he shot me a look.

"What was that for?"

"You always do this."

"What are you talking about?"

"This!" Drystan signed the word in a jerky movement before throwing his arms out to the sides, gesturing to the cavern we remained trapped inside.

"I have never done *this*," I snapped back at him.

"You never *wait*. You must be the first for everything. Every lecture, every discovery. You think you know best, and you don't. We are not safe here."

The copper of Drystan's face had lightened by several shades as the minutes wore on. I swallowed the guilt that crept up.

"Drystan, we will get out of here. My father will—"

"You don't know that. People disappear in these mountains all the time. I know you've heard the tales."

My eyes rolled as I shook my head.

"The Stone Witch, Drystan? Really? Fairytales like that have no place in the minds of scholars. The fabled witch is north of the river anyways. We are south."

"And the disappearances?" he countered, raising his brows.

"Rumors," I replied, shrugging my shoulders despite the

unease his words brought. People *were* disappearing in the kingdom. New bulletins appeared on the street corners of Aedrialis each week, pleas for help in finding missing persons. And though plagues or pirates seemed to be the most reasonable explanations, the disappearances sowed distrust.

My answer did nothing to quell the anger and fear that radiated off Drystan as he held me in his gaze.

"I'm *sorry*," I continued, "I just..."

"You *just* feel you're entitled to this because you found it. Because you're *Lady Lyvia Cantor*."

The words stung, slicing through my chest like the sharp edge of a scroll.

"I'm entitled to *none* of this, asshole," I seethed back at him. "When you are donning your black robes and walking the famed halls of the Stynguard library, I will be bedding a lord of the king's choosing."

Emotions slammed through me at the regret, the pity that now shown through Drystan's eyes. They glimmered in the dimming light, and he moved to reach for me. I backpedaled to avoid him when the back of my knees knocked against the edge of the mound at the center of the cavern. I tripped, my hand moving to its edge to catch my fall.

It slammed onto a blooming flower, breaking open the cut on my palm. The flower sank into the rock as a deep grating sounded from the center. Drystan paused mid-stride, eyes snapping to the stone mound as eight massive triangular sections of stone lifted away from the top of the mound.

The tips arched slowly through the air. They teetered upright for a moment, pointing to the cavern ceiling like giant arrowheads. A whining creak sounded, and I screamed for Drystan as the stone tipped and came crashing toward us.

CHAPTER TWO

And in the wake of the horrific acts of mortals, the gods saw fit to wipe the realm of Vael clean of unworthy kingdoms, striking the final blow that shattered the lands in the last war.

—From A Historic Recounting of the Great Purification, Chapter 56. Temple of the Sky, Aedrialis.

B reath sucked from my lungs as I slammed into Drystan and we crashed to the floor of the cavern, rolling out of the stone's path. The stone had slowed on its descent, landing with a soft puff of air an inch above the ground. Drystan coughed into the dust that had been kicked up and we staggered to our feet at the back of the chamber.

Silence filled the space, dust shimmering in the light as it floated and settled. My heart thumped wildly as my eyes registered what lay before us.

The carved mound had opened like a blooming flower, the

eight triangular sections splaying around a large circular stone like rays of an enormous sun. And inside the lidless mound...

The bones were bright, glowing in the refracted sunlight like misshapen stars in the night. The dry, stale air that accompanied old bones mingled with some metallic scent. Two bodies lay carefully positioned in the tomb.

I slid between two sections of the stone lid that had lifted away and approached the massive sarcophagus. Snowflakes and delicate flowering vines adorned the elaborate hilt of a blade which lay positioned in the hands of a human skeleton, whose body was arced to follow the shape of the tomb.

The second body, a massive dead horse that lay beside it, only made the discovery more perplexing. His size was like no living horse, not even those of the agrippa. Hooves the size of dinner plates rose above its head as if he were positioned to defend even in death. There was something beautiful about how they lay there together. A team who lived and died together. I smiled, my mind drifting to my own horse likely still waiting outside, untied. Tiberius was *my* agrippa. A young stallion I'd raised since birth and more weapon than mount.

Drystan approached, pulling free his journal as he blew out a breath. He nodded his head as he surveyed the bodies and various chests that lay carefully positioned throughout the tomb as if answering some unspoken question of his own.

"This might be enough," he signed, a resigned smile tugging on his lips.

"Enough for what?"

"To change your fate. To get you into Stynguard and out of the Match," he replied, eyes softening as they met mine.

Everything stilled.

I stared at him, wide eyed, not daring to believe it might be possible. Was this what I'd been searching for all along? Some way to cheat the system, to become so indispensable to the order that they'd have to keep me. Why I'd ridden and searched for these sites so arduously.

Drys's smile widened into a grin.

"Let's get to work."

MY FINGERNAILS BLACKENED as I brushed and scraped away the grime from the ancient humerus. I rubbed my thumb against the smooth bone, a creeping sense of excitement sending birds flapping in my gut. This body was strange, *wrong*, in some ways.

The inconsistent aging markers made it impossible to conclude age at the time of death.

Drystan scribbled in his journal before adjusting one of the mirrors to get better lighting. The sun had begun to set, the light streaming into the cavern now casting an orange hue.

"Look at the depth of the muscle footprints," he signed, motioning me to his side.

The origins of where the muscle attached to bone were extreme. The markings were *crevasses*, boring into the bone at severe angles and depths.

"Could this have been caused by trauma?" he continued.

I shook my head, blowing the dusty sediment away with my breath. "I don't think so," I replied. "I think these abnormalities suggest extreme strength. Though I've never seen anything like this. Even in the records kept from the Great Purification."

Drystan nodded as he continued his notes and sketches. Skeletal injuries peppered the remains, and I relayed a few plausible causes of death to Drystan. Spinal injury or internal bleeding were the most likely based on the trauma to the vertebrae and third and fourth ribs.

My mind spun as I worked my way down the body. I cleared away some grime off the pelvis, signing my measurements to Drys when my breath caught. These angles were all wrong. Narrow and heart-shaped, that's what I should have been seeing. My fingers slid over the inside of the broad, open pelvis.

"Female," I signed with certainty.

Drystan blinked at me before dropping his notebook and kneeling carefully next to the woman.

"A mother," I noted, eyeing the childbearing evidence which was at complete odds with the lack of wear and tear we should have been seeing on a woman of childbearing age. None of it made any sense, but the thrill of the discovery sent my heart hammering.

"And a warrior," Drystan noted, again eyeing the intricate blade in the woman's hand. "There are more weapons in the chest near the horse. And scrolls in the second. Come see."

Drystan carefully unfurled a scroll. My fingers slid over its edge which was soft like leather and caramel in color. Not far from the hue of my eyes, the one trait I'd gotten from my mother, whom I'd lost as a child. The familiar, lilting tune of a night-blooming flower filled my mind's ear, as it often did when I thought of her.

I studied the withering images and text, noting the similarity to the markings on the blade and those on the walls and arches of the tomb. Black ink dotted what I assumed was the coastline of our lands, Sultira. But the rivers were all wrong, and there were mountain ranges in the wrong places and missing lakes. Not to mention the other continents and islands I didn't recognize.

"There are extra bones on the horse," he continued, motioning to the massive body behind us. I adjusted my seat and pulled my attention back to the bones.

Indeed, a second long humerus swept behind the horse's back, connecting to what looked like a radius behind his neck.

"These look aerial," I noted.

"Wings from a large bird," Drystan mused. "A ceremonial offering, perhaps?"

I leaned forward, pulling my hand from the second radius to the enormous skull when realization hit me. I whipped my hand back before scurrying across the sarcophagus and hopping over its edge.

A loud *thunk* sounded from high above as I reached the edge of the chamber. Muffled shouting followed. My father had returned.

I scooped up the octahedron, rotating the puzzle in my hands for what had to have been the hundredth time in the past two hours. I twisted its edges, the tiny triangles rearranging as I did so, certain I knew what lay on at least one of the last faces of the diamond.

Hum, hum, hum.

The feeling returned, this time accompanied by something like anticipation, encouragement, even.

A small blast echoed from the top of the stairs as bits of rock came trickling down. I twisted the final piece into place, the top of the horse skull lining up with the bottom, as the strange constellation beneath it fell perfectly into place.

A blooming sense of satisfaction spread within my chest as I stared at the solved puzzle resting atop my palm. Drystan paused on his way to the stairwell, turning to me as a sudden breeze wafted through the chamber.

My hair once again flitted across my vision. Muffled shouting continued from above followed by pounding rock. My name was being called, but the wind had vanished.

I stared, unblinking, as the diamond-shaped stone atop my palm began to open. The four faces with skulls lifted away

14

from the tip of the diamond in the same manner as the top of the sarcophagus.

Hum, hum, hum.

The air stilled further. I barely registered the flurry of movement to my left as my eyes landed on the onyx stone sitting at its center. Blacker than night and the deepest sea, the stone seemed to *look back* at me, as if it were the eye of death itself. The stone devoured the light in the chamber, the afternoon sunshine vanishing as it bounced off the mirrors above. The soft *hum* returned, and my lips slowly parted.

"*Lyvia.*" My father's voice had hardened, drawing my attention away. He stood between Drystan and Father Marcus, all of their eyes pinned on the black stone.

"Do not touch anything," Father Marcus murmured as he moved slowly toward my side. I had the inexplicable urge to pull away as his gloved hands reached for the puzzle.

Hum, hum, hum, the stone called. *Come back.*

I opened my mouth to protest when my father's hand gripped my shoulder.

"This is not what I meant when I said, '*Don't move.*'" He cast a wary gaze over the tomb, eyes flashing to Father Marcus's back.

"This is the discovery of a lifetime," I countered, my voice hoarse after hours of disuse.

He returned his gaze to me, eyes softening a bit. "Indeed, Badger."

Warmth bloomed in my chest. *Badger*, my nickname since I was a child. I had always been digging, searching for secrets hiding in the ground, my father often accompanying me on my rides.

His tan hand rested atop the elaborate horse-head hilt of his blade. His deep blue eyes narrowed as he approached the sarcophagus and murmured something to Father Marcus.

The old priest paled, eyes slicing to me. He winced as he straightened and glanced between Drystan and me. He was a good man. I didn't often say that of the scholars at the temple, but he showed me kindness and shared his knowledge without hesitation. I was simply a student in his eyes.

"We need to return to Aedrialis," my father murmured. "I need to speak with Lord Pavel."

"Go. Do not mention this to anyone." Father Marcus nodded, turning to me and signing the words to Drystan. "I'll stay to conduct my own examination. We'll meet in my scholar room first thing tomorrow morning."

My chin dipped in a resigned nod, the warning leaving a twisting feeling in my gut as I climbed the stairs and exited the vast chamber of death.

I BARELY REGISTERED PASSING through the city gates at sundown. Tiberius's inky coat warmed my thighs, my agrippa stallion's rolling gait lulling me into a trance. My mind skipped between undisputed, scientific evidence and the fairytales my father recited to me and my brother as children. The discoveries of today were too mysterious, too illogical. The stuff of myth and legend warred with the scholarly logic woven into my brain.

The acres of sprawling pastures that were home to our agrippa herd butted up to the city walls. The Cantor House had trained the agrippa war horses for centuries, providing the kingdom with one of their greatest weapons.

I gently pulled Ti's bridle off his face, running my fingers along the braided leather and fortissa chain, careful not to wrap the smooth silver around my wrist. While it appeared delicate, it was the strongest and most expensive metal known to our world.

I led Ti to his pasture for a well-deserved rest before returning to the stables. I took a deep inhale, the scent of leather and cedar as calming as any tonic. I made my way to the corral to work one of the many colts still in training. My lips tugged upward at the sound of his nicker, and I led him to the pen where we began a series of commands on the ground before I hopped on his back. We trained the agrippa to respond to the slightest touch of our bodies, the twist of a hip, the slide of a leg.

We raced up and down the field, sliding and stopping, pivoting and passing. My leggings became sticky as they rubbed against his side, the dirt and sweat creating a mucky mixture on his neck and belly.

Twin moons rose in the sky, casting a blue hue over the city walls when the baying of our hounds reached my ears. I followed their howls, trotting the colt over to the side of the manor as shouts erupted in the night.

Steel on steel crashed as men in black armor and white cloaks slashed at our guards. Silver embroidery caught my eye, the outline of a brilliant sun and two interlocking crescent moons. The king's men. Not only part of the royal guard, but the *king's* guard.

A sword flew through the air, the kingsguard landing a lethal blow as the other went down with a dagger in his thigh. Our remaining guard's hesitation gave the attacker enough time to slice through his abdomen and a sickening scream filled the night.

My shock came out in a small yelp and the kingsguard turned to me. An unnatural, silvery light flashed across his eyes as he took me in. My stomach dropped as he focused a predatory gaze on me. I twisted my hips, launching the fatigued colt into a gallop away from the manor.

My pursuers wasted no time as they mounted their own

war horses. We flew through the torchlit, narrow streets of the capital, dodging parked carriages along the way. I slammed my heels and hips forward, slowing the horse enough to skid into a side alley. Three of the four remaining kingsguards flew past the small opening, catching my move too late and missing the turn. The last slammed to a stop, the tight corner costing him momentum and speed.

Panic fueled my flight, and though I had no idea where I was going, I pushed the poor colt, my heels digging harshly into his sides. I was cut off at an intersecting alley by a kingsguard and my agrippa's hooves shot into the air. He was so young, not trained for battle or real pursuit like Tiberius was. Seizing his opportunity, the kingsguard's longsword swept out and sliced through the horse's chest. His whinnying scream ripped through the night, and I flew off his back as he crashed down onto the cobblestones.

A sob choked up my throat as I scrambled up and fled down the adjacent alley. My face smacked the side of a stone building as I was tackled to the ground, the crush of my attacker like a boulder flattening a flower. A gush of warm liquid filled my mouth and leaked from my nose. The weight of the kingsguard knocked the breath from me, and as I scrambled to turn around, the hilt of his sword slammed into the side of my head.

Pain and darkness.

MY PULSE DRUMMED behind my eyelids, an ache growing with each beat. I swallowed against my fear, the mixture of blood and saliva doing nothing to quell the growing nausea. The cell reeked with an iron tang. The damp staleness of mildew hung in the air, mingling with whatever rancid liquid wept from the ceiling, each drip a sinister countdown to my fate. It collected in the small bucket in the corner I assumed to be my new toilet, though I could hardly see the corner of the small space, the single, dimming torch at the end of the hall the only source of light. The air down here was so dank I could *taste* the smell with every breath.

Flashes of unconscious memory danced across my mind. A towering white castle. A darkened, domed ceiling. I'd been here before. Though the hall I'd been dragged through was a stark contrast to the one that housed the Sun Dance, the solstice ball, only a few months ago. Empty fireplaces. Stairs. And then a dungeon.

I'd been taken to Mount Telum.

My eyes pinched shut as I tried to replay the events of the prior day. The cave. The bodies. The scrolls. The stone. How much time had passed? My mind raced as the pounding in my head matched the beat of my fist against the iron bars that separated me from my freedom. From my privileged, unappreciated life.

My breaths shot too quickly from my lungs and my head started to spin, to feel lighter. Darkness crept into my vision as the edge of consciousness neared.

I shut my eyes, blowing out a hard tunnel of breath as I forced the words into my mind.

I am not afraid of the dark.

My pulse evened out and my breaths slowly returned to a normal pace. The *plop, plop, plop* of that rancid liquid dripping in the corner bucket suddenly ceased as the deafening boom of drums sounded above.

CHAPTER THREE

Four in the great pantheon of gods deigned to remain after the Great Purification. The Father and Mother long since perished, only the eldest and youngest Brothers, along with their twin Sisters, cared for the salvation of mortals.
— From A Historic Recounting of the Great Purification, Chapter 78, Aedrialis.

The deep steady beat sent chills down my spine as blaring horns joined the chorus. Aedrialis was under attack. Shock was quickly snuffed out by intense fear. The capital hadn't been attacked in over a century. Despite the distance, I could hear guards on the floors above my cell shouting and the clash of steel. A thud sounded near the top of the stairs. I squinted in the dark cell, looking for anything to grab as a weapon or somewhere to conceal myself, coming to the devastating conclusion that there was nowhere to hide.

The hairs on the back of my neck rose like the hackles of a

hound as two hooded figures sprinted noiselessly down the hall, glancing in each cell until the tall one spotted me. I backpedaled, the cold, wet stone of my cell halting my retreat. My heart leaped into my throat when he made eye contact. Hazel eyes above a black mask stared out from under the dark hood.

He pulled a set of keys from his blood-stained cloak and promptly swung the door open. I was a rabbit cornered by a wolf. A stab of envy twisted in my gut as my mind drifted to the female warrior.

The man in the back stepped forward.

"It would be in your best interest, Lady, to come with us." His voice was low and soft. Western Sultiran, if I had to guess.

My lips clamped shut.

"Grab her and let's go. We're wasting seconds and we only have minutes," the other said.

I whipped my head to him and stared back at the hazel eyes. Definitely *not* Sultiran, with that lilting accent.

The three of us spun around as a third hooded figure flew down the hall with unnatural speed.

"He knows what we're after. We leave now. Take her."

The command in the thickly accented female voice indicated their leader had joined us. The tall one launched himself at me and I threw my fist up, instinct taking over. He dodged to the side as irritation growled out of him and he flung me over his shoulder. My fists pounded on his back, and I briefly looked up as I was hauled out, catching a glimpse of the neighboring cell. Bile threatened to rise as my gaze caught on the pool of dark, fresh blood.

My body jostled as we raced down the hall, deeper into the dungeon. We entered the last cell on the right and their leader knelt in the corner, surveying the stones in the wall.

"Nerissa..." the tall one warned.

"Quiet," she snapped back.

"Are you sure this is the spot?"

Nerissa straightened and leveled a deadly stare at the tall one.

"My time here has not been forgotten, *Vulcan*. I haven't forgotten what got me here," she seethed, her eyes casting daggers at him, "or what got me out."

She turned and plucked a small stone out of the wall before dislodging an entire brick. My knees buckled as he sat me down, and the other two began hacking away against the dungeon wall. Nerissa stepped toward me.

"Don't think about trying to run. You face a similar fate to your neighbor if you do. *Move*."

I glanced behind her and a small opening in the wall appeared, large enough to crawl through. The walls of Mount Telum were *inescapable*. Supposedly. With a dagger at my back, I did as she said.

We wiggled through a hard, cold tunnel that must have been dug ages ago. An escape route long since forgotten. The pitch-black tunnel was barely wide enough to bend one knee at a time to shimmy through. I felt a heaviness then, like the tunnel was closing in on me. Air rushed into my lungs, not allowing them to fully empty. My limited vision became fuzzy with that familiar feeling of dizzying panic.

"Just breathe," the Sultiran murmured from behind.

"I am not afraid of the dark," I breathed, the words forming on my lips instead of my mind as I closed my eyes against the hysteria.

"You should be," Nerissa's reply came a moment later.

I kept the growing tide of unease at bay. We continued this way for what felt like an eternity. Finally, ahead of me, Vulcan pounded through dirt and rock, a splash sounding as he dropped out of the tunnel. Soft green light gleamed in through the opening, and a rancid stench overwhelmed the small space. The air caught in my throat, and the limited contents of my stomach began to rise.

Vulcan beckoned to me as I neared the exit. I splashed headfirst into the wet slime and gagged as I landed in the sludge. We were in a small round tunnel. The sewers, I realized, trying not to think about the thickness of what we trudged through.

I followed willingly. Where would I run? I could try to swim away if this entered out into the Ripped River. But then where would I go? I needed to find my father, but had he been arrested too? I could go west to find my brother. Aeriden was only a year my senior and a soldier in the royal guard. He was stationed on the West Coast to deal with the pirate problem.

Was that who these people were? My father had money, so a ransom made sense. That was if he wasn't arrested already. *West.* I'd go west the first chance I got. I could run. And I could ride hard. I'd find a horse and figure it out once I was out of the city.

We waded for hours in an uncomfortable silence. My pruned feet were numb in my water-logged boots. The sludge thinned as a small light appeared ahead.

Nerissa whirled toward me. "Can you swim?"

I nodded, eyeing her closely. There was something lethal and strangely familiar about her. We neared the opening, and a sweet salty mist kissed my face. I inhaled deeply as the fresh sea air filled my lungs, drinking it in. The night wind was like the whisper of freedom, its breeze clearing my senses. Stars flecked the clear sky, and Renova's crescent moon rose high above her sister, casting a soft blue glow on the Juniper's waves as they raced to shore.

The Juniper Sea. Not the river. *Shit.* My stomach dropped. We'd made it to the coast outside the city gates, the entrance to

Aedrialis miles away. The rocky shoreline rose at least fifty feet high to my right and left. There was no way I'd be able to make a run for it here. There was only the sea and the tunnel of filth. My stomach turned as I realized we'd be swimming. The twin moons moved across the sky toward each other and crossed paths each night creating tidal bulges. Only the most skilled sailors could navigate the perilous waters and swimming at night was always discouraged.

I removed my sheepskin coat and tossed it onto the rocky shore, knowing its thickness would only weigh me down. We waded into the surf, the slime washing away as I dove under the water and kicked through an oncoming wave. The freeze was a welcome shock to my system. Within twenty minutes my lungs burned, my billowy shirt and heavy riding boots dragging me down further with each swell.

"Where are we going?" I rasped, spitting the words with bits of salty water. "Is there a boat? I can swim, but I don't know how—"

I stopped mid-sentence as a massive ship appeared out of nowhere.

The colossal hull and sails loomed in front of us, and a ladder clanked as it was thrown over the side. I grasped the smooth wood as I climbed, the ropes shaking as my muscles strained to pull myself up. I flopped over the side like a limp fish as I reached the top, aching everywhere.

"Welcome aboard, Lyvia Cantor," the older man said.

I threw a wary glance in his direction at the use of my name. They didn't abduct a random prisoner. Abduct? Or liberate?

A flash of white caught my eye, and I staggered back, hitting the base of the mast as I stared at a kingsguard. No, *queens*guard, designated by the deep crimson trim bordering his cape.

I gaped at Sir Ronan Merik. The ladies at court gawked at the tanned, muscled queensguard every time he entered the room, not unlike how I gawked at him now. It was rumored he was more to the queen than her protector and muscle, and after eyeing him this closely, I couldn't blame her. She was the king's fourth wife as he had outlived the three before her along with the would-be heirs they produced. Ronan's curly light brown hair bounced, and his lips turned up in a grin I'd seen him give her majesty, as he swaggered over to where I stood.

"Lady Cantor." He bowed.

I backed up a step, wary of the amusement dancing in his sapphire eyes.

"What do you want with me?" The familiar face cleared my head.

The corner of his mouth tugged up, and he raised a suggestive eyebrow. I blinked, and it was gone.

"Later," Nerissa snapped. "Bayne will be offshore by morning, so we need to move now. This was an unintended pitstop, and now that you've been discovered, Ronan, you can take off that ridiculous cape."

"Trying to disrobe me already, Nissy?" Ronan drawled, giving her a heated stare.

"Don't call me that," she seethed, cutting a glance at me.

Ronan caught the rope she tossed at him before she stalked up the deck.

Nerissa pulled her mask down revealing a nearly flawless face, save for the scar that ran through her eyebrow. Striking eyes with irises of every shade of green shone brightly in the night. Plaited brown hair draped over her shoulder.

She began barking orders at the crew, which seemed to be limited to only five people as far as I could tell. Most ships this size needed a crew of thirty or forty men. She made her way about the deck and pulled off her sopping cloak. As her hood slipped down, I spotted them. My lips parted, jaw dropping as I took in the slightly pointed ears.

I stared at her, watching her move with unnatural grace across the deck. She was tall, but there was something ethereal and deadly about her. My mind drifted to the bones I'd been carefully examining only the day before. I jumped as Ronan stepped beside me.

"They are not like us," he murmured. "*Elf* is the word they use."

My head shook as I stared in disbelief.

A throaty chuckle escaped Ronan's lips. "Believe what you will. But I don't think she's the first one you've seen, is she?" he asked, his voice a quiet murmur. Feeling his stare in the dark, I pulled my eyes from her and sucked in a quick breath, acutely aware of how close I was to the queensguard.

"There are two others on board. Vulcan, the tall blonde one with the face tattoo and the dramatic chip on his shoulder."

I eyed the man who had lobbed me over his shoulder. With his mask and hood removed, a thin fern followed the curve of his chin up to his temple, a beautiful work of art in black ink. It was a stark contrast to the blonde shoulder-length hair tied at his nape. He prowled about the deck getting ready to sail off, his gait unnaturally graceful.

"Isla is the only other elf on board," he nodded toward a young woman who hopped down from the upper deck, positioning herself at the center of the ship.

The young woman flashed a curious glance at me before closing her amber eyes. I noted the slightly pointed ears adorned with tiny pink and white rings. A matching, single ring ran through the nostril of her small nose. She placed the tips of her fingers together as if she held an invisible orb between her bronze hands.

The crew had gone quiet, and as she exhaled, she began to

shake. Small tremors began at her fingertips and slowly spread to her arms as if she were holding onto something moving fast, attempting to escape. Barely perceptible sparks of light danced around her hands and scattered up to our sails and over the side of the ship as if jumping into the water.

Disbelief flooded my senses. I could feel Vulcan's eyes on me from where he stood in the distance. Isla's tremors ceased as the ship lurched into the night at a speed I wasn't prepared for. I yelped as I stumbled back, falling flat on my ass.

A foreign wind filled the air. Not the same cool autumn breeze off the sea when we left the tunnels. That breeze was soft and salty and smelled like the seeds from the lapis trees that dotted the coastline. This was a warm, strong wind, summoned from a place far from here that smelled like green meadows and jasmine.

What was happening was not natural. I searched my memories of countless lectures at the temple that might be able to explain what I'd witnessed and came up short. I bristled at my ignorance. The answer felt simple yet wholly unknown to me.

"We call that *magic*, Lady Cantor. I suppose we have a bit to fill you in on," Ronan drawled, pulling me to my feet. "I am sorry about this though."

Before I knew what was happening, Ronan's broad hands had my wrists in a vice grip. I tugged without thinking and was met with a sharp pain as he dug his thumbs into their center. He quickly wrapped the rope around my wrists before tying it into a tight knot.

"Oslo, you can take Lady Cantor down to—"

"I'm your captive?" I spat.

"You could choose to see it that way," Ronan said, turning toward me.

I jerked my fists up, displaying my bound wrists. "What other way is there to see it?" I snapped.

"I don't make the rules," he murmured, shrugging his shoulders. "You could try to jump ship and swim to shore, but Nerissa will send Vulcan out to retrieve you. I can tell you from experience, it's not pleasant being hunted by him." He rubbed his hand against the back of his neck as he watched the elf in the distance.

"Or you could accept that you've recently suffered a concussion, you haven't eaten in a day, your muscles are depleted of energy, and you're in no position to escape. You could also accept the fact that if we hadn't gotten to you before the king began questioning you, you'd likely be dead. You could also accept the offer I was about to give," he said with a wink.

He *winked*. I bristled.

"Some food?"

He motioned to Oslo, the older man offering a small smile. A soldier, perhaps, based on the way he moved and carried himself. Smile lines bordered his soft brown eyes, his tan Sultiran skin weathered from years of sun.

I tugged at my bounds, the rough edges of rope already chafing my wrists. Without much choice, I followed Oslo below deck.

Breathe.

This had to be better than a cell.

make myself smaller as I began to feel it *looking* at me. Dread snuffed out all awareness.

The crew remained frozen for what felt like an eternity. I didn't dare wipe the sweat that slid down my temple until finally, the fog dissipated, and Nerissa's shoulders relaxed.

"What in Tynan's hell was that?" I asked.

"The Mortis Shroud," Isla murmured. Her face had gone pale. "An evil that prowls the lands and waters of Kayj. It answers to no one, but I suspect it's drawn to the scent of death and pain on these lands."

"It also means we're getting close," added Nerissa, assessing the now visible skies.

"I can't hold the shield any longer," said Isla, her eyebrows tilting up in worry.

"It will be fine. Save your strength for our departure," Nerissa replied, not taking her eyes off the horizon.

I found Ronan at the prow of the ship peering through a spyglass.

"Two o'clock," he said, handing it to me as if we were old acquaintances, and he hadn't just bound my hands. Though he'd replaced the queensguard cape, he held himself like a soldier. Tall, broad shoulders. My eyes drifted over the skin that peeked through the loose laces over his chest, and I caught myself admiring the curls that blew in the sea breeze. His eyes caught mine, and I snatched the instrument from him.

I gazed through the clear glass, the sea rising quickly as I scanned the horizon. I almost missed the dark island below as my attention snagged on the odd cloud that hung over the land like a veil. The kind of cloud you saw coming before a great snowstorm, one that would bring the spinners. Layer upon layer of menacing plumes rose beyond sight into the sky, casting a shadow over the land. Parts of the cloud were as

CHAPTER FOUR

> For blood and for bonds. May the sacrifice of our house never
> be forgotten.
>   —From the Cantor Family Crest. Cantor Manor,
>   Aedrialis.

E*lf.*

Magic.

The words stuck out like beacons in the night as I
traced them through the pages of my memory, searching for
some logical explanation for all of this.

I followed Oslo and Ronan into a small, dimly lit chamber
below deck where the two of them sat, the former tossing a
handful of mendaci cards to the latter.

"I have questions," I said to the queensguard.

"Take a seat and we'll see what we can do," he said, "And
relax, we're not here to gut you."

I remained standing. An older woman with haunted brown

eyes and light hair dotted with gray approached with a glass of wine and some bread, offering me a soft smile before walking away.

"Thank you, Marian," Oslo murmured, his chin dipping toward the retreating woman.

I followed his gaze, the warmth of the goblet seeping into my frigid fingers. I stifled a groan. I normally did not enjoy winter wine, but the heat warmed my belly and the alcohol calmed my mind.

"I have questions," I said again.

Ronan sighed. "Starting with?"

"Why am I here and what do you want from me?"

"Well, you're here because three members of our crew sprung you from your jail cell and you *willingly* climbed aboard this ship."

I leveled a stare at him.

"Ronan, the lady's been beaten, dragged through shit, and has had her world flipped on its ass. Just talk," Oslo muttered.

Ronan shifted in his seat, clearing his throat as he eyed the cards he'd been dealt. It was strange to see the queensguard spoken to in such a casual way.

"You have information. And your discovery could save a lot of people."

"From what? We're not at war. Pirates hardly count."

Oslo and Ronan exchanged a look.

"We've been *at war* for a thousand years... Oslo, maybe you can give her the history lesson."

Oslo glanced at me before saying, "Lady, all is not as it would seem in the kingdom."

I clamped my mouth shut, not sure I should believe a single thing these people said.

Oslo continued unfazed, "King Saros has been searching

for something very specific, for a very long time, which we believe you may have stumbled upon yesterday."

He waited a moment, eyes meeting mine. I wasn't sure if he was referring to the bones, the scrolls, or the mysterious stone. Holy gods, there was a lot to unpack there. It couldn't be a good idea to give them all that information right away. The only thing keeping them from throwing me overboard was the fact that they thought I had information they needed.

After I didn't offer up any information, he continued, "There is an object..." He paused as I shifted on my feet. The stone. He had to be referring to the stone. He gave me a knowing look. *Dammit.* There was a reason I didn't play cards.

He glanced at Ronan.

"So, Saros has the stone then?" he said, pinning his eyes on me again.

"What is it?" I asked.

Ronan cleared his throat before saying, "A weapon. One that could drastically tilt the favor of the war to our hands."

"And who are we supposedly at war with?" I asked, raising my eyebrows.

Oslo laid his cards flat on the table, conceding the win to Ronan who smirked before gathering them up.

"There is an island, northeast of Sultira, called Kayj where a dark king rules the dead. His reign in the north has lasted hundreds of years, and he is perhaps one of the most powerful mystics to have ever existed."

I blinked, processing his words.

"A thousand years ago, during the War of Ruin, the kingdoms across the Vael clashed in a war that left the world forever changed. You would know it as the Great Purification."

Oslo's eyes were hard on mine. Of course, I knew it. The last war was so terrible the gods themselves intervened, saving those they deemed worthy and erasing all others from the realm of Vael. Though most of the names of generals and commanders had long been forgotten, King Saros was a direct descendant of the Hidden Hero, the savior of our kingdom.

"Do you ever wonder why there are no records of the kingdoms that existed outside of Sultira before the Great Purification? Doesn't that seem odd to you, as a student?" he said, voice becoming animated, gesturing to me. "To know that in a kingdom so *obsessed* with knowledge, a massive part of our history has been... erased? Along with the rest of the world? Do you ever wonder what was left out of the texts, Lyvia?"

I stifled the doubt that crept into my chest at his words. Could this be possible? Or were these people pirates? The disappearances... The murders... I had to stop and think critically about this.

"But you of all people know that there is truth in death. And a war like that, with so many dead, left its mark on the world. Fields were left scorched. Mountains were leveled. The evidence is out there. We're just not allowed to see it." He paused, collecting himself.

"The world was permanently changed," he continued. "There's a reason the history is vague. And it's not because it's a thousand years old. It wasn't the gods who altered the topography of the world. Not only did humans and elves fight alongside each other, but they used mystics and mages who waged battle with magic and beings who—"

Oslo paused. He and Ronan exchanged a glance that suggested there was more to be said. Ronan's chin dipped to the side, and Oslo cleared his throat. Having spent enough time in the Court of Two Moons and observing its politics taking place, I knew a signal when I saw one. Important details were about to be left out of the discussion.

"We believe at some point during this great conflict, Saros, a young commander at the time, struck a deal with a young elf prince who usurped his grandmother in a northern kingdom. This deal probably wasn't what ended the war, but it saved a small population of humans in Sultira and doomed the rest of the world to suffer at the dark king's hands for hundreds of years."

I lifted an eyebrow.

"Impossible," I said, shaking my head, "King Saros would have to be—"

"Over a thousand years old," Oslo cut in, narrowing his gaze on me. "He is a mystic with incredible power. And yes, he was there a *thousand* years ago. How he's stayed alive, we don't know. Perhaps complex spells... It's also why scarce few in Sultira remember or know anything about the outside world. His shield has hidden us from the world, and *the world* from us. His bargain during the war allowed his kingdom to thrive *almost* untouched by the darkness in the north, while the rest of the world has bled and sacrificed."

Oslo gritted his teeth, eyes flicking briefly to the door Marian had disappeared in.

"Almost?" I asked, despite myself.

Ronan answered me, lightning dancing in his cobalt-blue eyes.

"Almost. Because unbeknownst to most in the capital, hundreds of humans are sent to Kayj each year in tribute to the dark king."

My stomach pitched at the thought. I frowned and shook my head in an attempt to shake my uncertainty. I knew the history of Sultira like the back of my hand. To believe this... To even consider what they said might be true would upend my entire world. I turned to leave when Ronan gripped my arm, spinning me toward him.

"*Yes*, Lyvia. Our good King Saros rounds up towns of people each month to trade to the dark king. I know you've seen them.

The bulletins on the corners. Missing families and, *Aelius*, entire fucking *towns* disappearing. This is it, Lyvia. The slaves are sent to the work camps and most end up—"

"That's enough for now, Ronan," Oslo said, voice surprisingly soft.

I blanched at Ronan, unease mingling with irritation as I wrenched my arm free from his grip.

"The rest Nerissa or Bayne will need to discuss with you," Oslo finished.

"Who?"

"Bayne is our captain," Ronan replied, running a hand through his hair. A faint look of admiration flashed across his face and was gone in an instant.

"We'll be picking him up shortly," he continued, meeting my eyes.

"Hopefully," Oslo added.

Light footsteps sounded in the hall and the beautiful, black-haired, bronze-skinned elf poked her head in the doorway.

"Hello," she said. "Lyvia, is it?" She had a slight accent, and her voice sounded hoarse like she'd been screaming. She was petite. Thin, but strongly built as I noted the muscle in her legs highlighted by the leathers she wore.

I nodded, taken off guard by the jasmine scent that followed her into the room like a breeze.

"My name is Isla," she continued, a broad smile stretching across her face. "We're glad you're here." She gripped my hand with both of hers in a swift shake. I stared back at her, taken aback by her warmth. I sure as hell wasn't glad to be here.

She turned to Ronan and Oslo. "Aquila is here."

I followed the group up the stairs to find the sun beginning to rise, Aelius's golden fingers drifting across the deck. We had traveled an immense distance in just a couple of hours. I could

34

no longer see the coastline of Aedrialis. My heart dipped. This was the farthest I'd ever been from my beautiful home. My chest tightened with worry and dread as my thoughts drifted to Drystan, Father Marcus, and my father.

Nerissa stood at the helm, facing an enormous seahawk. Its eyes were a spattering of gold and green flecks, and its ten-foot wingspan was draped with long, thick feathers, a tapestry of ash, rust, and honey. Its sharp beak hooked down as it clicked twice and looked over at us. I shifted on my feet when its clever eyes found mine. Nerissa said something to it before it lifted off, wings sending blasts of air through the loose tendrils of my hair as it rose high above the sails and out of sight.

Nerissa approached us. "He's heading east. We should be able to intercept him before the enemy realizes he's missing if we move a little faster. Isla, can you get us there any quicker?"

"I can try, but the closer we get to Kayj, my influence of the wind weakens. His power controls most of the forces once we're within hawk sight of the island," Isla croaked, her voice ragged.

"Damn it. You sound terrible." Nerissa's brows pinched in what could have been concern—the only other emotion aside from pissed off I'd seen on her.

"I find that insulting," Isla said with a grin. "Let me see what I can do." She walked to the center of the ship, her focus narrowing.

Ronan eyed Nerissa.

"What?" she snapped.

"What else did Aquila say? How *is* he?" His eyebrows tilted up in concern for a split second.

"He's alive. And alone."

She sounded grim, striding off with Ronan following closely behind. I watched as they stalked off, more questions forming in my head.

Oslo turned toward me. "Bayne is Nerissa's twin brother. He's one of the bravest men I know. If we find him... *When* we find him," he corrected, "he will likely be close to death. The first person ever, human or elf, to have escaped Kayj with blood still circulating his body. *Bayne the Unbroken*, as they say. It would be best for you to stay back when we bring him aboard."

I followed as Oslo made his way to a cabin below deck, my stomach twisting as he gathered medical supplies, ropes, and weapons.

"What happened to the others from the burial chamber?" I asked, a sliver of desperation seeping into the question.

Oslo glanced at me, and his shoulders tensed. "The Death Scholar is likely dead or will be soon. They were questioning him when we arrived. I would imagine anyone else will be questioned and executed."

My stomach dropped.

Father Marcus would be *dead* soon. Guilt scraped at my chest. And Drystan... If he'd been held captive, would they understand his ears didn't work? Nausea churned in my stomach at the thought of my friend in the hands of the kings-guards. And my father...

A shout drew our attention above deck, and Oslo raced up the stairs. I followed in his wake before stopping in my tracks on the main deck where the crew had gathered, gazing ahead as a black wave of clouds choked out the golden morning sky. Our speed slowed. No one uttered a word.

The crew stood with their posture taught as if ready for battle. The deck rocked slowly against the lapping waves as a thick black fog enveloped the ship. My heart thumped wildly against my chest, every inch of my being urging me to flee as tendrils of fog climbed their way up and down the masts, a serpent made of mist and shadow.

CHAPTER FIVE

Once upon a time, there lived a young maiden who fell in love with a god.

— From Fabia's Fables, "People of the Stars". Cantor Manor, Aedrialis.

There was something unnatural about the way the fog snaked around the vessel as if it were aware. It circled us like a predator, searching for the smallest vulnerability it could exploit. But something kept the evil at bay. Did it have something to do with the strange power Isla displayed? A barrier, perhaps? I sent up a silent prayer of thanks for the elf.

Every penetrating coil crept upon my senses. Within seconds, it surrounded us, choking out what was left of the gray light seeping through the black clouds.

I slowed my breathing as the air became sticky and oppressive, the weight of the fog pressing down from above. I tried to

black as night while others, illuminated by lightning, glowed violet with a ghostly beauty.

Nerissa still scanned the skies, which began to drizzle, slickly coating the deck. I began to feel the weight of all that had happened crush down on me.

Nerissa's shout pulled me out of my stupor as our ship lurched to the west and picked up an unnatural speed. In the distance, Aquila made soaring circles over the water, only a couple hundred yards offshore. Oslo rushed to where Ronan stood at the prow, taking the spyglass from me and peering through it.

"He did it," Ronan called. He swore and began racing around the deck, gathering ropes and tying them off on the mast, making some type of harness. Marian came up from below with a pack full of medical supplies and instruments I'd seen many of the Life Scholars using. My stomach churned at the sight of a long, thin saw connected to a wooden handle.

Oslo pulled my attention away as he screamed, voice laced with a trace of panic, "ASHEN FROM THE NORTHEAST!"

He ran below and returned with a trunk full of arrows, tossing a quiver to each crew member on deck. Vulcan snatched his out of the air as he climbed the taut ropes connected to the masts. He tiptoed across the mast and squatted on the balls of his feet, balancing on the beam that swooped and dropped as we raced across the waves, an arrow already nocked.

Oslo and Nerissa took up positions on the starboard side of the bow while Isla remained center deck, concentrating on the power flowing through her fingertips as the wind whipped through her loose hair. What in the gods' names were ashen? I ran to the edge to get a better view.

About a hundred yards out, I spotted something bobbing in the surf, the swell rising high enough to block my view every few seconds. I grabbed the spyglass Ronan had abandoned and saw a dark-haired man barely treading water. Twenty feet above him, Aquila called to the ship in warning. I panned the horizon until my eye snagged on a wave of white fins. Some type of sea beasts? They moved through the water with incredible speed. Adrenaline pulsed through my body, making my senses fuzzy. I panned back to the man floating in the water, barely conscious. The gap between man and beast closed.

Aquila dove for him. His talons wrapped around the man's arm, giant wings pumping wildly into the air. He couldn't pull him out of the water completely, but he slowly dragged him closer to the ship. We were so close. I panned back to the sea beasts in pursuit and nearly dropped the spyglass as I realized they were *humans*, not beasts.

My gaze narrowed on the horizon. Not *quite* human. Ghostly white limbs flew out of the water, camouflaged in the spray of the surf. It was as if mountain river rapids suddenly materialized in the middle of the sea.

Feeling utterly useless, I ran to Ronan's side as he began taking up position on the opposite side of the boat with the harness.

"Untie me," I demanded, urging the shaking of my voice to settle.

He looked as if he was about to dismiss me and hesitated.

"Please," I begged. "I can help."

He shot a quick look at Nerissa before drawing a concealed dagger and slicing through my bounds.

"Below deck, there is a room, down the hall and fourth door on the left." He instructed, before reluctantly adding, "Bring up both sets of shackles."

I shook my hands out and gave him a swift nod before sprinting for the stairs. I returned with the heavy iron chains. Marian joined Ronan at the edge. Aquila was close but began to falter, the deadweight of the captain pulling him so low that the tips of his wings hit the lapping waves. The ashen would be on them in seconds.

As they neared, arrows rained down from above. Vulcan's hands moved faster than humanly possible. He cast down arrow after arrow, each one hitting its mark. Nerissa and Oslo added their bolts to the volley, and the wave of ashen thinned as they approached. Before I registered what happened, Ronan leaped off the side of the boat, the makeshift harness secured around his hips and thighs, diving into the crushing waves below.

He swam to where Aquila struggled to stay airborne. He reached the flailing seahawk at the same moment three ashen broke through the onslaught, one grappling at its wing. An arrow sliced through the ashen's neck as the other two reached for Ronan and the captain. He hooked an arm around the barely conscious captain's chest, wielding his dagger in the other, all while trying to stay afloat in the wild swell ripping off the ship.

Vulcan focused his arrows on the ashen nearest the captain, buying Ronan enough time to tie a rope around his waist. Vulcan's attention shifted to the other side of the boat, where, to my horror, the creatures began to climb aboard.

Oh, gods. My stomach dropped as the first set of milky white hands reached above the edge of the ship. The whine of a blade being unsheathed sounded before a shout from Ronan pulled me out of my stupor.

"PULL!"

Marian had hold of the rope. I grabbed hold with her and pulled with my limited remaining strength. I glanced over the edge. The captain was deadweight. Ronan had slain the two ashen that were upon him and now climbed up his own rope. I braced my foot against the side of the ship and threw my weight back, hands shaking as the rope slipped, burning through my calluses. Ronan was over the edge and back on deck seconds before Marian and I nearly lost hold of the captain, catching the rope as it slid back.

I risked a glance over my shoulder, horror making my insides turn. The ghostly creatures moved with animalistic speed and ferocity as they boarded the ship. They weren't the type of enemy met on a battlefield. There was no intelligence in their attack—just a raw need to kill. Pure violence. They were so human-looking, save for the paleness of their complexion and the dimmed, unnatural hue of their irises. Below haunted eyes devoid of life, sat deep gray circles. They carried no weapons, attacking with their teeth and elongated nails. Every fiber of my being urged me to get as far away from these creatures as possible.

Nerissa clashed with four ashen as Vulcan flew down from the mast, swinging on a rope to join the fray. I glanced at Nerissa with a mix of awe and horror. Save for the bones in the chamber, I'd never seen a female warrior before. She spun between her attackers, her sword moving too fast to track. She sliced through two before beheading a third. Vulcan was there for the fourth as he shoved his arrow through the back of its head. Oslo was now at the back of the ship, longsword in hand, cutting through three more. The ashen kept coming, invading the ship like locusts.

Ronan yelled my name, drawing my attention back. I heaved one last time, falling hard on my back as the captain lurched over the side of the ship and onto the deck with a loud thud.

I noted the slightly pointed ears poking through his shaggy dark hair first. His clothes hung in tatters off a chiseled body marked with rows of old scars and fresh wounds. Swirls of black ink lined the space of skin that showed through his tattered shirt. Fresh scratches and tears covered his face and long, deep slits, recently cauterized, ran down his corded forearms making my stomach turn. He moaned and Ronan moved. Shackles snapped on his hands and ankles.

"We've got him! Let's go!" he called to Isla. She looked at the others, still fighting off the remaining ashen.

"Just go!" screamed Nerissa.

With that, Isla threw her remaining strength into the wind, which sent our ship hurtling away from the island and the remaining ashen. Nerissa rushed to the captain's side, leaving the three remaining ashen to Vulcan and Oslo.

Nerissa knelt by her brother's head, turning his face to the now-clearing sky as we made our escape. Shadows formed under his closed eyes, the same dark circles the ashen had. She held his head in her lap as Marian examined him.

A gut-curdling scream sounded from across the deck. I whirled to see an ashen rip through Oslo's right arm as Vulcan tossed the other overboard. He turned and skewered the last ashen through the chest, but not before it had shredded through the tendons and muscle of Oslo's forearm.

He staggered back, and Vulcan pinned him to the ground in seconds. Ronan left the captain and raced to Oslo's side, shoving the hilt of his dagger in Oslo's mouth before moving to hold down his kicking legs. Marian followed, grabbing the thin saw from her medical kit before swiftly tying a tourniquet beneath his elbow. Nerissa left her brother's side to hold down Oslo's right arm. Bile rose in my stomach as I realized what was about to happen.

My eyes tore back to the captain, and I suddenly realized I was the only one by his side. Brilliant green eyes opened, his gaze boring into me. I suppressed a shudder, gaping at eyes shining like a sunlit forest. Lethal intelligence sparked through them, and though my senses were on high alert, my breath had been stolen.

A long moment later, I remembered the irons, glancing down at the shackles. His striking eyes followed mine, and he tugged, causing me to flinch. A gut-wrenching scream ripped through the air, and I glanced over my shoulder as Marian sawed through Oslo's flesh, her own arm quivering with strength. The sound of muscle tearing and bone grinding was lost in the agony of Oslo's pleas. The blood and gore that followed suddenly put me over the edge. I met the captain's eyes once more before darkness took me.

CHAPTER SIX

Between the Marisarma scum and the treacherous waters of the Crimson Sea, we've failed to explore what lies beyond the Votruvian Islands. How many ships is he willing to sacrifice?
—Correspondence to General Calvus, 28th of Summer, 061.3E. Aedrialis.

The piercing call of gulls drew me from sleep in the room below deck. Small shimmers of light bounced around the ceiling, reflecting off the water outside the tiny window. My tongue felt like sandpaper as I tried to swallow. My muscles ached as I gingerly rolled to my side. The burning on my palms brought back the memory of rough, wet rope.

All that had transpired came hurtling back into view. We must have made it far enough away from that godsforsaken island if I lay here in bed. A shiver crept up my spine as I remembered the look on Oslo's face when the ashen was on him, ripping at his flesh. And the one that followed as Marian approached with the saw.

I'd passed out. I knew it had to do with all the events leading up to it, but there was a reason I had no desire to study with the Life Scholars. I couldn't handle the gore. A tiny pathetic part of me was impressed I hadn't vomited first. My headache dulled to a light throb. How long had I been asleep? Where were we going now that we had the captain?

The captain. His gaze left an odd feeling in my gut. After being chased down and beaten, thrown in a dungeon, forced to flee through sewers and surf, all to end up on a ship heading for hell on Vael with people I didn't know, to rescue some elf who shouldn't even exist, to fight a war that has apparently been underway for hundreds of years, I hadn't had time to sift through fact and fiction.

A knock sounded at the door. I sat up too quickly, my head spinning and throbbing behind my temple. He didn't wait for a reply before stepping inside.

"We don't have time for a beauty sleep," Ronan said with a wink. Iron clinked in his hands.

"Are those for me?" I asked, gritting my teeth as I eyed the shackles he carried.

"No, just returning them. I convinced the others you were trustworthy enough. You're welcome," he replied, sketching a bow.

"How long was I out?" I asked, ignoring his request for my gratitude.

"About a day and a half," he said, tossing me a skin of water and some type of jerky. I devoured it all, choking on the water and savoring the salt in the dried meat. Leaning against the doorframe, he watched me for a moment.

"Nerissa wants sketches," he said, tossing a pen and parchment onto my lap.

"Sketches of what?"

"The burial site. The findings. All of it."

"*Nerissa*," I snapped, tossing the pen and parchment aside, "can come speak to me herself."

Ronan snickered, a dimple forming on his left cheek. "I promise that's a conversation you don't want to have."

Ronan turned and strode out the door.

I stared at the parchment, anger replacing the irritation. I let them take me without so much as an introduction to who these people were. I'd taken orders. I'd *obeyed*. Gods, I was so *complacent*. I deserved more than to be shut down in this fucking room without a clue about where we were heading.

Irritated with myself, I tossed the parchment and pen to the floor and flew after him, my emotions getting the best of me. I whirled around the corner to the stairs and smacked into a wall of muscle that smelled of pine and salty sea. I yelped, bringing my hand to the pain in my chest, the wind completely knocked out of me. I looked up and found those striking green eyes staring down at me.

"Good morning," he said.

I glanced at the captain's pale, corded arms. The ragged cuts and gashes that lined his face and arms had begun to heal. A lock of dark hair fell over an old scar on his temple. Clean clothes had replaced the scraps, and he was clean-shaven.

I stood there dumbly for a moment holding my chest. "What?" I breathed.

"I said good morning. I'm Bayne Ravindra, Captain of the *Evecta*," he said, his voice like velvet sliding over my skin.

Heat rose to my cheeks as my mind stupidly searched for my next move. I blinked and took a breath, shaking off my stupor, irritation and purpose returning to my muddled mind. Right. I needed to get off this damn ship. My mind drifted to my father as I chose my next words.

"I demand answers and safe passage to the nearest port in Sultira. I've been beaten, arrested, taken against my will, and—"

"Forced to rescue a man you've never met?" Bayne cut in. "You're also a wanted woman, Lady Cantor."

A betrayal of warmth slid down my abdomen as my name rolled off his tongue in that accent, and I blinked, replaying his words. I was a fugitive now.

"Come with me."

My nostrils flared with indignation at yet another command. He turned, making his way to the captain's quarters.

I debated ignoring him. But what would I do? Go back to that little room? I followed, urging myself to keep my courage —that tiny fire kindling in my chest—alive.

"I *said* I have questions."

"So do I," he said, leveling a stare at me.

I met his gaze, refusing to balk at it. Though I couldn't help but study the facets of green that reflected in his irises. He was clearly related to Nerissa, but his eyes were brighter.

"Take a seat," he growled, gesturing to a chair across his desk.

The desk was strewn with maps and notes in a language I didn't recognize. My eyes snagged on the drawing of five ships, all with different monsters carved into their figureheads.

"An answer for an answer," the captain continued, drawing my attention back. "You start."

"How is Oslo?" I blurted out, unsure why it was the first question that popped into my mind.

His dark brows narrowed, and he peered at me curiously.

"Recovering. As I'm sure you can imagine, getting mauled by the undead is unpleasant, and then, to have your arm removed without even a tonic... Oslo's a soldier. One of the bravest I know. I am sorry it happened." He looked down, and for an instant, a hint of guilt flashed across his face.

"He filled me in on what he told you... I'm sorry for the circumstances you were thrown in," he murmured. "You are Lyvia Cantor, daughter of Sultira's Horse Lord, Willem Cantor."

"Has he been arrested?"

My stomach twisted as I thought of my father being questioned. He wouldn't go in without a fight. And he was persuasive. Maybe he'd talk his way out of this and persuade the king to take the price off my head.

"Ah, an answer for an answer, yes?" He raised his eyebrows at me.

I ground my teeth and sat back, waiting.

"Describe the map to me. What markings did it show?"

I shifted in my seat.

"It was inaccurate," I began. "While it looked like Sultira and its bordering seas, the major geographical markers were in the wrong places."

"Like what?"

"An answer for an answer," I said, unable to help the smugness in my voice.

"Lord Cantor has not been seen since you were arrested," he replied. "We're not sure if that means he's been taken by the kingsguards or if he fled. Our knowledge from the walls inside Mount Telum is limited now that Ronan can't return."

"So, Sir Ronan was just a spy? For your kind?"

His chin lifted, and I couldn't help but admire the angles of his face. Right. His turn.

"Which geographical markers were in the wrong places and what markings did it show?"

"The markings I couldn't read, and there was more wrong than I could catch in the short amount of time I had to examine it. Aside from the additional islands I didn't recognize, a large isthmus ran east connecting Sultira to another continent. The Lake of Light was out of place as were the Lumerians." The mountain lake was unmistakable, its eight fingers stretching out in different directions made it look like a star from the highest peak.

The captain didn't pull his gaze from me as I spoke, making it oddly difficult to concentrate. I shook my head trying to make sense of it and realized I'd rattled off more than I intended to. I stopped talking and waited for him to answer my question.

"Ronan is a member of my crew, and as such, he is a defender of all beings, humans and elves alike. But yes, he's a spy."

I opened my mouth to ask more, but he held up his hand.

"It's not my story to tell." He rubbed his eyebrows and sat back. "Did your Death Scholar friends tell you how old they thought the map was?"

Drystan. Father Marcus. My gut twisted thinking of their fates. Father Marcus was so frail and weathered. And Drystan... The thought of them being dragged in and potentially harmed made my mouth dry.

"Drystan thought perhaps first Epoch, but I'm not sure if Father Marcus even had a chance to run tests to confirm."

"That means it would be two thousand years old."

"Yes." I didn't say more.

"Tell me about the body."

I opened my mouth to reply, excitement bubbling at the memory of discovering it was female, and clamped it shut. My turn.

"What are the ashen?"

Darkness flashed across his face, and he glanced out the window which seemed to clear away any demons that haunted his memory. He cleared his throat. "The ashen are weapons of

Dark King Daimos. They were once humans and elves. Some were taken captive. Others were willingly given."

My stomach twisted despite my doubt as I thought of what Oslo and Ronan had told me about King Saros and the tribute.

"We're not sure how he does it. Possibly a curse, some dark spell used to turn mortals into the undead. However he does it, it renders their minds and bodies under his control. They have no intelligence or mind left, just a basic need to kill and consume. He's building an army of them, collecting them for hundreds of years. Your good King Saros has essentially *given* him an army with which to destroy Sultira and the rest of the world."

My stomach threatened to bottom out.

"The only silver lining is that the creatures have no intelligence." The captain scratched at his short beard as his eyes took on a glassy effect. "They act purely out of a need to kill. There's no thinking involved. And with the volume, he can only stretch his influence over them so far. He can't control individual ashen. At least, we don't believe so. We expect he can only send hoards in general directions, destroying anything in their path."

I stared at him, clearly missing his point. "*That's* the silver lining?"

"My point is there is no strategy. And we know how to kill them. You saw the ones on the ship. Head or heart. Simple."

"Could they be saved? Turned back?"

Bayne's features turned dark and distant. "There is no saving them," he said flatly. His eyelashes shuddered for a moment before his eyes met mine again. "Our only hope is to fight fire with fire."

"Or magic with magic you mean," I murmured, finishing his thought.

He nodded. "A long time ago, there were mystics powerful

enough to imbue ordinary objects with magical properties. The magic was stored and could be used later by anyone who knew how to unlock it."

The captain's gaze locked on mine, and the blood drained from my face as I realized the ordinary object he referred to was the onyx stone we'd found in the burial chamber. He didn't need to say it.

"King Saros probably has it already if he took the others in for questioning. Oslo said he was a mystic. Maybe he's planning to use it to stop the dark king," I replied.

"Perhaps." The captain shrugged. "But regardless of what you believe of the king, his shield over Sultira is weakening. He can't hold it forever. He's likely using all his remaining strength to keep that in place. To stop any non-human from entering your lands. But my crew got through. We're small, which is probably why it wasn't too difficult, but it's weak, nonetheless. I'm also certain that while he might use it to protect *his* people, he would let the rest of the world fall to ashes."

His gaze grew icy. Fury smoldered in his pupils, darkening his eyes to a deep emerald. "What did it look like?" he asked, voice quiet. "And how did it feel?"

My heart hammered. That last question... I had the inexplicable urge to clamp my mouth shut and swallow any words that rose to my lips. He held my gaze for a moment, waiting. Silence would not do. I inhaled slowly through my nose, choosing my next words carefully.

"Black. Darker than a moonless and starless midnight, as if it devoured light from the sun itself."

The captain went utterly still, his pupils dilating.

"And it felt," I said slowly, pausing as I thought about the look on Drystan's face when he eyed the stone from a distance, "dangerous. It felt dangerous."

I held the captain's gaze for two heartbeats, waiting for him to call me on the lie. His lips parted for a moment as if he was about to say something.

I blurted out, "What about the elves? Is there someone powerful from your land who could stop the dark king?"

A shadow of distaste appeared on his face for the briefest moment. "Not a king, but a queen. Queen Antares of Lotrennia, the *Land of Light and Life*." He shifted in his seat, and his gaze drifted to the maps strewn across his desk. He sighed. "I believe that was four."

I blinked, caught off guard. "What?"

"You asked me four questions."

"Oh," I stammered, sifting through my memory for his last question.

"The body was female. A warrior. And she..."

He raised his eyebrows in question.

"And she was... different. I'm not sure what it was I saw."

"You know what it was," he responded, eyes pinning me to my seat.

I didn't respond immediately, instead leaning back in my chair and feeling suddenly heavy.

"One of your kind, I suppose."

"I suspect so. And I would imagine you have more questions to follow that up. But for now, you have a choice, Lady Cantor. We can help you find a horse in Aedrialis. I suppose you would want to go west to see your brother, yes? We have no news of him, but since you're considered an enemy of the kingdom now, it's not implausible that he's been arrested or even executed." He paused and stood. His frame loomed in the small cabin.

My stomach dropped.

"Or you can stay with us. Help us. Sultira will not remain unscathed for long. War is coming, and we could save millions by retrieving the Obscura Stone before Dark King Daimos does. Because make no mistake, he will come for it."

Obscura Stone. The words sounded wrong in my head like we were missing something obvious.

"You want to steal the stone from King Saros?" I asked, incredulous.

"Yes. It's that or find another burial site containing a long-lost powerful rock that could reduce thousands to ashes," he said, eyeing me expectantly.

I sat back. Was that what that little stone could do?

He walked to the door. I stood, recognizing the dismissal.

"Either way, while you are on this ship, you are a part of the crew. We aren't in the transportation business—"

"No, Captain, I'd say abduction business is more accurate," I cut in with a glare, pausing at his desk.

He stopped and slowly turned, eyes flicking to my crossed arms.

"Find some work to do, Lady Cantor," the captain continued. "I'm sure Marian could use help in the kitchens. We'll be at the coast in a few days."

He paused in the doorway.

"Oh, and the sketches. Take it from someone who has known Nerissa her entire existence, it's best not to keep her waiting."

CHAPTER SEVEN

O slo and Ronan stopped talking as I paused at the doorway of the little cabin below deck. I did my best not to look at Oslo's arm, now wrapped in soiled dressings that needed to be changed. In part because I didn't want to offend him, but I also knew I might need a bucket if I stared at the bloody stump too long.

"Settle a debate, Cantor," Ronan began. "Do we get Oslo a pipe or a pint to attach to his stump?"

Humor danced in his eyes. He was so different from the serious queensguard I'd observed inside the castle gates at

Mount Telum. The smoldering and stone-faced guard appeared at ease here, perhaps even at home.

"Why not a blade?" I asked.

"I knew I liked you," he said, huffing a laugh. Heat tinged my cheeks.

"How are you?" I asked Oslo.

"I've been through worse, Lady. Thank you for asking."

"You can call me Lyvia. I've never been very good at being a lady."

"I think you're damn good at being a lady." Ronan's sensuous lips twitched up in a smirk, sending birds flapping in my stomach.

Isla blew through the door with that jasmine breeze and hopped on the table, taking a seat on its edge.

"I think you should get a broom so you don't have an excuse not to pitch in around here more often," she teased.

"Isn't that what your lovely breeze is for?" Ronan cut in, throwing her a wink.

She stuck her tongue out at him.

I stood watching, unsure of my place in all of this. The warmth in this room made the little group almost likable. Were they my kidnappers or liberators? The elves above deck did little to quell my uncertainty. The attack yesterday had proved my instincts about Vulcan and Nerissa were correct. The two of them were lethal.

And then there was the captain. *Bayne the Unbroken*, I recalled, rolling my eyes. How *had* he escaped the island of Kayj? And would he truly let me leave when we reached Aedrialis?

Unease crept its way from my stomach into my chest as I thought about what that might mean. The captain said I'd have a choice to make, but I had already made it. I had to find my father. Somehow free Drystan and Father Marcus. They had to be okay. And what then?

My hope of being a Death Scholar... of Stynguard... All of it seemed so far away, so out of reach, like a strange, deflated dream. One thing at a time. I had to get off this ship.

"How does it work?" I asked, turning my attention back to Isla, whose legs swung at Ronan in a halfhearted kick, a response to some bold remark he must have made. "The magic, I mean."

"It's simple, in truth. At its most basic level, it's a give and take with the threads of power and energy that connect us all. I give some of myself, and the forces I am dipping into return a bit."

My brows furrowed at the simplicity she implied. It had to be more complicated than that.

She laughed. "If you'd like, I can give you more of a lesson later. Right now, I need to check our bearings with Bayne."

"Are you controlling the ship now?"

"I am. But I'm only giving it a nudge." She winked and hopped off the table, blowing the door shut behind her with a slight tug on that breeze.

"Show off," Ronan called after her.

The raw strength of her power was a stark contrast to her petite frame and bouncy personality. Oslo had said she was just a mage. What did that say of the power King Saros wielded? Or the other mystics? I shuddered thinking of its use in the wrong hands.

"Well, I'd better get these changed," Oslo said, as he moved to the exit. "Otherwise, Marian will be on me."

"On you?" Ronan smirked, raising his eyebrows at the soldier.

"You're indecent," Oslo scoffed, shaking his head, though his cheeks reddened.

"I'll come with you," I murmured, and we found our way to the kitchens.

MARIAN DROPPED the foul rags in a bucket of water, the slosh splattering the wall with pink droplets as she finished changing Oslo's dressings. I swallowed the gag that rose up my throat with the stench in the room. She pulled out a little booklet and pen from her apron and jotted down a note, handing it to Oslo.

"I'll be sure to let you know sooner next time." He laughed and made his way out of the kitchen.

I gaped at the notebook, realizing this was her way of communicating. She had working ears, that much was evident, but she either couldn't speak or wouldn't. And she didn't know how to sign.

"The captain thought you could use a hand down here while I'm on board?"

She peered at me for a moment and jotted something down in her notebook before sliding it over.

Got one already.

I lifted an eyebrow as I glanced up. She grinned, little wrinkles forming around the edge of her amused eyes as she gestured to another bucket on the table in the corner.

I blanched, realizing it was Oslo's severed *hand*. The shock must have shown on my face because she started scribbling again.

We will learn from it. There is truth in the death of things.

I paused, nodding slowly. She clearly had experience with Life Scholars if she was a healer, but I had never heard those words uttered from anyone other than a Death Scholar.

She handed me another note.

58

Bad joke. Yes, I could use some help.

"My best friend has ears that don't work. He can't speak," I blurted out.

A haunted look flashed across her face, filled with fear and pain... And anger.

"I could teach you the signs if you want. It's faster than writing things down," I signed as I spoke to her.

She continued staring at me for a few moments as the darkness slowly dissipated from her eyes. Finally, she nodded. Turning on her heel, she moved briskly through the kitchen, pointing to some potatoes. I got to work peeling and chopping.

NERISSA FOUND me alone a few hours later below deck.

"Do you have my sketches?" she said, voice clipped and eyes unapologetic.

"I haven't had the time," I said, gritting my teeth.

"Liar," she said, sitting down on the small stool in the corner of the room. She narrowed her eyes and crossed her arms, the black outline of a wolf skull flexing on her shoulder. "Isla said you had questions about her magic. And you've been helping Marian. I want to see what you saw."

"I can't remember it all," I lied, tapping my head where the fresh scab of the kingsguard's blow had begun to form.

"*Liar*," she repeated, eyes bearing into me.

I held her gaze, forcing bravado into my own. Before I registered her movement, a dagger was at my throat.

"I suppose we don't need you anymore, then," she breathed into my face. She leaned in, pressing the dagger further into my neck. The edge met with my skin in a sharp sting, a warm drip of blood slithering down my neck. *Shit.*

"Fine," I breathed, trying my best not to move my throat as I spoke the word. "FINE!"

Triumph glimmered in her eyes for a moment, but she didn't move. "You're hiding something, Lyvia Cantor. I will find out what it is," she breathed before pulling away.

My heart thumped a wild beat against my ribs, the drip of blood drawing a cold line down my chest.

"Never think about lying to me again," she spat before starting down the hall.

I was acutely aware of the throbbing pulse under the skin of my neck as I steadied my breathing, still reeling from the touch of Nerissa's blade. I eyed the pen and parchment. While I might be a shit artist, I'd sketch all day if it meant staying alive.

AFTER A FEW HOURS of tedious sketching, I wandered above deck, following the scent of salted pork. The crew had gathered for dinner. Isla's warm breeze and thin barrier kept the ship deck warm and comfortable, despite the chill autumn air we sailed through. I lingered at the edge, eyeing their togetherness.

Oslo's weathered fingers on his remaining hand strung quickly over his lute as Marian handed me a small plate. Isla grabbed Ronan's hand and pulled him into a bouncy jig. He eyed Nerissa as he swept Isla around the deck. Oslo whistled as they went. A small smile tugged on Marian's lips as she watched, clapping her hands to the beat. Even the captain shrugged off some of his seriousness.

At the end of the night, the crew quieted and looked toward Vulcan. The somber elf stepped to the center of the deck, eyes closed, and filled the air with an ethereal voice. His tenor vibrato reverberated through the wind, and the sails themselves shuddered against the graceful notes. It was a heavenly lullaby that made my eyelids heavy. Despite my position on board and the events leading up to that moment, I slept like the dead that night.

DAYS AFTER THE ATTACK, Oslo's detached forearm had become bone white and chilled but had yet to decay. The color had leached from the marrow, but it remained spongy and gelatinous as I examined it. Marian sliced off a thin strip of flesh which she viewed under a flea glass with not two, but three lenses that magnified the details, a sophisticated instrument I'd never seen.

"Where did you get that?" I asked.

"Stynguard," she spelled the word, unsure of the sign for the university city.

A pang of jealousy pitted in my stomach. I moved my hands slowly in a sign like that of a serpent, demonstrating the correct sign for the city. She'd memorized the signs quickly, and I'd taught a few of the others when I had the chance.

"I studied midwifery for a time. My husband was a Death Scholar, like you," she continued.

"I'm not a Death Scholar," I corrected her, turning back to the flesh.

"You could be," she signed out of the corner of my eye.

The blood had bizarrely disappeared hours after the amputation, leaving shreds of white flesh hanging off the limb where the ashen had ripped and torn into the arm. The limb had stiffened yet hadn't yet begun to self-digest, typically seen in dying flesh.

Most unnerving was what happened when Marian gently prodded the nerve on the inside of the arm, opposite the thumb, and the fourth and fifth fingers reacted in response. They didn't just twitch. They flexed and stretched.

"It's still alive in some ways," I murmured next to her.

Marian's head bobbed in confirmation.

"The captain said they cannot be saved though."

"Alive in some ways, dead in others. Perhaps their brain, or even their soul..." she paused her signing as she considered. "Perhaps the part of them that makes them human or elf is dead. And only bits of their flesh remain living."

ISLA TRIED EXPLAINING THE MAGIC, but without logic, the art made no sense to me. She spoke of her energy like an offering, rambling on about its push and pull. I listened, trying to focus on her words and ignore the fact that I enjoyed her company. Drys was my only real friend in Aedrialis.

The rest of the crew spent their time training. Strike, parry, block, strike, parry. And on it went. When they weren't attempting to hack each other to bits at the stern of the ship, they often disappeared into the captain's quarters for hours on end.

Curiosity got the best of me on more than one occasion, and I found myself cleaning a little corner of the ship outside of his room when he was consulting with the others. I shouldn't have been surprised when I'd overheard multiple conversations and understood none of it. Of course, they'd have their own language. *Elvish.* Occasionally Ronan and the others would join, but I was always conveniently preoccupied with Marian when that happened.

Nerissa continued to question me relentlessly on the burial site. Her manners hadn't improved since her threat, yet despite the real danger I knew she posed, it only made me match her iciness.

"Cantor's going in first." Ronan chuckled the next morning as I stormed onto the deck after another infuriating interrogation with Nerissa. He sat on a barrel, sliding his dagger across a whetting stone on his lap.

"I don't know," Isla challenged, throwing me a wink. "I think Lyvia's tougher than she looks."

"What are you talking about?" I asked, frowning at the pair as they smirked at me.

"Isla and I have a bet going on who will throw the other overboard first. You or Nerissa." Ronan's lips tugged up as he sliced the freshly sharpened dagger over his muscled forearms, shearing the tiniest bit of arm hair to test its edge.

"Well, that's a joke. Considering I have no idea how to fight," I murmured, snatching a piece of dried meat from the queensguard's stash sitting next to him.

"Your brother never taught you?" he asked, raising a light brow.

I frowned, shaking my head. "You know my brother?"

Ronan eyed his blade as he flipped it to the other hand and nodded. "Aeriden Cantor's the best swordsman to enter the king's royal army in the last ten years." He wiggled his eyebrows at Isla whose lips tilted into a small grin.

"*Oooh*, sounds dreamy," she murmured, winking at me.

"Yeah, just ask him." I snorted, rolling my eyes. "And no, he didn't teach me... Well, I guess he tried to once, but I was already breaking enough courtly rules..."

My thoughts drifted to that summer when Aeriden insisted I learn how to throw a proper punch after what had transpired with the stable hand. Of course, I'd refused, pretending I was fine. Aer had done the honors eventually, anyway.

Stupid. I'd been stupid.

"Even if I did," I continued, "you know I'd be at the bottom of the Juniper Sea in no time." I eyed the door Nerissa had entered after our argument. "*She* is abnormally fast and *freakishly* strong. I wouldn't stand a chance." My voice lowered as I kept my eye on the door, remembering the feel of her blade against my neck.

Ronan chuckled, stretching as he stood.

"Better late than never, Cantor," he said, flipping the dagger once more, this time offering me its hilt. "You're a fugitive now. You'd better prepare for it."

CHAPTER EIGHT

The orders of Sultiran Academia shall be reduced to seven, all scholars and priests falling into one of the following categories: Life, Death, Vael, Sky, Civil, Culture, and War.

—Official Modification to the Sultiran Academic Sects, 197.2E, Private Library. Mount Telum, Aedrialis.

Though it left my body aching, training with the queensguard was... enjoyable. I was so sore after the first afternoon training with Ronan that I winced every time I reached up to put away dried rags or squatted to scrub the deck. It was like learning how to ride all over again. A new kind of sore in tender muscles I didn't know I had.

We focused on defense. How to use the base of my palm, knees, and elbows instead of my fists, which I apparently didn't know how to close properly without injuring myself in a strike. How to use my weight against an attacker while my wrists were tied and the sensitive parts on both men and women.

It felt good to move. I itched to get in a saddle and fly across the plains outside the capital gates, but I supposed this was a good alternative considering where we were. And that's where we spent the morning before we were to make landfall at Aedrialis.

"How did the captain get captured by the dark king? Was he taken as a prisoner of war?"

Ronan loosened his chokehold at the question, and I took advantage of the momentary distraction by inching my chin toward the crook of his elbow, sliding my foot next to his, and twisting, using the momentum to throw him to the ground. Even caught off guard, he landed in a crouch and hopped back up. Surprise flashed across his face, quickly replaced by a smirk.

"Better, Cantor, but next time, get that foot directly behind mine. You'll need less force to knock me down, and I won't be able to catch myself as easily."

I nodded, satisfied I was able to accomplish that much.

"Bayne wasn't captured."

"What do you mean?"

"He went in for someone."

Of course. *Bayne the Brave*, so it would seem.

"He snuck in with a tribute from the north last month. A group gathered from several villages in the northern cliffs."

My stomach churned at the idea of people being rounded up like cattle and gifted to Dark King Daimos. I didn't know King Saros well, but I had met him on a few occasions at the castle, and I suppose I learned, or was taught, to admire him. It felt like such a betrayal.

"Who was he looking for?"

I got in position again. This time Ronan grabbed me

around the neck in a side headlock. Despite the position, I couldn't help but enjoy the contact with the tall soldier. He smelled like citrus and something loamy I couldn't place. I tried to reach around to hook him in a particularly sensitive area, but my fist slammed into a wall of muscle, his thigh blocking my way. I twisted my head, moving my mouth toward his forearm, ready to snap my teeth, but he squeezed tightly, cutting off my air for a moment.

"No. You just exposed your neck to me and made it that much easier for me to suffocate you. Try again. Use your momentum and weight to your advantage."

We reset.

"Her name was Lida," he said softly, reverently. Something twinged in my chest. Jealousy? Confusion mingled with guilt at the thought. How selfish to feel something like that, even for a fleeting moment.

"Did you know her?"

"Yes." He stopped then and loosened his grip, leaning back against the edge of the ship.

"We've all lost someone. Either to the tribute or in war." His features dampened with grief as he said, "Bayne went in to save her."

I didn't need him to go on to know that she couldn't be saved. The captain had told me as much, and if that weren't enough, he hadn't brought anyone back with him.

"I'm sorry."

I didn't know what else to say. The heartbreak that must come from losing someone in that way—to lose their soul and have their bodies transformed into something barely recognizable.

"How did he escape?"

Ronan shook his head, clarity returning to his features.

"He *leached* himself one night, disguised himself as one of their own. Lost an unimaginable amount of blood and well, you know what happened after that."

I stared at him, dumbfounded, then remembered the long, vertical gashes along the inside of Bayne's forearms when we'd pulled him aboard.

"How did he swim that far after losing so much blood?"

"*Bayne the Unbroken*." He shrugged. "The things he's capable of are hard to believe. I've known him for ten years, and I'd follow him anywhere. That goes for all of us on this ship."

I leaned back against the edge of the ship next to him, chewing on his words as we took a brief break.

"Where did Nerissa learn to fight?"

"Nis was a Lotrennial War Slayer, a special force of assassins used for espionage. The wolf skull on her shoulder marks her as one. It dates back to the War of Ruin," he said, a hint of admiration entering his voice.

Breath shot through my lips.

"How old are they? Were they *there*?"

Ronan chuckled. "Younger than the good king of ours, but old enough to have fought in the War of the Elders," he said, pausing at my look of confusion. "Lotrennia's first real push against Dark King Daimos after the War of Ruin," he clarified. "About a century ago. They lost. Miserably."

I stopped moving and contemplated what he'd told me— to be that old, to have seen and experienced so much. I realized then that their physical features—the ears, swiftness, and strength—were not what truly made them different from humans. It was their lives and experiences that made it impossible to compare.

"*She* was a prisoner of war." He glanced out at the waves. "She was held in Mount Telum for sixteen years and escaped."

That was how she'd gotten us out. I'd only been there a few

hours. The thought of surviving underground in a cell for that long. And who knew what other horrors she'd endured at the hands of her captors. *My* king.

"Why was she held at Mount Telum if Sultira wasn't involved in that war?" I asked, confused.

"Why, indeed?" Ronan said, grimacing.

"Did Vulcan have something to do with it?"

Ronan tipped his head to the side. "He did. He was a part of her team and—" He stopped abruptly as Aquila swooped down from the main mast.

"I'll fill you in later," he murmured.

We followed Aquila as he banked around the back of the ship and landed center deck about fifty feet away, where the rest of the crew waited. The captain walked swiftly up the stairs from below deck. He hopped up the last four sets of stairs as lithe and predatory as a mountain cat.

Dressed in dark brown leathers adorned with belts of daggers and laced with pockets, Bayne cast a striking portrait, a prince of the sea. Pigment had returned to his skin, and the vivid green of his eyes was a striking contrast to the dark attire. An odd awareness that I hadn't felt in a long while coiled around my midsection. Distant sensations brushed against my memories of hot damp skin and smooth lips bordered with prickly unshaven cheeks.

"We should make landfall in five hours." His words pulled me out of my momentary trance.

"Isla will stay on the ship with Marian and Oslo to keep the cloak in place and ready for our departure, which should be six hours after we land if all goes as planned." They nodded, though Oslo sat back, his head lowering in disappointment.

A bristle of nerves fluttered in my belly, replacing the pleasant feeling that was there only moments before. They planned to be out and back in only six hours.

"The rest of us will swim ashore. We'll enter the city over the north wall and head to Mount Telum."

"Lyvia, we'll need you to join us in the castle to identify the map and any other artifacts found at the burial site. After we find the stone, you are free to go if you wish."

Vulcan and Isla gaped at him. Nerissa sucked in a sharp, furious breath. Even Ronan, Oslo, and Marian blinked in surprise. I knew too much. But the captain's gaze didn't falter as he made eye contact with me.

I had one task to complete. Stick with this crew until we got to the castle. I had no doubt they'd be able to get us in with what I'd seen already, and I'd thought about my choice over the last few days. I wasn't thrown into these circumstances by choice, and while some of these people were easy to like, I wasn't a part of this crew. They were not my family. I *had* a family. They were out there somewhere, and I needed to find them. I'd stay with the crew and then find my father, Drystan, and Father Marcus. If I didn't, I'd make it to the manor and flee with Tiberius. I'd head west and find my brother.

I nodded.

"Good. We get in and out without being seen. Ronan, you'll have maybe five minutes with her."

Ronan gave an affirmative tilt of his chin. I looked at him in question, and he didn't return my gaze. As much as I'd spoken to the queensguard over the past days, I never really learned anything about him or his past. I glanced at Nerissa, searching for a reaction, but only saw raw determination in her eyes as she listened to her brother.

"Aquila will be our eyes and ears as we enter the city, and should things change, he'll notify the ship and we'll rendezvous at the normal spot in two days," the captain said, making it sound like they'd done this a time or two.

"Lyvia, a moment." He pinned me to the spot with that

stare of his while the others departed, recognizing the dismissal.

He approached me, stopping only a foot away and wafting notes of pine, sea, and sunshine in my direction.

"It's not guaranteed we find out what happened to your father tonight when we go back for the stone. We will not pass near the ranch on the way in or out of the city. If you choose to approach your home and have a look around, that's up to you, but I won't risk my crew remaining in the capital longer than necessary. What I said before still stands. You can join us if you wish. Or we can part ways tonight."

He then stepped closer and leveled a quiet stare at me. "We've told you quite a lot these past few days. I'm not in the business of silencing young women for fear they might share my secrets..."

My insides turned at the intent behind his words and the lethal quietness with which he spoke them.

"But there will be consequences for any words spoken that result in harm to my crew."

I nodded, suppressing a shudder at the blatant threat. "I won't say a word."

CHAPTER NINE

*We have reached the bottom. The last shipment of larimer
stone has left Kayj and shall arrive in Aedrialis next month.
—Correspondence to King Saros, 3rd of his name, dated
15th of Spring, 233.2E. Aedrialis.*

The Cascada Arches loomed high above the black
shore. The five, massive stone structures towered
over the Ripped River in the distance, only a few
hundred feet from where the *Evecta* dropped anchor. From this
angle, the giant marble structure resembled fingers, tipped and
touching together as if reaching from the dark river below. Not
unlike the way Isla steepled her fingers while controlling the
wind. I furrowed my brows, pulling my thoughts back.

I felt indecent, dressed in nothing but my leggings and
undershirt. I stood at the edge of the ship, arms folded across
my chest, close enough to feel the heat of the shirtless captain
next to me.

My stupid jaw hung open when he'd stepped from the captain's quarters, upper body bare save for the intricate swirls of black that inked across his chiseled chest and abdomen. Whorls of various thickness spiraled across his chest to a large circle in the center that somewhat resembled the sun, framed with feathery ferns. Waves crashed in its center, and I thought if I got close enough, I might see the outline of mountains on a distant coastline.

My cheeks had heated in embarrassment as Isla nudged me in the side and I clamped my mouth shut, averting my eyes which caught on Ronan's equally impressive physique before landing on Vulcan. The elf's entire torso and arms were covered with leafy whorls of ink, and his shoulder bore a matching wolf skull to the one on Nerissa's.

I sucked in a deep breath as I braced myself for the jump. What came next was a shock to my entire system. The blast of chill air that flew up to greet me as my feet left the wood stunned me before I plunged into icy black water. I'd gotten so used to the warmth of Isla's summer breeze aboard the ship, I forgot autumn had landed.

My body responded with instinct, and I kicked. Crisp air stung my face as I broke the surface. Muscles starving for heat, I swam as hard as I could through the rough waves, fighting against the tide moving out. I was the last to make it to shore, lungs drinking in the lapis-scented air. The others were already dressing and drying off their weapons. I spotted similar whorls of ink snaking up Nerissa's chest before she tugged her leather vest tight.

We dressed swiftly and silently. I donned the black cloak, pulling the hood up and draping the mask across my face, pinning it behind my ear. I eyed the others feeling small, a doe among wolves. The captain gave the signal, and we were off at a trot.

It took us thirty minutes to get through the gnarled trees of the shore to the northern gates of Aedrialis. Hidden among the brush, I observed as two patrol guards approached the watch tower and two left. The bone-white colossal walls rose eighty feet into the air, and as the changing of the guards commenced, Vulcan lassoed a rope onto one of the empty pikes just below the tower.

Amusement bubbled as I thought of the irony. The pike, meant for enemies of Sultira, was now a tool for our entry to the capital. It quickly died as I recalled the nature of how they were used. Images of spiked bodies and blood raining down the sides of the marble white walls flashed through my memories.

Vulcan scaled the wall, rendering both guards unconscious in a matter of seconds. Ronan fashioned another one of his handy harnesses for me as the rest climbed like an invasion of eight-legged insects I wasn't fond of. I felt more than inadequate as Vulcan hauled me up the side of the wall. We ran the length of the wall and down the guard stairs into a part of the capital I'd never seen. We moved at such a fast speed my lungs and thighs burned by the time the gates of Mount Telum were in view.

Apprehension danced with my nerves as I took in the sight. Was I truly about to break into Mount Telum as a fugitive? Though our manor sat miles to the southeast, I'd spent countless hours in the castle as a lady-in-waiting. *Fortress* was more accurate, as my eyes climbed its walls to the turrets that scraped the sky.

It rose from the center of the city like a spear thrust through an enemy's chest.

Its gleaming white exterior reflected the light of our gods, golden in the daylight and blue in the night. The stone used for its construction, over six hundred years ago, was called larimer. It was harder than most rock and so rare that most believed no more existed outside of the city.

Ronan took the lead as we neared the castle, weaving in and out of the alleys until we came to a small service door on the eastern side of the fortress, two guards chatting in the darkness. It was Nerissa, this time, who silently put them to sleep. As I tiptoed past, I now noticed the empty bottles she'd placed in their hands.

We stole through the gates and were inside the castle walls within minutes. We raced up the servants' stairwell stopping after four flights, where I greedily chugged from my waterskin as Ronan and the captain exchanged a few mumbled words.

Ronan turned to me, giving my shoulder a squeeze and nodding a quiet farewell before disappearing into the dim hallway. The rest of us continued up another three flights. We flew through a small room into another hall, finally coming to a stop outside the castle's shrine to Aelius, god of the sun. Nerissa disappeared down the hall to the left to check for guards. She was back within seconds and motioned us toward a small door next to the entrance to the shrine room.

Desks strewn with unfinished work lined the walls and tools used for analyzing various objects neatly adorned the shelves. Chests full of artifacts, each carefully labeled and coded, sat at the front.

"Be quick. We need anything you recognize from the burial chamber." The captain glanced at me and nodded at the others. "The rest of us will look for the stone until Ronan returns."

I scanned the room, straining to see in the dark, not daring to light any tapers. I ruffled through chest after chest looking for anything. The scrolls were nowhere to be found. I checked the long stone benches containing salt, typically used to preserve artifacts found on the digs, and found nothing.

My heart leaped as I spied a bookcase of scholar journals. I rushed to the wall and began running my fingers over them, searching... Maybe it was here. It wouldn't have surprised me if Father Marcus had come here first to notify High Priest Helmar of our discovery. He was meticulous and a creature of habit, even in the way he stuffed his pipe with enderleaf on the ride home once finished for the day. If he came here first, he might have placed his journal in with the rest.

My fingers raced over the spines reading name after name until footsteps sounded and the door to the shrine next to us opened with a whoosh.

The captain moved so fast I didn't see him until he pinned me to the corner of the room. Our backs flat against the wall, he signed something to Vulcan and Nerissa at the other end. Vulcan signed back and realization hit me. They *signed*. They were using the signs I taught them for Marian. A warm feeling briefly rushed into my chest, quickly replaced with unease as I remembered where we stood.

"I'll find Ronan," Nerissa signed back as she slipped out the door with lethal grace before I could blink.

Mumbled talking began on the other side of the wall.

King Saros.

Vulcan moved across the room to where a servant's door connected to the shrine room, silently sliding a chair under the handle and pressing his ear to the door. The captain motioned me to follow.

"—unfortunate circumstances, but necessary."

I could barely hear the king's voice. He was so frail and withered. I still wasn't sure if I believed what Ronan and the others had shared about him. A scraping noise sounded as his staff slid across the room. He always had it with him. The silver-lined scepter stretched seven feet long spinning into the sigil of our kingdom: a softly glowing sun with two overlapping crescent moons and at its top, a sharp, white arrowhead. He always held it in his left hand, his right too weak with its missing fingers.

Someone with heavy boots walked closer to our wall.

"Unfortunate or not, Your Grace, the kingsguard's actions from the other night have left us in a precarious position."

I stopped breathing entirely as the shock of hearing my father's voice froze my body and mind. The wave of relief that flowed through me at the discovery of his safety was momentary, as confusion and uncertainty filled my gut with lead. What was he doing here? The captain's iron grip was over my mouth before I could release a breath.

"I'm not sure what you want me to do, Lord Cantor. We had to bring her in. And with those brown eyes of hers... I don't take threats to the kingdom lightly..."

"Threat or not, I'm certain she can find the rest. She is the key, Your Grace." My father's voice had taken on that tone I'd heard so many times. So persuasive. He had a way of getting what he wanted, from anyone.

"What of the mother? Was she?"

"Blessed with blue? No."

"And the father?"

"Unknown."

The king's sigh was barely audible through the door. Who were they talking about? The captain released his hand, and I slumped. He put a finger to his lips. I nodded and pressed my ear to the door.

"Tell me again about the process."

"We'd start with the elixir from High Priest Helmar, usually in her tea before our rides beyond the capital gates..."

Unease slowly coiled its way through my gut.

"—and I'd get her talking about the history of Sultira or her recent digs..."

My heart thumped rapidly in my chest as if trying to escape, making my long braid tremble despite being frozen in place.

The king interrupted, "And she'd just *find* them?"

"Yes. Every time. Lyvia always said there was something in the way the ground beneath the grass moved and 'whispered of a hidden past.'"

I could feel the color drain from my face, bile rising to my throat. My father's words were like a match hitting the barrel in the scope of everything that had transpired since my discovery of the tomb.

I didn't have to look up to know that Vulcan and the captain stared at me. I couldn't meet their eyes. The burn of salty tears rose behind my own, and some part of me inside that had always been soft and safe, hardened, shoving them back down. I steadied my breath.

Something inside brought me back to reality and the realization of the danger I was in. It was as if I'd been floating along in some dream, or nightmare, and I'd wake up as soon as I found my father. I didn't allow the devastation or shock of what could only be a lifelong betrayal sink into my gut.

"I'm wondering why, Lord Cantor, you've only just now shared this information with me. How long have you and High Priest Helmar been testing her?" Icy fury coated his words, not unlike the ice frosting my heart. I'd never heard the king sound so dangerous.

"I had to be sure, Your Grace. I was on my way to consult with Lord Pavel when your *dogs* arrived at my manor," my father said, words dripping with disgust.

The king didn't respond for a long moment. My heart continued to drum wildly in my chest. "Lord Cantor, if she *is* the one Olienna spoke of... She needs to be found and brought in—or silenced."

The words settled in my gut.

"You're certain the mother has been taken care of?"

My father's next words were clipped. "Yes, Your Grace. She was given as tribute twenty years ago."

An eerie stillness seeped through my veins as my father confirmed the devastating truth of what the *Evecta's* crew had shared with me. The tribute was indeed real, and the king, perhaps even my own father, was complicit.

"Very well. We'll discuss this in the morning with the Grand Counsel. High Priest Helmar is almost finished with the stone at the Temple of the Sky. He'll leave for Stynguard tomorrow. Come."

I was numb by the time they'd finished and left the room, the door thudding closed. A heavy silence filled the scholar room. The captain and Vulcan signed to each other as I stared blankly at the bookshelf I'd rummaged through minutes ago.

Vulcan moved toward the exit, and the captain motioned me to follow. I pulled my eyes from the bookshelf, and they snagged on a small ivory triangle, just beneath. I stopped and quickly shot across the room, pulling the opened journal from under the large stand. I didn't need to check the name to know whose handwriting it was. *Father Marcus.*

Vulcan and the captain were almost out of the door as I began signing frantically trying to get their attention. "Dungeons!"

I reached out and the captain whipped around, his hand flying to my wrist before I could so much as grasp his cloak. "We need to stop at the dungeons," I hissed in the dark. "We have to look for Drystan and Father Marcus. They could be alive."

He shook his head. "That's not part of the plan."

I yanked my arm attempting to break free, but his grip tightened.

"You're free to return and search for them after we find the stone," he breathed, "Move."

He released my wrist, sending me after Vulcan with a slight shove. I gritted my teeth, knowing Vulcan would simply throw me over a shoulder if I tried to stay. A sickening twist sank into my gut at the thought of leaving Father Marcus and Drystan behind.

We met Nerissa and Ronan at the top of the stairs. The grim expression on Ronan's face told me enough about how his encounter had gone. We exited the castle the way we came in and ran east toward the Temple of the Sky. I trotted along, gripping Father Marcus's journal so hard my nails dug divots into the leather. Nerissa and Ronan left a trail of unconscious guards in our wake. Too many for it to look like a coincidence.

We approached the black-marbled temple from the rear. Its outer columns rose fifty feet into the air like beams of black night shooting down from the sky. I'd been here countless times for lectures and other lessons, but tonight, the familiar hall that once brought excitement and anticipation, loomed dark and ominous as if it could sense outsiders in its walls. The numerous waterfalls in the center of the hall drowned out the pitter-patter of our steps on the marble floor. We flew to the second level, not passing a single guard, the temple eerily empty.

Then I felt it.

CHAPTER TEN

A warrior may someday find himself without saddle or rope.
When that time comes, he'd better hope he speaks the same
language as his mount.
— From A Horseman's Duty, *Chapter 2, first edition*
written by Lord Willem Cantor.

The deep thrumming of the stone vibrated and pulsed.
Hum, hum, hum.

My heart slowed, matching its beat as an ache formed in my chest, pulling me toward the small bit of darkness.

At some point, I'd stopped running. I stood in the center of the hall as the others raced toward the entrance of the high priest's room. The captain skidded to a stop and looked back. Our eyes met for a moment before chaos erupted outside the entryway. Ten guards burst from the door and attacked with such fury, I was certain we wouldn't make it out of the temple, let alone the capital, alive.

Vulcan and Nerissa cut through the fray with lethal grace and unnatural accuracy. They downed four guards before the captain flew in from behind and sliced through three more. Ronan ran toward me, gripping my elbow and hauling me away from the fight. My feet felt like lead as I tried to run, but the ache in my chest screamed in protest as I pulled myself farther from the room.

It wasn't right. It didn't feel right. We shouldn't go this way.

Turn around.

I needed it. I stopped, skidding on my heels, and twisted out of Ronan's grasp, using the defensive move he'd taught me only days before. I rushed forward before a solid arm wrapped around my stomach, knocking the wind out of me. I doubled over. My feet left the floor as he heaved me up.

His grip loosened, and I dropped to the floor. The scream that reverberated in my ears suddenly snapped me from my stupor. I wheeled around to find a guard standing over Ronan, who lay face down on the marble floor, with his blade held high above his head ready for the killing blow. The sword flew down, but was met by another before it could slice into Ronan's back. The captain attacked with such fury that some primal part of me cowered. He carved him up quickly, slicing up the center of the guard's abdomen before twisting around and taking his head off.

Silence followed.

Vulcan rushed to pick up Ronan, whose blood drenched through his black cloak. The captain grabbed his other shoulder, and Nerissa sprinted forward, searching for another way out.

We followed a back staircase down to the main hall where the distant clatter of boots met our ears. More guards. A sharp right took us out to the back alley.

Why had I turned around? If I hadn't... Guilt hit me like the kingsguard's fist. It was my fault Ronan was being dragged out of the Temple of the Sky, leaving a bloody trail in our wake. Nausea roiled in my gut. How would we escape? Had this been a trap? I had to get us out.

"Stop! Stop! Turn here!" I shouted, my voice hoarse. We weren't that far from our land. If we could get to the agrippa herd, we'd get out of Aedrialis.

To my surprise, they stopped and followed me. Gripped by new determination, I flew down the cobbled streets, past the alley where they'd gutted that poor colt, and around the corner. I slowed as we approached Cantor Manor. Royal guards replaced our family guards. The sight of my home left a knot of unease in my gut.

I turned to Nerissa. "They will have guards at the stables. If you can take care of them, I'll find our rides out of here. Let me handle the hounds," I whispered through ragged breath.

She nodded.

"Meet us by the last pasture in the back. There's a trail to the southeastern gate that connects to our land."

The captain gave a firm nod. I sprinted toward the stables, Nerissa in tow. A low growl sounded from the gates, and I let out a soft whistle. Padded steps sounded in the dirt, and I gave the two brindle hounds a scratch under the chin. They eyed Nerissa warily but let us pass.

The ex-war slayer made quick work of the two guards on duty, silencing them before they knew she was there. I flew down the main aisle and out the back, aiming for a small paddock of land where a massive black stud stood.

Tiberius turned and nickered as he walked over to the gate. The sound filled me with warmth as I realized there was still a part of my home untainted.

I threw open the gate and grabbed a fistful of mane. My back leg screamed in protest as I swung it over his back, burning from the strain I'd already put on it and barely making it high enough to hook over his spine and pull myself up.

Not bothering with tack, I pulled Nerissa up behind me and we flew to a neighboring paddock that housed three agrippa mares. Tiberius whinnied suggestively and danced, his enormous hooves stomping back and forth.

"Not now, boy." I patted his withers.

Nerissa slid off Ti's back and haltered the mares before mounting the last. She pulled the other two in tow, and we galloped along the remaining pastures. I scanned the darkness as we approached the trailhead.

"There!"

I followed Nerissa's gaze as the dark figures came into view. They staggered along, slower than when we left them minutes before. Vulcan and the captain carried Ronan. Dread sank in. He *couldn't* be dead. A shout erupted from the stables, and three guards sprinted for us. Nerissa slowed at the sight of Ronan's limp body, torn between pursuing the guards or stopping to help.

"Get him up!" I shouted to her.

I might not have been trained to fight, but Tiberius was.

Leaning left, I twisted as we reached the corner, and he pivoted around my leg. I bent forward, grabbed a fistful of mane as my calves wrapped around his body, and whispered "*Impetum.*"

My intentions made clear, he thundered toward the guards, ears pinned, and teeth bared. Within seconds, he was on the first guard who didn't have time to react, massive black hooves crunching through armor. He stomped through his shield and chest plate, leaving the guard heaving as he choked on his blood.

Anticipating the attack of the two remaining guards, he lashed out with his front legs, hooves coming down on the helmet of the first, knocking him down. He crashed into the second, knocking him off balance before throwing a buck to land a crushing blow to his face. The first was back on his feet, long sword in position to slice across Tiberius's chest.

Unlike the young, untrained colt, Ti kept his front feet planted and swung his head into the guard's sword arm before ripping at the weak point in his armor beneath his armpit. The guard's scream echoed in the darkness before Ti finished him off with a crushing blow to the face.

The sound rang in my ears as I twisted on his broad back, urging us toward the crew now waiting at the head of the trail. I'd spent half my life training Tiberius. I'd given him that command countless times in the arena and always walked away feeling uneasy, stomach churning at the sight of the shredded, straw dummies.

I felt absolutely nothing as we galloped back to the crew through the darkness. I had no remorse toward the guards we slew. The guards *I* slew. Ti might have delivered the blow, but it was on my command.

I could feel their eyes on me as we approached.

"This way!" I shouted without slowing.

The royal guard had to know where we were headed as there was only one way out of the city from this trail.

We rode hard. The captain in tow behind me, Vulcan holding the unconscious Ronan, and Nerissa in the rear. We sped down the dark trail lined with fir trees, the pounding of the agrippa's hooves filling the air like thunder in the night.

The city walls loomed ahead over a small service gate. The

four guards, two at the top of the wall and two at the gate, turned their attention toward us as they took in our party. Realizing we weren't slowing, they scrambled, shouting orders and taking up defensive positions. Arrows rained from above.

I urged Ti faster, spurring him on with my legs, leaning into the side of his neck, and staying as low as possible. The guards at the gate drew their longswords. This time, the captain and Nerissa flanked me, blades out, and sliced through the soldiers. I aimed Ti straight at the gate. He crashed through the wooden beams, the blow making my teeth clank together. We flew into the night, arrows following our trail as the city walls loomed behind us.

Our freedom was short-lived as a team of soldiers, astride their own war horses, galloped after us. We flew through the vast plain, guided by moonslight as the dim hue of the city faded behind us, heading straight for the Lumerian Mountain range.

The resounding beat of the soldiers deepened as they closed in. I spurred Ti faster. Cold autumn air stung my eyes, a line of tears running across my temple. I risked a glance behind, my stomach pitching. We couldn't outrun them. Not with Vulcan holding Ronan. His mare couldn't keep pace.

Ahead, a looming dark shape materialized out of the black sky. Ti's ears pinned and he tensed, readying himself for an attack as he thundered harder toward the shape flapping in our direction. I braced myself for the collision and instead felt an enormous whoosh of cold air as Aquila soared down from above, barely clearing my head.

Someone screamed in surprise and armor thunked from behind as Aquila began his attack. I risked another glance. Half of the soldiers had slowed their pursuit attempting to fight off the massive hawk. Aquila dodged their blades and aimed for another, his dagger-like talons piercing the armor and ripping him from his steed.

The captain barked an order from behind. He and Nerissa split, heading opposite directions, and circled back for a flank attack. Steel clashed, and I slowed Tiberius to a gallop, allowing Vulcan's mare to catch up.

"Keep going! We head for the foothills!"

His command was cut off by a gut-wrenching screech from behind. Aquila was hurt.

I raced Tiberius forward, the massive Lumerian peaks looming over the foothills as we approached. A dense forest covered the slopes, dotted with large outcroppings of rock.

The sound of battle quieted, and I slowed Tiberius to a trot as we approached the thick trees. A quiet moan escaped Ronan as Vulcan eased his mare to a halt. Their heavy breathing matched my own, and my heart pounded with Tiberius's as we took in the dark forest.

Vulcan hopped off his mare and gently pulled Ronan to the ground. He set him behind a small group of trees, propping him up on a boulder. I balked at the amount of blood that soaked the ground in his wake. He was going to die if we didn't stop the bleeding.

Vulcan gathered some brush and laid it across Ronan's body, camouflaging him among the thick trees. He mounted his mare and turned to face the plains as distant galloping filled the night.

Ti heaved a sigh. I suppressed a shiver as a cool breeze blew the braid off my neck, my pants cold and soaked with Ti's foamy sweat.

Vulcan unsheathed his blade and moved his mare forward, readying for an attack. I positioned Ti about fifteen feet away, my heart continuing its thunder in my chest. We waited, hardly breathing. Vulcan's shoulders relaxed seconds before I realized there were only two horses heading toward us and I immediately recognized their riders.

Our relief was short-lived after the captain's next words.

"Aquila is injured, but he should make it back to the ship." He paused for a moment. "And two of the guards retreated."

Nerissa fumed.

The captain leveled a stare at her. "We didn't have time to pursue them. We need to get Ronan somewhere safe."

"If two escaped then we can be sure they know who was in the capital tonight," Vulcan cut in. "This mission was a disaster. What the fuck happened?"

The captain threw me a glance and dismounted to kneel by Ronan. Suffocating guilt filled my chest.

"It was my fault. I'm sorry. He came to lead me away from the fighting, but I..."

What did I do? I'd stopped. I'd practically thrown him off me to be near the Obscura Stone.

"I hesitated. I'm sorry."

"I told you she was a liability," Vulcan snapped at the captain before turning to me. "And you have some explaining to do. What was King Saros referring to? It would seem you know more than you've let on."

Nerissa's head snapped toward me at the accusation.

"I knew she was hiding something," she said quietly.

I gritted my teeth, doing my best not to shrink beneath her stare. Alone. I felt utterly alone. I didn't know these people. I didn't even know my father.

Not my father, I remembered. *Lord Cantor.*

The amalgamation of memories with him, the words exchanged with King Saros, and the events of the last week swirled in my mind and behind my eyes like a cauldron boiling over. They rose up and up until my head started to spin and an ache formed. I squeezed Ti's mane, my fingernails digging painfully into my palm. And I shoved the thoughts back, plunging them down as if they were a ship sinking into the depths of the sea—down into the darkness where I could lose them forever. I slowly released Ti's mane.

"Why should I trust any of you?" I snapped back at her.

"Enough." The captain's voice rang with authority as he cut me a glare. "We don't have time for this right now. The coast will be watched too closely to return. We make for Crown Peak."

I blinked. Crown Peak led to a part of the mountain few dared to trek and even fewer returned from. Rumors of a haunting in that part of the mountain circulated throughout Aedrialis. *Stone Witch*, people whispered. I shoved down the fear that slipped into my throat.

Ronan moaned as the captain and Nerissa mumbled and moved their hands over his back. Small bits of light, brighter and more brilliant than Isla's, bounced around Ronan's body. The sickening smell of burning flesh wafted into my nostrils, and I suppressed a shudder. The captain hunched over Ronan, his dark hair dripping with cold sweat as brother and sister used their own form of magic I had yet to see.

Nerissa brought a waterskin to Ronan's lips, coaxing it in. To my shock, he coughed before chugging it down, blinking his eyes open.

"What the hell happened?"

"We'll talk later. Can you ride?" The captain reached an arm around him.

"I think so."

"Let's go. They'll be sending a search party. You're on this mare."

Ronan winced as the captain gave him a leg up on the tall mare, whose black coat was slick with sweat.

"I'm riding with you," he said as his eyes met mine with

that sudden intensity. A statement, not a question. Yet he waited. Even in the dimmest dawn, I could see the little facets of green dancing in his gaze.

I nodded.

The captain approached Tiberius with a closed fist, allowing him to step forward and meet it with his soft muzzle. I eyed him warily as he whispered something to him and gave him a pat on the neck.

He swung a leg up and settled in behind me. I tensed, waiting for the touch of his body behind mine and an arm that would wrap around my waist, but neither came. He sat close enough for the heat of his body to brush against mine, but not the touch. It felt strangely... polite.

I nudged Ti forward. We trundled through the thick trees and rocky outcropping, making surprisingly quick progress up through the foothills considering the fatigue of our party.

A hazy mist shrouded the rising sun by the time we'd made it up the first two slopes of the mountain and approached the entrance to Crown Peak. The pathway leading to the entrance pass narrowed, its edge a sharp cut against the steep cliff.

"You good, Nis?" Ronan croaked from behind.

Nerissa slowly turned around, and the glare he received in return was enough to turn my stomach. Was she... afraid of heights? The notion that she could be afraid of anything seemed preposterous.

Elevation cooled the air. I tugged my coat tighter across my chest, grateful for the protection it provided against the wind. The entrance was dark—as two steep slopes of the mountain rose up on either side—and narrower than I'd expected. I scanned the footing.

It would be impossible for horses to trek through that treacherous crevasse, not to mention the massive agrippa. Realization hit. They intended to leave the horses.

I could go, though. Finally break free from this group. But we were still so close to Aedrialis, the coast an inky smudge on the horizon. If Saros sent scouts, he'd find me. I was sure of it. My heart squeezed hard enough to crack as I realized I'd taken my last ride on Tiberius.

"We send the horses north at the split and cover our trail," the captain announced from behind.

I hopped down, my feet stinging as I hit the hard rocky ground. My thighs ached after the night of running and riding. Ti nudged me with his big head. I gave him a little scratch under the chin as the captain approached the others and surveyed the entrance to the pass.

"Thank you," I whispered to Ti, hoping none of the others could hear. A burning sensation rose behind my eyes, and I quickly shoved it down. I kissed him on the nose before taking a step back. The mares had gathered behind, eyeing their leader.

I pointed down the northern slope and clucked my tongue. The dim hue of the early morning sun illuminated the trees and plains below.

"*Dimitte*," I said.

Questioning the dismissal, Tiberius stomped his hoof, his dark eyes surveying me. I groaned despite warmth blooming in my chest at his refusal.

I clucked again. "*Dimitte*."

Stomp.

"*Go*," I commanded.

Stomp.

"Please," I whispered, voice breaking. I retreated a step before slapping his rear hard enough for the sting to burn across my hand. He pinned his ears before stomping again, but this time he trotted off, the four mares in tow. I watched as they picked up speed, freedom fueling their flight. The agrippa of the Lumerians finally returned home.

Nerissa and Vulcan slipped into the ominous crevasse. Ronan gave me a half grin before following. The captain met my eyes with an uncomfortable, knowing look. I pulled mine away before I could read into it and stepped into the dark, narrow mountain passageway with a single reminder.

I am not afraid of the dark.

CHAPTER ELEVEN

The Sending: on Sultira's official day of mourning, death prayers shall be collected prior to the Sending Ceremony where the high priest will commend the souls of the deceased to Tynan, god of death.
—From the Religious Protocol Records, Temple of the Sky, Aedrialis.

The sun was blocked from view in the pass. Cold, wet air drew moisture onto the rocky walls we passed, dripping onto the leather of my coat as we squeezed and scraped through rock. Silence hung heavily in the air. My mind now matched my body in numbness, unfazed by the eeriness of the dank trail.

We hiked for a few hours before we made it to a small clearing where the steep walls of rock opened up, letting a sliver of light illuminate the wider trail. We stopped to rest.

Nerissa pulled provisions from her pack and began distributing. I sucked down a few mouthfuls of water from my almost empty waterskin.

Ronan closed his eyes as he leaned against the side of the mountain. I could feel the blood rush into my feet and legs as I slunk next to him, painfully pumping to the beat of my heart. My daze wore off as muffled arguing reached me, and I glanced up to see the three elves approach.

The captain squatted on the balls of his feet across from me. "We need to talk about what happened last night."

"Which part?" I muttered, certain I didn't want to discuss this.

"Let's start with the conversation between your father and King Saros."

I waited for the unease to twist in my gut, but any normal emotional response to what we'd overheard the night prior was blocked. Snuffed out like the mountain's mist clouding the skies from the sun. My eyes remained pinned to the leather laces of my boots and my lips shut. I felt... nothing.

A growl of annoyance escaped Vulcan's lips. "You're not going to talk now? You didn't tell us *you* found the burial site. What else are you withholding?"

"Why does that matter?"

"Did you not hear the Horse Lord? He's been *testing* you, drugging you, and using whatever power it is you've been hiding from us to find the Obscura Stone. For the *king*."

Drugged. It hadn't felt that way. I'd felt alive and aware. Always so aware when we'd scout for excavation sites. "I have no idea what power you're talking about! My father—"

"He's not your father if you didn't catch that," Vulcan spat. His sneer met his eyes as he cut me off.

Fiery anger sluiced through the numbness, his words cutting like daggers. "Fuck you," I snapped back at him, searching my memories with Aeriden for the best string of

94

curses to add on when the captain jerked his chin, shooting Vulcan a look that promised pain.

Vulcan pushed off the mountain wall with a scoff and retreated to the darkness.

"How did you find them?" the captain murmured, turning back to me. Despite his calm voice, it was firm, more demand in the question than kindness.

I ground my teeth, debating whether I'd answer, but something in the captain's gaze made me pause. A desperation lay in his eyes, a deep, long-seated need to unravel some riddle. "We would go for a ride. Just me and my..." I finally replied, the word *father* catching in my throat. "Me and him. And I'd get a feeling."

"A feeling?" he asked, raising a brow.

"Yes," I replied, unable to keep the irritation from my voice, "a feeling. Like the truth was waiting."

"And you found all of the Death Scholar sites, not just the one with the stone?" he continued.

I nodded in the darkness. "I suppose I'm drawn to death."

There is truth in death, I reminded myself. Father Marcus's words steadied me before the dread of his fate sunk in. *Father Marcus.* I had gotten distracted with questions about the conversation we'd overheard and trying to survive the night that I'd forgotten about the journal. My hand went to the concealed pocket in my coat, and I felt the thin leather journal. I pulled my attention back to the elves.

"If she is in any way connected to the prophecy of Olienna, she will be hunted by more than the kings and queens of this world." Nerissa paused and looked at me as if I were infected. "The Lords of Marisarma will come, Bayne. *We* will be hunted."

The captain turned to Nerissa with a knowing look. "We

don't know if she's connected to the prophecy. And if she is, we may yet find there's a reason—"

"What prophecy?" I interrupted, feeling increasingly blinded by new information.

"Shortly after the War of Ruin," the captain began, "a seer prophesized the coming of the next generation of Bella–"

But Nerissa had cut him off. Her voice was soft and song-like as she recited:

> *"Bloodless armies from below*
> *circle the carrion from the crow.*
> *The Sisters shield us from the Brother*
> *and signal the coming of another.*
> *From the stars, there will rise*
> *a spark that beats in the warrior's eyes.*
> *Blessed with blue*
> *the heart is true.*
> *If shadowed and dark,*
> *Death to the monarch.*
> *Saviors return from beyond*
> *and shape our fate with the bond."*

NERISSA'S EYES had taken on a glassy look as she finished. She blinked, looking back at me. She truly looked at me, not dismissing me for the burdensome human she thought I was. Her gaze pierced my soul, and I had the disarming sense she knew more about me than I did. The captain watched her for a moment, and turned to me, his face thoughtful yet tense.

"As I'm sure you have devised, bloodless armies refer to the ashen. There is debate on who the crow is. Some, your king included, believe it to be Dark King Daimos and the piles of bodies he leaves behind. Others argue it might be someone less obvious. The Sisters—"

"Are Ganmira and Renova," I said, cutting him off, "The Sending. It's talking about the twin solar eclipse when the moons cross paths with one another, blocking the sun."

I knew enough about the patterns from my basic studies with the Sky Scholars to know the event was an astrological phenomenon. The moons traveled across the sky toward each other, and once every twenty-four years, their paths crossed directly in front of the sun at the same exact time, shading the world from Aelius's penetrating rays and shrouding the Vael in a shadow of darkness.

The Sending was a day of mourning. A day of death. The one day we recognized or paid tribute to Tynan, the god of death. Aelius's brother. Ironically, I'd been born on the evening of a twin eclipse. It was a secret I kept most of my life, as those born on a twin eclipse were considered unlucky. The next Sending wouldn't take place for another two years.

The captain peered at me curiously before nodding. "Yes. And then it speaks of the return of the Bellators."

Ronan's eyes were open now, frowning as he watched the captain.

"The Bellators were guardians of light and life. They were beings who possessed great power. Not the sort of magic that we use today. Something older." The captain stared at the path before us, and his emerald eyes grew distant.

"They were gifts to human and elf-kind from the gods and the unifiers of our two peoples, protecting the world from an enemy so fearsome, not even our histories will name them. The Bellators guarded against this force for hundreds of years, the last of them dying out during the War of Ruin. Their power was amplified when they were bonded with their *caeluma*, extraordinary creatures, some say from other worlds, though they've long been forgotten. Some even believed the Bellators themselves were not of this world."

My thoughts drifted to Aquila. The massive bird seemed too intelligent and ancient for something of this world.

Ronan cleared his throat before saying, "The Bellator powers were godlike. They had a responsibility to the beings of this world. To defend and protect." His eyes slid from Bayne's to my own. "And the Bellator who wielded the Obscura Stone betrayed the others, bringing about their downfall."

A knot formed in my throat, my thoughts drifting to the stone. I glanced up, Nerissa's eyes still pinned on me. The captain drew my attention back.

"The prophecy speaks of the return of the Bellators. They'll come on a twin eclipse. King Saros believes that those blessed with blue will be our salvation and those with dark eyes... Well, you can imagine King Saros believes them to be a threat to himself since it references the monarch. Although the prophecy could just as easily be referring to Dark King Daimos. This is all assuming that the return of the Bellators even happens in our lifetime. Or the king's. He is not immortal."

"Close enough," Ronan scoffed.

I rubbed my eyes, taking in the information. Seers, magic, godlike power...

"Prophecies are tricky things. They're often not as straight-forward as one might assume." The captain stood then and stretched, cracking his neck.

"If this is true, why is none of it in our histories?" I turned to Ronan.

"You didn't know elves or magic existed up until a week ago. Knowledge is power, Lyvia. Few in our kingdom know about any of this, and those who do are either serving King Saros's agenda or they are excellent at hiding."

"In plain sight, some would say." Nerissa finally pulled her eyes away from me and raised her scarred brow at Ronan.

"I played my role well. As long as I could," he said, straightening and wincing at the movement.

"We need to get moving." Nerissa approached the captain as she gave her blade one last polish before sheathing it.

"Where exactly are we going?" I asked. The mountain pass sent a chill down my spine.

Nerissa and the captain exchanged a look.

"We are paying a visit to the Stone Witch," the captain said, his voice going deathly quiet.

Ronan swore as Vulcan inhaled sharply through his nose, a look of disgust passing over his features.

I swallowed the lump that formed in my throat. "She's real?" I asked, not sure I wanted to know the answer. Anyone who made this group grow deathly quiet after slaughtering tens of ashen and kingsguards without flinching would surely make me cower.

"She is a disgrace," Vulcan muttered as he stalked off to gather his things.

"She was an elf mage, long ago. She made her way to the human lands years ago. Not much is truly known about her, except that she practices dark magic. There are few we can turn to in Sultira right now. King Saros fears her enough that we stand a better chance of escaping into her mountain than we do trekking across the countryside. For now." The captain put his scarred hand on the sharp wall of the mountain.

"She knows we are coming." The mountain seemed to shudder as he pulled it away.

"Let's move." An order. The rest of the crew sheathed their weapons and started down the path. My body barked in protest as I stood and stretched. I winced as the burning sensation of newly formed blisters rubbed against my riding boots and took a step down the path.

THE LITTLE LIGHT that had found its way into the opening during our break quickly faded from view as our trail became narrower and treacherous. I picked up my pace until I reached Ronan.

"I'm sorry," I murmured, guilt still gnawing at my core.

He didn't respond immediately.

"Why did you stop?"

"To be honest, I don't know."

He pulled his gaze from mine, returning its focus to the pass.

"It's okay, Cantor. Comes with the territory," he said, eyeing the brother and sister as we walked several paces behind them.

"What they did... Their magic looked different from Isla's."

My voice was barely a whisper. I watched them, waiting for any indication that they'd heard me.

"You slipped my hold," he murmured, shaking his head.

"What?"

"You used the move I taught you. You used it better than when we practiced on the *Evecta*. It worked flawlessly." He peered at me, and his gaze traced my body beneath my coat, something primal passing over his features. I suppressed a shudder.

Unsure of what else to say, we continued our trek in silence. The only sound was the scuff of our coats against the rock and the padding of our feet. The trail began to descend, slightly at first, and then steeply, as if we were walking into the mouth of a beast. I steadied myself against the rocky wall with both hands on either side, unease coiling its way into my gut as the captain's words replayed. *She knows we're coming.* I wrenched my hands away, willing my heart to calm.

At some point, the light above disappeared entirely. We were underneath the mountain, or inside of it, I didn't know. I was lightheaded from the trek and the exhaustion from the night before began to take over.

Then we heard it. A spine-stiffening cackle echoed off the walls from every direction. It started soft and grew louder as the sound bounced off the rock and chased away any remaining light. The tensed outlines of the others slowed to a halt, and a moment later, a chilling voice filled my mind.

Hello, Death Digger. Your list of traitors grows bigger.

CHAPTER TWELVE

Legend claims the agrippa came down from clouded Lumeri-
ans; a thundering torrent of black, crushing everything in
their path.

— From A Horseman's Duty, *Chapter 1, first edition*
written by Lord Willem Cantor.

T
he voice of the Stone Witch was like gravel, grinding
and sickening and undoubtedly deadly. I couldn't
move, unsure if it was because she'd cast a spell on
me or if my nerves forbade my body from working.

You clean the bones yet know no home.

You've found what was lost but be wary the cost.

Who are you, I wonder? Bringer of sunshine or thunder?

My heart hammered in my chest as I willed my mind to go
blank, the riddles in my head like a sick violation of my
thoughts. The pass, or cave... wherever we were, had dropped

ten degrees. The crew froze. I could hear nothing but her voice resounding in my ears and the refrain of her cackle, still reverberating along the walls.

Time passed. Minutes? Hours? A loud thump sounded behind me. *Ronan.* He must have fallen. I stared ahead at the other crew members mere feet in front of me as something powerful pulled on my fatigue. They strained against some invisible force, their bodies going rigid. A bead of sweat dripped down my temple despite the chill air. The sudden drowsiness threatened to consume me. Some primal, instinctual part of me screamed against the threat of sleep. I had to stay awake. Stay awake. Stay awake.

My heart stopped when, to my horror, Vulcan and Nerissa collapsed. My sluggish gaze followed their limp bodies. I looked up to find the captain staring at me, his eyes equally heavy, and something like shock strewn across his features. He opened his mouth to speak and instead heaved a sigh as he crumpled to the ground.

Real, raw fear like nothing I'd ever experienced, even given the events of the last week, climbed its way up my spine as I realized I was the last one standing. I was helpless and weak, exhausted from the night before, with no knowledge of how to fight or defend myself against magic. I stood there for ten long heartbeats, each one coming slower than the one before. Footsteps made their way toward me. They stopped too far ahead to glimpse the evil that lurked in the darkness.

A deep, throaty growl rolled off the walls followed by a flash of blinding white light. For a split second, the lingering impression of two violet stars filled the space behind my eyelids before darkness consumed me.

I WAS FREE. We soared over cobalt blue waters, savoring the feeling of open air and endless space, the sky my true home. The curve of the world glowed a dim orange as brilliant rays peeked over the horizon, the sun bringing the dawn of a new day. The eastern wind ushered in misty clouds. Gulls shrieked in the distance followed by the bay of an ancient beast deep below the surface.

We banked left and dove below the gathering clouds, the land to the west coming into view in the distance. A moment later, a quiet hiss sounded from below. Realization hit and we banked right as a bolt of iron fired past, narrowly missing her left wing. We climbed, higher and higher until the misty clouds blocked all line of sight.

The scent of iron lingered in my nostrils. I ground my teeth, anger replacing the surprise at the unexpected attack.

Another bolt came flying out of nowhere, narrowly missing. Shit. *How were they tracking us? How did I not hear them coming?*

More arrows chased us. Faster. Fly faster. *Panic threatened to claw its way into my mind, and in an instant, decades of discipline snuffed it out.*

We do not flee.

Our upward momentum slowed, and for a heartbeat, we hung midair before making the gut-flipping rotation to dive. Headfirst, through the clouds, dodging arrow after iron arrow straight toward a ship, bracing for impact, I drew the sword behind my back...

I opened my eyes. Cold sweat soaked the shirt beneath my coat. My cloak was gone and I shivered against an icy rock. *What was that?* My heart thudded like a frightened bunny in my chest. I tried to sit up but was so disoriented I stumbled forward, and my hands hit the damp dirt ground. No. Not dirt. Dirty wood? My fingers slid along the ribbed panels. Where the hell was I?

The events of the last twenty-four hours came hurtling into view. My fingers followed the wooden floor to its edge and up the wall to its short ceiling, searching for any type of door or latch and coming up empty. I was in some type of room or container. Where were the others? Oh, gods were they dead? I'd been taken captive. Again. Dread formed a pit in my stomach. The Stone Witch was here. I was likely in her lair, deep within the mountain. My heart thundered in my chest, my breathing rapid.

Unable to exhale completely, my mind raced to my father. But as the image of my loyal, wonderful father came into view, the ache of betrayal swarmed my chest and *squeezed*. His words in Mount Telum played on repeat, like a taunting, spiteful song pushing my heart to thump faster. Fuzziness crept into the space behind my eyes. My lips went numb.

I am Lyvia. I am not afraid of the dark.

I blinked through the fog as the outline of a door appeared before my eyes and slowly swung open into a dimly lit stone hall. The shock of it was enough to reset my heart and catch my breath.

My hands braced against the roughly hewn walls of the cave as I stumbled out of the small space I'd been kept in. A single taper had been stuck in a sharp, jagged edge of the rocky wall casting a dim light in the gray space. Urging my sluggish steps to become quicker, I followed the curve of the hall, the drive to escape edging me forward.

Keep moving.

A door appeared as I rounded another corner.

I skidded to a stop, willing my heart to calm as I backed against the sharp, uneven wall. Sliding along its edge, I crept as silently as I could, inching closer to the closed door. My breathing stopped as I pressed my ear to it. Muffled talking sounded beyond.

It is rude to spy when you're trying not to die.

The graveled voice sounded in my ears. I jumped, my heart leaping into my chest as the hairs on the back of my neck stood.

Get out! I screamed back at it, my mind's voice loud and frantic.

A resounding cackle was the only response as the door swung open and I toppled inside.

I didn't know what to make of the scene before me.

Relief filled my senses for a brief moment as I spotted the captain sitting on a chair in the center of the stone room. *Alive.* Where were the others?

The space was small. A ramshackle kitchen in the corner, a filthy sitting space at the opposite end. Cages lined the far wall with bats, rats, and other small animals poking their heads through the bars to peer at me.

The captain looked at me with those piercing green eyes with an expression I couldn't read. Concern? Surprise? A quick sweep of the small, dimly lit room gave the impression that we were alone.

"May I introduce you to Lady Lyvia Cantor of Aedrialis."

Confusion settled over my features. The same spine-tingling cackle filled the room, coming from every direction. I searched frantically for the source, unable to spot the witch.

"Behind you," he murmured.

I tensed, slowly turning around. A small, ancient woman with crunchy gray hair that matched the stone around us stood a few feet from me. Scars and patches of discolored skin dotted her face. A large mole sprouting a few silver hairs grew from the center of her long, hooked nose. She gave me a gut-curdling smile, flashing several yellow teeth that were sharpened, like the canines of a wolf. I caught a whiff of her breath and nearly doubled over from the stench of rotten meat. I finally gazed at her eyes, unable to hide my surprise, when I was met with two beautiful irises of violet staring back at me, the only lovely thing about her.

"Lyvia, the infamous Stone Witch," the captain finished his introductions.

The woman surveyed me, murmuring riddles beneath her breath. A chair appeared out of nowhere, knocking the back of my knees and causing me to plop down on my butt. A rush of foreign rancid wind blew me back in line with the captain.

He glanced at me and shrugged as if this were any normal house visit.

"Can we please get back to the issue at hand?" he asked the Stone Witch.

"Clouds and veils her future holds, but she seeks a truth yet untold," she replied as she pointed her long, sharp fingernails toward me.

"She's not your concern and will have no part in the bargain."

The Stone Witch's gaze lingered on my hands, the dirt still crusted beneath my fingernails.

What are you digging for, girl? Tell the witch, your path may unfurl.

"Enough of that," the captain snapped. His words rang with warning.

She bristled at him and flashed her teeth with a click.

"What will it take?" he continued.

"To see beyond is something rare," she croaked. "Enemies and lovers, plans laid bare." She raised her bristly eyebrows at him, a look of hunger flashing over them.

"Access to the Waters of Ascendiel in Lotrennia?" the captain scoffed. "I cannot give that. I haven't the authority."

"Forgotten One, you may be," she said through gurgles in her throat. "My price as high as your sacred tree."

The captain shifted next to me. "Fine," he said at last.

She eyed him, seeming to savor his discomfort.

"What of the queensguard? Handsome and strong. Dear Saros wants blood, my captivity too long." Her mouth curled up in a wicked grin.

"Ronan is not for sale."

"His white cape is gone but are you quite sure?" she asked with a cruel smile. "Blades may be bought, is his honor secure?"

The captain leveled a stare at her.

She opened her mouth, and the captain cut her off. "Non-negotiable. And King Saros wouldn't free you from this mountain if you delivered the veil of Olienna herself."

The witch stilled, amusement dancing in her violet eyes for the briefest moment before being replaced by irritation.

The Stone Witch turned on her heel and paced slowly back and forth as she contemplated what to do with us. The filthy rags on her back swung in tatters as she hobbled. Her foul stench caused a wave of nausea to wash over me at each pass. The captain sat annoyingly calm and at ease during the whole encounter.

She finally stopped.

"Gork! Come here," she barked. "Join us now or I'll slice off an ear."

Muffled scraping and a thud came from the other side of the door. It swung open, revealing a creature I'd never seen in my life. A small, pig-nosed beast with beady black eyes and pointed ears stood in the doorway. He was covered in fur but wore a pair of knit trousers and his left leg ended in a stump. He carried a spear in one hand and a lamp in the other. Limp, almost see-through wings hung off his back and dragged on the ground. He leered at us with malevolent eyes.

"Fetch the Ravindra twin," she ordered. "Agreement from both and we may begin."

He sauntered off down the hall. A moment later, Nerissa walked slowly in, blinking and wiping the sleep crumbs from her eyes. She stared at the captain for a moment before glancing in my direction. Confusion flicked over her features, no doubt wondering what the hell I was doing here. She walked to the other side of the captain and turned to face the Stone Witch.

"Chair," she said, her command laced with pomp and entitlement. I could only think she meant to irritate the Stone Witch.

The witch stared at her for a long moment, nostrils flared.

"Pretentious like the first," she hissed through her pointed teeth. "The sun I wish I'd cursed." Yet a chair did appear behind Nerissa, and she delicately took a seat, crossing her ankles.

The captain cleared his throat before repeating the terms of the deal out loud for Nerissa to hear. She was careful not to react. She continued staring at the Stone Witch, who met her gaze and whose pale lips slowly started to curl into an evil smile.

"Agreed." Nerissa's voice was firm and confident.

The Stone Witch turned to the door where Gork had remained, standing at attention. "Gork, we shall have company soon. Remind them his soldiers are not immune."

He responded with a firm nod and a bloodthirsty grin before hobbling off down the hall. She turned to us.

"Come now, out the back," she instructed. "Light and safety the tunnels lack."

I staggered upright, following the captain's gaze as a second door appeared at the back of the room, swinging open.

"The others wait at the turn. Mind the waters, his sting will burn." She said the last words with a malevolent chuckle.

Will you find what's needed to unlock your might? Some keys are lost, their locks hold tight.

Her voice graveled in my mind before she disappeared through the door we came in.

The captain swore.

"The Kryax Pool?" Nerissa hissed at him.

CHAPTER THIRTEEN

The Ravindra twins took off at a run, my feet struggling to keep pace as we sprinted down the steep tunnel, the temperature continuing to drop. Ronan and Vulcan lay sprawled at the end of the first curve, just coming to.

"What the fuck?" Ronan rubbed his eyes.

Vulcan sprang to his feet hauling Ronan with him.

"We follow this to the Kryax Pool. The rest we'll fill you in on later," Nerissa said. "Let's move."

Vulcan let out a soft curse.

We ran down the dark tunnel, zigzagging our way through the side of the mountain. Minutes later, the dimness of the tunnel glowed as it opened to a wide, cavernous lake. The swell of illuminated water sloshed back and forth, hiding more than its depth. A narrow river flowed down a tunnel, illuminated from above by tiny blue-green specks in the ceiling of the cave.

We filed onto the narrow shoreline. As Vulcan, the last to exit, stepped out of the tunnel, it vanished. No way back. An unnatural glow radiated from the center of the small lake.

"Get to the river," the captain murmured, shuffling along the lake's edge.

"Do not let the water touch you," he added as it lapped playfully near our feet, enticing us to dip a toe in.

Do not let *it* touch *you*, I replayed his words. As if it had a mind of its own.

We slowly made our way around the lake, single file. The walls of the cave were streaked in different shades of gray and smooth, unlike the jagged edges of the Stone Witch's lair. I kept one hand on the stone, an anchor to keep me from wading into the water, resisting the strange urge to submerge myself in it. Like it was the warm, welcoming bath my aching muscles craved. A look behind me confirmed Ronan felt the same as he raised his light eyebrows.

A slow churn of the water began in the center of the lake. The captain held up a fist, a command to stop. The swirl of water and light quickened, violently dancing as droplets splashed and sprayed in every direction. It was a mesmerizing show I couldn't pull my gaze from. I began to take a step out when Ronan caught my arm, warning in his gaze. I closed my eyes, attempting to shake off the effect of the lake.

I offered a smile of thanks and turned back to find Vulcan, hazel eyes glassy, falling forward into the illuminated water. Nerissa's shocked yelp filled the cave as she reached for him, nearly plummeting into the water herself had it not been for the captain's outstretched hand.

The moment Vulcan's body hit the water, two glowing tentacles wrapped around his torso, ripping him below the surface. I froze as chaos erupted. The others began shouting. The captain launched into the water, and Nerissa waved her hands in a circular motion as she began muttering under her breath. A massive blast of wind followed the movements of her arms, spearing toward the bright water. It split down the center and water shot toward the ceiling of the cavern, unveiling the nightmare that sat below the surface.

A massive beast covered in tiny black scales lounged at the bottom of the lake. *The kryax.* Six long, thick appendages splayed across the floor of the lake, dotted with rows and rows of thinner, smaller tentacles that stretched and climbed in all directions. At the center lay a large bulbous body, the source of the eerie glow. A single, opaque gray eye narrowed at us in the center of its head, which opened into an enormous black beak, lined with hundreds of blunt, rocky teeth. The type that wouldn't slice quickly and swiftly, but instead slowly crushed and ground the bodies of its victims.

Vulcan's limp body was wrapped in hundreds of tiny tentacles, like a fly encased in the cocoon of a spider's web. The kryax let out an ear-splitting roar as it held him high over its head and the captain sprinted down the center of the lake, slicing through the thin tentacles that attempted to snatch him up. Two giant appendages hurtled toward the captain from both directions. He sliced a gap through the tiny tentacles as he leaped over one and impaled the other with his blade. He tore through them with a roar of his own.

Ronan wrapped his arm around my waist with an iron grip that knocked the wind out of me. I couldn't have maneuvered out of his grasp if I tried this time. He yanked me back, and we slammed into the rock wall of the cavern. He grabbed my wrist, and we sprinted toward the other end of the lake where the water gushed through a wide tunnel in the rock, the river our only salvation.

We stopped short as a scream of pain blared from behind. Ronan spun on his heel as I skidded to a stop, slamming into the queensguard. Terror rippled across his face as he looked back and cried, "Nerissa!"

I followed his gaze to see the elf's limp body hoisted high above the waves that crashed down around the kryax. The captain and Vulcan were out of sight, and the creature started to spin.

The chaotic swell of the lake began to settle and follow the command of its master as the kryax moved faster, creating a massive whirlpool. Nerissa came to, squirming and freeing a dagger from her pants. She sliced through the sticky tentacles encasing her body. The creature let out a roar of frustration as she dropped headfirst into the spinning water, her body quickly disappearing. The creature spun faster, the water inching further up the shoreline.

Ronan's gaze fixed to the spot where she dropped. He cast a wary glance back at me for a split second before diving in headfirst.

"Ronan!" I screamed after him, the water now sloshing up my knees. I took a step toward where he vanished when a magnificent blast of light and wind threw me back against the wall of the cavern.

Stars danced in my vision as my ears hollowed out. A ringing whined in them, amplifying the pounding in my head. Sandy rock scratched beneath my cheek, and I blearily opened my eyes to see an enormous wave of white water hurtling toward me.

For the briefest second, water stretched toward the ceiling

and thinned enough that I caught a glimpse of Nerissa at the bottom of the lake, arms stretched out in both directions, pushing the water away with the strength of the wind. The captain hurtled toward the monster in the center before leaping through the air as he swung his sword with both hands over his head.

What came next was a violent crash of solid water that shoved the air from my lungs. It battered me like a rag doll in a storm. The water tossed me in a savage dance, stealing my sense of direction. My lungs burned and screamed for several long seconds as I tried to swim. My arms flayed in the water like limp noodles and a wild swell knocked my shins back with every kick.

I bounced off something hard before slamming into solid rock, my shoulder blazing in pain. I screamed, the sound lost in the loud slosh of water and distant noise of battle. A mistake. I instinctively took a breath of cool water, and my lungs were met with a torturous burn that was made worse when I tried to cough. Panic flooded my senses. For a moment, the events of the last few weeks came crashing through my mind until I was again seeing through the eyes of another.

PAIN WAS NOW A DISTANT THING. My body was broken, I realized. It would soon stop working entirely. Smoke and ash floated and mingled with the rotting scent of battle, stagnant in the humid air.

The click, click, click of his metal war boots beat on the ground as he leisurely strode to where I lay. An insufferable snicker escaped his lips as he gazed upon my shattered body. I could feel his indecent, greedy eyes slowly rove over me until they reached my own, barely open now.

"It didn't have to come to this, Enya Natara. I tried to get you to see."

The smugness in his voice made me sick. I would have spit on him if I could have moved my mouth. Instead, I stared, unable to wipe the warm dribble leaking from the corner of my lips, cooling as it slid down my cheek.

"Cantor."

He knelt beside me and leaned over, placing both hands on the ground on either side of my face. Whatever part of me that was left recoiled at the proximity. He leaned in close.

"You have no idea how much I'm going to enjoy this."

He thought he'd won. The weakest chuckle escaped my lips, blood gurgling up in response. Momentary confusion flashed across his features, replaced quickly with determined hate. He dragged his gaze from my own to the crest of my helmet.

"Cantor. Can you hear me?"

He reached up...

"Lyvia!"

Pain erupted in my forehead. I opened my eyes, meeting the cobalt blue of Ronan's as he leaned over me, concern etched across his face. He held my gaze for a split second before I sat up and hurled a gallon of river water.

I heaved and wretched for several minutes. As I caught my breath, I took in our surroundings. The calls of mountain wrens sang above the rush of the river. The Lumerian mountains stretched in every direction, blanketed with pines and dotted with pockets of autumn leaves. The sun began to set, casting a violet hue on the distant, rocky peaks.

"What happened?" I finally asked, my voice hoarse.

Ronan's normally bright eyes were shaded, like a lake on a cloudy day. He shook his head.

"I don't know." He shook his head as he stood. "I don't know where the others are."

He surveyed the land. "We need to find shelter. It'll be getting dark soon, and there are more than wolves and mountain cats prowling these mountains at night."

"What about the others?" I asked, pulling my riding boots off and dumping the water out.

"I've been searching for the past half hour, and you're the first I've found," he said as he stared at the water dripping down from his coat, knuckles lightening as he squeezed. "We'll look again tomorrow." He shook out his coat and flung it over his shoulders before reaching a hand to me.

I gripped it, welcoming the heat on my icy fingers. I gingerly got to my feet. My shoulder throbbed, but the headache started to subside.

"Can you walk?" he asked.

"I suppose we'll find out," I murmured, eyeing the thick brush and rocky edges of the riverbank.

Though he set a brisk pace, the hike did little to warm my body. The air was cooler at this latitude in the mountains, and with the sun beginning to set, the temperature continued to drop.

Ronan boosted me up to a rocky outcropping as the last rays of light dipped behind the horizon. His hands were warm against the back of my thighs. "Let's make camp here. We'll have some shelter from the wind with that inlet. I'll be back with some firewood."

I nodded, the movement shaky as I attempted to keep my teeth from clattering. Ronan returned a short time later, cursing as he tried to light the kindling with a bit of flint and steel. After several minutes, a small fire sparked to life. I held my hands at the edge of the flames, wincing as the orange light jumped up to touch my fingertips before dancing away.

Ronan eyed me for a moment before murmuring, "Come here."

I slid my questioning gaze to the queensguard.

"You're freezing. Come here. You need body heat."

I eyed him warily.

"I don't bite," he crooned with a wink. "Not unless you like that sort of thing."

Heat rushed to my face, my gaze darting back to the fire. Though I was out of practice, the queensguard was flirting, and despite recent events, I couldn't deny I savored the feeling.

I rolled my eyes and slid next to him, shuddering as he draped an arm over my shoulder.

"You never told us what happened when you went to see Queen Galena," I said as his warmth melted into me. "I'm assuming that's where you went at Mount Telum."

He was quiet for a moment.

"She wasn't particularly pleased to see me. Felt betrayed. Understandably so. But Galena isn't stupid. She knows King Saros is dangerous and has... secrets. After a few minutes of punching me in the chest and cussing me out, she heard me out."

"They say you and the queen are..." I paused and glanced at him, raising an eyebrow.

He chuckled, a deep throaty laugh.

"I know what people think. I care about Galena but not like that. I've been her queensguard for almost ten years since the night of her wedding." His eyes grew distant.

"Who guards her when you aren't around? Do you have a backup?" I asked, curious where he went as his mind wandered.

He slid his eyes back to mine and nodded. "Yes," he murmured with a slight shake of his head, "I trained him myself. He's honorable. He'll take care of her."

We sat in silence for a few minutes.

"Do you think they're dead?" I whispered into the dark.

"I hope they aren't," he murmured.

"What do we do now?"

"We try to get some rest. Tomorrow, we'll double back and see if we can find any trace of them. If not, we head to West-wyn. It's the closest thing to civilization at this point."

The decrepit, tiny mountain town was of little significance, except that it sat on one of the few roads that led through the mountain range.

"Is it safe?" I asked.

"Probably not."

CHAPTER FOURTEEN

The remaining records of the Bellators, and any Bellatorian powers, have vanished. And if the Living Library wants something hidden, it shall remain so.
—Journal of the Master of Spells, Lotrennia.

I curled up near the flames and closed my eyes. My body was exhausted, but my mind raced. I cataloged the events of the last several days, attempting to sort fact from fiction.

The realm of Vael was far bigger and more dangerous than I ever knew. Magic was real, yet illogical. People were disappearing in Sultira. I was now a fugitive. I had some connection to the stone. My father manipulated me into finding it...

My father.

His conversation with King Saros left a gaping hole in my soul, the secrets and betrayal slicing into it as sharp and damaging as any blade. And from the wound dripped doubt and fear. It festered, a crisis warring at the deepest level of my being. Who was I? Where did I come from? What do I do now?

I swallowed against the rising panic.

Think.

Order. Logic. Facts.

My father spoke of the tribute with the king. That much confirmed it was real and that the king was involved. My mind spun... I wish I had something to write with to sort through this all.

The journal.

I'd completely forgotten, not having time to look through it. I frantically felt around the pockets of my coat as my gut filled with lead.

It was gone.

The last piece of evidence must have washed away in the surge from the lake. I felt sick. Father Marcus's last words were the single positive thing that came out of the disastrous trip to the capital. My heart stammered.

"Everything okay?" Ronan asked, casting a wary glance at me.

"I... yes. Everything's fine. I just... I feel a little wired, that's all."

What was the point in telling him? It was gone. I didn't think I could face the disappointment of someone else in addition to how I now saw myself. Which was what?

Failure. I felt like a failure.

I closed my eyes once again, my mind drifting in and out of that place that wasn't quite sleep. The place where the line between dreams and conscious thought blurs. My thoughts eddied and flowed, true sleep eluding me the remainder of the night.

A HAND GRIPPED MY ARM, giving it a gentle shake.

"Lyvia, we need to go."

My eyes blearily peeled open. The fire had been reduced to embers, and night still blanketed the sky with stars.

"What's wrong?" I croaked.

"Soldiers from the capital at the eastern pass. We need to move now."

I scrambled up, the alarm in Ronan's voice fueling my movement.

He gripped my hand as I stood, placing a few small berries into my palm, which I shoved quickly into my mouth. Gods, it was like eating air. Ronan kicked dirt over the embers, stomping them out with his boot before we hurried through the woods.

"What about the others?" I asked through my ragged breathing.

"We'll have to count on them finding us. They're excellent trackers so it shouldn't be difficult."

HOURS LATER, sinister clouds swept over the mountains, blotting out the pink morning sky. A torrent of icy rain and wind followed. We found shelter in an abandoned barn in a small valley. I took shallow breaths. The air was heavy with the scent of rotted wood and moldy hay.

My body shivered against Ronan, whose broad hand ran quickly up and down my shoulder as he puffed breath into his fist. Despite the current predicament, I had to admit I was getting used to viewing the queensguard as a source of heat.

The relentless rain hammered on the old roof, sending frequent large drips landing atop our heads. The downpour obscured our view of the valley, replacing the autumn trees with a solid gray mist that could almost make me forget where we were.

"What was it Vulcan said about your father?"

My stomach pitched. I was quiet for a long moment, wondering how much the queensguard knew about my father. Or if he actually *knew* him. Willem Cantor was a lord, after all. They both would have regularly been in the king and queen's company.

"Aside from insinuating he is not my father?" I finally said, a knot forming in my throat. "He manipulated me into finding the excavation sites, apparently."

Ronan's hand paused, squeezing the top of my shoulder.

"And you'd just... find them?"

I nodded, staring out at the wet gray scene. He shifted in his seat.

"Well, it's remarkable. You found the Obscura Stone. The powers of the world have searched for that for hundreds of years."

I didn't respond, feeling more blind than remarkable. Like I wasn't seeing the full picture. Like I was missing some critical information for this all to make sense.

"You know there are others," he said, turning to face me. His azure eyes sparkled in the dimness of the barn. Blessed with blue, indeed.

"What do you mean?" I asked.

"There are other stones. The Obscura Stone is rumored to be one of the most powerful Bellator Stones. It is also one of the most dangerous and deadly."

"And the others?" I asked.

"No one knows for certain, but there are legends that speak of a stone that grants healing powers to the mage that wields it. Another that enables the mage to forge great weapons not seen for thousands of years. Some with the power of the sun and stars and planets. There were eight Bellators, so most believe there are eight stones of power. Think about what these could do in the war."

My stomach pitted, my mind drifting to that strange dream on the battlefield. I continued to chew on my cheek, the inside getting rather sore.

"So, if the so-called tribute is to blame for the disappearances in the Sultira, why would they send Aeriden to the West? If pirates aren't a problem, then what is he doing there?" I finally asked, skirting around his comment.

Droplets of rain bounced off Ronan's hair as he shook his head. "No, there's still a pirate problem. The Lords of Marisarma, as they call themselves. But their focus is typically on supplies. Saros cut ties with the Votruvian Islands about a century ago, and since then, the Lords of Marisarma have focused their efforts on raiding parties. They've hit Sultiran naval ships, towns along the coast, even Demon's Door Prison in the last fifty years."

My stomach churned at the thought of Aeriden dealing with the like of pirates.

"If what you say is true and King Saros has indeed struck a deal with Dark King Daimos," I began, "who fights for Sultira? The crew of the *Evecta*? The elves?"

Ronan's brows narrowed, his focus growing distant as the rain softened to a hush.

"We may yet find allies in unlikely places," he murmured. "And... if you found the Obscura Stone, you might be able to find the others."

I threw him a wary glance, feeling too much like a child playing with sharp knives. I wasn't entirely sure I wanted to find others. And how would I even begin as a fugitive? It wasn't as if I could waltz into Stynguard's library and begin researching the topic.

And as much as I feared the dark king and his ashen, as much as the mere notion of our king trading his own people into slavery made my stomach turn, the primal need to simply *survive* continued to outweigh the possibility of anything else. My dreams of proving myself to the order of Death Scholars, of becoming one myself, felt as distant and fleeting as the mysterious show of lights above the Lake of Light. I'd come to the conclusion I had to first find Aeriden.

"Not now, of course," Ronan continued, the dimple returning to his cheek at the tilt of his lips. His eyes followed his fingers as they ran over my braid, and for a moment, I let myself wonder what that gentle caress would feel like on my skin.

"Do you think the others made it out?" I asked, looking for any change of subject. Guilt continued to claw its way through my chest. I kept leaving people behind.

As if reading my thoughts he said, "Don't feel guilty for surviving, Lyvia. If they did, they all have years of experience surviving under worse circumstances." He turned his gaze forward, his brows pinching in some emotion I couldn't place.

"Looks like the rain is letting up. We can make it to Westwyn by nightfall. Let's go."

THE REMAINDER of our damp and muddy trek had my thoughts drifting to Tiberius. I would have given anything for a ride on him. To feel the heat of his warm coat and his easy, sure-footed gait. My heart squeezed.

We stopped once before reaching the outskirts of the small mountain village. I hid in a small alcove of trees while Ronan went into town to scout for rooms and gauge the danger ahead. He returned thirty minutes later tossing a fresh pink apple through the air. My icy fingers fumbled, the fruit slipping and tumbling into the mud. I threw him a rude gesture, which he returned with a devilish grin.

"No sign of soldiers and no news from the capital," he said, "*And*, I found us horses and a place to stay."

"Thank the gods."

We made our way through the small village, which was little more than a handful of run-down houses, a general store, a brothel, and an inn. The muddy road was lit by a few oil lamps, and we saw a few withdrawn passersby as we made our way through the village.

The innkeeper nodded *hello* as we entered, and Ronan led us to a room on the second floor. A small table with two tapers and a bed crowded the little space.

One bed.

CHAPTER FIFTEEN

It is with great pleasure I give my highest recommendations for Captain Ronan Merik as he is transferred to the kings-guard commanding unit in Aedrialis. There is no better soldier suited to the task. I'm honored to have him join the Elite Forty-Eight.

—Correspondence to General Calvus, 16th of Spring 061.3E. Aedrialis.

A soft groan escaped my lips in anticipation and relief when I saw it. I squeezed into the room next to Ronan, the slow realization that we'd be sharing one now dawning on me. Those familiar butterflies returned to my stomach, creating an uncomfortable mixture of nerves and hunger.

"Sorry, Cantor. Probably not what you're used to," he murmured with a wink. "I'll sleep on the floor." He sketched a mock bow before pinching me in the side.

I resisted the tug of my lips, slapping his hand away. My eyes shot to the sliver of wooden beamed floor, barely wide enough to extend the door.

"There's a washroom on the main level. I'll get us some food." He turned, offering a half grin before leaving.

Alone.

I sat down on the straw mattress and rubbed my eyes. A wash was a good idea. I was filthy. And I was sure I smelled like it.

The situation with the bed took up so much space in my mind that I had no room for the rest of it as I bathed. And despite the chill water, I felt quite warm by the time I'd finished.

I quickly toweled off and tugged on my damp undershirt and leggings before hurrying back upstairs. I'd given them a good scrub before setting them to dry by the hearth as I'd bathed. I wrapped a quilt around my shoulders as I sat and waited for Ronan. The rain had begun again, pitter-pattering against the roof, clouding the view from the tiny window.

I started as the door creaked open, Ronan poking his head around the corner with a small tray of food. My stomach let out an embarrassingly loud roar as the scent of minced pie wafted over to me. Heat rose to my cheeks as he sat down next to me on the bed, his thigh pressed against mine. He handed me the pie and a cup of wine, which I quickly downed.

As the heat settled in my stomach, I dove into the pie. I stopped after a moment, remembering who I was with and where. Ronan was accustomed to eating and dining with the queen while I clawed at my plate like a starved orphan. I glanced up, catching his eye. A smile tugged at his lips.

"Eat up, Cantor," he said through a mouthful.

I coughed an uncomfortable laugh and forced myself to slow down to an acceptable pace of inhaling my food. I devoured every crumb on my tray before slugging down half of my remaining water.

"I'm going to get cleaned up. Get some rest," he said with his eyes lingering on the outline of my leg beneath the quilt.

Heat pooled in my lower abdomen, a sensation I'd not felt in some time. I'd been with a man only a few times before. My rendezvous with the stable hand in the back stalls lasted throughout the summer. Looking back, it had been a silly fling, but I thought maybe I'd been in love. He'd made me feel that way. And then I caught him making not one, but two lady's maids feel the same way.

I'd confided in Aeriden, unable to keep the tears from flowing. He, in true elder brother fashion, offered to kill him. When I declined, he insisted I learn to fight, so I could at least leave a mark on his face that matched the one on my heart.

The hurt was brief, but it was one of those significant moments I'd felt the stinging absence of my mother. I never knew her, but I'd imagined it would be her I'd turn to in such a circumstance. Aeriden tried, but he wasn't her. I brushed it off, and after a few weeks, our dalliances in the back stalls picked up again. He'd been a boy.

The queensguard was a man. Ronan spun on his heel, leaving me alone.

I lay down on the crunchy straw mattress and dowsed one of the candles. I curled up on the far side of the bed and closed my eyes, blaming my restlessness on the little bits of hay sticking out beneath. I lay there, frustrated that my stupid body wouldn't settle down for twenty long minutes until Ronan returned. The door creaked open as he stepped inside the small, now chilled room.

The soft sigh of fabric slipping over skin sounded behind me followed by the thunk of boots hitting the ground as Ronan shuffled around the small space. I rolled over, my eyes drifting over his tanned body. He was indeed trying to sleep on the floor. His head cranked to one side against the small table and his knees tucked up against the bed as he shifted around trying to get comfortable.

"Ronan," I said into the dimness. "I don't bite. Unless you like that sort of thing."

Shocked at the gall I had to repeat his own words, I waited for his response. Where in *Tynan's hell* did that come from? I waited a few heartbeats for his response.

A throaty chuckle sounded from below that sent my toes curling. I rolled to the side, making room for him as he slipped in beside me. His hand slid under the pillow where he placed his dagger. Smooth warmth soaked into my back as he curled around me. His arm draped over the covers, and I couldn't help but lean into him. A hot awareness spread through my body, and I stilled as something hard pressed against my backside.

"You seem tense, Cantor," he murmured into my ear.

My heart hammered in my chest, and I willed my breathing to calm.

"Who knew the queensguard was such a flirt?" I said back, barely able to keep the trembling from my voice.

"Only when I can't help myself, my lady."

His breath tickled the edge of my ear, and I shuddered in response. I leaned my head back and arched into him. His fingers drifted over my thin undershirt, grazing my ribs. The skin on my arm pebbled as he placed a delicate, small kiss on the nape of my neck.

A small surge of doubt edged its way into my thoughts. What the hell was I doing? The heat forming at the center of my legs quickly squashed the intrusive thoughts. I needed this —needed a distraction after everything that had transpired.

My hand drifted back and slid into his curls, locking onto a few soft strands. I tugged gently, turning my face toward him.

His hand cupped the side of my face, and I met his cobalt-blue eyes shining in the dark. Close enough to share breath, I inhaled citrus as he leaned forward and planted a soft kiss on my lower lip. A small sound caught in my throat, and a relentless pulsing began at the apex of my thighs, desperate for any friction he could give. His lips parted, and I felt my own respond in turn. His hand dropped from my cheek and slowly moved down my side, fingers grazing the outside of my thigh.

He dragged the tips of his fingers above my leathers, closer to the relentless pulsing, stopping inches away and making a torturous stroke down my thigh. He deepened his kiss, now slowly exploring with his tongue.

More, my body seemed to shout. I wanted *more*. I wanted *him*. My mind blurred, lost in the desperate need of pleasure. It began to climb, faster and faster until his movement stopped, and he went utterly still.

He pulled away and abruptly hopped out of bed. I blinked, trying to shake myself out of the fog of lust that had come over me as the pulsing slowly subsided. I opened my mouth to speak, and he held a finger up to my lips. The hairs on the back of my neck stood on end. Something was wrong. He leaned over me to peer out the window.

"Fuck. We have company. I'll be right back."

Flustered, he tugged on his boots and grabbed his coat before hurrying out the door. I sat there for a moment, collecting myself. What the hell had I been thinking? I allowed my brain to take over and process the danger we were still in.

I knelt on the floor to reach for a boot that had slid under the bed. I ducked my head under and caught sight of a small leather pack.

It had thin straps with various buckles as if they hooked around one's shoulders and waist. I hadn't noticed Ronan carrying a pack, though this could have been easily concealed.

Curiosity nagged at me. I pulled it out and flipped the latch open, revealing a handful of papers and a journal.

My heart stopped.

The journal. Father Marcus's journal. Unease coiled its way through my gut, and a cold realization settled through me. I ran my hands over the leather cover. Ronan must have taken it from me. Maybe he found it washed up on the river shore and didn't realize it was mine. Annoyance at my wishful thinking, my naivety, made me grimace. Of course, he knew it was mine. He took it.

I set it aside and rifled through the other papers. There were military charts and logs of the movements of the king's army. Death Scholar analyses from the Temple of the Sky and lectures I'd attended myself. And a copy of the map—the map I'd drawn for Nerissa.

My heart fluttered. I had the sinking feeling I was being played. Ronan had been somewhat cryptic about where we were going. Could he be playing both sides? Was he truly an agent of the king? I replayed every conversation I'd had with the queensguard since we'd met with the sudden realization that his relentless flirting hadn't begun until we'd separated from the others. A mixture of hurt and shame collided in my chest at my naivety.

I had to get out of here. I was going west to find Aeriden. My brother would know what to do. He'd get me into hiding.

I formed a plan as I remembered Ronan had secured us a couple of horses. Gripped by new determination, I shoved the contents back into the pack and strapped it to my chest. I dressed again and snuck downstairs to the kitchens. I would need provisions, especially with winter rounding the corner.

I finished stuffing the pack when I remembered the dagger under the pillow. I had no weapons. While I admittedly didn't know how to use it, I was certain I was better off having a dagger on hand. Despite the knowledge that Ronan would be back any moment, I tiptoed up the stairs and listened against the door.

Hearing nothing, I quietly pushed the door open making for the bed. As my hand slid beneath the small pillow, a hand clasped over my mouth.

CHAPTER SIXTEEN

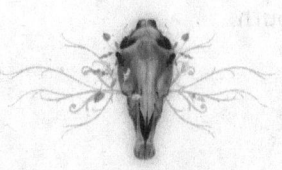

The sacred wolves of Lotrennia are all but gone, their
existence a mere legend.

–Journal of the Master of Spells, Lotrennia.

A cry caught in my throat as panic sent my heart leaping
into my chest. I grabbed at the hand and thrashed.
Any self-defense training Ronan had given me sank
below waves of hysteria.

The hand softened, and a deep voice whispered, "Lyvia!
Lyvia, it's me. It's Bayne!"

The shock of hearing the captain's voice was enough to
shake me out of my frenzy.

His hand slid from my mouth to my shoulders, turning me
to face him. My heart slowed as I took in his rugged features.
That paralyzing gaze pinned me to the spot.

"You're alive," I breathed.

His eyes searched mine for a moment as he nodded.

"So are you," he said.

"What about the others?" I whispered.

Bayne's dark brows drew together as he murmured, "Alive, but not here." His eyes darted to the door. "We need to go."

I paused, turning toward the bed again. I ran my hands under the pillow just in case. Gone. I should have known he wouldn't have left his dagger.

Bayne moved to the side of the small window and stared at the village street below. His eyes narrowed as they caught mine, pressing a finger to his lips. He signaled me to look, holding up three fingers. I hurried to the other side and peeked out the dirty window.

I scanned the dark street, stopping my gaze at three o'clock, and found two men talking beneath the sign of the neighboring brothel. I caught the side of Ronan's face as he glanced to the right. The other man, barely visible, stood under the overhang of the roof. I tiptoed to Bayne's side and caught sight of his white cape. *Kingsguard*. And Ronan was not under arrest.

Bayne gave me a knowing look. I cringed at the sympathy that passed briefly across his face. As if he could see the dark shadow of betrayal lurking behind me, continuing to stalk its prey.

Ronan turned and walked toward the inn. Bayne nodded to the door, and I followed as he snuck out, quietly closing it behind us. We hurried down the stairs to the first level, ducking into the washroom. The inn door creaked open, followed by Ronan's steps up the stairs. We moved out the back and raced down the dark path to the stables where Ronan had claimed to secure horses for our trek.

We found two, tacked and ready to go at the front paddock.

Bayne approached the tall one, cautious of the rider, but not skittish. I brought my fist up to meet the second and paused after glancing at his hooves. Cracks split down the center and sides. *Shit.* While the gelding wasn't lame now, he would be soon. I had to find another.

I hurried down the stable aisle peeking in stalls as I ran. Empty except for one. The lone dark horse whinnied as I approached. I grabbed a bridle and moved to open the door, and a little black head popped out from behind the mare, looking too much like Tiberius. The foal eyed me warily, and I sighed, something squeezing in my chest. I couldn't take the mother.

As I was about to check the back paddock, commotion from the inn drew my attention. Ronan would have discovered I left. And that I'd taken the satchel. Guards shouted orders, and the loud bay of hounds filled the air.

No time for a second horse. I ran out the back and caught sight of Bayne urging the gelding into a gallop toward me. The horse picked up speed. I started running the same direction, as fast as I could, glancing back to find Bayne's arm outstretched. I reached up, ever grateful for my height, and grabbed hold of his forearm while kicking off the ground as hard as I could. He hauled me up with the momentum of the gelding's gait. I wrapped my arms around Bayne's torso, and we took off.

The beating hooves of pursuit echoed through the night. Five at least, if I had to guess, but the sorrel gelding was fast and sure-footed. We sped down the dim, narrow road to the outskirts of Westwyn. We were lucky it was still the early hours of the night, but this meant we had to rely almost entirely on the gelding's intuition and direction.

After an hour of hard riding, we found a narrow trail that wound its way up the southern face of the mountain. Bayne slowed the gelding, now slick with sweat, to an easy walk. We heard nothing but the heavy breathing of the sorrel and the clopping of his hooves on the now rocky ground. I loosened my grip on Bayne's waist and wiped my eyes, watery from the cold air during our escape.

"Are you all right?" Bayne asked, voice soft.

I closed my eyes and listened to the gelding's breathing as it finally slowed, sifting through the layers of his simple question.

"I don't know," I said quietly. I hadn't allowed myself to think about that question since the day I found that burial chamber.

He nodded. "Do you want to talk about it?"

I didn't respond. How could I trust anyone? I kept coming back to the same thought. I didn't truly know these people, didn't know the people in the life I'd left behind.

I was alone.

⁂

WE RODE in silence for the remainder of the night. I found myself drifting in and out of sleep as I rocked along with the gelding's smooth gait, listening to his hooves clop quietly among the frosted leaves.

After a few hours, the sun began its rise over the looming peaks, casting a blue-green hue through the thick pines.

"I can feel them," Bayne said, finally breaking the silence.

I blinked, confused. "I'm sorry?"

"Nerissa. And Aquila. That's how I know they are alive. And fine, more or less," he said.

Interest piqued, I sat up straighter, and the autumn frigid-ness quickly filled the space between us. I dropped my hands to my thighs, realizing I'd been huddled against him most of the night.

"A result of our parents' soulbinding, we think," he added in explanation. "And they were both mystics which made the pairing, their bond, that much more powerful. Nerissa and I have always shared this connection with each other, with Aquila. It allows us to feel each other's emotions if we wish."

My gaze drifted through the thick trees as I pondered the sudden confession.

"The closer we are, the clearer the feeling. If they want you to feel anything, that is. It is possible to guard your emotions around others if you wish. The further away you get, it becomes more like a curtain has been draped. You can still sense some movement and sometimes the general impression. Are they feeling good or bad? That sort of thing."

I reeled at what sounded more like an invasion of privacy.

"That sounds overwhelming," I murmured, scanning the emerald forest of pines. The sun brightened the woods, the occasional yellow aspen shining like a flame in the sea.

"It does. That's what the guard is for. It helps to block out those incoming sensations. But it's the three of us, so it's not so bad."

"So, your parents could feel each other's emotions with this soulbinding? Is it common?" I asked.

His dark head shook in front of me. "Not exactly. The soulbinding connection is deeper than that. I'm not sure they felt each other's emotions. They were a part of each other. I sometimes think they could get inside each other's heads. Soulbinding isn't a common practice among elves anymore. Rare, even, to find those whose souls might be compatible, and for *both* to make the conscious choice to bind themselves, their entire being, body and soul, to another. There are other bonds that are more common. Oaths that can be taken to bind you to another that allow some type of connection, but ours is different."

The gelding's footing slipped on a smooth rock, and he tripped forward a few steps. I clutched Bayne's sides out of instinct before quickly dropping my hands.

Soulbound. To give yourself to someone else to that extent... Marriage alone seemed daunting, stifling, even. I supposed I no longer needed to worry about the Match.

"What happened to your parents?" I asked quietly.

He was silent for a moment. "They were killed. A long time ago."

"By the dark king?"

"No." His response was quiet enough I knew this part of the conversation was over. "Let's stop for a quick break and try to gain some distance between us and Westwyn."

Morning birds twittered across the treetops, their serenade twining with the soft crunch of leaves beneath the mount's hooves. Bayne shifted, and the gelding slowed to a stop. I swung down first, my feet stinging from the impact of the frozen ground. Bayne swiftly followed before reaching behind the gelding's knee and gently pulling his leg forward, stretching the sore horse.

"You're good with him," I noted as he pulled out a full waterskin, offering it to the horse. "You were good with Tiberius too. Most men think they need to be broken."

Bayne glanced my way. "Most *Sultirans* think they need to be broken. But that's not what your father taught you, was it?"

I shook my head. "No. It's more about speaking their language. It's why the agrippa only respond to riders who respect them. They aren't complete order-takers."

He looked thoughtful as he stroked the sorrel's neck. "We don't use tack in Lotrennia. If you must rely on physical equipment to control your steed, you're not worthy of the ride."

He held the waterskin open to the gelding who took long gulps of the cool water for a couple of minutes, pausing as he lifted his head, his wide tongue hanging between his front teeth as the water dripped down. I stifled a grin, the exhaustion of our pursuit beginning to wear off. Even the agrippa looked funny as they drank.

My hands slid into the cushiony fur under the horse's mane, thickening with the approaching winter. The thought of winter in the mountains gripped me with a new determination. Bayne's eyes were on mine when I looked up.

I cleared my throat and eventually pulled my gaze away. I pulled out my own waterskin and handed him some dried meat.

"How did you find us?" I asked. "And what happened in the Pool of Kryax? We thought you were dead."

Bayne pursed his lips and shook his head.

"*You* thought I was dead," he said, jerking his chin toward me. "Ronan knew I was alive. At least he did that first night when I picked up your trail."

The fresh queasiness of recent betrayal returned to my insides. That was why Ronan kept us moving so fast.

"Why did he... I thought you were close? He was a part of your crew."

Bayne gathered up our things, shoulders tight. "He *was* a part of our crew. More than that. He was like a brother. I have suspicions as to why he did what he did, but my head isn't clear enough to sort it all out." He peered at me then, an icy fury dancing in his eyes. No, definitely not clear.

"And what happened at the lake?"

"The kryax is dead. I'm sure that was part of the Stone Witch's plan. A way of ridding her mountain of the beast. The magic it possessed caused a tidal wave after it was killed. It swept all of us up. Nerissa is... I know she is alive, but I can barely sense her. I don't think she's in danger. I searched for the others and only found your tracks, which makes me think she found a different route in the mountain. She'll head north."

The magnitude of power, of courage it must have taken... It painted the captain and Nerissa in a new light. And while it edged along the lines of respect, my fear of the two deepened.

"Vulcan," he continued, "I'm less sure about. He's resilient. A survivor. Though apparently not resilient enough to resist a fainting spell from the Stone Witch."

"She needed a way to get the beast's attention," I muttered, connecting the dots.

The captain grunted his confirmation. The stench of the bottom of the lake still filled my nostrils when I thought of it. I closed my eyes and took a deep breath of the fresh mountain air, crisp and dewy. No rain today, thank the gods.

"How did you track us in the rain?"

He averted his eyes before saying, "I scented you."

I blanched.

He quickly added, "Your scent was familiar enough. And Ronan's. Elves have heightened senses. At least in comparison to humans."

I squirmed at the confession and reminder of my ignorance. "Why did you come for me?"

His expression shifted between confusion and frustration. "I came for Ronan," he clarified. "At first, I thought someone or something was after you both. I saw the hurried tracks and assumed that would be the only reason you'd run off. After not finding another set, I suspected Ronan had other ideas. With his cover blown, he's either playing both sides or has motives of his own we don't yet understand. Either way, we can't trust him."

"And can I trust you, Captain?"

Bayne eyes darkened for a moment before he took one last swig from his waterskin.

"Yes," he answered, his unblinking gaze never leaving mine.

"Where are you going now then?"

Bayne tied the waterskin to the back of the saddle before checking the tightness of the cinch. "I need to get north. The fastest way to do that is finding a ship at the Lake of Light and taking it up the Rhew."

"And I imagine you think you're taking my horse?"

Bayne's fingers paused fidgeting with the knot, and he turned to me with a raised brow.

"Your horse?"

"Anchor," I answered, straightening my spine. Anchor seemed the perfect name for the sure-footed sorrel. Steady and stable. "Ronan secured him for me. And I've named him, so he's mine."

Bayne's lips twitched for a moment before nodding his head slowly.

"And I'll be taking him west to find my brother." I stepped around the captain and fixed the knot he'd loosened.

Bayne's biceps flexed beneath his thin jacket as he crossed his arms and took a step back. I tore my eyes away, irritated with the way they continued to rove over him.

"The Lake of Light is west," he said, tilting his head, "perhaps we could travel together."

Despite his earnest gaze, doubt gnawed at the back of my mind. If I'd learned anything the past few days, it was that I was terrible at reading people. On the other hand, his survival skills would be invaluable in these mountains. I didn't want to be out here on my own.

"I suppose you may tag along," I murmured, fitting my boot into the stirrup and hoisting myself up. I reached a hand down for Bayne. His eyes met mine as he gripped it, the gesture feeling more natural than expected, before swinging a leg up behind me and settling into place.

Fate had thrown daggers my way for long enough. I was ready to take back the reins of my life.

"West," I said again, giving Anchor a gentle nudge with my legs. The sorrel took off at a steady trot over the rocky trail and up the side of the mountain.

CHAPTER SEVENTEEN

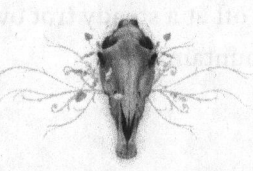

The Kingdom of Sultira will henceforth cease to conduct trade with the Isles of Votruvia. The trade winds have been severed.
—Correspondence to the Trade Council of Votruvia, 1ˢᵗ of Winter, 969.2E. Votruvia.

We continued at a steady pace for most of the day, stopping occasionally to rest. We didn't speak much, the two of us content with silence. Anchor's easy pace and the gentle rocking of his gait sent my mind to a calm, accepting state.

After making camp that night, I watched until the rise and fall of Bayne's chest slowed, his breath deepening. When I was certain he slept, I pulled out Father Marcus's journal. I ran my hands over the soft, worn leather. The texture and scent of it called on bittersweet memories. Father Marcus had been a guiding light in my life. His lectures, the excavations, all of it fed my growing need for discovery. I'd felt more alive in the past four years than I had the prior eighteen.

I inched near the fire the captain had easily kept alive and flipped through the pages until I came upon the date of my discovery.

Light notes littered the page detailing the layout and cataloging the weapons and bodies. I flipped through, scanning the details I knew well enough. Several scrolls had been discovered that I hadn't had a chance to examine.

I paused a page later, staring at the Death Scholar's handwriting which became frantic and disorganized. The Obscura Stone stared up at me from the page, its depiction as dark and dangerous as the object itself.

The stone gives off a dysphoric repellent to any who near it, I read, my insides churning at the conflicting pull I'd felt toward the object. I shoved it below the surface and continued on, the final pages the climax of the frantic, crazed writing.

Warned them not to touch the stone...

Porous properties... Evidence of canals...

A relic of the forgotten arts...

Not stone.

I squinted in the dimness of the crackling fire, scooting closer to the flames, trying to make out the barely legible scribbles on the final page. My heart leaped in my chest as I made out four words.

Twin Eclipse.

Lyvia Cantor.

How much had Father Marcus known about my history? Did he know about my father? Was that the only reason he had extended an invitation to me? A quiet sadness crept its way into my chest at the thought that my entire scholarly life had been a manipulation and a lie. I moved to close the journal when a thin, folded piece of darkened paper fell out, and my heart stopped.

As gently as possible, I unfolded the ancient text, fingers trembling. He had hidden one of the scrolls from the burial chamber. This was entirely unlike him. Folding the ancient text like this would destroy it, damaging the fibers too much after being rolled so carefully for hundreds of years.

I stared at the caramel page, eyes scanning the ancient words. There were eight of them, each with a small symbol carefully etched next to them. My eyes snagged on one of the symbols in the center, something nagging at my memory before they caught on the second to last word. *Obscura.* Alongside a circle with eight elaborate, twisting swirls and something small in the center I couldn't see.

> *Palaega.*
> *Advetis.*
> *Ramadiel.*
> *Celestyn.*
> *Soleia.*
> *Transcindiel.*
> *Obscura.*
> *Aeterna.*

I BURNED the words and symbols into my mind, willing myself not to forget as I knew this scroll wouldn't survive for long without the proper equipment. It was remarkable it hadn't disintegrated after its trip through the Pool of Kryax.

I gently folded the scroll, careful to follow the crease lines from Father Marcus. Had Ronan seen this? I had almost missed it myself. I rubbed my eyes and quietly tucked the page back in the notebook and returned it to the satchel. I leaned back on a boulder as I continued my watch, glancing at Bayne, whose shoulders continued to rise and fall in his deep sleep.

DAYS LATER, Bayne nicked a bow and some arrows from a guard as we passed a small mountain village. The day he brought back the first rabbit, he offered to teach me to use it. The pang of hunger twisted cruelly in my gut as we sat quietly in a bushy alcove, peering into the tangle of roots and fallen trees. For *two hours.*

The growl that erupted from my stomach sent pink flying to my cheeks. Bayne's mouth quirked to the side, but he kept his eye and his arrowhead aimed at the dark entrance of a tunnel. Moments later, a fuzzy black and white-striped face peered out. The plump badger waddled out of his den, and Bayne barely moved as he drew his bow tighter.

Badger, my father's voice whispered from the depths of memory.

"No," I breathed. "Please, no."

Bayne's emerald eyes flashed to mine, narrowing in confused irritation, but he lowered his bow.

Hours later, we'd settled for two scrawny squirrels.

WEEKS PASSED as we continued our trek and eventually made camp not far from the western tip of the Ripped River, which connected to one of the eight sunken valleys belonging to the Lake of Light. The lake stood at the center of the vast Lumerian Mountain range in the shape of an eight-pointed star, spanning two hundred miles from tip to tip. Forested hills rose sharply around an intricate coastline of bays and sheltered inlets.

The name also stemmed from the magnificent natural light display in the sky. Waves and spirals of brilliant violet-white light would periodically pass over the lake, resulting in a breathtaking reflection of star-like light off its waters.

I poked the now smoldering fire that Bayne started before he left to find food. Despite the nausea that rose every time I sliced them open, I'd learned to cut and clean our kills these last couple of weeks. I placed the makeshift grid of sticks over the open fire to roast whatever small animal he brought back.

A rustle sounded in the brush behind me, and my hand went to the dagger Bayne left behind. Every time he left, he'd press the hilt of his dagger in my hand and repeat the maneuvers and vulnerable body parts. Bayne's fighting style was different from Ronan's, but no less lethal. Every maneuver was painstakingly precise, like a step in a dance. An action and a reaction that positioned you for the next. The only difference was a misstep might mean the loss of an arm or even your life, not an invitation or proposal.

Another rustle, loud and seemingly larger. Rustle, slide, rustle, slide. My heart quickened in my chest, and I scooted behind a tree, dagger in hand and feet apart, braced for a potential attack.

My eyes scanned the thick forest. It had to be Bayne, though my thoughts drifted to the large tracks we spotted only a day before. My shoulders sagged in relief as I spotted the back of his dark hair as he stepped backward, dragging something large.

He glanced over his shoulder and flashed a wide grin that sent butterflies dancing in my belly. It was the first time I'd seen a full smile on him. I looked at the ground, and there in the brush, sprawled out in front of him was a massive moose. He had it by the antlers. The bull had to be six feet tall and weigh more than a ton. I'd forgotten how strong he was. How different the elves were from humans. My thoughts drifted to the muscle footprints on the remains I'd poured over two months ago.

"I had to take the shot," he said, flashing that smile again.

I couldn't help but grin back. "What are we going to do with all of it?"

He heaved the bull into the clearing, and I handed him the dagger.

"We're about half a day's ride from Rivaner. Maybe longer with this load. We can butcher it and bring the meat and pelts to sell in town."

I nodded my agreement. Rivaner, a settlement off the Lake of Light, was small enough that we were hopeful they wouldn't hear much from the capital, but large enough that we'd blend in with other passing caravans. Bayne also had a contact there.

It took hours to process the moose, during which, I filled our waterskins and collected some nuts and berries. It was well past dark by the time Bayne had finished half the bull. I made a makeshift sled out of some downed branches and stinging nettle. Bayne would pull the sled while we packed the remainder on Anchor.

We sat next to the fire, my mouth watering as I took a bite of the smoky moose loin, salty juice dribbling down my chin. I stifled a moan, certain I'd never tasted anything so good.

"This beats squirrel and rabbit meat," I said through a mouthful.

He groaned in agreement, the sound sending a shiver dancing up my spine. I forced my attention on the fire.

He left camp to wash up in the icy mountain river. Weeks

of living in the wild left us feeling grimy and foul-smelling. I caught a glimpse of his chiseled chest and the whorls of black that stretched up to his collarbone as he made his way back to the fire, tugging on his shirt. I glanced away as he looked toward me.

"That was less than pleasant," he said, sitting down next to the fire.

"Will you be offended if I wait until tomorrow?"

He huffed a laugh. "Not at all. You could even wait until we get to Rivaner," he said, his eyes growing distant with memory.

"I'm sure I'd scare away any hospitality if I arrived like this," I said, holding up my gritty, bloodstained hands.

He chuckled, the sound warm and inviting. Despite acclimating to the proximity to the captain these past weeks, I was guarded, the recent sting of betrayals still fresh. It kept me from revealing the satchel contents to Bayne.

"I need to keep heading west, anyways," I continued, my thoughts drifting to Aeriden.

"You should at least stay a night," Bayne replied. "If we can find Belgar Hunt, he'll share provisions for your journey west as well as my journey north."

I eyed him warily.

"Belgar," he said with a reassuring smile, "is an old friend. I spent some time with him off the western coast many years ago."

"How long is *many*?" I asked, pointedly raising my eyebrows.

He paused at that. While he indeed seemed honest, there were certain things Bayne was often vague about. That included his age.

"Twenty," he said, meeting my eyes.

Bayne looked to *be* in his late twenties.

"Did you run into any pirates?" I asked.

Another pause.

"You *were* the pirates," I finished for him.

He threw me a devilish smirk. "It's all a matter of perspective. Though not the type of pirates you're thinking of. The Lords of Marisarma are something else entirely. Belgar and I were part of a crew tasked with recovering some goods taken from Lotrennia."

"On behalf of the queen?"

Another long pause, during which he stared intently at the dancing flames as he weighed his response.

"Not exactly..." he said, finally meeting my eyes. There was no shame or defensiveness in them. Just fierce honesty.

I waited.

"We were working more on *behalf* of Lotrennia. Not necessarily its queen."

Truth, I decided, but the type that had some holes in it.

"So, Belgar Hunt works for the elves?"

"Belgar works for whoever pays him best," he said with a chuckle.

"So, he's a mercenary?"

"I think he prefers *contractor*."

I sipped some water as I considered. "Ronan won't suspect we're heading to Rivaner? Does he know Belgar?" I asked.

Bayne shook his head. "He won't know we're heading there. This was years before Ronan joined the crew. Either way, it's best not to linger more than a couple of days."

I gave him a nod, aching for any semblance of comfort before my journey across the Lake of Light to find Aeriden. If we could find Belgar Hunt and just breathe for a moment without kingsguards on our tails, I'd be grateful for it. I curled up on the hard ground next to the flames and let my mind drift to sensations of wind and flashes of wings in the open sky.

CHAPTER EIGHTEEN

*They call him Astraeus. The new Lord of Marisarma sank six
from our fleet. My captain claimed he downed the pirate with
three arrows, but he's been seen twice since. We require more
ships, more soldiers. Send them west.*

*—Correspondence from General Calvus, dated 15th of
Spring, 066.3E, Aedrialis.*

The savory scent of roasting meat pulled me from a
deep sleep, the snapping of a fresh fire interrupted by
the occasional sizzle of meaty juices. Daylight peeked
its rays over the mountain tops, the air frosty as winter
hovered nearby. I shivered, anticipating the frigid dip I'd yet to
take in the river.

I glanced around, taking in my surroundings as I searched
for Bayne. Anchor gave me a soft, friendly nicker as I sat up.
Bayne let me sleep the entire night. I was grateful, confused,

and unsure why he'd break our steady routine that had been working for the past few weeks.

I stood and stretched, pulling my coat tight around me. My huff of breath clouded in the air. I tiptoed over to the fire where two flank strips lay roasting. I sucked in a long breath through my nose, savoring the scents of spicy moose and mountain pine.

"Good morning," a warm, deep voice said behind me. I turned to find Bayne standing a few feet away, wearing the half grin that I'd begun to see more of.

"Should be ready in about ten minutes," he murmured, pointing to the fire. I nodded. Enough time for an icy dip. I gave him a half smile back and made my way to the river.

The icy plunge was a wicked shock to my system. I gasped for air as my face breached the surface, and a chill breeze sent tiny icicles dancing across my skin. I kept it quick, long enough to scrub off the obvious blood and dirt from my hands and face. Then I jumped out and shook myself as dry as I could before struggling to slide dry clothes on my wet body.

When I returned to camp, Bayne had packed up the meat, pelts, and antlers and sat near the ashes of the fire he'd doused. He'd finished cleaning the moose in the night as well. I sat across from him as he handed me the other strip of meat.

We ate in silence and left the camp within a few minutes. I didn't miss walking. And I could tell Anchor would rather have a rider than three hundred pounds of meat on his back. I patted his neck as we walked side by side down the mountain trail.

As we began our descent to the lake town of Rivaner, we passed a rocky outcropping a few yards off the trail. Bayne dropped his sled and took Anchor's reins from me before offering me his hand. I paused a moment as I stared at his outstretched, calloused palm, too aware of the butterflies dancing in my belly and what they meant. We would be parting soon. I'd be done with him. Done with the nonsense of the stone. Done with magic and elves and all of it.

My life had been upended, my dreams shattered. And the only path that lay ahead of me ended with Aeriden. With finding my brother in hopes we could keep each other safe.

The captain waited, his eyes beckoning. I resisted the urge to take his hand, clenching my fist instead and nodding toward the outcropping. I stepped past him, pulling my gaze away before the breath was knocked from me at the sight.

The Lake of Light lay sprawled out below, glittering in the autumn sun like an azure jewel cut from a star. The bordering mountains stood guard as if they'd marched down to gaze upon this sacred place. I was transfixed, certain I'd never seen anything as lovely in my entire life. I stared for several minutes without moving a muscle.

I turned to him, searching his eyes for... I don't know what. The image struck a chord in me, deep in a place long forgotten.

He regarded me steadily for a long moment.

"I thought you needed to see it from above," he said quietly. "We should get going."

I stared at the magnificent portrait of twinkling water for a moment longer, willing myself to forever embed the image in my mind before returning to the trail.

THE SMALL LAKE town of Rivaner sat on a relatively level valley on the shores of the easternmost tip of the star. We found a small, concealed cave where we stashed the sled of meat while we made our way into town with Anchor carrying the rest. It would look strange to see a man pulling four hundred pounds of meat on a sled by himself.

Autumn strained against the winds of winter as the air in the mountains grew frigid. It gave us a good reason to keep our hoods up, concealing Bayne's ears and our general appearances if word from Aedrialis about our status had reached the small town.

We stopped at the local market first and made a killing off the meat and pelts, save for a large roast that Bayne planned on gifting our unbeknownst host. We got a handful of looks as we made our way through town, but no one seemed overly interested in our business. In fact, the people of Rivaner were skittish, like deer in the woods with an approaching, unseen wolfpack.

Curtains were drawn, people spoke in low voices, and a dry wind blew the fallen leaves through a mostly deserted road. I glanced at Bayne who scanned the streets, eyebrows pinched.

"We should stop here," I said, jerking my chin toward the blacksmith's shop. "Anchor needs to be reshod."

Bayne murmured his agreement, and I led the gelding to the small stable in the back and returned to find the captain in conversation with the smith.

"We're also in the market for a bow and a quiver of arrows," Bayne said. "Is that something you can help us with, or do we need to head to the next town over? Something smaller would do."

The blacksmith side-eyed me before looking back at Bayne. Women did not hunt or fight in Sultira. Bayne wrapped his thick arm around my waist, giving it a slight squeeze, awakening the butterflies in my stomach. It was an intimate, slightly inappropriate gesture in a public place.

He gazed down at me with a mask of complete devotion that set my heart and something else on fire. "It's a gift. For our son. He'll be turning eight soon."

For a moment, I was lost in his gaze, imagining my life as

he suggested before the town bell rang and sent my thoughts scattering.

The blacksmith nodded, relief and understanding on his features, likely thanking the gods he wasn't selling a weapon to a woman.

"Mine is twenty now," he said grinning at Bayne. "Off to fight for the good King Saros in the north. I think I have something that should work for your lad. Let me check the back."

Bayne released my waist, and I suddenly felt cold. His deep green eyes flickered at me before the smith returned. A wink, perhaps. I had the uneasy feeling that I'd been down this road before. Irritated at my inability to not fall for handsome men who wink at me, I turned away from him and perused the blacksmith's workshop.

He returned with a small bow and quiver of arrows. Bayne laid on the compliments, a swagger entering his voice I'd yet to hear. He was convincing. Within minutes, he had the craggy blacksmith grinning and talking about his work and life. My father would have approved. The thought of him opened the rip in my heart I'd been getting used to ignoring. I shoved it back down with the anger burning from my chest.

"Any news from the capital?" Bayne asked quietly.

"No, we don't hear much from the capital in these parts. Except when we get passersby such as yourselves."

I caught Bayne's eye. We should be relatively safe here for a night or two.

"We're looking for a man who goes by the name of Belgar Hunt. Any idea where we might find him?"

I watched from across the shop as the blacksmith shook his head.

"No one around here goes by that name, son."

"He's a rather big fellow. Would be difficult to miss. Dark skin, light brown eyes, about the size of a—"

"You're not talking about the Bear?" the blacksmith interrupted him.

Amusement and delight danced in Bayne's eyes for the briefest second. A month ago, I would have missed the look before spending so much time with him. He quickly donned a mask of confusion and uncertainty.

"The Bear and his family keep to their home in the southern woods. We don't see the likes of them often. I hope for your sake that's not the man you're seeking. You'd do well to stay far away from him. He's dangerous folk. Rumor has it he's torn a man in two with his bare hands for looking at him the wrong way."

I gaped as Bayne visibly struggled not to laugh. So much so that he turned to the side to fake a cough. An amateur move my father would *not* approve of.

"That doesn't sound like the man we are looking for, but thank you for the warning."

The blacksmith gruffed in response, and we parted ways. Bayne's mood improved dramatically as we made our way through the town.

It was past sundown. We'd need to find Belgar or shelter soon. We passed a dark alleyway where a fresh notice caught my eye. I stepped up to the building it was nailed to and my stomach sank. Plastered on the Sultiran wanted poster was my face, along with Bayne, Nerissa, and Vulcan. No sign of Ronan. Fiery anger squashed the growing nausea. Our likeness was eerily accurate, minus the ears of my companions. Nothing marking them as elves.

I stared at the poster for a few heartbeats when they practically stopped as a deep, dangerous voice boomed from behind.

"Looks like you two wandered into the wrong town."

CHAPTER NINETEEN

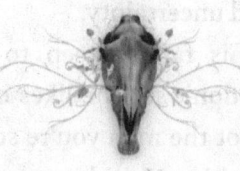

I humbly ask, no beg, you to send Lotrennian forces to Kayj now, while the dark king has eyes elsewhere. Should you agree, I will return to Lotrennia and face the consequences.
— Correspondence from Captain Bayne Ravindra to Queen Antares. Date Unknown.

Bayne moved faster than lightning as he snatched the poster from the wall and turned to face the figure behind us, sword unsheathed and dagger in his other hand. The man was on Bayne with a dagger at his throat before I knew what happened. Bayne nicked him on the forearm, and they swung at each other, dancing out of the other's grasp.

I was utterly useless. I gaped at them, my heart fluttering in my chest. Fuck. I had to *do* something. It took me too long to remember my new bow was strapped to my chest. I worked its way off, painstakingly slow, before hearing gruff curses and laughter. Bayne playfully punched the man in the chest, smiling with joy I'd yet to see in him.

The man was enormous, his appearance exactly as Bayne described. He donned a thick belt lined with sinister-looking axes and towered over both of us, filling the alley with a deep, booming laugh.

"Come, we should get out of here before someone notices you're on a godsdamned wanted poster from Aedrialis," Belgar Hunt said, still shaking with laughter.

I gaped at them both, unamused. We needed to get the hell out of here.

Belgar gestured us to follow. Bayne caught my eye, noting my seriousness. He sobered up, allowing his laughter to die off, and waved me on to follow the giant man. *The Bear.*

DARKNESS LOOMED when we arrived at the small stone cottage that stood at the center of the thick trees in the southern woods, its tall chimney sending puffs of smoke into the cool night air. The inside was larger than expected, and the giant man tossed a handful of wanted posters into the fire as we entered. He turned and gave what could only be appropriately described as a bear hug to Bayne, who in turn squeezed the man's tree trunk shoulders. I stood inside the entryway, watching awkwardly.

Bayne turned toward me.

"Lyvia Cantor, may I introduce you to Belgar Hunt, otherwise known as *Bear*," he said shooting an amusing look to Belgar, who shrugged in return.

"I needed a reputation. These lake folk are so nosy. I need them out of my business," he said, plastering a big smile on his face.

"*Bear*," Bayne said pointedly, rolling his eyes, "Lady Lyvia Cantor."

I had the inexplicable urge to curtsey at the use of my formal name, which I resisted. Instead, I simply gave Belgar a small, awkward wave. A curtsey would have been better.

Belgar approached and took my cold hand in his, giving it a firm shake. He followed it with a surprisingly graceful bow for such a large man.

"At your service, Lady Cantor. Any friend to Bayne is welcome here," he said, a grin stretching his gruff face into a handsome mask. "You're safe here."

"So, you haven't torn a man in two with your bare hands for looking at you the wrong way?" I asked, still wary of the large man.

"No, that's half true. But he did more than look at me the wrong way," he said with a wink.

I swallowed, sizing him up.

Clanking sounded in the other room, the kitchen, based on the enticing smell wafting from it. A woman, maybe ten years my senior, with bright red hair and even brighter blue eyes stepped from around the corner, closely followed by a younger version of herself.

Her face lit up as it landed on the captain. She crinkled her freckle-covered nose as a wide grin stretched across her lips. "Bayne."

She moved swiftly across the room and wrapped him in a tight embrace before grabbing hold of his shoulders to look him over. Bayne greeted her with the same warmth.

"It's good to see you, Winnie," he murmured into her thick, curly red hair, his arms dwarfing her petite body. She pulled away, still beaming as she turned toward the teenage girl behind her.

"You must be Evony," Bayne said, his striking green eyes

landing on the girl, whose light brown cheeks turned a shade pink at his stare, her freckles becoming more visible.

Her crystal blue eyes widened as they took Bayne in, and she swallowed. I suppressed a chuckle, sure I knew *exactly* what she was thinking.

"Pleasure," she said quietly as she met Bayne's outstretched hand with her own.

Bayne smiled softly as he shook her hand, earning a shy smile in return before Evony quickly averted her eyes.

A grumbling sound escaped Belgar's throat, sending Evony scooting back to her mother, her arms crossing as if she needed more distance between her and the handsome elf. The whites of Belgar's eyes flashed briefly as he gave an exaggerated eye roll, shook his head, and at last turned toward me.

"Morwyn, Belgar's blessing of a wife, and their daughter Evony," Bayne began, gesturing to the two in front of me, "This is Lady–"

"Just Lyvia," I interrupted, offering yet another awkward half-wave.

The warmth in Morwyn's eyes made me want to melt. I offered a small smile, and she reached forward, giving me a tight hug.

"Where is Ezrich?" Bayne asked.

"Our son," Belgar clarified, turning toward me, "is beyond the docks now." A hint of warm, fatherly pride entered his voice. "He's hoping to captain one of the barges in a year or so. He'll be back at the week's end."

"In just a year?" Bayne asked, seeming genuinely impressed.

Both proud parents nodded.

"Come, let me get us some food and you can tell us what in the gods' names you've gotten yourselves into," Morwyn said, motioning us to follow them into the kitchen.

My body thawed as we dug into the bowls of stew. The family watched as we devoured our meals. I resisted the urge to lick my bowl clean. Finally, Belgar crossed his arms and cleared his throat expectantly.

Bayne peered at me.

"It might be best to start with you, Lyvia," he said.

Morwyn and Belgar watched Bayne carefully. Evony's eyes shot between her parents and him. They slowly pulled their gazes away to meet my own. Morwyn gave me a small encouraging nod.

And so, I told my story from the beginning. Morwyn and Evony were a captivated audience. They huffed and sighed with animated facial expressions as I spoke. Belgar kept a blank, unblinking face, but by the time I'd finished, he sagged and let out a soft curse.

I suddenly felt the enormity of my situation after speaking it out loud from start to finish. It left me deflated. I sank into my chair, feeling exhausted. Belgar peered at Bayne, all amusement and cheerfulness gone from his features.

"And why the fuck were you on Kayj?"

"Belgar!" Morwyn chided, slapping him halfheartedly on his solid arm and looking pointedly at their daughter.

"She's fifteen!" He looked at her incredulously. "And you're one to talk with your sailor's mouth."

All humor vanished from the room at Bayne's next words. "Lida was taken."

"How? When?" Morwyn let out a strangled gasp, her hands shooting to her mouth.

Belgar's face blanched.

"Two years ago. During a run from the Cielo Islands. We took the Shungite Straits to avoid the Sultiran navy and ran into a tribute ship heading to Kayj. You know Lida. She

162

wouldn't let it drop. The children were on the upper deck, freezing."

My heart froze at the word.

Children.

They'd taken *children*. Gathered them up like cattle to be gifted to the dark king. Nausea churned in my stomach. Belgar cussed under his breath, shaking his head.

"We attacked in the night, but it went all wrong. The ship had to be carrying more than tributes because they had two mages and twice the number of soldiers."

"Lida insisted on being the one to board the ship to convince the tributes of our safety. Not a minute later, they torched our sails and smashed into our hull, nearly sinking the *Evecta*. Next thing I knew, Isla was screaming and pulling Nerissa out of the water. The tributes and ship were gone, Lida with them."

Bayne stared at the wall as he spoke, words emotionless and empty.

"And you went back for her," Belgar finally said.

Bayne nodded. "I went back. *Two years* later," he murmured, shaking his head, guilt etched across his face. "I went to Antares for help first."

Belgar's thick brows narrowed.

"I know. I was desperate though."

"Does she—"

"No," Bayne cut him off, voice clipped.

My senses prickled. Bayne didn't meet my eyes, not wanting me to know whatever it was Belgar was about to ask.

"How did you make it to Kayj?"

Bayne looked at me. "Saros's queensguard is a member of our crew."

Belgar leaned back in his chair. "You mean the queen's cockpuppet?"

My jaw dropped. Morwyn cleared her throat while Evony snorted out a giggle before clamping her mouth shut, eyes darting toward Bayne.

"Sorry, milady. I just meant..." Belgar shrugged, looking somewhat embarrassed, opening his hands to me.

Bayne cut in quickly. "I met Ronan eleven years ago during a run-in with some of the king's soldiers on the east coast. Most of what we see is what he wants us to see."

"And this is the same Ronan you mentioned from Westwyn?"

I frowned at Bayne's words, unable to fathom a reason for Ronan's actions. And I realized I didn't care. I had no more room for games or betrayal.

"One and the same," Bayne continued. "I knew when and where I needed to be thanks to Ronan. I lingered in a crowd of tributes and was taken with the rest of them."

Bayne paused then, a long uneasy silence stretching across the room.

Finally, he said, "Once I was there, I searched. The mines first and then the children's camp. She would be one to stick closely to them. The one person who recognized her description said she'd been taken by guards not two weeks prior."

His voice, like gravel, wavered as he spoke the last few words.

"So that's where I went. I knew I probably wouldn't leave. If she was one of them, that would be my fate as well. The ashen camp was foul. I caught a small one and tried everything I could to unravel the spell, spending nearly all the magic in my bones and nothing would do it. No change.

"I had to know if she was there," Bayne's eyes flicked to his forearms before continuing. "I found a way to blend in, not caring how weak it made me. I found her."

He looked away, silver slowly pooling on his lower eyelids.

Morwyn stretched out a hand and firmly clamped his in hers. Evony's mouth parted, her eyes transfixed.

"And I broke. I tried to take her to the shores with me. She just snarled and started to stir up the rest."

He paused, his throat bobbing. "Two weeks. If I had gotten there two weeks sooner..." Bayne's words were a broken rasp.

"And I just... I just left her."

He blinked away tears threatening to form. In that moment, he wasn't Bayne the Unbroken. Bayne *had* been broken. Bayne was still broken, his grief raw and agonizing.

"I left her and called Aquila. I didn't even give her the decency of a true death. I'd gone into that camp ready to die. I can't explain it, but after seeing her, something in me snapped. The coward in me snapped and... And I didn't want to die. I made it to the shores and saw Aquila in the distance. I knew the *Evecta* would be close, and I dove.

"Home was calling me. I felt it. The *Evecta*. And much after that was a blur. I swam as hard and fast as I could. There's not much that Dark King Daimos misses in his lands, and once he learned I'd snuck into the ashen camp, he quickly turned his forces on me. The next thing I knew I was..."

He glanced at me and away quickly.

"I was on board the *Evecta*," he murmured, sinking back in his chair.

"Oh, and Marian was sawing Oslo's right arm off," he finished, wiping a hand over his face.

Belgar choked on his beer before dropping another colorful curse. "*Bayne the Unbroken*," he muttered after a few moments.

Bayne shook his head and murmured something under his breath.

"It is not cowardice to want to live," I offered, my voice ringing through the silent room.

The four of them peered at me like they'd forgotten I was

there. Shocked at hearing my own voice, I simply stared back. Bayne regarded me steadily for a few moments before Belgar stood and grabbed a few small glasses, which he filled with a dark amber liquid.

"Indeed," Morwyn replied as Belgar handed a glass to us. Evony scowled as he deliberately passed her.

"To live," Belgar added, holding up a glass before downing its contents.

The rest of us followed suit. Bayne's eyes sliced to mine as he murmured the toast. The thick liquid slid down my throat like honey, burning at the pit of my stomach. Its spicy after-taste had me licking my lips, my head already feeling lighter.

"Belgar," Bayne drawled as his eyes slid to the round bottle of liquid. "Is this *ridecus*?" He leveled a hard stare at the large man, looking somehow pleased and stern at the same time.

I'd never heard of such a drink, but many were illegal in Sultira.

Belgar returned his stare with a large grin. "I take my business seriously," he said with a wink before pouring another glass for us.

"On that note," Morwyn interrupted. "This one ought to go to bed." She wrapped her arm around Evony's shoulders, who in turn opened her mouth to protest but was met with a stern jerk of her mother's chin toward the door.

"Good night," Evony murmured as she sullenly left the room.

Morwyn turned to us before following her out. "Stay as long as you'd like. It's good to see you, Captain," she said with a wink.

Bear grinned and turned to Bayne to raise his glass. "To BAYNE!" he bellowed. "Bayne, the unbroken! Bayne, the brave!" He staggered back. "Bayne, my old friend. I would follow *you* to the Kayj and back."

I lifted my glass and downed a swig. My lips tingled, an unexpected silliness wafting over my senses, lightening the weight that had settled during Bayne's story. The warm liquid pooled in my stomach, and my thoughts wandered to the handsome captain to my right. Belgar swiftly refilled our glasses.

I raised mine before saying, "To Bayne the *Brilliant!* Bayne the *Bright!* Bayne... Bayne the... *Buoyant,*" I stuttered, thinking of him swimming away from those atrocious ashen. I flung my hair over my shoulder in the most exaggerated and ridiculous way, like the names he collected.

Bayne doubled over in laughter, and Belgar's roar shook the house. I smiled and an uncontrollable giggle burst from my lips. The first since my arrest, I realized, and I couldn't stop. Moist droplets formed at the corner of my eyes that I didn't bother to wipe away.

I finally caught my breath to find Bayne gleaming at me.

"For the record, I didn't give these names to myself, unlike someone I know." He looked pointedly at Belgar, smiling.

The two of them took turns toasting people and places I didn't know. With each drink, Belgar became louder, eventually insisting we call him Bear. Morwyn came down to quiet him but was easily convinced to stay for another drink. Bear pulled her onto his lap, and she slung a lazy arm around his shoulder.

My thoughts drifted to Aeriden when the jokes started, not any jokes, but indecent, filthy ones. Despite the burn that snaked up my nostrils when I unwittingly spurted ridecus from my nose, it felt freeing to laugh again.

I retired to a small bedroom on the main level after a couple hours, savoring the feel of the cotton blanket and a real bed. Sometime in the night, I awoke to relieve myself, tiptoeing through the main sitting room, where I spotted the two men sleeping. Bayne lay slumped in a chair, glass still in hand. And Belgar, ironically, lay sprawled on a giant bear skin in front of the hearth, glowing orange with the last bit of embers holding on.

As I made my way back to my small room, a hand reached out and softly grabbed mine. The soft glow of the dying embers cast dark shadows against the barely visible panes of Bayne's face.

"Angel," he murmured in the dark.

I stood there frozen, my hand in his, for several heartbeats, staring at him. His eyes remained shut, the dark lashes a smudge above his cheeks. My gaze followed the soft curve of his lips, and I imagined for a heartbeat what they might feel like.

And in that moment, a *pull*, a wanting so deep I thought I might drown in it. A possibility blossomed in my thoughts, in my soul. A need to know what it might be like to *be* his angel. His fingers loosened, my hand falling from his grasp.

My fingers flexed before curling into a fist, feeling cold again. I glanced quickly at Bear, still asleep, before sneaking back to my room.

CHAPTER TWENTY

The wee bow and arrows might make my heart combust.
She'll love it once she's big enough to pick up the damn thing.
Thank you.

— Correspondence from Morwyn Hunt to Captain Bayne
Ravindra, date unknown, Captain's Quarters, Evecta.

I laid in bed for an hour before the sun finally came up, eyes open, thinking about what I'd heard the previous night and the captain sleeping in the neighboring room. *Angel.* Was he dreaming of Lida? I felt a strange mixture of jealousy and emptiness I couldn't explain.

Muffled movement sounded in the living room. I dressed and found Bear in the kitchen, a pot of tea steeping on the stove. He grinned at me.

"Years of being married to an early riser has taught me to always have the tea going by sunrise," he said.

"Morwyn seems lovely," I replied, smiling.

"She is more than I deserve. And to whom I owe everything," he added. His face turned sober before saying, "We'll give Bayne a little extra time to sleep off the ridecus. Elves have a hard time recovering from the drink, but they sure love it. It's stronger than their sparkly wine. We have more we need to discuss."

I helped Bear prepare breakfast while Bayne slept off the hangover, his jokes just as witty in the early morning but perhaps not as crude.

Morwyn followed a grumbling Evony into the kitchen. The former looked bright-eyed and full of energy, a stark contrast to the latter, who merely rubbed the sleep from her eyes before plopping onto a chair when I said good morning.

"I'm impressed, Lyvia," Morwyn said, giving me a wink. "Not many who have their first taste of ridecus look so chipper in the morning."

I shrugged in response, never being one to drink much unless Aeriden was home. He'd become a bit of a wine snob, I had to admit. He'd gone on and on about the various notes from a bottle of red we'd taken home from our last trip to the Rellenor Fields. And while I'd told him to buy a case of the sweet white one that tasted like peaches, he informed me only "empty-headed ladies of Khasimir" drank the stuff. I rolled my eyes, my mouth tugging into a small grin at the memory.

Morwyn was striking in the morning autumn light, as if she herself were the essence of the season. Her light skin was a stark contrast to the dark brown of Belgar and the tan olive seen in Aedrialis.

I opened my mouth to ask where she was from when Evony cut in, "So, do the horses in the capital really kill you?"

I choked on the tea I'd begun to swallow as she stared at me. "Not unless they're told to, I suppose," I answered, clearing my throat and shaking my head. "My family actually trains them."

Evony's eyes widened as she leaned forward. "I want you to tell me everything. About the agrippa, the capital, all of it."

I chuckled, finishing a bite of cheese, and nodded "Sure. Though, it's probably not as exciting as you may think."

Morwyn huffed a laugh as she filled her plate, Belgar rolling his eyes once again.

Bayne slowly wandered into the kitchen as the bacon started sizzling. I handed him a warm mug of tea, which he accepted with a pinched brow and a nod before slumping down in a chair at the table. I searched his face for any recollection of what he'd said, finding none.

"You're a bastard," he said to Bear.

"Language, Bayne. We're not on the *Evecta*," Morwyn scolded.

He placed a hand to his heart. "Apologies," he said, nodding toward Morwyn and Evony, the latter swallowing a large bite she'd taken and quickly brushing her hair to the side, along with the crumbs collecting on her lap.

Bayne turned back to Bear. "You—" He glanced at Morwyn and shook his head, the obvious retort still not appropriate enough to be muttered in front of their daughter.

"You're getting soft, old friend," Bear replied, handing him some bread. "Eat."

"Now. Where are you two heading?" he asked, looking between us.

"North," Bayne replied, rubbing the bridge of his nose. "The *Evecta* will be waiting near Stynguard."

"*Bayne* is heading north," I clarified before taking another luxurious sip of tea, my head still light from the ridecus. "I need to cross the Lake of Light. I'm headed west to find my brother."

"So, you'll both need a boat," Bear replied.

"Can you help us find something discrete?" Bayne asked.

"Yes. If we can't find a passenger vessel, Ezrich can ferry you to the northern port during the next run." Bear nodded as he dished out bacon. "You're welcome to stay as long as you'd like though. Sounds like you've been on the road long enough. It's worth gathering your strength before setting out again. I took care of the most recent shipment of wanted posters with your lovely faces on them," he said with a wink. "The next shipment from the capital isn't due for another two weeks, so you should be relatively safe with us in the woods."

Bear made a pointed look at Morwyn, who caught his eye and dragged a reluctant Evony from the room. Bayne's brows pinched together as he regarded Bear.

"Bayne," he said, face growing serious, "there's rumor of the tribute reaching the northern lake towns."

Bayne's features tightened with shock. "This far south? Since when?"

"Since about a month ago. Rumors at this point. But I'm considering sending Morwyn and Evony away for the winter."

Bayne nodded, deep in thought. "Think he's growing desperate? Have the numbers increased?"

"Not that we know of."

"What does he need them for?" I asked, still feeling like there was so much I was missing.

Bear regarded me for a moment. "The dark king has many uses for the tributes," he scoffed as he said the word. "*Tributes*. That's not the right word. They're slaves, really. They either end up as the godsforsaken ashen or they end up working the mines."

I glanced at him expectantly.

"The mines are home to some of the most valued

gemstones in the world. And believed to be the last remaining source of larimer. Larimer is—"

"What Mount Telum was constructed from," I finished for him.

He regarded me for a moment before nodding. "Yes. And do you know why King Saros used that particular rock for the construction of his mountain?"

I shook my head.

"Some believe larimer has astro properties."

I perked up, sitting higher in my chair, recalling none of this information from my Sky Scholar lectures.

"An innate attraction to the stars," he continued. "We don't know why that's important or what he needs it for, but he's been around long enough..." He paused, shaking his head. "Who knows what knowledge he's kept to himself?"

Bear sat back, looking pensive.

"If he's reaching for tributes this far into Sultira," Bayne said, "the people won't stand for it. It's only a matter of time before the rumors spread throughout the rest of the kingdom and the people revolt. Saros must know that."

Bear was silent. Bayne looked at him expectantly before understanding spread across his features.

"There's already a revolution underway," the captain concluded, nodding. "And I take it *you* are involved already?"

"Aye. Not sure I'd call it a revolution at this point, but there have been enough towns and villages ravaged by the tribute over the last fifty years that people are remembering. They aren't as subtle as they used to be. They come in, take half the town or more, blaming it on 'relocation for health and safety.' There are enough of us who know the truth. And the seeds have been sown in the royal army as well."

"A coup?" Bayne asked, leaning forward.

"I'm not privy to that knowledge. But we will fight back.

Soon." Bear sat with his shoulders forward, eyes set with determination and grit. Bayne met his stare, all evidence of the recent hangover gone in an instant.

"I still don't understand why he does it. Is he allied with Dark King Daimos?" I asked.

Bayne turned to me. "Some think he is. Others speculate it's all part of a grand plan to overthrow the dark king. I can't help but think there's something we're missing."

"Whatever his reason, we'll end it soon," Bear gruffed in response.

BEAR LEFT for business in town, and I found Bayne returning from the washroom. My eyes roved over his chiseled and scarred chest as he pulled his black shirt down. For a moment, I caught myself imagining what it would feel like to run my fingers over the intricate black design with waves of sunbeams and leaves on his chest and stomach. I jerked my gaze away, shoving the thoughts aside.

"I need to talk to you," I told him and turned around, leading him into my small room.

I tossed him a small towel he used to tousle his hair as he plopped down on the small chair once inside. I stood in silence for several long moments, my mind continuing its internal debate that had begun weeks ago when he'd found me in Westwyn. My self-preservation and distrust warred with the need to confide in him, the urge to open up.

My throat bobbed as I finally conceded.

"Before we left Westwyn," I began, "I found Ronan's satchel." I pulled the bag out from under the mattress, Bayne's eyes following the movement. "I want to show you what's inside." I pulled out the map first and laid it on the bed.

"I drew this for Nerissa," I said, "but no one ever explained it."

Bayne moved to stand next to me, the fresh scent of pine and sea wafting over with the movement of his arm as it stretched over the map.

"This," he murmured, "is the realm of Vael prior to the War of Ruin. The few sources that remain suggest there was an event during the war that caused some type of blast or explosion. Tsunamis and vaelquakes wreaked havoc across the lands, flooding an enormous part of Sultira and the connecting isthmus to Lotrennia." He paused, watching me.

I leaned closer, tracing the jagged lines connecting the two continents.

"Everything you've drawn here," he said, pointing to the section of land to the south and east of today's Sultira, "is now beneath the Juniper Sea."

"And you think that blast was connected to the stones of the Bellators."

A nod.

"What if the Bellators returned somehow? If Saros doesn't fight for his people, maybe they could."

Bayne's green eyes flashed, yet he yielded no emotion as he held my gaze for a few silent moments.

"It could certainly turn the tide in our favor, assuming they'd fight *with* us and not against us," he finally said.

"Does the name Enya Natara mean anything to you?"

Bayne blinked and cocked his head, staring at me curiously.

"Where did you hear that name?"

I scanned his eyes, searching for something. They sparkled in response. I finally divulged the details of my recent dreams, certain they'd been about the warrior I'd discovered in the burial chamber two months ago. His brow pinched together as a wariness entered his eyes.

"Enya Natara was the Bellator," he said, eyes searching mine, "who many believe was to blame for their demise. 'Enya the Betrayer.' What did she look like?"

My heart picked up a rapid beat as I considered how much to share with him.

"I was dreaming I *was* her," I finally said, averting my eyes. "But there was another there. A human, I think. I don't know if he was a Bellator, but she was terrified of him. And I think he did something terrible. And I think he killed her. He was after the stone."

Bayne pinned me with his gaze, but this time, I couldn't meet it. My eyes locked on my hands for a few moments as he contemplated what I said.

He shifted next to me. "My mother was a seer. She always said it was unwise to ignore messages gifted in your sleep."

I nodded, feeling relief in finally sharing these dreams with someone. And I *was* beginning to trust him, despite the warning bells that hadn't ceased ringing since the words my father had spoken in Mount Telum.

I sat next to him on the edge of the bed and finally pulled out the military logs. Bayne's eyes narrowed as he scanned the documents.

"These are troop movements. Plans. These are either inaccurate, and he left the satchel on purpose hoping to throw us off. Or," he said, turning to me and lifting a dark eyebrow, "he was *quite* distracted."

"We..." I began, sputtering and utterly flustered at how close he was to the truth. "It didn't get that far. Not that you care, but for the record, nothing *really* happened. Between me and Ronan."

The stammering in my words was as bad as the heat that

raced to my cheeks. He scanned my face, eyes drifting to my neck. His mouth opened, the tips of his teeth pressing into his lower lip.

He refocused on my eyes and gave me a half-shrug. "No? Ronan is a good-looking guy. I wouldn't judge you if something had."

He turned back to the military logs. I sagged a little as he released me from his gaze. "What do you think?"

"These look authentic, but it's difficult to say whether they are out of date. Based on the information here, there hasn't been much movement on the west coast. If you think your brother was stationed there, it's likely he still is," he said, handing me the logs.

Good. This was good. I had no idea how I'd manage on my own until I found Aeriden. Bayne and I would go our separate ways at the tail of the Rhew River, but at least I was heading in the right direction. A small, strange twisting formed in the pit of my stomach at the thought of parting with the elf. I folded the logs and tucked them away.

"There was one other thing," I said, pulling out Father Marcus's journal. "I found this in the scholar room at Mount Telum. I thought I'd lost it in the Pool of Kryax, but I think Ronan took it off me when he pulled me from the water."

Saying it out loud made the boiling rage return, and I unclenched my jaw.

"I know," he said, watching me carefully. He glanced at my hands, bunched in fists.

"What do you mean you know?" I said, slowly biting out each word.

"I knew you took something from the scholar room, but I wasn't sure what. I thought it best to wait for you to share it if you wanted." He grinned, holding his hands up. "May I see the journal?"

Of course, he knew. He had super senses. My eyes rolled, earning me a chuckle in response. The sound danced along my limbs. He carefully opened the journal and paged through the notes. He stopped where I had, his expression grim.

"He was scared. That much is clear."

I nodded. The frenetic handwriting and increasingly sloppy notes confirmed as much. A paralyzing wave of guilt rolled over me. We'd left him. We'd left Drystan.

"I, uh," he paused, eyes flicking to mine, "I'm sorry we didn't stop to search the dungeons for him." The strong column of his neck worked as his throat bobbed.

I finally brought my gaze to his. He held it for a moment, conveying what felt like regret. The urge to quell his unease formed in my chest, but I bit my lip.

I nodded instead, my own guilty conscience in need of a crutch, and murmured, "They both could still be alive."

"Will you go back for them?"

"Yes," I answered before thinking. How would I even do it? Could Aeriden and I possibly free them on our own?

Bayne's eyes sparkled for a moment before they returned to the journal. He frowned as he read out loud, "'Not stone?'"

He scratched the stubble on his chin as he read until he stopped at the delicate scroll. I cringed, the edges of the parchment nearly disintegrating as he gently unfolded it. Bayne's expression turned blank as he studied the words and symbols. His eyes lingered halfway down the page.

"What are they?"

He didn't respond for a few moments. I shifted on the bed.

"You said I could trust you," I reminded him. I wasn't a fool. I knew he'd lie to me if he thought it was necessary. Or if he didn't lie, he was at least willing to withhold information and provide incomplete truths.

"The stones of power. But," he paused, eyeing the words,

"most of the names of the stones have been lost for hundreds of years." His fingers hovered above the parchment, almost touching the delicate scroll.

"These others haven't been uttered for hundreds of years. These powers were lost. Long forgotten." He shook his head and rubbed his eyes. "This is the key to identifying the lost powers. This could be catastrophic in the wrong hands."

"Well, it won't survive much longer," I said, a despair entering my voice at the inevitable loss of history.

Bayne nodded his head in agreement, not taking his eyes off the page.

"Thank you," I added, "for not prying. For letting me come to you with this."

I sat back, contemplating what he'd said, feeling relieved to be able to share the mental load of all that I'd discovered with someone. Bayne's lashes fluttered for a moment as he crossed his arms and gazed up at me.

"Friends don't pry," he murmured, his lips tilting up in a half grin.

CHAPTER TWENTY-ONE

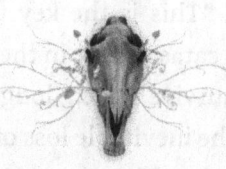

Morwyn Eghan, age ten, under elder brother's charge, to remain on board the Siren *until released by Lord Haro of Marisarma.*

— Notes from Votruvian bill of sale, Captain's Quarters, Evecta.

M orwyn found me soon after and dragged me from the small cottage, claiming she had an urgent task she needed my help with.

"Where are we going?" I asked as we began our hike up the mountain. I eyed the horses in the barn, longing to hop on one of their backs.

"Into the mountain," she said, her voice giddy as she glanced back with a wink, "for a surprise."

I couldn't help but return her grin despite the burn in my backside.

"How did you meet Belgar?" I asked as we wove our way

through the trees. I shivered despite the warmth spreading from my working muscles. Winter would be here soon. A chill breeze whispered through the near bare branches of birches and aspens we wound around.

"I met Belgar on the *Evecta* about twenty years ago. You could say I tricked Bayne into letting me join the crew," Morwyn said.

I couldn't see her face as she trekked a few paces ahead of me, but I could hear the smile in her voice.

"Twenty years ago?" I asked. "You must have only been, what, fifteen?"

"Sixteen," she said, continuing the rigorous trek up the slope, "Although I lied about that at the time. Said I was eighteen. Truth be told, I would have said anything to get off that godsforsaken island."

"Your home?"

"Not sure I'd ever called it that, but yes, where I was born. Where my family was from. Votruvia. It's west of Sultira. Beautiful. Greener than you could possibly imagine. Well, except for maybe Lotrennia, though I've never been. Beautiful. And brutal."

I bristled at the discomfort that arose every time I was reminded of the history erased from Sultira. The knowledge kept hidden. The kingdoms and continents that I never knew existed.

"Anyways, Bayne and his crew had a run-in with one of the Lords of Marisarma. The pirate lords rule over the Votruvian Islands," she clarified, looking back at me. "There was a disagreement over the retrieval of an artifact of some value, though I never learned what. My older brother was indebted to said sea lord, which meant servitude... slavery, really, as no laws exist in Votruvia to prevent it. And as his younger sister, I was too."

My stomach churned at the thought of what that might mean. Morwyn continued her trek ahead of me, unfaltering.

"My brother saw an opportunity with the *Evecta* and tried to leverage our freedom with some information. It's a long story, but my brother was gutted in the process. There was a lot of blood, in the end. But Bayne and his crew got what they were after, and I found my freedom."

"I'm sorry about your brother," I said in between breaths as our incline steepened.

"Don't be," she said, a hint of bitterness entering her words. "He was a piece of shit, for the most part. I had a younger brother too. Gone now, thanks to my older brother. He tried to make it right in the end, but..." She shook her head and picked up the pace.

"Here we are," Morwyn rasped as she pulled herself up a rocky ledge.

I scrambled after her, my elbows barking in protest at the sharp rock. I stood at the edge, catching my breath from the vigorous trek up the side of the mountain. Glancing around the rocky outcropping we stood on, there was nothing in sight except more rock and a stunning view of autumn colors dotted throughout the deep green pines down the steep mountain face.

"Wouldn't it have been faster to have gone further east and then up?" I asked, pointing to the smoke rising from her little cottage.

"Aye, but the path to the southeast cuts a little too near the mountain cat's territory. I am pretty sure that big girl has cubs in her. Best to steer clear."

She walked straight at the side of the mountain, and her hand slid into the side of the rocky wall. A sharp *click* sounded, and a massive wall of rock slid to the side, revealing the entrance to a dark tunnel.

My stomach pitted.

Another. Fucking. Tunnel.

The not-so-distant memories of sewage and grimy walls filled my mind, replaced by the all-consuming, spine-tingling fear I'd felt in Crown Peak.

Morwyn turned to me, concern etched across her face. "Are you all right, Lyvia?"

I didn't meet her gaze, only stared at the dark entrance to the tunnel, waiting for the glowing violet eyes of the Stone Witch to appear.

Morwyn stepped to my side and gently grasped my arm.

"Oh, Lyvia. I'm an idiot. I'm sorry. The last tunnel you entered in this mountain range..." She nodded in understanding and pulled me toward her. "I promise no evil lurks here. Trust me," she said, her twinkling eyes and warm smile returning.

I am not afraid of the dark, I reminded myself before following her in. I jumped as the stone door slid shut behind us, and the rancid scent of rotten eggs filled my nostrils. I held my breath for a moment, and Morwyn paused in front of me.

"You'll get used to the scent," she said, lighting a torch.

Orange light danced off the walls of the tunnel, which were as smooth as glass. We continued down the dark tunnel for a short while before it opened into a vast cavern containing a system of small pools. I paused at the entrance, taking in the sight.

Morwyn moved across the cavern, lighting little torches along the walls so the massive space glowed with a soft, warm light. Before us lay several small pools of steaming water and others with something dark and bubbling. My stomach churned, thoughts drifting to the kryax.

"What is this place?" I called to her across the cave. The massive space had low ceilings but stretched at least a couple hundred yards in both directions. The interconnecting pools led to a sharp drop-off at the end, and I could hear the whooshing swell of a waterfall far beyond.

"Welcome to my haven, Lyvia Cantor," Morwyn said with a wink, stretching her arms out to the sides. "I'm sure this was something more sacred at a different time," she continued, glancing at the polished walls.

I stepped closer to the torch sconces on the wall. They were made of iron but had the tiniest chains wrapped around them in delicate intricate patterns. I ran my fingers over the design. Fortissa.

"Belgar and I stumbled upon this place when we first built our house. It had long been abandoned. To our knowledge, no one knows it's here except for us. The baths are purifying. Hot springs feed them from the tunnels below. And the mud," she said, gesturing to the dark, murky pools, "we believe is ash mixed with the springs. Stay away from the ones with bubbles, of course."

Morwyn set her pack down and twisted her hair up above her head. She pulled out a few waterskins and some fruit and then, to my shock, began undressing. I averted my eyes, suddenly feeling shy and uncomfortable. She approached the dark bath and dipped a toe in. She let out a soft groan and slowly slid into the thick, steaming mud.

"I promise, you won't regret it," she murmured. Her pale white skin was a stark contrast to the dark pool. She slid in up to her neck before sitting up. The mud covered her body like a dark, black paint. She raised her eyebrows at me expectantly.

I shifted awkwardly on my feet.

"Oh shit, I'm sorry. Forgive me, Sultirans aren't as free-spirited as Votruvians," she teased and turned around.

I quickly disrobed and tied my hair into a knot above my

head. I sat on the edge of the pool and slowly slipped my feet and legs into the sludge.

It was so unlike water, the thickness coating my limbs like a spoon moving through batter. Gods, did it feel good though. I didn't sink to the bottom of the pool like I would have in water. I floated, suspended in the warm muck. I let my head fall back on the edge of the pool and breathed out a long exhale. Morwyn turned toward me with a wide grin.

"Drink plenty of water," she said, passing me a waterskin. She pulled out the fruit, slicing off green circles with her dagger. She handed me two before placing two on her own eyes.

"Tell me about your brother," she said.

I closed my eyes beneath the cool slices, smiling at the thought of him.

"Aeriden is my rock. Exactly what you would think of when you picture the son of a lord of Sultira, minus the pomp and arrogance. Cocky sometimes, yes, but mostly when it comes to women. You should hear some of the lines he's used." I chuckled, my mind flitting to the summer we'd spent in Khasimir and the countless ladies-in-waiting he'd had drooling over him.

"*'Did you injure your wings when you plummeted from stars?'*" I recited, doing my best imitation of his voice. "*'The entire agrippa herd couldn't stop me from mounting you.'*"

Morwyn snorted out a laugh.

I continued in a giggle, "*'My father made me shave to look more presentable for you and now my upper lip is cold. Could you warm it for me?'*"

Morwyn's laugh erupted, her bright cackle bouncing off the cave walls.

"We spent a summer in Khasimir while our father had business with Lord Pavel. And the ladies there—" I smiled, shaking my head at the memory. "He had them crawling over each other to get to him. And one night, he snuck out of one of their balconies for a midnight wiz off its edge, unaware that the doors were built with an automatic locking mechanism..." I paused, laughing as I remembered Aeriden's urgent whispers. I'd led a young Tiberius down the road and caught sight of his naked ass shivering in the early hours of dawn.

"Well, you can imagine how pleased my father was. But no, never truly arrogant, unlike so many of them. He pushed my father to allow me to study with the Death Scholars. Bought me a ridiculous black cloak since I'd never wear their robes. But I have always been a digger. Hands in the dirt," I said with a smile.

"Not what you think of when you picture a Sultiran lord's daughter," Morwyn replied softly with a chuckle.

"He is one of the few friends I have left." My thoughts drifted to Drystan, my smile disappearing.

"My mother always said life will bring people into your world and take people away in unexpected ways," Morwyn said softly. "I've found it best to remember there's usually a reason for it. Though you may never find out why."

She was right, of course. The steady rush of the waterfall in the distance and the cool fruit on my eyelids quieted the questions that bubbled up every time I thought about the events that had taken place.

"Everything that's happened in the last couple months," I said quietly. "It's like I can't process it. There's so much... darkness. How do you go on with your life after you see the truth? After a shadow falls across it all?"

Morwyn's soft sigh sounded from across the pool.

"There is darkness in the world, Lyvia. There is no doubt about that. But there is also light. And I find it helps to remember that *somewhere* in the world, something good is happening. A mother is reading to her child. A father is teaching his son. Two people are falling in love. Or maybe someone's just getting laid."

I snorted as a giggle rose up. Some good *was* happening now. We sat in silence for a while longer until Morwyn deemed it time to have some water and move on. She led us to a small pool, closer to the edge of the cavern where the thunder of the waterfall echoed off the rock walls. The thick sludge dripped down her curved body as she sauntered over to the pool. She turned to me, flashing a wicked grin, before saying, "It's best to make this one quick."

She winked and jumped into the pool, splashing me with frigid water. Her head shot through the surface, and she let out a loud yipe.

"Oh, holy gods, that is cold!" she yelled. "Come on, then!"

Well, shit. I thought I was done with cold baths for a while. I closed my eyes, steeling myself for the icy plunge. Sucking in a breath, I jumped.

"Fuck!" I shouted as my face broke the surface.

Morwyn threw her head back, curling wine-red hair splashing in the water, and barked out a laugh.

"I'm done in here!"

"No! One minute, Lyvia! Suck it up."

I turned and splashed her in the face. She laughed and hopped out on the edge. I made to follow, and she planted a hand on my head, shoving me back down.

"Hey!" I shouted.

She laughed as she turned and walked over to a hot spring a few pools down. I groaned as I slid in after her, savoring the heat that was fire against my icy skin. She tossed me another water skin.

"Okay, this is amazing," I finally said, after soaking for a few minutes.

"Aye," she agreed. "You know, you can stay longer if you'd like, Lyvia. It's been a few years since I had a girlfriend close by."

My heart warmed. A girlfriend. And as tempting as it was to stay, I needed to find Aeriden. He was family.

"Thank you," I said.

We sat a few minutes longer before the grinding rock on rock sounded at the entrance to the tunnel causing my heart to leap into my throat. Morwyn splashed across the pool, reaching for the blade that sat on the edge.

CHAPTER TWENTY-TWO

Congremar, *the gathering of the Sea Lords of Marisarma,*
will take place on the Sixteenth of Spring in the Burning Sea
Mountains. You didn't hear it from me.
— *Anonymous correspondence to Captain Bayne Ravin-*
dra. Date unknown. Captain's quarters, Evecta.

A dark figure stalked through the end of the tunnel and entrance to the cavern several yards away.

"For fuck's sake, Bayne!" Morwyn shouted at him as she heaved a sigh of relief and slid back into the pool. "You about made my heart stop! Knock next time, you ass."

Bayne's throaty chuckle reverberated along my bones. He slowly moved across the cavern, winding his way through the dim light on the slick rock separating the pools. I watched him closely, a rabbit eyeing a fox on the hunt.

I moved to the edge of the bath, suddenly very aware of my naked body in the clear spring. I tucked my knees into my chest dipping lower into the water. He stepped to the edge of the pool, eyes dark as he locked them onto mine. They slid over the water where I sat submerged, and I felt a stir in my lower abdomen.

"Can we help you?" Morwyn asked him as she slid next to me, perching her white elbows on the edge of the pool and leaning her head on her hand as if he bored her.

A dark brow raised in response.

"Not like that," she snapped. "How did you find us? I told Belgar not to tell you where we went."

"You think I need Belgar to track the two of you? I'm offended, Winnie," he said, placing a hand on his heart, pulling his gaze from mine to Morwyn's.

She rolled her eyes. "Right. Elf eyes."

"I was just curious," he said, a soft grin tugging on his lips.

"Well, you're not invited. Girls only. Go away," she said, giving him a splash before turning around and dismissing him.

He chuckled and turned back to me.

"Why is that? I'm just as sore as you. More so, after lugging half that moose all the way to Rivaner," he said, raising his eyebrows at me. "I could use a soak and a back rub."

"I'm sure Belgar will be happy to oblige," Morwyn said, closing her eyes and settling back into the bath. "Out, you pirate."

"Enjoy your soak," he said, voice low.

My toes curled in response, heat rushing to my cheeks, all too aware that it had nothing to do with the spring I sat in. He sketched a mocking bow before retreating.

BY THE TIME Morwyn and I toweled off and trekked back down the mountain, the sun began its descent across the sky. After spending an hour pouring over Father Marcus's journal once again, I left my small room to get some fresh air. Bayne had disappeared and Bear was nowhere to be found.

I found myself wandering through the small barn when the zip of an arrow sounded. Another whoosh, and then, "Fuck."

I stepped from the back of the barn to find Evony trudging down the woods to a target eighty feet away. She ripped the three arrows out of the target, two of which had hit its center with incredible precision. The third sat only an inch to the left.

She stalked back toward the barn and jumped as she caught sight of me.

"That was incredible," I called as she approached.

She picked up a jog and shrugged as she slowed to where I stood.

"Thanks," she grumbled. "I'm missing more than usual."

"Missed? Your aim is next to perfect," I said, shaking my head.

Evony was silent as she drew her bow once more. Her body stilled for the breath she slowly blew out before letting the arrow fly once more.

"Would you," I began, eyes still on the arrow that once again found its mark. "If I stayed another day or two, would you teach me?"

Evony whipped her face toward me, eyes alight. "Yes!" She nodded. "Yes, I'd love to. Here."

I took the bow and arrow she shoved at me with reluctance, suddenly remembering how terrible I was.

"You may want to stand behind me," I murmured.

She giggled, adjusting my stance and tipping my elbow up and back. I let the first arrow fly, its tip embedding in a tall oak several feet to the right of a much closer target. A grumble escaped my lips as she offered a correction on my breathing before handing me another.

"So, you and Bayne," she began as I drew the bow, the muscles between my shoulder blades straining as I held it in place for a longer breath this time. I let it fly, the blur of the arrow zipping past the target but missing by only a foot this time.

"He's..." I started, thinking back to our conversation from the previous night. "A friend," I said with a solid nod.

"So, he's available?"

I choked on a laugh, certain Bear would murder them if that type of relationship developed. I coughed, doing my best to disguise my reaction, and shrugged.

"I suppose," I answered. "Though I think he's still pretty hung up on Lida. You heard him talking about her last night."

"Yeah," Evony muttered. "Suppose you're right."

Evony spent hours with me that afternoon, coaching and adjusting my posture. She peppered me with questions about Aedrialis between shots before we retired for the night to the small cottage.

———

THOUGH I'D PLANNED to rest with Bear and his family for only two days, we awoke to snow the next morning. As if laughing at our plans, the winds of winter brought a blizzard that lasted two months. Mountain roads and trails were impassable, and the Lake of Light shipyard shut down passenger travel, saving all ships for fishing and supply runs.

Bayne and Bear went back for the remaining moose, and we sold it off in the village to contribute to our stay. While my mornings were split between chores and archery with Evony, Bayne insisted on continuing our training sessions in the small barn where we kept Anchor. Bear hung a sand-filled dummy from the rafters that we pummeled repeatedly until bruises peppered my knuckles, knees, elbows, and shins.

"Stop," Bayne said as I landed a kick on the giant bag.

"You're kicking with your leg."

I gaped at him. We'd been at it for over an hour. While I had improved in hand-to-hand combat, it exhausted me to the bone.

"I'm kicking," I said, irritation flaring. "What the hell am I supposed to kick with?"

Bayne smirked and sauntered over to where I stood panting in the chilly barn. "Your hips," he said as he stepped behind me, hands sliding over my sweater and onto my hip bones.

I stirred beneath his touch, urging myself to ignore the speed of my quickening pulse.

"Your power comes from here," he said, twisting and repositioning my hips so they angled to the side of the barn, away from the dummy. "Angle that step out to the side, keep this tight," his hand slid up from my hips to the dip in my waist where my muscles contracted, "and let the momentum slam your leg forward. Your shin is the weapon."

He paused, hands still on me, as a slight intake of breath hissed through his lips.

"Again."

I took a breath as he pulled his hands away, finally free from the distraction to actually think about what he had said. I lined up and allowed my leg to follow the motion of my hips as I spun into the dummy, ripping it free from the rope. Satisfaction bloomed in my chest. I glanced behind me, and Bayne gave me a half smile before leaving me to it.

Morwyn and Bear joined us often to train. Morwyn was surprisingly deadly with the short sword. She threw a few cheap shots at us as we sparred, shrugging off our comments that she was a dirty fighter, claiming it came from years of living with pirates.

Despite the forced proximity, I loved spending time with them. Laughter and stories filled our days at the little stone cottage. Evony stared dreamily at Bayne as she peppered me with questions during our dinners. She was enamored with the idea of going to the capital, which her father scoffed and rolled his eyes at. I hoped someday she would make it there.

AFTER NEARLY THREE months of relentless snow, I made my way through the knee-deep powder to feed the horses and goats. Raucous laughter and shouts came from behind the barn, and I caught Bayne and Bear in the middle of a snow fight, throwing balls of it through the air or tackling each other before smashing it in the other's face.

A flying chunk of snow crashed into my chest from across the yard.

"Look out!" Bear bellowed from behind.

Another icy ball smashed into my face.

"Hey!" I yelled at the hidden attacker, wiping the icy melt from my face as the wind whipped through the trees.

"Sorry!" Bayne called back from behind a mound of snow.

"Children," I muttered and shook my head as I made my way to the barn.

A third was lobbed through the air and connected with the back of my neck before I finally stopped to turn around. I could barely see the outline of Bayne's charcoal coat through the heavy downfall, but I could tell he grinned like a child.

He knelt and packed another.

"I dare you," I warned.

The huff of his laugh was lost through the howl of the

wind. He threw it so fast I didn't have time to duck, the ball of snow bursting against my forearms. I ran, or rather trudged, toward him, trying my best to gather up a snowball of my own. The mounds were so deep I couldn't get there before he smashed another into my face. Bear's booming laugh crumpled into a nervous chuckle as I surged forward, my clothes sopping wet.

"You're on your own with this one, Cap!" he called before hurrying back inside the cabin.

Another flew through the air and connected with my shoulder. I stopped and gathered up one of my own. As I flung it in his direction, he dodged and lobbed another at me, snow exploding in my vision. As I rushed through the snow, Bayne's breathless laugh sounded as he scooted out of my reach. His confidence distracted him, and I dodged to the right, forcing him to round a pine where I finally caught his ankle.

His laugh echoed in the wind as we crashed into feet of soft, frigid snow.

"You!" I yelled, climbing my way up him. I reached my hand around to swipe some snow in his face, and he caught it, easily flipping me to my back.

I was utterly helpless against his strength. Even with weeks, now months, of his training, I could do nothing against his maneuvers. I lay on my back with his body and gaze locking me in place.

He gave me a boyish grin. "You, Lyvia, dear, have lost."

"I never said I wanted to play."

"Sometimes, we are thrown into the game before we realize it," he replied, eyeing me under his thick lashes. Snow dripped off his nose onto my lips. He looked down as I licked the droplet that slid down my lower lip. His gaze traveled to my neck, bare against the cold and wet with snow.

"This might be considered indecent, you know," he said, eyes darkening.

"*You* are indecent," I replied, voice a bit breathless.

"Would you like me to get up?" he asked, the warmth of his breath melting the flakes landing on my skin. His scent filled my lungs as heat pooled in my lower abdomen. A blaze entered his pupils, his nostrils flaring for a moment.

Could he sense it? I dared a slight shift in my hips, repositioning us, and felt him long and hard against me. The sensation sent fire rippling through my body. Icy wind whipped the snow into a blinding white flurry so dense that his face disappeared for a moment.

"Oi! You two better get back in here before another spinner starts up!" Bear called from the cottage.

He held me in that gaze for another heartbeat, and I realized then that I wanted him. Despite feeling like I was playing with fire, I needed him. Unsure I'd get another chance, I locked my lips onto his and held them there for a heartbeat as he firmly kissed me back. I pulled away for a moment, eyes pinned on his. My lips parted as he met them again, his tongue dancing along mine, exploring and tender. The kiss was brief but deep.

He pulled away and jumped to his feet, hands sliding to mine. He scooped me up, my heart leaping at the sudden movement as my feet left the ground and dashed us through the thick snow back to the stone cottage.

We pulled off our sopping wet furs in the entryway, feeling somehow cooler inside than we did in the feet of snow outside. Bear flashed Bayne a knowing look and shot me a wink, which I returned with a scowl. I quickly dashed to my room and changed into dry clothes, sobering up from Bayne's intoxicating scent.

THE SNOW SPINNER lasted for three more days, in which we were truly stuck in the house. I could feel Bayne's eyes undress me as I walked to bed. And each night, I resisted the unrelenting urge to ask him to come with me. By the end of the third day of the snow spinner, I was truly going to lose my mind if I didn't put some air between us, our tension as taught as a halyard on the *Evecta*. Every movement, every breath from him, felt like a message, a promise. He was hunting. And though I knew I was his prey, the thrill of it sent my blood roaring.

Bayne sat next to me at dinner that night, his knee sliding closer to mine as we devoured our meal. I did my best to hide the relentless pulsing in my veins every time Bayne shifted in his seat, his thigh now pressed against mine. Morwyn and Evony retired to bed early that night, and Bear leveled a stare at us before he went up.

"You two should get a quick fuck in and get it over with already," he grumbled.

Heat quickly disappeared from my lower abdomen and rushed to my cheeks, the pleasant sensation of anticipation dissipating into cold embarrassment.

Regret flashed in Bear's eyes, and I quickly looked away.

Bayne casually stood from the table, clearing away the dishes. "I have no idea what you're talking about, old man. But you should get some sleep," he said, patting Bear on his massive shoulder.

"Indeed," he gruffed in response, rolling his eyes. "Good night."

And with that, we were alone again.

"He's just being a pirate," he said.

I cleared my throat.

"Indecent and rude, aren't they? Filthy mouths," I replied.

He flashed a wicked grin, locking me in place as if he knew exactly what I imagined he might be able to do with that filthy mouth.

"Indeed."

I joined him at the sink and began scrubbing the dishes while he dried.

Without looking at me, he quietly purred, "For the record, it wouldn't be quick. It would be slow and torturous in the best possible way. I would worship every inch of you," he paused, turning to me now, eyes drifting to my lips, "starting with those. And when I tasted you for the first time..."

His eyes drifted lower, tongue sliding over his lips, which sent my blood raging beneath my skin. "I'd wring you out until you were begging me to finish you off."

Heat flooded my entire being. I wanted him to ravish me right here in this kitchen. On the floor, the counter, the table, the wall, anywhere and everywhere.

As if reading my mind, he huffed a sultry laugh, shaking his head, and said, "Not here though. It wouldn't be right to do the things I want to do to you in my old friend's house. Indecent things with my... *filthy mouth*, as you say."

His last words sent my heart fluttering in my chest and butterflies chasing in my gut. I had to get the hell out of this kitchen.

I took a deep breath and bid him "goodnight" in barely a whisper. He shot me a shameless smirk and turned back to putting the dishes away.

That night, I left my door ajar. I waited and waited, but he didn't come. Some primal part of me still held out hope he simply couldn't resist me waiting in bed for him. The ache pooling between my legs made my breasts heavy and tight.

After tossing and turning for two hours, I finally poked my head out of my room and spied him sleeping in his usual spot in front of the dying embers of the fireplace. I tiptoed over to where he lay, examining his features. He was still as a statue except for the slow rise and fall of his bare chest. Asleep then. Damn.

I snuck back into my room and closed the door. Breathing in his scent did nothing to quell the maddening ache that started to consume my entire being, so I did what any sensible young woman would do and found my fingers drifting between my legs.

Bayne's words replayed over and over in my mind, and I found my thoughts wandering to the image of him climbing out of that river. My mind's eye drifted below his navel, something my real eyes didn't dare. His hardness against me... Our heat melting the freezing snow flying all around us... The wild pulsing between my legs quickened and crashed as I fell into luxurious, quiet pleasure.

CHAPTER TWENTY-THREE

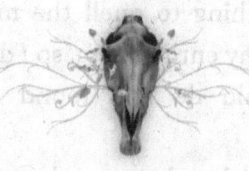

Bayne Ravindra, Captain of the Evecta.

— *Kill on Sight Order, Lords of Marisarma, dated 18th of Spring, 050.3E.*

C lear skies greeted us in the morning. Although winter neared its end, it tended to tighten its grip in the mountains for a few more weeks. A strange mixture of relief and apprehension grappled within me. We could be on our way. I could search for Aeriden. And that part of me that had itched to get away, to put distance between anything and everything that had happened in the fall, suddenly stilled at the thought of leaving this little family—of leaving Bayne.

The captain eyed me like the predator he was as I stepped from my room, pack in hand. His gaze met mine for a split second before it shot to my fingers. Heat rushed through my veins. A knowing look swept across his face before it was replaced with feral desire. Damn him. Could he possibly know? I tore my gaze away and joined Morwyn in the kitchen.

The Hunts helped us gather supplies for our respective trips, and Bear contacted Ezrich to secure a space on the transporter barge leaving Rivaner that day. The three of them escorted us to the docks, where we met Ezrich for the first time. He was the double of his large father, minus the auburn hair he had cut to his scalp, and slightly lighter skin tone. He greeted us with the warmth of his mother before he was devoured in her kisses.

Our farewells were drawn out and truly painful. My heart ached at the thought of leaving their little family. Morwyn teared up as she asked us not to go.

"You," she said, turning to Bayne. "Don't you dare go another sixteen years without seeing us."

Bayne smiled and pulled her into a tight hug. Her kind eyes found mine as he released her.

"You are welcome back anytime. Do you hear me? With or without that one," she said with a nod toward Bayne. She squeezed the breath from me, whispering in my ear, "Take care of yourself, Lyvia."

My friend held me in her arms for several heartbeats. A deep ache filled my chest as I blinked away a few tears. My *friend*. Morwyn had become more than a friend. Almost what I had imagined a sister to be like. Her bright blue eyes welled with tears as she squeezed my arms before finally releasing me.

We stood at the stern of the ship and waved, the gray-blue of the lake filling the space between us as the barge drifted away from the docks. Her words from months ago echoed in my ears. *Life brings people in and out of our world for different reasons.* And I knew finding Bear, Morwyn, and Evony in my life meant something good. Even if it was short-lived.

THE SAIL to the tail of the Rhew River would take all of two days on the lazy barge, so we settled into our new quarters, a small room below deck. We didn't see much of Ezrich, who was busy bustling about and following orders.

That night, we sat above deck in silence for several long minutes and stared up at the stars for which the massive lake was named. They blinked in the sky as our moons peeked over opposite horizons.

My chest tightened as I took a deep breath, uneasy at the question I knew I had to ask the man next to me.

"I've been meaning to say something to you," Bayne said, a moment before the words could form on my lips.

I clamped them shut, swallowing my nerves. He turned to me as he leaned a forearm against the rail.

"I am sorry," he said, throat bobbing as if he were fighting his own nerves. "You were right, on the *Evecta*. The others may have sprung you from your cell, but we took you without your consent. And we forced you to return to Mount Telum with us. We left your friends, dragged you to Crown Peak..." His voice trailed off as his eyes went distant.

"You didn't ask for any of this, and I—" he paused, searching my eyes for something. "War is unforgiving. It's harsh, and it's cruel, and it's hardened me in ways I never knew were possible. I've been fighting this war for too long."

He turned, placing both forearms against the rail. I joined him, my arm brushing against his.

"I will do whatever it takes to save my people," he continued. "And I think, that when you're so focused on saving the kingdom, saving the godsdamned *realm*, it can be easy to miss the impact it has on one person."

His arm inched toward mine, the heat of it like the teasing

lick of fire. He turned to face me. "Even if they're standing right in front of you."

Bayne's green eyes glowed in the night, their facets transformed into an ethereal turquoise in the reflection of the blue moons.

"I think I understand you a little better, Captain," I finally said, still transfixed. "And I think that had things gone differently, in any of those cases, I would have likely ended up dead. Or worse."

Bayne swallowed and gave a shallow nod as he released me from his gaze and turned it back to the skies. "What will you do when you find Aeriden? Where will you go?" he asked.

I heaved a shaky sigh, unable to calm my nerves. "Well," I began, acutely aware of the racing of my heart, "Saros is still after me. We can't trust my father. Assuming Aeriden stays with me, he'll be considered a fugitive as well. I can either stay in the wild, hiding, or..." I trailed off, unsure I'd be able to ask the question.

Bayne's head snapped in my direction. "Would you fight? Would you come with us?" he asked, straightening.

Warmth bloomed in my chest, and I gave the captain a shaky nod. "I mean, I'm not a great fighter, you know that. But if I could help in some way... I have nowhere else to go. And if Saros won't fight for his own people, then someone should."

Bayne's lips curved into a grin.

"I have two conditions though," I murmured, glancing back at the sky. "Aeriden has to be on board. And we go back for Drystan and Father Marcus."

Bayne was quiet for a moment.

"What do you think?" I pressed, nudging him with my elbow. "Can I save the realm with you?"

The captain finally turned toward me. "I suppose I'll let

you tag along," he repeated my words from months ago in a low voice before flicking my nose.

I batted his hand away, resisting the upward tug of my lips.

"Though I'll warn you, life as a fugitive is far less satisfying than you may expect."

I turned to him, raising my eyebrows. "Care to elaborate?"

He let out an exasperated sigh.

"Bayne! Truth please." I scowled, reminding myself I was still getting to know him. Despite being enormously attracted to him, it had only been a few months since we'd pulled him from the water. Yet I found myself *wanting* to throw caution to the wind when I was near him.

He rolled his eyes as I cut him a glare.

"I didn't lie, Lyv. I haven't had a chance to tell my story."

Lyv. He started calling me Lyv instead of Lyvia, and damn, if it didn't make me want to climb him like a tree.

"Haven't had the chance?" I asked, incredulously. "We've been on our own for months now! I can think of plenty of chances."

"Maybe that was the wrong way of saying it. I haven't felt ready to tell you my story yet," he gruffed.

Despite understanding too well what he meant, a small part of me wilted.

"Do you trust me?" I whispered.

He pinned me with his piercing gaze, and for a moment, I was lost in layers and layers of green ferns and forest waters.

"Yes," he said, voice unwavering. "Do you trust me?"

I stayed lost in those eyes, holding his stare, feeling safer and more content looking into them over the past few weeks.

"Yes."

I waited expectantly. He cleared his throat and pulled his eyes to the deep, velvety night sky.

"Nerissa and I come from a royal line of mystics. We are not royalty," he said, holding up his hand before I could ask the question forming on my lips. "We are just related. My father was second in line to the throne of Lotrennia before Queen Antares married my widowed uncle—the king at the time. He died shortly after the birth of my cousin. After his death, Queen Antares outlawed the act of divination."

I pinched my brows at his dark form. He glanced at me noting my confusion.

"The act of foreseeing. Magic is highly regulated in the elven world. There is an accounting of every elf who practices, whether they were born with the gift or have studied. And magic always leaves a fingerprint.

"Trained eyes can identify what type of magic has been used and *whose* magic has been used. After my uncle's death, the prophecies turned dark, most of them predicting the ruin of Lotrennia."

"And your mother was one?"

"Yes. A true seer cannot stop the visions from coming. And one day, my mother saw the Living Library, the sacred tree of Lotrennia, burning. 'White flames freezing from the north,' she said, 'and demons from the west,'" he peered at me, "and black wings in the sky. And death that would *'end all or bless all'* is what she said.

"My father tried to convince her to keep quiet, but she went to Antares, trying to convince her of some future threat. She was convinced this had some connection to the prophecy of Olienna and the return of the Bellators, but no one had seen nor heard from Olienna for hundreds of years. We still don't know what happened to her."

"Antares lost her mind. She tortured her, mangling her body and mind so completely my mother was nothing but a shell when she'd finished. My father was in a rage. And because they were soulbound, her death destroyed him. It didn't simply break his heart and shatter his soul. He was in *physical* pain with her loss. He *felt* it with his entire being. He tried to kill Antares and was taken prisoner. They tortured him for weeks before drowning him in the Juniper Sea."

Emotions slammed into me. The coiling horror in my gut was second only to the deep ache I felt for him in my heart. Without realizing it, I reached out and grasped his hand in mine, staring up at his face, now lost in the skies above.

"Two months later, Dark King Daimos attacked the northern shores of Lotrennia. That's where Isla and her family were from. Her village was one of the first to be attacked. Nearly all of them ended up as ashen. She saw her parents and five sisters turn before her eyes."

I blanched. Isla was so cheerful and warm. I'd never have thought she suffered so much.

"Nerissa and I went into hiding. We were young at the time. Nerissa had been a war slayer commander, and I was a captain in the navy. We found each other and Aquila. Vulcan was part of Nerissa's squad, second-in-command, so he came with." He sighed, rubbing his eyes.

"That's why neither of you use your magic. Or at least, you try not to. To stay hidden."

He gave a quiet nod. "We aren't exactly welcome back in Lotrennia at this time. But the queen has enough on her plate that she hasn't bothered to come looking for us, yet."

"Is that why the Stone Witch called you the Forgotten One?" I asked.

He glanced up at me. "You caught that, huh?" he asked, a wry smile forming on his lips in confirmation.

I took a moment to digest everything he said. The pain and loss he must have endured would easily overwhelm a person. My hand still held his, and I realized then I was happy to share the burden with him. I gave it a squeeze and pressed my side against his. Heat rippled from where he stood, and I leaned into his warmth.

"If what Bear says is true and there is an uprising in Sultira, they could use our help. And you," he said turning to face me. "You have some connection to this. I don't know what it is, but your threads are woven in events yet to come."

I opened my mouth to object.

He said, "I won't ask you to look for the stones. But I want you to know this. Your life is a part of all of this. Destiny, fate, whatever you want to call it. What you do with it is up to you."

His eyes were hard on mine.

"How will I find you?" I asked, my eyes sliding to his lips in the dark.

"I could come with you," he murmured. "Help you find Aeriden first."

I blinked. He would postpone reuniting with his crew? Leaving the captain had left a quiet unease that lingered in my heart for several weeks now. His words doused it like a flame.

"What about the others? The *Evecta*?" I asked, swallowing my relief.

"I can communicate well enough with Aquila from a distance," he said. "We can make it work."

I pulled my eyes back to the sky. More and more stars blinked into existence like the sliver of hope that now spread through me. We sat in silence for several minutes. The gentle rock of the lake and the lapping of the water cleared my mind, and an icy breeze sent shivers skating along my limbs.

"Let's get below deck. It's getting cold up here," he said, giving my hand a squeeze.

I stood, ready to make my way below deck when the sight from the north stole my breath. Violet and blue-white lights blanketed the sky. Swirls and swaths of color danced high above as the light show slowly made its journey over the lake.

Bayne muttered something under his breath I didn't bother to hear. I was transfixed by the breathtaking phenomenon. We stood there silent, watching the show of lights swirl and sway above us for the next thirty minutes before it finally disappeared to the south, beyond the horizon.

At last, I looked back to find Bayne's piercing gaze holding me in place. It slowly traveled down my body and up to my mouth, as if seeing exactly what his proximity did to the blood in my veins.

His lips found mine, and he locked me in an iron embrace, one hand gripping my lower back while the fingers of the other slid through my windblown hair. This kiss was deep, wild, and wanting.

We stopped between breaths, enough for me to murmur against his mouth, "Take me below, Captain."

His responding growl set me ablaze further, and I wrapped my legs around his waist as his lips continued to ravage me. Unaware of others above deck, some primal part of me had taken over—its only focus was his lips and what lay beneath his layers of clothes.

He flung open the door to the small cabin and quickly scanned the room. The two cots wouldn't do. He tossed a fur wrap on the ground before laying me down gently. Warm, wet lips peppered my neck with soft kisses as he slowly undid the ties of my shirt and pants.

My fingers found his laces, and I tugged them loose, letting my hand brush against the hardness of him. He released a shuddering breath that gave me a sudden sense of satisfaction, and I slowed the movement. His eyes traveled from my neck to my navel and dipped below where the heat pooled between my legs. A guttural sound escaped his throat, and I lost my mind.

I took his face in my hands as he crawled up to me. My

fingers slid through his soft hair, brushing the tips of his pointed ears. He shook his head, trembling. "Not yet," he breathed.

His mouth found mine, and he slowed its movement for a few heartbeats. Then he dragged his lips to my neck, where his tongue slipped out and began tracing its way down my chest to my breast. His mouth wrapped around my nipple as his fingers grazed the inside of my thigh. He made soft, teasing strokes with his fingers that had me opening my legs for him.

His mouth traveled to meet them, a flood of warmth rushing in its wake. His lips found the sensitive spot at the apex of my thighs and, soon after, his tongue. I arched my back in response to the sensation that followed, letting out a soft whine. I could feel his lips curl into a smile and he moved slower.

His fingers continued their lazy tease on my thighs as his tongue delighted me in between. The pulsing quickened, and my breasts tightened with anticipation. Bayne responded by sliding one and then two fingers into me as his tongue continued wandering lazily over me.

I pressed my hips further down as he moved his fingers in a steady manner, his tongue keeping pace and making quick circles around me. The heat in my veins consumed me as the pulsing between my legs became overwhelming.

I wasn't beyond begging. His name ripped from my lips, and he moved faster, reacting to me, and reached up with his other hand to squeeze my breast as he sent me over the edge, waves of convulsions racking my body as I cried out.

He let out a primal groan as he slid his fingers out and kissed his way back up to my neck. My fingers locked into his hair as I pulled his face to mine, tasting myself on his tongue. My hand slid below his waist to free the hardness pressing from inside his leathers. A sound escaped my throat as my hand found the impressive length of him. Oh, gods. Thick, velvety, and ready. He twitched in response as I began moving for him.

I pressed my other hand on his chest, silently demanding he flip to his back. My eyes devoured him as I worked him. His body was as much a work of art as the intricate black ink that covered his chest. My gaze slid down to the place where his hips met with his abdomen, cutting a sharp V shape, to the massive length of him in my hand. My mouth watered as I wrapped my lips around him. I worshipped him. Slowly at first, and faster in response to his breathing and the most visceral noises escaping him. Heat flooded back between my legs.

Before I knew what had happened, he had me back on the floor splayed open for him like a feast. His lips and fingers found their way back to the center of my legs for a few moments as I grabbed his hair with one hand, moving against his mouth.

I needed all of him, needed his fullness. I pulled his face up as I adjusted myself beneath. He understood the command and slowly inched himself between my legs. I gasped as he entered me fully, taking in the size of him. I found his gaze on me as I looked up, a wicked, satisfying grin formed on his lips, which I locked in mine.

He filled me to the brim and began moving, responding to every uncontrollable noise I made. I was lost in a sea of waves, pleasure pounding its way through my body. The throbbing was so intense I thought I'd drown in the passion, and then his finger found that spot at the top. I was sent over the edge again, waves crashing through me, this time crying out his name as heat pleasantly melted its way down my hips.

His eyes locked hard on mine, the look of victory and devilish delight spread across his features as his tongue found mine, and my hands slid into his hair, brushing the tips of his pointed ears with my fingers. He roared in his own waves of pleasure, his body hammering me until he shook with completion. His ragged breath slowed to match my soft, lazy inhales as he placed his forehead on mine. Little droplets of sweat dripped onto my neck and chest, each one kissed away as he eased himself out.

He slumped beside me, cradling me in one arm and pulling me close. Drunk on our own pleasure, we quietly lay against each other, arms and legs intertwined. His fingers drew slow circles on my forearm draped across his chest, my skin pebbling in its wake. We lay like that for a few minutes while our bodies cooled from release.

Bayne's fingers trailed down my forearm to my thigh, and we found ourselves feeling rather warm again. His hardness pressed against my leg, and I quickly climbed onto his lap like it was my saddle. I took him in me and moved slowly, teasingly. He groaned in response, hands finding my hips, demanding more. We fit together perfectly, like two missing pieces of a puzzle. He moved me faster, the fullness of him throwing me into a dizzying dream until we both shook with pleasure. This time, my eyes closed as I sprawled against his chest, utterly defeated. He wrapped his arms around me, and I drifted off into a dreamless sleep.

CHAPTER TWENTY-FOUR

Few Sky Scholars understand the noctilux, the cloud of lights that passes over the Lake of Light. Despite its beauty, the lights appear unremarkable when measured against various celestial and atmospheric phenomena.
— Journal of Father Marcus dated 8th of Winter, 057.3E, Aedrialis.

I awoke to Bayne's fingertips tracing soft lines on my bare back beneath the furs. The sky cast a shade of deep violet through the small window in the corner of our cabin. I nestled my face in the crook of his neck, earning me a tight squeeze around the shoulders.

He kissed the top of my head, breathing into my hair. A smile formed on my lips, and I looked up at him. He met my smile with his own before locking me into a slow kiss, his tongue quietly moving against mine. I felt calm. At peace. He sighed his own contentedness, laying his head back down. I settled my head back into the crook of his neck and began to hum.

"What is that?" he murmured against my hair, voice soft.

"I have few memories of my mother," I said, suddenly remembering what I'd overheard my father telling King Saros. The ease and pleasure that had filled my entire being suddenly threatened to escape my body as the memories of her fate flooded back. Sensing it, Bayne pulled me closer, placing a gentle kiss on my forehead.

"She had light brown eyes."

"Like yours," Bayne said, a smile in his voice.

"Yes, but very light hair. And she used to sing this song... I remember the melody but not all the words. Something about violet blooms in the dead of night."

Bayne's breathing stilled beneath me.

"I know that sounds odd," I chuckled and continued to hum its lovely melody.

Bayne gave me another tight squeeze. "Lyv..." he began and paused, hesitancy entering his voice. I sat up on my elbow, my brows pinching in question.

"There *are* violet flowers that bloom only at night," he continued, sitting up and adjusting a strand of ebony hair that had fallen across my face. "They are native to the glacial mountains of Nivis, the northern lands of Dark King Daimos's kingdom."

My brows creased, lips tightening at his words.

"I thought Dark King Daimos ruled Kayj?"

"Kayj is his stronghold. But the continent north of the island, Nivis, is where his subjects and his army come from."

Unease twisted in my gut. "You think my mother may have had a connection to Nivis?"

Bayne's hand found its way to my back, giving gentle strokes.

"I don't know," he said, shaking his head, "but I've heard of those flowers. They're beautiful, yes, but deadly."

My frown deepened. "What do you know about Nivis?"

"Only what I've heard in rumor, to be honest. The land is a mix of ice, rocky cliffs, and snow-covered mountains. The terrain is rich in gemstones but deadly. Not much has been heard from the people of Nivis since the War of Ruin. The land is well hidden from the rest of the world."

I sat back and stared at the low ceiling of our small barge. Nivis. I hadn't imagined the dark king to be a king of anything except death and that small, haunted island. And the question that had lingered in the darkness of my mind since our escape from Aedrialis snaked its way back into my thoughts. Who was I? And how did my mother fit into this? I chewed on his words a bit longer as Bayne brushed his fingers through my hair, lulling me into a few more hours of sleep.

TWO DAYS TURNED to three as we bypassed Bayne's intended stop at the tail of the Rhew River running north to Stynguard. It was a tiny escape from reality. I *knew* I was playing with fire, but I suddenly couldn't help myself. A dam had broken, and all the gritty thoughts and pent-up desire came crashing through in a cascade of lust. The flood that followed was unstoppable.

I'd wake to stretch my limbs and get some sunshine, and Bayne's hot gaze would slide up and down, pinning me to the spot. My body became a useless thing that refused to follow my brain's command, other than wrapping my limbs around him.

I might have been losing my mind. A new loneliness filled my soul, causing it to ache when he left the tiny room. And upon his return, I found myself ripping his clothes off, mouth searching desperately for his.

We made landfall at a small port town at the western edge of the Lake of Light. We'd barely seen Ezrich the entirety of our trip, and guilt gnawed at my gut as we said goodbye.

Stepping off the barge and into the busy town was like the lifting of a fog. A sex-soaked, pleasure-filled fog that had wiped away all our worries for the past few days. Though the fog had cleared, I still found myself drifting closer to Bayne as we walked the horses through town. Just as I found his hand drifting to my back in the most natural way. Something had changed between us. I tried to convince myself this was the result of the nonstop sex, but it seemed like more than a release of tension. It felt like a beginning.

We led the horses down the boarding plank past a man herding sheep up into the neighboring ship, earning a loud snort from the testy, bay mare Morwyn gifted us.

I froze as we passed the apothecary, and a heart-stopping thought crossed my mind. *Shit.* I turned to Bayne and whispered, "I haven't had the barren tea in months. Have you?"

I hadn't even considered the risk we took these past few days. Dread filled my chest at the thought of bringing a small child into the world while on the run. The herbal contraceptive, while frowned upon, was usually easy to come by. Bayne gave me a small, sad-looking smile.

"I'm not, but it won't be necessary, Lyv. It's impossible for humans and elves to produce children together. We are not the same."

A small, delicate part inside of me that had slowly bloomed in the light of possibility suddenly trembled, withering under the truth in his words. Of course. There weren't half-elves. I had never even thought to ask the question. The relief I should have felt was squandered under a strange sense of loss.

Stranger, even, when I thought about my utter lack of interest in marriage and starting a family. Learning, digging, and riding. That was all I had ever thought about. I blinked in an attempt to hide the reaction in my eyes.

"Good. That's good," I said, nodding.

We continued our walk. We tied the horses to a post outside of a pub, which they both protested. They itched to run after being caged up in a barge for three days.

We snuggled into a little corner in the back of the pub. Bayne's hood was up now that we were in a public place with watchful eyes. I thought of the ears he hid and memories of hot breath and wet touches flashed into my mind, causing my blood to heat.

His nostrils flared, and he tsked.

"You're going to drive me to insanity with this appetite of yours, Lyv," he said as his tongue slid over his lower lip.

The movement sent hot blood rushing to my lower abdomen. Under different circumstances, I might have jumped across the small table and torn at his clothes. Instead, I gripped my mug and slowly took a sip of ale, keeping my eyes on him.

Bayne made a soft sound that sent my toes curling and tipped his mug back, taking a long swig. Our lustful reverie was interrupted as the pub door swung open, letting in a gust of wind and five Sultiran soldiers followed by a short man in scholar robes. A chill not caused by the breeze entered my bones, quickly snuffing out any heat that had built.

Bayne reached out and grabbed my hands in his, leaning in close like two courting lovers. "Look only at me, Lyv," he whispered under his breath. I focused my eyes on his, searching for any signs of worry or unease. I found only easy confidence and determination. He smoothly slid his hand in my hair, untucking it from behind my ear so that it fell more naturally across the side of my face. He brought his hands back down and brushed his thumbs over mine in small circles.

The soldiers ordered pints and sat down two tables away from us while the scholar began questioning the barkeep.

"And you can bet he'll up recruiting after what happened at Crown Peak," a soldier with a gruff voice said before taking a swig.

Bayne's hands stiffened in mine.

"Aye, but from where? These relocations aren't making the people any more loyal," another said.

"Quiet. Both of you. This is not the place," a third man said.

I peeked out of the corner of my eye and noted the large, black-haired leader scanning the rest of the pub. I refocused on Bayne and plastered a love-sick look on my face before his eyes scanned our table. Amusement danced in the captain's eyes. He planted a gentle kiss on my hand that disguised a playful nip. He tried to distract me from the unease that snaked its way up my spine. It almost worked.

The soldier sitting with his back to us then asked about the properties of the lake, and I choked on my ale. Bayne let out a soft, fake chuckle and finished the joke he never started. I followed suit, giggling quietly. His eyes searched mine for the cause of my startle, but I kept quiet. He brushed the back of his fingers against my cheek.

"Is it Aeriden?" he breathed with a smile on his face as if he were quoting me poetry. I shook my head, not trusting my voice with how wildly my heart beat.

One of the soldiers said something, and their table rocked the pub with laughter. That laugh. *Unmistakable.* I tightened the grip on my mug and took a long sip of ale, feeling confident that I knew exactly who sat two tables over from me.

Vander Stryke was my brother's dearest friend in Aedrialis. They joined the royal army together six years ago, and I'd not seen him since. I trusted him. And he could give us some answers to Aeriden's whereabouts. Hope flooded my system.

We didn't have much time. If the scholar was from the capital, they no doubt knew we were wanted fugitives. We sat in the pub until their table cleared out and quietly followed the group as they split. I quickly told Bayne who he was.

"Are you sure you can trust him?" he murmured.

I gave him a firm nod. "He's like a brother to me."

"You'll need a distraction," he muttered as we followed Vander and another soldier down the muddy, frozen road.

"Keep your distance until you see smoke from the east. I can buy you five minutes. I'll meet you behind the inn we passed," Bayne said. He turned to me, grasped my shoulder, and gave me a quick warm kiss before turning down an alleyway, leaving me with that familiar longing in his wake.

I shook my head in hopes of clearing it, needing to figure out how I would get Vander's attention away from Bayne's distraction. I quickened my pace to keep the two soldiers in eyesight and noted a busy general store to my right. The sudden arrival of warm spring air had melted the mounds of snow, and there were goods set out on display in the front of the shop and several people perusing them. A quaint little sign marking half-off dried goods leaned against the side of the building.

Without thinking, my boot connected with the sign, knocking a display of jams into the mud. I scooted into the small crowd and grabbed a basket of dried fruits. I retreated down the road as if nothing had happened as the patrons scrambled to help the poor shop owner gather up the goods.

I might not have fit the mold of a lady-in-waiting, but I'd never stolen a thing in my life. The thought of it sent wings flapping in my stomach. I grinned and refocused my attention on the two soldiers ahead of me, who thankfully hadn't noticed the scuffle behind them.

Two blocks later, smoke rose from the east. Shouts of alarm sounded, and I picked up the pace. I needed to time this just right. The two soldiers stopped, attention drawn to the east, and turned that way. I banked on Vander being the kind-hearted boy I'd known as a small girl.

They turned down a street when I let out an exaggerated cry and tripped over nothing, my dried fruit flying out of my basket. Head down, I bent over on all fours, clumsily trying to gather them all up.

Vander's tall outline paused down the road, followed by brief, argued murmurs. The second soldier hurried down the street, and Vander turned my direction. He knelt beside me, reaching for a handful of fruit.

"Here, let me help you with that," a soft voice said.

I glanced up from underneath my hood and met his light green eyes. I grabbed his hand before he could fully react. Shock shot across his features, and he quietly swore.

"Van, please. I need your help."

"Lyvia, what in Tynan's Hell are you doing here? What the fuck happened in Aedrialis? Your face is on a godsdamned wanted poster!" He glanced around and slowly returned to putting the dried fruit back in the basket.

"I know, I know," I said hastily. "It's a long story. Look, I need your help. I'm trying to find Aeriden."

He glanced up and said, "Aeriden was stationed with me in Krestwood. A few weeks ago, he was sent back to the capital, so he's likely reaching the western peaks of the Lumerians at this point. We'd heard about you and your...friends." He stopped and looked at me.

"Lyvia, are they—"

"It's best you don't know all the details," I cut in.

He nodded, but his eyes darted between mine. "At first, he thought you were kidnapped, and it took him everything not to come after you. He got a letter from your father urging him to come back to Aedrialis. It had the king's seal on it, so nobody questioned it. And then I was reassigned to escort the Civil Scholar to these rural towns to—" He paused, looking around. "Lyvia, you need to get out of here."

I scanned his face, noting the concern and the trace of guilt that caught in his voice.

"What are you doing here?" I asked, realizing for the first time how strange it was for a small group of soldiers to be accompanying a Civil Scholar.

Van ground his teeth. "He's taking the census of these rural towns," he said, eyes dropping to focus on what his hands were doing.

A twisting sensation entered my stomach. "Why would the capital be interested in knowing that?" I asked as he tensed, his grip on the dried fruit giving away some hidden, deep rage.

"Look, you need to get out of these towns. And soon. Trust me."

"Where is the next tribute ship headed?" I breathed.

He dropped the sack of berries, eyes shooting to mine.

"I know about all of it. Please, Van. Do you know where it's going? Is it coming for the lake towns?"

He glanced around quickly. "Yes. It will have passed through the small ones on the northern tip. Its next stop is Rivaner. We were there two days ago."

My stomach plummeted. Dread coiled its way into my chest as I thought about Morwyn and Evony being forced onto the slave ship. They would kill Bear.

"How soon will it be there?" I urged.

We slowly stood, doing our best to delay the end of the

conversion now that the fruit was back in my basket. He glanced around.

"Two days. Three maybe. Look, Lyvia whatever you're thinking... You want to stay far away from here." He eyed me, a protectiveness entering his voice. "Find Aeriden. He'll get you to safety."

"Thank you, Van," I whispered, holding his stare. I turned on my heel and headed down the opposite side of the street, looking quickly over my shoulder to find him staring at me before trotting off to join his group.

I ditched the basket in an alley and quickly made my way to the inn Bayne referenced. I spotted him already atop the mare, ponying Anchor in their wake. A look of relief passed over his features as he took in my form, hurrying down the road.

His dark brows creased as I relayed everything to him after mounting Anchor and making our way to the lake's shore. He was silent for a minute, the clopping of our horses' hooves like the countdown to a canon blast. He didn't have to say it. I had a choice to make.

Despite being a fugitive, in some ways, I was free now, wasn't I? And hadn't that been what I'd wanted all along? The yearning to break free of the shackles that locked me into forced fate at the hands of the Match. That longing had masqueraded as the student. The desire to learn and dig and prove myself so impossibly valuable, the Death Scholar order would have no choice but to accept me. But at its most basic level, it wasn't about becoming a Death Scholar. It was about taking command of my life.

And now that I knew the truth of our world, the marred and scrubbed history of our kingdom, how could I possibly put my freedom above others? Above the souls trapped on Kayj, above the little family I'd grown to love in Rivaner. We were so close to finding Aeriden. All I had to do was follow the king's road and I'd find him. But a tribute ship headed for Rivaner. For our friends.

Find Aeriden, my family, my blood, or fight for our friends. Friends I'd known but three months. A pained guilt at leaving Aeriden melded with apprehension. I'd already decided. A fire had been lit months ago when I was taken by the kingsguards. Those embers had slowly been fanned by the wild events and vael-shattering revelations over the past few months.

No. This wasn't a question of if we'd fight, but how. How fast could we get back to Rivaner and how might we be able to stop the ship from leaving the dock? How would we connect with the rebellion and what could I do to help? Ronan's voice sounded in my head. I could find the stones. No. I wouldn't find them for him. But I could find them for the rebellion.

I might not know who I was, but I knew what I had to do. The enormity, the certainty of it pressed down on me. Of doing anything I could to stop the two kings, to save the people of Sultira. It steadied my breathing and calmed my heart. Bayne watched me carefully, waiting for me to voice the decision I was sure he already knew.

"How do we get back?" I asked.

Fire sparked in his eyes as he gave me a half grin.

"We're going to need a faster ship," he responded with a wink and nudged the mare into a trot toward the harbor.

CHAPTER TWENTY-FIVE

I've sent the two laborers who touched the onyx stone to the
Life Scholars. No word of their condition yet.
—Journal of Father Marcus, dated 7th of Autumn,
070.3E. Aedrialis.

While the idea of stealing a ship turned my stomach into knots, Bayne eyed the line of vessels in the harbor with the hunger of a winter wolf.

I tied the horses near the far end of the port and followed his gaze across the harbor yard where it landed on the livestock ship that we passed on our way in. Surely, we weren't going to try to steal that ship, fully loaded with goats, sheep, and gods knew what else.

"That is our ticket out," he said, jerking his head toward the ship so packed with livestock it hummed different notes of bleating.

"Did you sneak some of Bear's ridecus into your pack and not tell me?" I asked him, incredulously.

He chuckled. "No, darling, but that wouldn't have been such a bad idea." He gently grabbed my chin in his thumb and fingers and lifted my lips to his.

"We're not going to steal that ship. That ship is going to get us access to that one," he said, pulling his lips away and turning my chin to a small ship at the northern edge of the harbor.

I eyed the small ship, wary that such a little pile of timber would suffice after our trip on the barge. He watched me carefully.

"Trust me," he said.

And I did.

Ten minutes later, I lingered at the northern edge of the harbor pretending to pick out Anchor's hooves on the side of the road when a shout arose from several boats down.

Sheep and a handful of cattle filled the roads and alleyways connecting to the harbor, heading toward the market. They knocked over stands as they pushed through the small alleyways, leaving nothing short of chaos behind them.

The horses trailed after me as I led them away from the madness and toward the small ship at the edge of the harbor where three men rushed out, eyeing up the scene. A dark cloak flapped behind the helm as the anchor lifted, seemingly on its own accord.

I quickened my pace as the three men rushed past us. The horses picked up an edgy jog, sensing my anticipation. We stepped over the boarding ramp and onto the deck while my stomach leaped into my chest. The ship began moving before I even had the horses below deck.

A man with a high voice shouted, "Oi! What're ye doin', ye filthy whore?"

I finished tying the horses and yelped in surprise, stumbling back a step as a tall, wiry, and drunk man staggered his way to me with the empty bottle still in hand. I blanched at the insult, images of the prior three days flashing through my mind.

It took me two shaky steps and bumping into a wooden beam before other memories of striking and dodging flew into my mind. I veered to the side before striking him with my elbow under his chin as he launched himself at me. He cried out in surprise and swayed as he turned, swinging a long limb toward me. I ducked and caught him in the gut, quickly followed by a fast jab of my knee to a particularly sensitive part.

He howled, doubling over, and I brought both elbows down on the back of his head. He slumped to the floor as the empty bottle clanged to the ground. I stared at him, wide-eyed, while I caught my breath, unsure what I was supposed to do now.

A soft chuckle sounded to my left, and I looked over to find Bayne, casually leaning against the wall.

"How long have you been there?" I demanded, a different kind of heat now filling my veins.

"Only a minute!" he replied, throwing his hands up in defense. "You had it covered. I was here if you needed me."

He winked, and I hurled a nearby empty glass in his direction which he casually dodged. He stepped over to me, gently taking my arms.

"You are a good student," he said. "I knew you had it. And it is good to get some practice in before we reach Rivaner."

I shoved out of his arms, outrage and fear still pulsing through my chest. How was I supposed to fight when a half-conscious drunken buffoon shook me so much? The sudden realization that I wasn't ready for what lay ahead of us caused me to shrink beneath his gaze.

His eyes softened. "Lyvia, you will be scared. But fear can be a feeling with purpose. It can fuel you into action or freeze you into inaction. You proved you can take down a man twice your size, albeit a drunken one."

My eyes narrowed at him. "I'm serious. I'm not sure I'm ready for this."

His hands slid down my arms to mine. "Maybe not. But time isn't always on our side. I can get us to Rivaner in a day and a half. We can spend that time training. Unless you have other things in mind." His eyes drifted to my lips, darkening.

"You're not very good at pep talks," I grumbled.

"Would you rather I take your mind off it?" he drawled, his intention clearly written across his face as his eyes drifted from my lips to my neck.

I rolled my eyes, intent on staying irritated with him and annoyed that my body responded so intensely to that stare.

"What do we do about him?" I asked, gesturing to the man on the floor.

Bayne sighed. "Well, I suppose it is his ship. We probably shouldn't kill him, but I don't expect him to be supportive when he wakes." He drummed his fingers on the floor as he knelt beside him. He lifted one eyelid and let it droop shut.

"You really took him out," he said, a note of admiration in his voice.

I resisted the upward tug on my lips.

"For now, let's keep him in the back cabin, tied up. I think I can keep him unconscious for a while longer," he added with a wink.

A strong but subtle gust of wind rocked the ship as he set to work brewing whatever concoction he had in mind for our unwitting host. I caught a glimpse of him muttering a spell under his breath, and the wind picked up speed, as did our boat.

We made our way back across the Lake of Light at twice the speed of the large barge. I spent all morning dueling with Bayne, first with the short sword and then moving on to hand-to-hand combat, the captain intentionally slowing his counterattacks to be more human-like.

We broke for lunch, and I spent a couple hours with the bow I'd become fond of. I smiled as I adjusted my form, thinking of sweet Evony who spent so much time with me over the winter months. I still wasn't particularly good at any of it, but I knew how to use it.

That evening, we went over our plans at least five different times. We were to dock at the neighboring port, about an hour's ride away. Our first goal was to ensure Bear and his family were safe. Our secondary goal was to sabotage the tribute ship, hopefully with Bear's help.

Bayne's playful flirting did nothing to quell the growing anxiety and doubt that formed a pit in my stomach. I settled into the main cabin that night while Bayne worked his spell above deck. I tightly wrapped a fur around me and curled up on the floor of the cabin, making my intentions for the night clear. But sleep eluded me for hours, as the growing knot in my gut became tighter with angst.

The cabin door creaked open. Bayne walked over to where I lay, pretending to be asleep, and gently threw another fur over my huddled-up form before laying a soft kiss on my temple. I took a deep inhale of the pine wafting off his sea-kissed skin, loosening the knot that had been growing.

He stepped back and quietly left the room, turning down the oil lamp as he left. His absence hit me as if a chill entered the room on his exit. I continued to toss and turn for the better part of the night, wondering when or if he might come back. I gave up on sleep soon after and made my way above deck where I found him lying in the center of the deck, shirtless, both hands folded beneath his head, gazing up at the clear night sky.

He'd created a similar barrier to the wind that Isla had on my first few nights onboard the *Evecta* and the air above deck was warm. Unlike Isla's jasmine field breeze, Bayne's was the wind that whispered through trees. The kind that wound itself through thick forests, making the green leaves rustle and branches dance as it sailed through the woods and out to sea.

I dropped the fur I had wrapped around me and curled up next to him as he extended an arm, pulling me close.

"I'm sorry you can't sleep," he murmured, planting a kiss on my temple.

"Seems it makes two of us," I replied. The sky was clear, and the two moons shone a deep ocean blue tonight, barely lighting up the sky.

"It's normal not to sleep well before a fight," he said, stroking my arm with his fingers. "I find I get more rest if I just let myself *be*. Be here. Be now. Be under the stars... with you." He tugged me closer as I melted into him.

I sighed, savoring the warmth and hardness of his body. I traced the little swirls on his chest and down his abdomen. My fingers drifted over the spot where the black waves crossed in the center of his chest and I felt raised skin, like a large scar hidden beneath the ink. He shuddered in response.

"What happened here?" I asked, exploring the shape of the scar with my fingers. There was something familiar about it I couldn't quite place. Bayne stilled beneath my touch.

"A story for another night, perhaps," he said, a slight edge entering his voice.

I lightened my touch and let it drift further down, earning

me a deep guttural groan of approval. I had a sudden change of heart about my intentions for the night.

"Is there nothing else you can think of that can help me sleep the night before a fight?" I asked, fingers following their trail back toward his chest. He hardened beneath my thigh draped over him.

"Now that you mention it..." he whispered and flipped me on my stomach, swiftly removing my oversized shirt. The sudden, almost aggressive move surprised me, and I opened my mouth to protest when warm hands began making long, smooth strokes across my back. I groaned in response, not realizing how tight and sore I'd become over the last couple months of training. His thumbs made small, firm circles over my shoulder blades and swept toward my spine and down to my tailbone. I sank into the furs beneath me as he worked through the tightness of my muscles for the better part of an hour.

His hands slid up my arms, and his fingers intertwined with mine as he gave me a soft kiss on the cheek when he had finished. Though drowsy, the feel of his rough hands on my skin was too much. I arched my back in response, hips coming up to meet the hardness of him above me. A soft growl sounded in my ear that sent heat flying to my belly. He nipped my ear before hiking up my hips and widening my legs with his knee. His lips met the space between my legs, drawing a moan from my mouth.

He splayed me open, moving fast tonight, as if he had no time for unhurried teasing. Mere strokes away from breaking, I stood up on my knees, grabbed his hand, and pulled his body against mine. He seemed torn between continuing his work below and listening to the pulsing that hung between his own legs.

Giving in, he slipped inside me with a thrust that made my

blood sing in response. His hands found my hips, and he pumped hard and fast, causing a frenzy between my legs. His hands slid around my waist and up to my sternum, pulling me upright so that my back pressed against his chest. With one hand grasping my breast, the other drifted to the spot at the apex of my thighs where he drew small circles with his wet finger.

He continued this relentless movement until I broke, shattering into a million exhilarating pieces, further melting into him. I came back to my hands as he moved faster. He crashed into me, crying out as his body shook with release. In that moment, the wind shuddered in response, the barrier around the ship quivering before settling back into place.

He slipped out and tucked me against his body, arm wrapping around my waist, planting soft kisses on my neck and behind my ear. I sighed, melting into him and drifting off into sleep.

I awoke a few hours later, just before dawn, to the sound of lapping water and sea birds chirping right outside Bayne's barrier. I sat up, his arm sliding off me. I stared at his beautiful face for several minutes. He breathed deeply, mouth parted.

At that moment, I wanted nothing more than to stay forever on this ship with him in the Lake of Light, whose twinkling waters reflected the hundreds of stars shining like beacons above. But it was a moment. I wasn't stupid. No, I was a scholar. This was temporary for us. A much-needed distraction for me, and for him... For him it was similar. A diversion. Something to take his mind off the ache in his heart from losing Lida. I was a temporary patch on the hole that was left in his soul. He would grieve long and hard for her. While it had been over two years since she was ripped away on a tribute ship, he'd only truly lost her a few months ago.

These were the reminders I repeated to my foolish heart

over the past few days. But I'd been swept away into a dream. Into a romantic, adventure-packed novel whose heroine found true love at first sight. I needed to stop thinking about that day on the *Evecta* when we had pulled him from the water, and the gaze he locked me in and had yet to let me go.

It was as if my soul had fortifications as tall as the walls in Aedrialis, and he didn't even need to knock at the gates, they simply opened at the touch of his breath. I blinked, my vision becoming blurry as I stared at him in the glowing pink dawn. A warm tear slid down my face. Stupid heart. I hastily wiped it away and pulled my eyes from him.

I kissed him on the forehead, causing him to stir in his sleep, before returning below deck to dress and prepare for the day. Bear's laugh echoed in my mind as I pulled on my leggings and boots. I felt Morwyn's embrace as I donned my shirt and laced the bodice of my leather vest. I saw Evony's smile as I pulled my hair back into a long braid. We couldn't lose them. Anger rose to my chest, quickening my pulse as my mind drifted to the two kings bleeding the people of Sultira.

I released my jaw, sore from grinding my teeth. I glanced at where my short sword hung on the wall, watching me. Not fancy or pretty to look at but well-built and reliable. It had just begun to feel right in my hands. I stared back for several minutes before sheathing it and snatching my bow on my way above deck.

CHAPTER TWENTY-SIX

#87: Female, age forty-three. Signs of distress when Obscura Stone placed in close proximity. Shrieks upon direct contact. Able to maintain coherent conversation for approximately three minutes before her mind broke.

—Journal of High Priest Helmar, dated 67th of Winter, 071.3E. Stynguard.

We made landfall north of Rivaner three hours later, along with a thick morning fog brought on by the warm, early spring breeze. Solemnity had befallen the deck in those early morning hours as we prepared for what was to come. The flirty scoundrel I'd lain with the night before was replaced by a deadly captain, whose solemn face mirrored the busts of ancient war generals I'd passed hundreds of times in the Temple of the Sky. Silence stretched across the deck, hardening my heart.

We rode hard and fast to Rivaner through the land cloud.

The horses launched into an unrelenting gallop, flying over various creeks and downed trees we came across on the forest floor, muddy with the melting snow. The fork yawned open in the trail, and I slowed Anchor ahead of Bayne and his mare. He slowed for the briefest moment when his eyes met mine before taking off down the path to the right. I veered a reluctant Anchor to the left and urged him forward, away from Bayne, heading to the southern forest with hopes of catching Bear and his family before it was too late.

The months with the Hunt family replayed in my head as I flew through the trees. Days of being cooped up on a ship had Anchor edgy and flighty, but I kept hard legs on his side, spurring that energy into a forward direction.

We slowed, nearing the trail leading to the stone cottage, turning into the thick trees before reaching the path. The sight of smoke puffing from the chimney eased the growing tension that had built in my chest.

I passed the barn, noting two horses were missing, and nudged Anchor out from behind the trees when the front of the cottage came into view. The door was ajar, and the shudders on the windows pulled tight. Unease crept its way back into my gut as I slowed the gelding to a quick halt. I scanned the forest, my eyes catching a brief flash of white from behind the barn as a mild breeze snaked its way through the trees.

White cloak. Memories from Aedrialis all those months ago danced on the edge of my consciousness. The death of our men at the manor... Fleeing the kingsguards... The chase down the alley... and... Ronan.

The hair on my arms pricked up, and I readied Anchor for a fast departure. Ronan stepped out from behind the barn, arms clad in Sultiran black armor raised above his head.

"Cantor, it's just me," he called, staring at where I sat

behind a group of pines. My heart thundered in my chest. *Traitor*, it chanted.

"We need to talk. You are in serious danger coming back here," he called as he took slow steps in my direction.

My mind screamed at me to *go*, turn, and get back to the port where I would meet Bayne, but the part of my heart that ached from Ronan's betrayal had a chokehold on my reins.

I took several steadying breaths. He knew we had stayed here. We had put Bear and his family at risk. Guilt snaked its way into my chest, giving fuel to my heart pumping frantically in my ribs.

"You took it," I said, voice wavering. "You took the journal. You took it off my unconscious body, you ass." The words fed my anger, clearing my mind.

"Let me explain. Please, come down and we'll talk. This is important," he said, sounding as if he were soothing a caged animal. His pace quickened, raising my hackles. Suddenly feeling as if I were surrounded, I pulled my gaze from him for a split second, scanning the trees around me. Anchor danced in place, his hooves popping up as soon as they hit the ground.

I caught movement to my right, and when I looked back, Ronan was one step away from grabbing the reins. Twisting to my left, I leaned into the gelding's neck as I squeezed him into a run, darting between trees away from the small cottage.

Ronan barked a curse and shouted commands at the others hidden among the trees. The thunder of at least one agrippa pounded in the dirt behind me. Anchor couldn't outrun the agrippa on the plains outside of Aedrialis, but he was thin and wiry, darting through the trees and finding space in narrow openings the war horse wouldn't fit through.

The memory of our colt's whinnying scream swept in, along with a rising fear that I shoved right back down. I wouldn't let Anchor face the same fate as the first horse I rode fleeing a soldier in black.

I risked a glance over my shoulder and found two soldiers in pursuit on agrippa. Anchor knew mountain trails better than me, so I trusted his instincts, guiding him in the general direction of Rivaner as he raced through the trees. We flew over a stream, and thundering hooves crashed down several seconds later. Relief swelled in my system as I put distance between us.

Gray rooftops rose from below as we passed a small break in the trees. My heart skipped as Ronan appeared on his own agrippa, reaching for my cloak. I yanked Anchor to the side, earning me a quick buck that had me gripping his mane, but it was enough to angle out of his reach.

Ronan recovered quickly and came pounding after us as fast as my heart. I couldn't turn toward the town yet. As soon as we broke into the trail ahead, he'd be on us in seconds. A risky plan formed in my mind as we burst through the trees onto the flat trail. Ronan crashed through behind us and his mount closed the space between us in two strides before I veered Anchor back into the trees, heading up the side of the mountain.

He let out a snort of protest as I urged him toward the steep rocky face of the mountain, nerves fueling his flighty steps. I scanned the rocks. She *had* to be here. Morwyn said she stayed close to the den, and by now, she'd have cubs.

I slowed Anchor as we ran out of trekkable land. Ronan crashed through the trees from behind as two long, black tufts of fur peeked up behind the rocks. I twisted hard to the right, pulling the rein and sending Anchor staggering down steep, rocky footing as Ronan's agrippa slid to a stop, filling the space behind us. The horse gave a snort of surprise as the massive mountain cat leapt through the air with a throaty growl. Ronan was thrown off, his horse bucking against the giant cat.

I rocked wildly on Anchor's back as he trekked through the brush back to easier footing where we took off at a gallop. We raced toward the town for several minutes, free of pursuers. I hopped off and pulled my hood up as I tied him to a hitching post behind the pub with a pail of well-deserved water. After giving him a quick pat, his neck slick with sweat, I hurried into town, throwing wary glances behind me.

A familiar wanted poster hung on the door next to a town's meeting notice—currently underway. I cursed under my breath. The tribute ship was already here. I hurried past the pub toward the town square.

Several buildings bordered the gathering space. I broke through the back door of the nearest and seemingly empty building with surprising ease. Six months ago, I wouldn't have dreamed of committing such an act. Today, with what was at stake, it barely fazed me. Too much time spent with the captain, I supposed.

I took the stairs two at a time and quietly snuck through a room with a window and easy access to the roof. I pulled myself up the side of the building, where a spring breeze blew away a suffocating layer of fog just in time for a view of what transpired below. Frost melted beneath me as I inched my way to the edge of the roof.

A few hundred townsfolk gathered around a small, temporary stage. On the platform, a plump man stood with jet-black hair and scholar robes. I didn't recognize the markings on them. He spoke vehemently to the crowd who listened intently. I marked at least fifty soldiers stationed at various places throughout the town center, including two on either side of the scholar.

My eyes scanned the crowd for Bear and his family. There

were so many people packed into the small space. I noted a handful of hooded figures throughout the crowd, but none as large as Bear. Morwyn and Evony wouldn't have come without him. Relief filled my chest. They must have left. Bear must have gotten wind of the tribute's next stop. I sent a small prayer to the gods that was the case. Now to find Bayne.

Needing a better view, I slowly climbed up the side, bracing myself against the chimney when the words of the scholar drew my attention back to the people below.

"Death will come to Rivaner if we do not act now! The great plague is spreading. King Saros offers the good people here sanctuary and medicine in Stynguard. We must move now if we are to save the towns on the Lake of Light."

People shifted and murmured through the crowd. I paused, leaning against the sharp angle of the roof and peeking out from behind the brick chimney.

"We're not leaving our homes!" someone yelled from the crowd, among mumbles of agreement.

I searched for the source and found a small group of people who had turned toward the voice. The blacksmith.

"You, sir! Step forward," the scholar called back.

The blacksmith reluctantly moved to the front of the crowd.

"I understand your hesitancy. This is your home," he said, spreading his arms wide, "and your people. Do you have a family, good sir?"

"Aye," the blacksmith said, "and how do we even know what you say is true? Does King Saros offer any proof of this plague? None of us have heard this news."

Grumblings of agreement moved through the crowd. The scholar peered down at him, pity and disdain marking his features.

"Proof you ask?" he said quietly. A hush fell over the crowd at the shift in his voice. He tsked with his tongue. "Very well. Guards," he said, gesturing to the wagon at the edge of the square.

Two guards picked up a large crate from the wagon and carried it to the small stage at the center. A growing sense of unease flooded my stomach that echoed the nervous murmurs of the people.

"This plague is not prejudiced," the scholar called out, "it will come for everyone. Fathers or sons. Mothers or daughters. Old or young. Rich or poor. Soldiers or farmers. Scholars or... blacksmiths," he said, glancing at the man who dared question him.

My stomach twisted as two guards opened the top of the crate and dumped a bloodless, limp body onto the stage. Gasps of horror moved throughout the crowd. Bile rose to my throat as I gazed down on the body of a dead ashen, once a lovely, young girl. One that had been stabbed through the eye. I felt sick. And I wasn't alone, as the sound of sporadic retching interrupted the cries of shock and disgust.

"This," the scholar said, gesturing to the lifeless girl, "is what awaits Rivaner without the help and sanctuary of King Saros."

Anger swept over my senses. They were twisting the horrifying truth of King Saros's involvement with the ashen. These people, all of them, would live for the rest of their lives under threat of the ashen, working in the mines on Kayj, or becoming one themselves. My heart thumped angrily in my chest, my grip tightening on the chimney. I turned my attention back to the square.

People shoved each other in an attempt to get to the center stage. Shouts of help and desperate pleas for protection echoed through the agitated crowd. Soldiers pushed them back, throwing several to the ground.

Their commanding officer stepped forward and yelled, "Quiet!"

The scholar raised his hands. "Please, people of Rivaner. We will get you all to safety. We have room for you all. Please return to your homes and—"

An arrow ripped through his throat, cutting off any further lies. Screams erupted from the crowd. I dropped to the roof and scanned the other buildings surrounding the square. The soldiers below took up defensive positions, the large officer barking commands at his men. Another arrow whizzed through the air, striking a guard in the neck where their armor was weakest. He dropped to the ground.

Shit. Where were they coming from? What the hell was I doing? I should be the one firing arrows. I moved to the opposite edge of the roof, partially shielded by the overhang. I drew my bow, chest open and back strong, aiming for the kingsguard.

The crowd below was in a frenzy, tripping over each other to escape the impending fight. The whiz of arrows grew louder. I shifted, eyeing my target, and released mine, a crisp clean break making my fingers buzz. It clanged against the armor above his chest. He whipped his head around eyeing the building I was on. I drew a second arrow and released. His eyes found mine as he dodged. *Shit.*

He pointed, barking orders at a nearby soldier who sprinted to the base of the building I crouched upon. I had to go. The door creaked below, and I had seconds. I slung my bow and raced across the roof, grateful the early spring air had melted most of the ice. I eyed the neighboring roof. Not an ideal escape route but the only one I had. Armor clanged as the soldier climbed up the side of the building through the same window I'd used. I didn't look back as I sprinted across the roof and leaped, flying over empty space and oblivious pedestrians below before slamming onto the neighboring roof. My teeth clattered at the impact, and I scrambled up the side.

I risked a glance back as the soldier hurtled after me. He landed with a thump as I scrambled across the shingles on all fours. His sword hissed as he unsheathed it, closing the distance between us. I drew my own as I twisted onto my back, barely deflecting his attacking slash that came down hard on what would have been my neck. He let out a terrifying laugh as it knocked the blade from my hand.

He lifted his longsword with two hands overhead and swung it down with a menacing fury. It crashed into the roof as I rolled left. He let out a frustrating grunt, lifting it with one hand and reaching for my cloak with the other. He caught a fistful of fabric and pulled. My fingernails chipped against the tiles as I grappled for something stronger to hold onto. Panic flooded my system, and I rolled to my back as I came face to face with the soldier. My breathing became rapid, and my vision swam.

He raised his sword once more right as an arrow impaled him under the armpit. He howled in fury, dropping his blade. It clanged to the ground, shaking me out of my panic. I rolled, reaching for my own, in time to swing it into the space behind his calf at the break in armor. He screamed, kicking me in the gut with his other foot. I fell to the side and over the roof ridge, tumbling down the steep angle. The world was a blur of hazy sky, rough tiles, and a flurry of panicked people below as I rolled uncontrollably down the side. I flung my arms out, trying to slow my momentum, losing grip on my blade. I hit the edge of the roof, and my hands miraculously grasped onto the gutter.

My fingers were white from my grip as my legs dangled. I glanced down as my blade clanked against the stone road. My stomach dropped as I eyed the distance. A rusty pipe draped down the side of the building, and I shimmied to my left, hastily moving my hands along the gutter. I had nearly reached the pipe when a dagger flew over the edge of the roof, slicing my hand. I let out a yelp, dropping it before hastily recovering my painful grip. Blood dripped down my arm as I hurried my shimmy.

The spine-tingling clang of familiar armor sounded above as the soldier eased down the side of the roof. He leaned over its edge and peered down at me, the arrow still protruding out from his side.

"Let's see how many fingers you can hold on with, lake mouse," he said in a cruel whisper as he pulled out another dagger. He chuckled softly as he knelt above where I hung.

I glanced quickly at the pipe. Too far. I let go.

A look of surprise flashed across his face as I dropped three stories to the ground below. I screamed as I landed on the hard stone, pain ripping through my right ankle. I rolled and glanced up at the roof, blinking away tears, where the soldier had disappeared. Hobbling to my feet, ankle hot with pain, I snatched my sword and limped to the side of the building and scanned the wild crowd.

People screamed for loved ones and trampled over one another to get out of the square. I limped along the edge and spied a group of townsfolk being ushered toward the harbor by a soldier. Another group followed quickly behind. Saros would have his tributes. Anger slammed into me, numbing the pain in my ankle. I ran along the edge of the square, heading for the harbor.

Arrows continued to soar across the square. The clang of metal on metal crashed as I flew through the crowd. I glanced up and spotted a hooded figure in combat with two soldiers. Shouts from the west side of the square drew my attention away from the fight as black smoke rose from the harbor. It had to be Bayne.

A scream in the center of the square drew my attention back, and the hood of the fighter ripped back, red hair flying wildly as one soldier held her shoulders and a fist of black steel crashed into her cheek. Morwyn's mouth spewed blood, and she sagged in the soldier's grasp.

Fury rippled through me as I dodged through the frenzy. Another sickening crunch as the soldier's fist slammed into her jaw. I'd reach her in two heartbeats. His knee struck her stomach, and she doubled over before being pulled upright.

Before I realized what was happening, I had both hands on my blade and swung down in a large arc, slicing through the back of the soldier's knees. He let out a piercing scream as they buckled, and he crashed to the ground. The second soldier shoved Morwyn to the ground and launched into an attack. I parried the first blow of his longsword and barely kept hold of my blade, the clang of metal reverberating through my bones. He swung again, and I dodged, my own blade scraping against his armor.

Morwyn was on her feet, plunging her dagger into the first soldier's neck. I parried a few more blows before I nicked the second on his wrist. He hissed and twisted, faster than I expected, sword raised before an arrow came out of nowhere. It barely missed me as it tore through his eye. I spun, searching for the source of the arrow on the rooftops, and gasped. Morwyn followed my gaze and let out a soft cry as she spotted Evony. Anger, pride, and terror rippled across Morwyn's face.

"Go to her!" I shouted, grabbing Morwyn's shoulder and shoving her in that direction. She nodded, her eyes steeling in a raw determination only motherhood could bring. I tore my eyes away from Morwyn as she raced through the crowd. Evony rained arrows from above.

I frantically scanned the crowd for Bayne as soldiers continued to usher hordes to the lake. A massive figure tore through the west end of the square from the direction of the harbor, roaring as he knocked soldiers to the ground and ripped through their armor with two lethal axes. Ahead of Bear, Bayne sliced through two at a time as they made their way into the crowd. I caught Bayne's eye, a mix of relief and longing flashing across his face for the briefest moment before I hurried to join the fray.

"Cantor!" someone shouted from behind me. Whirling around, I spotted Ronan across the square, his three soldiers in tow. He looked like hell, and I felt a smug satisfaction imagining his encounter with the mountain cat. I turned away to join Bayne and Bear when a familiar scream echoed from above.

My head jerked to the roof where Evony had been. Horror sliced through me as a soldier shoved his blade through Morwyn's chest and tossed her off the roof. Another had Evony around the waist as she screamed and thrashed, fresh tears wetting her devastated face. A bellow sounded from behind as Bear witnessed the nightmare. The soldiers took advantage of his distraction and knocked him to the ground where they began a savage attack. Bayne leaped into action, cutting through half of them, allowing Bear to stagger to his feet. I turned back to the roof and spotted Evony being hauled away.

Bayne made eye contact with me for the briefest moment before I took off after Evony. I leaped over the bodies piling in the square, trying to keep my eyes on the young girl. They hauled her around the edge of the action toward the harbor.

The fog continued to lift, and my tension eased as I caught sight of a massive tribute ship alight with flames dancing wildly in the wind. I scanned the boat while keeping my mark on Evony as I sprinted toward the ship. Why would they be ushering people toward a burning ship? A strong gust of wind whipped off the lake, clearing the remaining fog and unveiling a second, massive tribute ship rocking in the distance. Dread filled my gut.

"Don't!" someone cried from several yards behind.

Ronan.

Bayne and Bear tore through the remaining soldiers, and the two of them rushed out of the crowd. Bear limped and bled heavily. I glanced back at Bayne and saw pain in his eyes, but also... confidence. He didn't slow his sprint, but he gave me a slight nod.

Go.

I pulled my gaze forward as the remaining soldiers loaded the last of the unsuspecting townsfolk, hauling in Evony against her will. She kicked and screamed, looking back as her mother's murderer loaded the gangplank and the ship began putting distance between it and the docks. *Faster.* My ankle screamed in protest as I threw as much momentum into my body as I could, leaping off the edge of the dock and grabbing hold of the mooring line.

My hands ripped as the thick, wet rope slid quickly through them. I tightened my grip as the ship picked up speed. A memory lurked at the edge of my consciousness. I turned back to find Bayne at the edge of the dock, arm outstretched.

CHAPTER TWENTY-SEVEN

Father Marcus's interrogation was a waste of time as his
mind had already shattered.
— Journal of High Priest Helmar, dated 10th of Autumn,
070.3E. Stynguard.

My cheek slammed down onto the cool ship deck as a soldier knelt on my back and stripped me of my weapons. I did all that I could to tense my muscles and press my knuckles together as he bound my hands and hoisted me to my feet. My ankle screamed in pain, buckling as I caught my footing.

I scanned the deck for Evony, finding only soldiers in black. The people from the town had to be below. The ship was large for the lake. Enough to stow at least one hundred extra bodies, maybe even two. Could they have taken that many? Bayne sabotaged the first ship. That had to count for something.

My heart ached as Morwyn's scream echoed in my ears. I

had to find Evony. The thought of that girl in the hands of these men lit a fire in my chest. We had to get off this ship. Could Evony swim? Growing up on the Lake of Light with sailor parents and a fisherman brother, that was a strong bet. We'd jump. The ship had to be heading to the Rhew River if the tributes were being sent to Kayj.

My mind raced as I continued to scan the upper deck. Soldiers moved about, and I spotted the leader who had gutted Morwyn at the stern. The guard gripping my wrists gave me a shove forward, and I hobbled along on one foot. I could feel the pressure of my ankle swelling in my boot, so tender now that I could barely touch it to the deck.

"General," the soldier behind me called, "look who decided to join us." I could hear a smile in his voice, and I ground my teeth. No doubt they knew who I was already.

The general peered down, a look of surprise flashing across his face. "The Cantor girl," he said, eyeing me. He looked at me curiously. "It seems fate has brought us a new opportunity, soldier. Take her below. I'll be there soon."

The soldier behind me grunted in reply, and I was shoved along, stumbling below deck into a long aisle lined with rooms. Murmurs sounded behind the padlocked doors. This had to be where the townspeople were. Did they know they were locked in? Did they have any idea they were slaves as soon as they stepped foot onto this ship? A tingling sense of awareness swept through me of my own position on this ship. Had I just walked myself into a life of slavery as well?

No. I had to stay focused. I was here to get Evony out. I steeled myself as the guard gave me another shove and threw me into an empty room at the end of the hall. I tripped and landed on my face, groaning as I wiggled around to face the door, which he promptly slammed shut.

I took in my surroundings. There was nothing in the room

except a small stool, which I had a feeling wasn't meant for me. I tried to sit up, but I couldn't figure out how to push myself up with my hands bound without putting weight on my ankle. I shimmied my wrists back and forth, trying to take advantage of the small bit of extra space I had created when they bound my hands. *Fuck.* Not enough. I lay there on my side for a minute before the door opened, and the general stepped in. He wiped the blood off his hands with a wet rag.

"Sit her up," he said to a soldier outside the door.

The soldier obeyed, and I bit my lip to not let out a cry as he plopped me on my butt and kicked my legs forward.

"Leave us."

The soldier stepped outside and closed the door. The general leaned forward, angry wrinkles lining his harsh, weathered features. His gray eyes met mine.

"Lady Cantor," he said, voice laced with authority. "You've racked up quite a record these past six months." He pulled out the wanted poster. "Not the best likeness. You've changed." He turned the poster around to face me.

I hadn't stopped to look at it since we saw it for the first time in Rivaner.

I scanned my face. It was me, but it was from last year. Before all this. My hair was tied back in an elegant twist, the common fashion for ladies of the court. I wore that lacey, off-the-shoulder dress for the Sun Dance and the earrings my father had given me. I wondered where they'd gotten so much detail.

Anxiety twisted in my belly. Of course, I knew where they'd gotten it. My father. I shoved down the thought of him and refocused on the man in front of me. The murderer. There must have been a stark difference between the face on the wanted poster and who he saw sitting here now. I could feel the blood crusted against my cheek from the fight and half of my hair had come loose from my braid. The earrings I'd sold months ago.

"'Breaking and entering, attempted theft, theft, destruction of property,'" he read out loud, pausing, and meeting my eyes before continuing. "'Attempted murder, *murder*, treason, and heresy.'" He tsked as he folded it up, pulling out three others.

"And your friends." He raised his eyebrows, and his eyes slid over the three other wanted posters.

"I am interested in hearing how you became acquainted with the elves." He leveled a hard stare at me, which I refused to shrink from.

"I'll tell you everything," I said, my voice gravelly and hoarse from the screaming and panting of the last couple of hours, "under one condition."

He shook his head and softly chuckled under his breath. "You are not in a position to set conditions or make negotiations, Lady Cantor."

"How much do you know about the Stones of the Bellators?" I asked, praying this would pique his interest.

A glint entered his eye, and he set down the wanted posters. "Go on," he said, watching me carefully.

"I can find them. I found one already. Saros has it. I can find more," I said, hoping he was as greedy as his king. "You can pry information out of me. I'm sure you have ways of doing that regardless of the conditions I set."

He watched me, the hand hanging near his dagger flinching.

"But I'm no good to you, or to King Saros, damaged. I can find the others. And I will. Under one condition."

He leaned forward.

"You stop this ship and allow one tribute of my choosing to exit."

"Well, Lady Cantor," the general said, shaking his head, "you've got one thing right. We *are* stopping this ship, and we will be letting one person off. But she was never intended for tribute."

He raised his eyebrows, and my gut filled with lead. They were going to deliver me to King Saros wrapped with a bow.

"I have no interest in the stones," he said waving a hand half-heartedly in the air as he stood up, "nor do I particularly care whether you share information about the whereabouts of your pointy-eared companions. As a fugitive, we'll deliver you to the kingsguards when we reach the mouth of the Rhew, and they will decide what to do with you."

"Coward," I spat before realizing the word had left my mouth.

"Watch your tongue. If you weren't a lady of the Court of Two Moons, I might not post a guard outside your door tonight," he said, a deadly glint entering his eyes.

My stomach twisted at the implication of his words.

"How can you do this?" I asked, unable to help myself. "Slavery was outlawed in Sultira over five hundred years ago. How can you so willingly round up these people like cattle and hand them over to the dark king for a life... A *non*-life of servitude? It's disgusting."

"King Saros keeps superior Sultirans safe," he said with a sneer. "*How* he does so matters not to those who matter *most*." He shook his head before slamming the door shut. His words sank beneath the disgust roiling in my gut. Mumbled talking sounded for a moment before silence.

I scanned the small, dark room for anything I could use to cut through the rope binding my wrist. I wriggled my sweaty hands and fingers back and forth, which only caused painful rubbing.

"Guard!" I called. "Guard! I have to pee!"

The door slid open a crack and a face peered in, eyeing me suspiciously.

"Please. I have to go. And it's..." I paused and took a breath, allowing some embarrassment to creep into my voice. "The Sisters are with me."

"For fuck's sake," he said, glancing away, clearly uncomfortable with the image I planted in his mind. He shook his head as if clearing it before opening the door fully and stepping inside. He drew a dagger and cut the bonds on my hands. It took everything in me not to gasp. *That easy.* Then he pointed to the corner of the room.

"No," I said, mustering up all the pomp of the Sultiran court I could. "I will require a lavatory room with clean rags." I motioned to the small pool of blood I'd smeared on the floor before calling for him. My nose had bled heavily, but he didn't seem to notice as he stared in disgust at the dark stain I sat in.

His hesitation was all I needed, and I barreled into him, knocking him off balance before I slammed my knee into his groin. I delivered two blows to his throat before throwing everything I had into my elbow against his temple. He slumped over, and I snagged his keys and dagger as I rushed past him before sliding the door shut on my way out.

I scanned the halls and sent a silent prayer up to the gods. Luck was on my side. No guards in sight. After locking the door, I wedged the stool he'd been sitting on outside my room against the handle of the door. I had minutes to find Evony.

I sprinted through the halls, trying each door as I ran. Padlocks on all of them, but I had a ring full of keys.

"Evony?" I called into each one. Panicked shouts answered me as I passed. None of them were Evony's voice. The people inside knew they were locked in. I'd have to come back for them.

Muffled arguing sounded around the corner. I stopped and

slipped into an insert in the wall, hastily stilling the various tools that I'd bumped into. Inching my way around a mop and bucket, I wedged myself further in. Two guards strode past, heading in the opposite direction. Shit, shit, *shit*. They would figure out what happened soon enough. I had to stop thinking like a fugitive and start thinking like the crew of the *Evecta*. What would Bayne do?

After scanning the tools, my eyes snagged on a small container of wallot soap. Highly flammable. Waiting until they rounded the corner, I grabbed the soap and sprinted in the opposite direction, heading for the animal crates I passed on the way in. I snatched an oil lamp off the wall as I ran and skidded to a stop as I reached the chicken crates.

After unlatching the crates, I dumped the bewildered chickens into the sheep pen and ran down the hall to the opposite end, smearing wallot grease along the walls as I ran. I coated the crates and stopped in a corner near a window, far away from the locked rooms and animals, and broke the oil lamp on the crates which quickly went up in flame. Daring not to think about the risk I put everyone in, I ran down the hall and up to the next level, setting another set of crates on fire near the kitchen. I ducked into an open room, my shaky breath steadying as my heart pounded in my chest. I waited.

Shouts erupted from the opposite end of the ship where I'd locked my guard in the room. Moments later, calls for water followed. If we were headed north, we wouldn't have strayed far offshore since we were on our way to the northernmost tip of the Lake of Light. The people on this ship were cargo. I banked on them saving as many as they could.

Peering around the corner, I continued my search of the rooms on this level. I found a similar set of doors and called for Evony. Hearing no sign of her, I moved to check the rooms past the kitchen when a rough male voice called out.

"Wait, wait! The girl? Is the girl Evony? There's a girl in here with a head injury."

I skidded to a stop, returned to the door, and began trying the various keys on the ring. My numb fingers fumbled through each one.

"What does she look like?" I asked in a shaky voice.

"Brown skin, freckles... Looks to be about... fourteen if I had to guess. She's been bloodied up pretty good though," he said.

My heart sank. If only my stupid hands would move faster. Shouts sounded from the level below. *Focus.* I steadied my breathing as the sound of the padlock's click sent a wave of relief over me. I threw the door open, and a group of townspeople gawked at me bewildered. The man who had been talking to me through the door eyed me up and down before he stepped outside the door, looked both ways, and ushered his family out.

"She's at the back," he said to me before hurrying out of the room.

At least a dozen people shuffled out of the room, and there, lying in the straw at the back, was an unconscious Evony. Warm tears quickly filled the corners of my eyes as I rushed to her. I grunted as I slung her slim form over my shoulder and hobbled out of the room into the smoke.

The townspeople had fled up the stairs to the upper deck and were met with shouts from the guards on deck. I limped along with Evony through the smoke-filled halls, ducking into a small vacant room with a window. I peered out and spotted land. We were only about one hundred yards from shore.

"Evony, wake up," I said quietly, brushing the hair back from her face and softly slapping her cheek.

One of her eyes was swollen shut, but she slowly flickered the other open. Rage like nothing I'd ever felt flooded my veins with heat.

"Are you okay? Can you hear me?" I whispered.

"Lyvia... Where are we? I... Mom..." she whimpered and began to cry.

My heart broke into a million pieces. "Evony, listen to me carefully. We are on a tribute ship. We need to get off. Do you think you can swim?"

She nodded. This wasn't going to be easy. I pulled out a piece of jerky I had stashed in my pack and handed it to her.

"Eat this. I will be back in a minute and then we are going to jump off this ship. Understand?"

She nodded, one bright blue eye meeting mine through silvery tears.

"Okay. Stay put."

The ship jerked suddenly, knocking us both off our feet. I peered out the window. We veered closer to shore. A slight sense of satisfaction settled over me. I peeked out the door and gently shut it. Smoke filled the halls, and I spied flames dancing around the corner. I returned to the rest of the rooms in the second hall and tried the same key that had unlocked Evony's cell. I was met with a satisfying *click*. Thank the gods. Scared and astonished faces peered at me as I flung the doors open.

"Hurry, the ship is on fire. You need to get off. Go!"

People scrambled through the doors, trampling one another to get above deck. I hurried to the lowest level and skidded to a stop by the tool closet, ducking inside. Guards dashed through the halls unlocking rooms and searching. Searching for me. A few people tried to rush out, and they slaughtered them without hesitation. My stomach turned. I marked six guards. If Bayne and Bear were here, we could take them and free these people. Guilt at what I'd done gnawed at my gut. I shoved it back down and turned on my heel, rushing to the next level. I was here for one thing.

Evony stood in a defensive position when I returned for her, ready for a fight. I gave her a nod, and she hobbled after me. We rounded the corner, heading to the top deck.

"Straight to the starboard side of the ship and off the edge," I whispered, "don't wait for me. Just swim. Got it?"

She nodded.

"Now!"

We ran above deck into a flurry of chaos. The townsfolk had grabbed tools or wrangled weapons from the guards and attacked those on deck. Others boarded the small lifeboats, cutting the ropes, and dropping fifty feet into the water with a crash. Several more in a panic threw themselves off the side.

We sprinted across the deck, dodging bodies when the general shouted, "YOU!"

I turned my head in response and met his gray eyes, full of fury. "Grab her!"

"Go, Evony!"

Footsteps sounded beside me, and a soldier lunged. I spun around and slashed at him with my stolen dagger, nicking him on the cheek. He let out a growl and swung his arm. I dodged and chased after Evony. She reached the edge of the deck and quickly scrambled up the side before risking a glance over her shoulder.

"GO!" I screamed, voice cracking.

She leaped and disappeared off the side of the ship. My ankle screamed at me as I ran as fast as I could, leaping over crates and bodies. I stretched my arm out to the side of the ship when a loud thump echoed in my ears followed by a blast of fiery pain before everything went dark.

CHAPTER TWENTY-EIGHT

The powder will be tasteless and can be dissolved into her tea.
An hour before your rides should do it.
— Correspondence from High Priest Helmar to Lord
Willem Cantor, dated 78th of Summer, 066.3E. Aedrialis.

H*um, hum, hum.*
I was flying again. This time over ruined cities and burned villages. Dusty gray wings swept out and softly kicked up the ash as we landed.

Hum, hum, hum.

I hopped off, feet sinking into inches of ash mixed with blood and mud. My boots squelched as I stepped over the devastated land. The skies glowed a gray, orange haze from the blast.

Hum, hum, hum.

My boot crunched onto something hard and brittle. Bones of a young child. Bile rose to my throat. My eyes scanned the scorched ground around me. The remains of a family lay strewn in broken pieces. Hot tears slid down my cheeks. Enough. This would end today.

Hum, hum, hum.

Muffled voices from nearby grew louder and sharper as pain slammed into my head. I groaned. A hand patted mine.

"There, there, Lyvia. All is right now. You're back in good hands."

Images of broken bodies and burned cities flashed between smoky wooden halls and white sails. I'd been chasing someone. I was worried and panicked. We were trying to escape. I needed to get her out.

"A little more of the celosia powder and that should do it," a voice said. It was familiar. The distant part of my mind slowly calling me back screamed into the darkness—*run*.

A sharp stinging sensation snaked its way through my nostrils and burned into the tender place behind my eyes. I choked on my spit, coughing until I gasped for air. The stinging quickly turned to itching, and I sneezed, my hands jerking upward and stopping too close to my thighs. Thick leather straps tugged on my wrists and forearms. The awareness of the bonds snapped me out of my dizzying dream state, and my eyes shot open. Evony.

Hum, hum, hum.

Where was Evony? Where was *I*? The lack of rocking beneath my feet told me I was no longer aboard the ship. I scanned the room full of familiar tools and charts hanging on the walls. A scholar room. Was I back in Aedrialis? Black stone tiled the floor, and I spied the long coiling tail of a serpent in the patterned stones. Stynguard?

I was at the university in the north. My head spun from the celosia powder. I must have been unconscious for days if we were truly in Stynguard. Small tidbits of memory crept back into my mind.

My heart leapt from my chest as my eyes lifted to a chair sitting opposite from me. He was bound, darkened blood crusted against the side of his head, his bright blue eyes staring at me through cracked spectacles. His hands trembled as he tried to sign to me.

Relief at seeing Drystan alive quickly sank beneath waves of panic and horror. He'd been tortured.

"Drys—" I began and stopped as my eyes settled on High Priest Helmar.

He peered at me from behind his workstation where he clicked together a few spy glasses and instruments with shifting gears. My eyes snagged on my pack laying on the table next to him. And Father Marcus's journal. *Fuck.*

High Priest Helmar appeared young, black hair slicked back against his head without a streak of gray, but most knew he was old. His opaque-blue eyes gleamed in the darkness of the room. He'd been high priest for the last fifty years, and one of King Saros's most trusted advisers. Friend to my father. And the one who had sanctioned my study with the Death Scholars.

His robes swished as he stood from behind his workstation and made his way to my side. I followed his nod toward the door, where a kingsguard returned it and quietly left the room, causing my insides to twist.

I met the high priest's eyes, painting an uninterested, bland look on my face. I relaxed my arms and took a slow steadying breath.

"Lady Cantor, I'm so glad we've found you," he said in a soft, deadly voice before looking back to Drystan. "Though I suppose this wasn't the reunion you were expecting."

Hatred sliced through the fear in Drystan's eyes as they slid to the high priest.

"Drystan Amando has great potential but has been less

cooperative than I would have expected from a man in the order." High Priest Helmar's words dripped venom, and he turned back to me.

"I hear you've been through quite a journey. It's a shame the foreigners kidnapped you before we had the chance to speak with King Saros about your... gift." He paused, watching me carefully.

I got the sense he knew more than he let on. My entire life had been manipulated, in part by this man.

"It is here," he said, his lips turning upward in a cold smile. "But I'm sure you knew that already." His dark eyebrows raised as he leaned in close.

The sickeningly sweet scent of licorice tea wafted off his breath. It churned my already twisting stomach. The pupils in his eyes constricted as though he tried to rip into my soul, tightening my throat and shortening my breath.

Hum, hum, hum.

Yes, I knew it was here. I could feel my heart beat in rhythm with it, the vibration of it so real and present in my chest that I knew if I spoke, my voice would quiver. His eerie smile broadened, and he slowly nodded.

"We are in Stynguard if you haven't figured that out. I've been studying the stone here for the past few months, testing the... *effect* it has on people."

My stomach churned. Drystan shifted in his bounds. Had he witnessed it all? Had it been used on him?

"It's fascinating how quickly the minds of peasants fracture in its presence."

Oh, gods. The tribute ships from the Lake of Light would pass directly through Stynguard from the Rhew River. Was he taking some of the tributes for his own, sick experiments?

"We're going to try something today," he murmured, close enough that I could feel his breath against my lips.

Enough.

I leaned my head back and crashed the hard space where my hairline met my forehead into his nose. He yelped and jumped backward, cursing. His hands flew to his face as crimson streaks ran down his lips and chin. He pulled them away, examining the blood. The sinister smile that appeared moments ago had vanished, replaced by a look of lethal calm. He stepped forward and slapped me across the face, the wetness from the blood adding a sharp sting to the tingling pain. Drystan jerked against his restraints.

"Cooperation would be advised," he growled as he wiped the blood off his hands and blotted his nose, "but it's not necessary."

He called the guards back in. Two large men entered the room, neither of them making eye contact with me. I recognized one of them as the kingsguard from Cantor Manor all those months ago. I scanned the dull blue eyes for signs of the swirling silver I'd seen, but the guard refused to meet my stare. I willed my pumping heart to calm, but it only grew more agitated, as if it knew what was coming.

Hum, hum, hum.

The vibrating pulse from the stone quickened. Blood trickled down the side of my chin from the corner of my mouth. I spat at the ground where the guards stood.

High Priest Helmar stepped through the door to an adjacent room where the whir of a tea kettle could be heard. I pulled my gaze back to Drystan. His bound hands moved in jerky patterns as he tried to communicate. I squinted at his hands, making out the words despite his limited movement.

"We finally made it to Stynguard," he signed, letting out a wet chuckle.

Tears formed in my eyes at the absurdity of his words.

"Not exactly what we had in mind. I'm sorry I called you an

asshole," I signed back, mouthing the words in case he couldn't read with my limited movement.

Drystan shook his head, eyebrows pinched upward in acceptance.

Before he could respond, High Priest Helmar returned murmuring quiet words as he added powder and liquids to a small cup. A flash of orange light sparked, and I realized he performed a spell. I fumed at the lie he and King Saros had spun these past hundreds of years. The twisted nature of keeping the magic to themselves, keeping the rest of the academic and spiritual world focused on the sciences and religion while they secretly benefited from the lost arts.

He carried the small mug of steaming tea across the room to where I sat.

"I would have offered you a biscuit. That's how your father said you take your tea," he said in a soft, mocking voice.

My chest caved at the words.

His cruel eyes scanned me up and down as if he knew. "But I can see any etiquette with you would be wasted time."

"We can agree on that," I said, voice clipped.

"Ah, the snake speaks! Very good."

He nodded to the guards who swiftly stepped forward. Panic shot down my veins, and I tugged on the straps. My feet and legs were tied down with similar bonds. I thrashed as one guard held my shoulders and the other stood behind me, thrusting my head back, one hand against my forehead, the other firmly gripping my chin. The soldier finally met my eyes, and I saw it.

Silver flashed, swirls of it dancing and writhing in his irises. A gut-churning grin crept on his lips for a split second before the silver melted back into dull blue.

"You can relax, Lyvia. You've experienced this before. I've been brewing this batch for your father for the last four years."

My heart raced through my chest as he approached.

Hum, hum, hum.

The stone's vibration picked up as my panic peaked. The high priest stepped in front of me while the guard forced my mouth open, his gaze blank. I did everything I could to cough and gurgle the burning tea, choking on it as the guard shook my head and pressed his hand against my mouth, forcing the liquid down my throat. I swallowed out of reflex, coughing, before snapping my teeth at the guard's hand.

"Agh, bitch," he said quietly, shaking his hand before bringing it down across my other cheek. My head rocked to the side.

Silence stretched. And then I felt it. A snaking anxiety sent my blood thundering through my veins and my heart jumping wildly in my chest. My eyes felt fuzzy and watery. My breath quickened to small, short inhales like the hot hounds panting at the manor in summer. The hairs on my arms stood straight, buzzing with energy.

I frantically looked around. This was unlike anything I had ever experienced in my life. *Unforgettable.* Between the frantic thoughts and tingling numbness, my mind whirred, out of control. A moment of clarity swept through my consciousness, and in that second, I knew my father had not given me the elixir High Priest Helmar thought he did. Yes, he'd concealed the truth. And there probably was some manipulation involved I wasn't aware of. But it wasn't the betrayal I thought it was. A small knot eased in my chest.

I buzzed through the universe, and in an instant, my attention was wholly focused on the humming coming from the next room. My watery eyes landed on the door connecting us to the adjoining room. Satisfied mumbling came from the direction of the high priest, and he moved toward the door. I couldn't take my eyes off it. He opened it, and my body reacted.

My back arched against the chair, and my arms tensed against the bonds, nearly ripping the leather. A distant part of my consciousness felt four hands press against my shoulders and arms, pinning me in place.

High Priest Helmar stepped from the room holding a small, velvet-lined box that he slowly opened as he approached me. The Obscura Stone called to me then. Crisp and clear.

Hum, hum, hum.

It was a queen summoning her most loyal subject. A goddess summoning her most devoted follower. I felt an urge to fall to my knees before it. Uncomfortable voices mumbled on either side of me. These guards were *weak*. All they had to do was take it. Its power would be all-consuming. The thoughts snaked through me, picking up more and more speed.

Water streamed from my face as he approached. Its blackness devoured the light in the small room. Time stood still as my eyes drank in its beauty. The high priest slammed the box shut.

I blinked away strange tears as a blast rocked through the door and a sharp wind spun through the scholar room, shattering glasses and knocking equipment off the tables. The guards left my side and scrambled across the room, engaging unknown attackers. I glanced back, and the high priest hurried to the room next door when a blast sent him flying back, the Obscura Stone soaring through the air and landing in front of my feet, like an offering.

Reluctantly, I pulled my eyes from the stone, barely aware the university was under attack, and noticed blood trickling down the side of High Priest Helmar's head as his white-blue eyes stared blankly at the ceiling. The humming slowed, and I took a shuddering breath. Drystan's chair had been knocked over, and he struggled to free himself.

Men in silver armor with the crest of a flower etched into the chest piece entered the room. Their leader, moving faster than expected, strode across the room and cut down the guards in one fell swoop. A small part of me felt a wave of relief as the dull-eyed kingsguard lay sprawled, mouth gaping open like a fish out of water on the rubble-ridden floor.

The soldiers stepped to the side of my chair and began undoing my restraints. This all seemed familiar. I'd been here six months ago. Been held against my will by the Sultiran kingsguards and sprung from my prison by unknown predators. But this was different. I had the sneaking sense that these people would not become my allies. *I* was different this time.

The soldiers removed my restraints but held my arms down on the chair, as a tall man with blonde-white hair and light brown eyes strode forward, his deep purple cape swishing behind him. I noted the pointed ears as his lips curled into an imperious grin that sent chills up my spine. He knelt before me and plucked the stone off the ground with a gloved hand, placing it in an intricate silver box. My heart hammered, and my hands twitched the moment he touched the stone. He glanced up and let out a soft chuckle.

"Bag her and bring her," he commanded the soldiers, voice thick with an accent I didn't recognize. I resisted the urge to look at Drystan, praying they'd think him dead. A black hood was shoved over my head, and I was hoisted to my feet, arms pinned to my sides. I stumbled, pain rippling as I put weight on my swollen ankle. The soldiers reacted, lifting me off the ground and hauling me forward.

They marched me through the eerily quiet halls of the university. I tripped over the rubble scattered across the obsidian floor as we swiftly made our way to the lower levels. A blast sounded, followed by ringing screams and clashing steel.

The blast cleared my mind. *Think.* It didn't matter who these people were. I wasn't going with them. I was stronger and more skilled than I was six months ago as I remembered the stench of the prison cell under Mount Telum.

Fresh, cool spring air tanged with salt wafted into my hood, and dimmed light shone through the dark fabric as they rushed me out the doors. Sounds of battle ensued, the thunder of agrippa racing down the streets as their riders defended the city. How many were here? It couldn't be many if Saros's shield still held. Smoke filled my lungs, and heat tinged my arms as an explosion sounded from behind. Screams echoed across the courtyard.

They shoved me over the cobblestones. A gust of sea air greeted me as we rounded the corner, and a familiar screech caught my attention. I jerked my head to the left, my eyes straining to see through the black hood. Another call and a blast of air. I didn't need my eyes to know the giant seahawk, Aquila was here. Relief swelled in my chest. Were the others here? The mere hope was enough to light a fire, dulling the throbbing in my ankle.

The vibrating whizz of arrows had my guard hauling me to one side, knocking me off balance. I hit the hard ground with a groan and kicked to the side, my boot meeting the side of my guard's knee. He side-stepped long enough to lose his grip on me, and with my arms finally free, I yanked my hood off. My eyes reeled from the blinding white light bouncing off the sea-cream buildings.

I blinked rapidly and backpedaled away from the group of six soldiers, bumping into the building behind me. Their caped leader barked orders, and a soldier came at me as more arrows rained down from above. I glanced up and caught sight of an elf twisting in a leap mid-air between buildings, stretching his bowstring back and releasing. His hazel eyes met mine for the briefest moment.

Vulcan.

I never thought I'd be so relieved to see the odious elf. Alive and fighting for me. I had to act. A soldier turned toward me and I took off at a sprint. My eyes darted to the rooftops as I ran, but the city was in chaos. Men and women screamed in every direction, shoving each other and calling for help. Fires burned and walls crumbled. I leaped over a pile of rubble that was once a stone sculpture of Aelius before skidding around a fallen boulder.

Looking up, I spotted movement to the left. A shadow running alongside me, four stories up. Pain ripped through my scalp as I rounded the corner. Tears welled in my eyes before I realized someone had a hold of my disheveled braid. I was yanked to a stop, and the man with the blonde-white hair had me bent over backward, forcing my face up to the heavens with his hand tangled in my hair. My hands scratched at his as he forced me to my knees. Armor clanged nearby as his pack of hounds joined us. My eyes darted from left to right, searching for any sign of the crew of the *Evecta*, terrified I might have imagined it.

The soldiers in silver took up positions on opposite sides of the smoking road while two others disappeared. He yanked me up by my hair and shoved me into the center of the road. The honed edge of an icy dagger bit against my bare throat.

I stilled as he whispered into my ear, "You slippery little doe." He panted, catching his breath against my hair. "Your friends are causing some trouble. Let's see if we can draw them out."

Strands of my hair snapped as he yanked my head further back. My breathing picked up as my pulse banged frantically against the blade. *Think.*

Bayne and Vulcan were too smart for this trap. These men wanted me alive. They had the stone. I had seconds. And there was one thing the others had to know. I didn't hesitate.

"Drystan is here!" I screamed.

His hand was so quick I didn't register what had happened. Cold steel bit into my neck so sharp that the sting of the blade was delayed. Warm liquid gushed down my neck followed by hot, blinding pain as he slid the dagger to the side. Too deep.

I coughed, choking, as my mouth flooded with warm liquid, spraying red droplets into the crisp air. The man dropped me, and I fell to my knees on the hard, blood-soaked cobblestone. My hands blindly slipped over the gash on my neck. My vision started to blur, and I caught a glimpse of a figure at the top of a building and another flying across the gap between the two. I dreamed he cried out. Devastation crashed into me. I was wrong. I wasn't needed alive. I would be dead soon. As would Bayne and the others.

CHAPTER TWENTY-NINE

*Lyvi, Our unit arrived in Krestwood last week. Van is here.
No sign of the so-called pirates. Tell Drystan I'm going to
kick his ass when I'm back. The enderleaf smokes he sent
landed me on full-time shit-shoveling duty. Love you. Take it
easy on pop. —Aer*

*—Correspondence from Aeriden to Lyvia Cantor. 56th of
Summer, 070.3E. Cantor Manor, Aedrialis.*

I floated on a wind that had no beginning and no end, through light and dark, life and death. Lines and swirls of glittering dust filled the universe. The stars beckoned, but the roots of Vael tugged me down. A cluster of islands shone like emeralds in the azure sea, their white shores stained with blood. Something tugged at my being, and I floated down from the stars. A ship rocked in the wild swells off the coast.

Dark eyes opened before me. The eyes of a young man. Younger, *perhaps. A teenage boy. Though he was surrounded by men, his arms held down and a leather strap thrust in his mouth, his hopeless gaze screamed, "I'm alone." Lines of dark blood dripped from his chest as he thrashed. A spark of fear shot through his gaze. I followed it to the orange glow of an approaching iron brand.*

Something stirred at the sight. I had no feeling here, but my consciousness, a distant, quiet thing, seemed to react, pulling me away from the scene about to unfold. He let out a desperate sound and two distant parts of me warred against each other. One rooting me in place, the other urging me onward.

His dark eyes shuddered as something pulled his attention away from the blazing iron. I felt myself slipping, and a faraway, voiceless part of myself called into the darkness. "I'm with you. You are not alone."

He blinked the tears away before they could form, a steely determination hardening his gaze, before I let the teenage boy and ship fall away into nothing.

Sun and moons rose and fell in reverse, streaking through the sky like shooting stars until everything slowed. I floated over the outline of Sultira, a solid mass of greens, browns, and whites, the Lake of Light shining like a beacon in its nest of mountains. I passed lives and moments until I came upon a familiar scene. I paused and focused my not-mind on the beings below.

Enya lay broken and shattered on a battlefield at the edge of a white cliff, the beautiful warrior defeated. Her white hair loose and singed at the ends, splayed out on the mud and wet ash like a crown of burned birch branches, topped with a resplendent helm. And at its center, the Obscura Stone, black as night and endless as the depths of the deepest sea. Its mesmerizing allure was dampened in this not-alive but not-quite-dead state. Whatever it was. I looked closer. I had no memory of the webbed structure or canals swirling at its center. A distant, curious part of me blinked an eye open.

Movement to the south pulled my attention away as the man approached. A bloody bandage wrapped around his left hand where only three fingers jutted out, holding the pommel of his sword as he swaggered to where Enya lay dying. I stared at the bandage. Not any man. Saros, the Hidden Hero.

There was no emotion in the revelation. Just calm observation. I hadn't noticed it in the first dream because I saw it through Enya's eyes. The left hand was missing his ring and pinky finger. Such a young face, but I knew now, it had to have been the Hidden Hero.

Words were exchanged, and he reached for the Obscura Stone. A blast of black fire and mist tore through the land, reducing the remaining plants and soldiers within miles to ash. All except for King Saros, who'd thrown up a magical barrier. Still, he'd been ripped back hundreds of feet and lay there unmoving. My eyes drifted over the gray and black wreckage that covered the land. No bones, just ash and metal.

I continued floating, unfeeling, as the dust settled. Enya's ocean-blue eyes had closed and her chest barely expanded as she took her final breaths. I wasn't sure why I was still here. It was time to keep floating. I began to pull my gaze away as I felt the tug of the wind that was not wind when her eyes shot open, and she gripped my forearm, which hadn't existed a moment ago.

Emotions flew back, slamming into my chest. What had happened? Fear flooded my system. She held me in an iron grip and an even harder gaze, her blue eyes alight with orange flame in the center.

"Get up," she rasped, the smoke choking her breath.

"Get up, Lyvia. GET UP!" she commanded, and her words threw me into the torrent of wind that was neither life nor death, spinning me away from the stars and the Vael and slamming me back into my last painful moments.

My eyes shot open as I sucked in cool, crisp air. My hands grasped at my throat where my neck had been sliced open. I felt the thick and smooth raised lip of a long, straight scar that ran from below my left ear to the right side of my throat. I jerked my hand away.

Impossible. No one would have survived that. I'd attended enough Life Scholar lectures to know the amount of blood I'd lost due to my severed artery should have put me in the ground. I raised shaking fingers to the patches of numb and tingling skin stretched taught above and below the scar. My throat had been slit. And someone had healed me.

I stared up at the dreamy canopy of the bed I lay on. White drapes of silk laced with beautiful, closed deep purple flowers twisted from one end of the black-wooden arches to the other, blocking the ceiling from view. My still-shaking hands dropped from my neck to the luxurious sheets around me. Crisp, white downy blankets and furs covered the bed.

I pushed up to my elbows, which I realized were bare. A violet chiffon night dress with split sleeves covered my body, tied loosely at the waist. A chill ran over my otherwise warm skin as realization washed over me. An embarrassed, vulnerable part of me bristled at the violation and the disregard for my privacy. I shoved it down.

I was in a large room. A *beautiful* room. The marble walls were covered in silver vines and gemstones of every color weaved in a tapestry of images. Mountains and flowers sprawled across them as if they were canvas, and swirls of snowflakes and water raced toward the ceiling, the night sky dotted with hundreds of stars, which had to be diamonds. Our beloved moons, depicted in glittering sapphires, aquamarines, and blue topaz, spun together in two twin spheres.

I tiptoed across the floor to the diamond-shaped window

which opened to a vast snow-capped mountain range. A small, white hawk caught an updraft of wind and soared past. I peeked down, and nausea churned. I was in a castle. No, a fortress, hundreds of feet up. I had to be north if the snow was still this thick. From what I knew about Lotrennia, there were only a handful of mountain ranges, and not many of them were high enough to boast so much snow, which meant I was north.

Unease snaked its way into my gut. I wasn't on Kayj. This didn't match the descriptions from Bayne. I had to be north of Kayj. The land of Dark King Daimos.

Nivis.

Dread pitted in my stomach as any hope of being rescued quickly diminished. If Bayne was still alive, he'd think I'd be on the island. No ships could pass through the torrential storms that swirled above Kayj, guarding Nivis. I stepped away from the window and as I did so, realized my ankle had been healed as well. I felt my chin and cheek. No bruising that I could feel there either. Even the nails I'd chipped on the roof in Rivaner had grown back, smooth and manicured.

A soft *hum* pulled my attention to the ornate armoire. I moved to the Obscura Stone, feeling my heartbeat adjust to the familiar rhythm. Gone was the frenzied effect from High Priest Helmar's elixir. Feeling entirely sober, the stone gave a gentle pull toward me.

Remembering Enya's vision, I saw it more clearly now. My fingers reached for the deep black etchings that danced and swirled. They stilled at my touch and settled into a familiar pattern. Calm certainty fell over me.

Bone.

That's what Father Marcus tried to tell me in his journal. Not stone. *Bone.* Striations of canals lined the black surface, and after feeling it under my fingers, I was even more certain. Father Marcus must have touched it and gone mad, trying to jot down as much as he could before he either lost his mind or the kingsguards took him. The Bellator Stones were bones.

My mind raced as I thought about the possibilities of the source of the bone. What ancient being had it come from? My fingers traced the soft, round edge of the bone. It felt like home. It was secured in an ornate silver setting, bedecked with diamonds and amethysts with silver chains looping and crossing, connecting in small places.

Footsteps sounded from outside the door, and I was snapped out of my reverie. Where the hell was I? I hadn't even checked the door for gods' sakes. I scanned the room for anything I could use as a weapon. There was nothing in the room except for the bone, which I didn't know how to use. I stood on the other side of the armoire in a battle-ready stance as a soft knock sounded on the door.

"Milady, it is time to dress," said a quiet voice before the door swung open. A young woman with a black veil wrapped around her head stepped in. She wore a matching black dress and had a large scar across her cheek. But that wasn't the first thing I noticed.

A thick, iron ring locked around her neck, connecting to a delicate chain and hung down her chest. A *collar*. All the beauty of the room was swept away as the realization hit me. The chain was more symbolic than practical, but the intent behind it was clear. Bile rose in my throat, and I swallowed, forcing myself to get a grip.

The slave timidly approached, keeping her eyes down. "I'm sorry for the intrusion, but King Daimos requests your presence tonight at dinner."

"Where am I?" I asked.

"This is the Crystal Castle, the Diamond of Nivis, Land of Ice and Gems. Home of the Great King Daimos."

Such a pretty picture clouded with such ugliness. I glanced out the window again. The brilliant sun bounced off the snowy peaks, brightening the room and reflecting off the gems in the walls. Such wealth was hidden beyond the clouds of Kayj, where Bayne had been.

My heart clenched at the thought of him. Be alive. *Please* be alive. I sent up a prayer to the Sisters and the Brother. He had survived so much. The kryax, the ashen, the island of Kayj itself. He had to be alive. I had to play this right if I was going to escape.

Turning back to the slave, I nodded. What choice did I have?

She led me into a small chamber off to the side where she leaned over a tub to draw my bath. A short thread of bleach white hair slipped free of her veil which she hastily tucked back in. I slid into the steaming, soapy water, resisting the urge to sigh. It exhumed comfort and luxury at such odds with the terror and panic in my heart. I soaked in the heat, deeply inhaling the eucalyptus steam which steadied my mind. The slave wrapped me in a towel as soft and as white as the feather-bed before motioning me to sit in front of the mirror.

Her hands slipped around my neck, pulling my hair back. I jerked reflexively as her fingers brushed the fresh scar on my neck. She pulled them back quickly, apologizing profusely, still refusing to meet my eyes.

"It's okay. I just..." I swallowed, the skin around the scar tight and foreign. The feeling of the blade slicing into my neck was so raw and fresh. I pinched my eyes shut for a moment.

"What is your name?" I asked.

She slowly twisted my hair back and up into an elaborate

braid. My black strands were a stark contrast to her own blonde-white head.

"I am called Pebble," she replied softly.

"Pebble?" I repeated.

She nodded her head, continuing to work on my hair.

"Is that the name your mother gave you?"

"No, milady."

"Why are you called Pebble?"

"All slaves are given ground names."

I understood. The word rang with insignificance. Something trodden or walked on. Pebble. Small, insignificant... kicked around. Blood rose in my veins. Sultira was far from perfect, with its hierarchy of classes and bias toward blue eyes, but at least we didn't have *this*.

"What is the name your mother gave you?"

She paused, hand holding a silver pin, and finally met my eyes in the mirror.

"Eira, milady. Though you may call me whatever you wish. It is an honor to serve you and serve here in the Crystal Castle."

"Do you know if anyone else was brought here with me?" I asked.

She shook her head, placing the final pin in my elaborate hair. Braided and twisted up, she adorned it with black pearls which stood out like dull stars in my dark hair. She dressed me in a deep, purple winter formal gown that was so dark it was nearly black, like looking into a moonless night sky. The long, sheer sleeves split at my shoulders and hung down like draped wings. She coated my lips with matching paint and drew heavy black lines on the top and bottom of my eyelids, making the caramel hue lighter and brighter.

I stared at myself in the mirror. The last time I had been this heavily done up was for the summer solstice ball, which felt like ages ago. My look today starkly contrasted the vision I portrayed then, clad in frills of white lace and soft pinks.

Another slave entered the room, not meeting my eyes and reverently picked up the velvet pillow the Obscura Bone sat upon. He flinched as he raised it, his haunted dark eyes pinned to the spot above the bone, not looking directly at it. He uttered a prayer beneath his breath.

Eira led us to the door, where we were greeted by a soldier in silver. We walked down winding glass stairs until we reached a wide hallway, bedecked with similar silver carvings on the walls. I was led into a massive throne room, filled with people dressed in formal winter wear. Elaborate silver vines and jewels sparkled off the walls, covering every inch of the room and meeting at a single point in the center of the ceiling where a huge diamond chandelier hung down, little lights reflecting rainbows on the white floor.

The court of blonde and blonde-white heads turned to me as I entered the room. My fluttering heart threatened to fly from my chest, but the bone grounded it, keeping it under its steady control. I lifted my chin higher, taking in the scene before me. A tall man with a crown of blood-red rubies lorded over the room, seated upon a throne of diamonds.

Dark King Daimos had the same blonde-white hair, long and flowing beneath the extravagant headpiece. He had sharp features and a crooked nose. Spine-stiffening, yellow eyes peered at me from across the room. Not the yellow of the hundreds of topazes and citrines that dotted the walls of the throne room. Nor the yellow of Aelius's brilliant sun. Nor the petals of the spring prairie flowers that bloomed on the plains outside of Aedrialis. No, this was the yellow of sickness. The yellow of decay, of puss and dying things.

He stood, holding his arms out with his palms toward the chandelier. He wore something on his hands. I couldn't tell from this far away, but it appeared to be some kind of glove with a jewel in the center. His deep, deadly voice echoed across the throne room as he slowly drew out the syllables of my name.

"*Liv-ee-yuh.*" A horrible smile appeared on his face as his eyes met mine. "Welcome, Daughter of Darkness, Tynan's Accepted."

The crowd responded in unison, "Welcome, Daughter of Darkness, Tynan's Accepted."

CHAPTER THIRTY

Lyvi, I ran into that stable hand when a passing unit came through our camp last week. I punched his teeth out. You're welcome. —Aer

—Correspondence from Aeriden to Lyvia Cantor. 54th of Autumn, 069.3E. Cantor Manor, Aedrialis.

The name sent an eerie sensation creeping into my gut. I held onto the connection with the bone, letting the steady *hum* be my anchor in a tumultuous sea. Silence followed as they walked me to the front of the dais. The guard and slaves bowed to the king, remaining on their knees as they waited.

The dark king regarded me with his cold, dead yellow eyes for a long moment before someone to my left scoffed. I pulled my eyes away and found myself looking at the man who slit my throat. It took everything in my power to keep my hands from flying to my neck. His eyes fell to the scar across my throat as he smirked. It was then that I noticed the healed gash across his cheek. He watched my eyes travel across his own scar, and his smirk turned into a scowl. An older woman beside him shifted on her feet.

"Bow to the king, you human whore," she spat.

I leveled a cold stare at her.

"Manners, Sister," Dark King Daimos said. He pulled his eyes from me, and they landed on her.

She cowered beneath their glow. "Yes, Your Grace," she murmured.

"Apologies, Daughter of Darkness. My sister-in-law is protective of her son. It appears Lieutenant Cyril bit off more than he could chew upon your retrieval in Sultira. Your friends left a mark."

My lips tugged upward. Cyril, who had been holding his arms behind his back at attention, dropped them to the side as he bunched up a fist and stepped toward me.

A fist.

My jaw dropped as my attention slid to the stump on his hand. He wasn't missing a hand when he'd taken me. It was his right, the one that had sliced through my neck. I stepped back as he moved toward me, rage rippling beneath his skin, and two guards stepped in front of me.

"There are some things I cannot heal," the dark king tsked, holding his palms up, shrugging nonchalantly. My eyes caught on his hands. Sitting at the center of his palms in a setting of intricate silver chains lay a bone in each. A deep blue with swirling, glittering sparkles lay on his left while a golden bone as brilliant as the setting sun shone on his right. They were tied in place with elaborate chains of silver bedecked with diamonds that wrapped between his fingers and around his hands and wrists, a unique merging of glove, ring, and bracelet.

The strangest sensations bounced between the two of them and the Obscura Bone to my left, each of them giving off their own unique aura. Neither of them hummed like the onyx bone next to me. The golden bone *sang* to me. Its melody lilting and light, calling me in like a lullaby. And though I felt no pull toward the blue bone, it pulsed. More of a drumming heartbeat than the darkness next to me.

Daimos had two of the Bellator Bones. And one of them contained powerful healing properties or I wouldn't be alive. I was frozen in place, the sensations of the three bones spinning together in a cacophony of power. I finally glanced up, meeting his cool gaze, and his smile widened.

"The Daughter of Darkness has brought us a gift," he said, gesturing to the onyx bone. "The Stone of Darkness."

A hushed murmur spread across the crowd. The king nodded to a soldier, and he held my shoulders in place as Eira put black gloves on and gently picked up the hand chain, careful not to touch the bone. I flipped my hand, palm up, knowing what was about to happen, certain there was no use in fighting it. I didn't fear the bone.

The humming intensified to a deafening roar as she slowly stepped toward me. As the bone hit my palm, its energy buzzed through my veins, the humming rapidly accelerating until it reached my chest, and then it stopped abruptly and calmed.

Eira wrapped the intricate silver chain around my hand. I stilled for a moment before letting my hand drop, careful not to show any reaction. I slowly lifted my gaze to the dark king. His lips pursed for a moment and a hushed murmur moved throughout the crowd.

"What makes you think I won't use this to destroy you?" I asked, my voice sounding stronger than expected, as if I'd subconsciously harnessed the strength of the bone's power.

"You'll find I can be persuasive," Dark King Daimos mused.

"And I can change... almost anything, Daughter of Darkness. Even people." He chuckled, the sound raspy and grotesque. "I should also think you'd want to take more care, given our other guests," he continued, raising a hand to the back of the room.

Four slaves shuffled down the aisle carrying a chest of pure ice. Intricate carvings lined the sides, making it difficult to discern its contents despite its transparent properties. They made their way to the front of the throne room, where they gently set it down between myself and the dark king. I blinked rapidly as a sinking sensation flooded my gut, certain that whatever lay inside was about to break me.

The slaves lifted the heavy top, and a cry escaped my lips as I registered the severed head. Vacant blue eyes stared at me, frozen blood smeared across his face. Tears welled in the corner of my eyes as my heart thundered in my chest, the bone on my palm humming rapidly to the beat. Dark King Daimos watched me carefully, his eyes moving between my own and the bone on my palm, waiting.

Aeriden.

My rock. My hope. One of the few remaining tethers to my life before the wretched discovery. My brother was dead. I abandoned my own family trying to help Bear, and the dark king had gotten to Aeriden first. A storm of emotions crashed through me. Horror and devastation collided with the guilt raking at my heart. I fell to my knees with a cry, my wails echoing off the walls of the jeweled throne room.

Guests.

He said *guests*. Terror tugged at my chest, and I looked around frantically.

"Tauruk," the dark king's voice cut through my sobs as he gestured to the back of the throne room.

The crowd parted as a massive figure draped in red robes approached. He wore a white-furred mask with large, gray horns, its snout sprouting long, massive canines. Behind him, two soldiers marched a tall, black-haired man from the back of the room.

Dread unfurled inside of me as they threw my father on the pristine floor. An iron collar wrapped around his neck, and he watched me, horror strewn across his face. Hands shackled and chained to his collar, he struggled to his feet, reaching for me. My heart crashed as I moved to rush to him. Soldiers appeared by my side at once, holding me in place.

"Papa!" I cried, straining for him.

"Lyvia... I—"

He was cut off as a long, curved metal scepter flew through the air connecting with the side of his head. I screamed as he let out a gut-wrenching cry, crimson mist spraying from the side of his face. I thrashed in the guards' arms as the Tauruk swung it over his head and slashed it across his back. No. *No.*

I screamed. This couldn't be happening. Tears poured down my cheeks as I witnessed a nightmare unfold before my eyes.

"Please! Please!" I screamed frantically at the dark king.

His yellow eyes narrowed as he observed. I was lost in waves of hysteria and horror as the beating continued for what felt like ages.

The Tauruk finally stepped away from my father's limp body, and the guards' grip slackened. I ripped free and rushed to my father's side, cradling his head in my lap.

Blood.

So much blood. He was going to die. What was the point of all of this? Had Aeriden faced a similar death? My heart shattered as he groaned, fluttering one sapphire eye open while the other remained swollen shut. Bruises and burns covered his strong arms. Blood trickled down from his nose and lips. My fingers drifted to his neck. A weak, barely detectable pulse flickered under my fingers. He lay there on the floor utterly broken. Dying.

My father. Protector. Teacher. *Papa*. The strength of my life, shattered and nearly dead, all thanks to me. Guilt as sharp as the Tauruk's scepter scraped through my chest as rage cut through my heart. Rage at the dark king, at the Tauruk, at myself. It collided in my chest, and my arms shook as I pulled my father onto my lap.

Angry tears streamed down my face. The first real ones to fall since I'd found the onyx bone all those months ago. I squeezed it in my hand and willed something, anything to happen. *Please*, I begged it. I gripped my father's hand as my mind spun through the memories Enya had sent me, searching for a way to activate the bone. I could kill the king for this. I could destroy this place.

Please. Let me save him. The heavy bone hummed steadily on my skin, useless and inactive. I slammed it on the cold ground next to me. My father coughed, blood gurgling from his lips. Short breaths escaped my lips, and my wrath morphed into desperation as I turned to Dark King Daimos.

"What do you want from me?" I asked, hysteria driving the words to my lips as panic rose in my chest. "I'll do anything if you let him go. Please. *Please*." The last word came out a begging whimper.

"I'm glad to see you're more agreeable to working with me. If not, I'm afraid your father will be spending more time with the Tauruk," he replied, icy threat in his words.

The pool of blood my father lay in spread to the bottom of the Tauruk's long, crimson robes, like an extension of his garb. He was still. I couldn't see his eyes, but I could sense them on me. What *was* he? Man or creature? Or some combination? The threat shivered down my spine.

"We have much to discuss. But for now," he paused, clapping his hands, "a dinner, to honor our guest."

A scream left my lips as the guards ripped my father from my grip, and his eye fluttered open, registering my face again. Pain of a different kind painted his face as he mouthed my name and was dragged away. I reached for him, sobs racking me as I stared back at my brother's pale face. Grief threatened to consume me. Aeriden was dead. And my father... My father had been given a fate worse than death.

Eira shifted on her feet. I looked up and caught the briefest look of pity flash across her face. I coughed, sitting back on my heels as the slaves picked up the chest with Aeriden's head and retreated. The guard lifted my limp body to my feet, and Eira led the way to the feast at the back of the hall.

They plopped me beside Dark King Daimos, a place of honor, as his court dined, and he exchanged light conversation with others nearby. Numbness spread over my blood-soaked body like a blanket of snow. I stared at the plate before me, the decadent scent wafting up to my lips, churning the growing nausea in my gut. I didn't eat. My eyes drifted to the silverware in front of me, the knife inches from my blood-encrusted fingers. A wave of clarity and focus washed over me at the proximity of the weapon.

I lifted my gaze and placed my hands on the table. My fingers trembled. I could do it. I could kill him. He was distracted. I slowed my breathing, willing my heart to steady. It would have to be quick...

Soft, firm hands landed on my shoulder, and I froze. A young woman, breathtakingly beautiful with crystal eyes and white hair like the rest, pinned me with a gaze.

"Daughter of Darkness," she said quietly. "What an honor it is to have you here with us in Nivis, Land of Ice and Gems."

I eyed her coolly through puffy eyes, sliding my hand away from the knife on my plate.

"I am Selvina, niece of Great King Daimos," she said, nodding to the dark king next to me.

He shifted and returned her nod.

"I believe you met my brother."

Cyril. I glanced at the elf sitting at the end of the table. His murderous gaze hadn't left me since my arrival.

"I'm looking forward to getting to know you. And witnessing the powers you bring to us." Her eyes greedily drifted to my palm.

My hand closed over the bone in reflex. Her eyebrows raised at the movement, and I could see the glint of sharp, white teeth peek between two red lips. A creeping awareness settled over me as I realized she might be more dangerous than the man seated to my right.

"Pebble," she said, voice clipped, "it's time for the Daughter of Darkness to retire. Take her back to her room."

I glanced at the knife one last time. My last chance. Selvina pinned me to the spot with her glare as if daring me to pick it up. If she was anything like the other female elves I'd met, she'd be fast. Faster than me. And my father would suffer for it. I swallowed, placing my hands in my lap.

Eira led me back to my quarters where she undressed me and undid my hair in silence. She tugged a nightgown over my head as I stared blankly at the armoire, leaving the hand chain on me.

"I'm sorry. Take this to sleep," she whispered, handing me a vial of milky, violet liquid. "And call if you need anything."

"What is it?" I croaked, my voice sounding foreign. I wasn't sure I even cared.

"Essence of Nyxteria," Eira murmured. "If taken from the buds of the flower, it aids in sleep. Though it's wise to remember that a blossoming nyxteria becomes dangerous. One in full bloom, deadly."

She left.

I sat in the chair for hours, unable to look myself in the eye. *I did this.*

Aeriden was dead because of *me*. My father... I couldn't even think it. All because of me. Because of this fucking thing on my hand. I ripped at the chain until the hand bracelet came loose and chucked it to the corner. My shoulders racked with sobs for hours until my tears finally dried up. I downed the vial and lay down on the soft feather bed, crying dry tears. Grief consumed me as I stared at the sparkling ornate wall shimmering in the soft blue moonlight until all my thoughts and emotions disappeared into nothing. Sleep finally found me and brought with it a torrent of bloody images.

Aeriden's head in the chest and behind it, several more lined up as Cyril lifted them by the hair one by one. Bayne. Drystan. Father Marcus. Morwyn. Evony. Bear. Isla. Oslo. Marian. Even Ronan. And last, my father's, whose eyes blinked up at me, mouth gaping.

A cold voice echoed in my ears. This is your fault... You did this... You could have attended to your music lessons instead of digging in the dirt, you stupid girl.

The Tauruk was back, and now, he gouged out my father's eyes with tools I'd use at the digs. His scream mixed with mine. I thrashed, and he turned toward me...

Soft, firm hands found their way to my shoulder and the side of my head. I thrashed violently until the music pulled me from the nightmare, the melody slowing my panicked heart.

"Blossom of night where the stars shine bright.

It dances with moons in the shadowed snow dunes..."

Eira's soft voice filled the chamber as her hands continued their smooth stroking against my wet, sweaty head. The thundering of my heart slowed, and I blinked my eyes open, blurry from the tears I'd cried in sleep.

I took a shuddering breath as I turned to face her, unable to make out her features in the dark.

"What is that?" I asked, voice hoarse from screaming.

"The song of the midnight bloom. Our kingdom's beloved nyxteria." She gestured to the blossoms adorning the bedposts. My heart stilled. The melody was more than familiar.

"My mother sang this to me," I mumbled into the darkness. Eira froze.

"A coincidence, perhaps," she whispered. "Sleep, milady."

CHAPTER THIRTY-ONE

Any scholar who breaks from their order may be given as
tribute.
—Revision to The Official Tribute Edicts made by High
Priest Helmar, dated 37th of Winter, 045.3E, Private
Library in Mount Telum, Aedrialis.

The next four days were a nightmare on repeat. I spent the day weeping in my bed or bath, mourning the loss of my brother and the pain I caused my father, and searching the room for anything that could be used as a weapon, coming up empty every time. I was inevitably left staring at the Obscura Bone on my palm.

I stood in the center of the room, placing my hands the way I'd seen Bayne, Nerissa, and Isla do, willing something to happen. *Anything.* I replayed Isla's words over and over in my head those first few days on the *Evecta* when she'd tried to teach me how magic worked. I cursed myself for not paying better attention or being more interested... And for not grilling Bayne about it.

I'd been so focused on what I thought was important for our survival and finding Aeriden that I'd gotten consumed in hunting and physical combat, never suspecting I might need to learn how to wield the forgotten arts. I evaluated my small window as the white hawk flew past again. I could squeeze through it, but I couldn't find a way around the two-hundred-foot drop.

In the evenings, I was dressed and walked to court where Dark King Daimos had my father hauled out to be beaten in front of the crowd where I wept and pleaded with him. Every evening was a new form of torture. Whips, fire, bludgeons. The Tauruk didn't lack imagination.

The Crystal Court blandly observed, barely taking notice of the nightmarish torment, as if this were simply another evening with the dark king. The only ones who seemed the least bit interested were Dark King Daimos and Cyril. The former watched me closely, not paying much attention to what happened to my father. The latter reveled in his torment, eyes bouncing between me and my bleeding father, enjoying every second of it. Enjoying it *too* much. Selvina was scarce, lingering at the edge, hunting—stalking me like some invisible predator.

The nights had me retching on the floor in front of the many lords and ladies. I begged and pleaded with the dark king, promising to give him anything he wanted. He spoke not a word, only watched and examined my reactions as he waited. Waited for me to somehow use the deadly weapon on my palm. To react, in some way that triggered its powers. And I tried. I willed all my pain and feelings into the bone, and it sat, undisturbed, dozing on my palm. He'd eventually storm out, scowling.

Only then would the torture stop, and they'd drag my

father from the throne room. Every night, Eira coaxed the essence of nyxteria to my lips, and I laid in bed, eyes closed, the echo of my father's screams too loud to sleep. The little sleep that did find me was ridden with nightmares of blood and pain.

On the fourth night, as Eira undid the pins in my hair, she murmured into my ear, "Nivis is a land full of strength, milady. The people who come here, people who survive here, are the strongest in this world. Ice and gems only thrive in unforgiving environments. People are soft, fragile things. They only survive if they adapt to their surroundings. Evolve. Change. If they are to be unbreakable."

My puffy, tear-soaked eyes drifted up to find her deep blue eyes watching me.

"I am already broken," I said, voice raw and cracked.

Her light brows pinched, eyes full of pity. I looked away, despising it.

"How is he still living after all of this?" I croaked, staring at the bone that had grown rather quiet on my hand. "He can't endure much more. Can he?"

She stilled, swallowing before meeting my gaze.

"Come, let's get you in a tub. It will clear your mind."

I blinked. I'd already bathed before being dressed for the nightmare that met me at court a few hours prior.

"Come," she repeated, more forcefully this time, taking my hand. She led me to the bath, turning on the water and pulling over a stool. She placed a finger to her lips and perched on the edge of the tub, motioning for me to sit.

"There are rumors, milady," she whispered, barely audible over the fall of the water.

My stomach twisted at her tone. "Go on."

"Some believe King Daimos may be partially healing him each night. So, he may continue with the... activities."

Nausea slammed into me, and I hurled into the tub. He was torturing him to near death and healing enough of him to keep him alive to do it over and over again. My vision spun. This couldn't be happening. This wasn't my life. None of this would have happened if I hadn't found this fucking bone. I clawed at my left wrist, ripping the chain, amethysts flying across the room as I tore off the wristlet and threw the onyx bone across the room where it bounced into the corner. Eira flinched.

"I think... I think he's waiting for something to happen with you and the..." She paused.

I knew without looking at her she watched the bone.

I shook my head. "I don't know how to use it. I've tried. It's useless to me."

"It's not," she said, voice stronger than I'd heard it before. "It's not. If it's anything like what he has on his hands, it is a gift from the gods. And he is afraid to use it."

I paused at this and took a shuddering, deep breath. "What do you mean?"

"Think about it. His men could have taken the Obscura Stone and killed or left you. But they brought you *with*. King Daimos could have used it himself, added it to his collection, but he didn't. I think he believes you may be the only one that can use it. And he's keeping your father hostage so that when you figure it out, he'll have leverage over you and can control you, who controls *it*."

I turned to her, eyes wide, taken off guard with the conviction in her voice. Her deep blue eyes met mine with calm confidence. This was not a simpering slave, beaten down by years of oppression. She was not *Pebble*. I had the growing sense that the woman standing before me was more than she let on. Eira was a tumultuous river, a fighter. One that rolled over stones and pebbles below.

"You have to figure out how to use it," she said, gaze hard.

"We must free my father. If what you say is true, even if I figure out how to use it, he's right. I'll do anything for my father. To stop this. To keep him safe."

She shook her head. "You're not listening, milady. Your father is as good as dead. King Daimos is healing him enough to keep this tormenting cycle alive. You've seen what's been done to his body. Without the king's magic, he will die. He cannot *live* without King Daimos. There is no ending where he walks out of here alive."

My head shook in denial, my heart breaking at her words. I glanced at my left hand, feeling strangely naked without the bone.

"I must get to him. I have to at least try," I said softly.

Eira shifted on her feet and looked down.

"Can you help me?"

She met my gaze, brows pinched.

"Please," I begged softly.

She glanced around and sighed. "Let me see what else I can learn."

She walked to where the bone lay splayed on the ground, picking up the broken chains, careful not to touch the bone itself.

"What does it feel like to you?" I asked her as she cautiously returned.

She eyed it with an uneasy suspicion before placing it on the velvet pillow.

"Death," she said in a quiet voice. "It feels like... I want to stay as far away from it as possible." She glanced at me. "But that's not how it feels to you, is it?"

I shook my head. "No. It is..." I began, not entirely sure words could describe its feeling.

Eira tilted her head.

"He calls you Tynan's Accepted. Tynan, the god of death.

Feared by most. So much so he's only acknowledged one day every twenty-four years. Do you know why?"

I blinked, shaking my head.

"Because *we* fear it. Mortals are fragile things. Afraid of death, afraid of the Beyond. Let go of it, Lyvia. *Embrace* it. Tynan fears no one. And his power waits for you. All you need to do is reach out and grab it."

I met her eyes, the weight of her words heavy.

"I'll see if I can get the setting repaired discreetly. If King Daimos finds out you broke it, he might think you unlocked some sort of power in the process."

"Thank you," I murmured as she made her way to the door carrying the broken wrist chain. A sickening thought suddenly occurred to me as I eyed the tiny, interwoven circlets and gems making up the chain.

"Eira, wait," I said, standing to turn the faucet back on. "Leave the chain. Just get me a new one."

She surveyed me curiously, tilting her head.

"This is fortissa, right?" I asked, taking the broken chain from her.

She nodded in reply. The actual chain hadn't broken, just the delicate circles of silver that had held it together. I examined it, running my fingers over the smooth, intertwining circlets.

"Just tell them I need another one with sapphires." She nodded in reply and left without a word.

EIRA ARRIVED in my chambers the next morning with a second, exquisite wrist chain. I clipped the Obscura Bone inside before she fastened it to my hand.

"A bath, milady? To ease your nerves," she said, an eagerness to her voice.

"Yes," I murmured, trying to sound as broken as I felt and hide the small bit of hope she'd ignited in me after our conversation last night.

Eira drew the bath, and we sat on the edge of the porcelain tub.

"What did you find out?" I whispered, barely audible over the running water.

"Your father isn't being held in the dungeons. He's in the north tower, in a guarded chamber not far from King Daimos's quarters."

"Why wouldn't they keep him in the dungeons?"

She shushed me as my voice had grown louder. "He's too valuable of a prisoner to keep so far from the king. He wants him close. He *needs* him close to keep him alive after everything he's endured. King Daimos's power through the stones weakens with distance."

Bayne had said something to the same effect. His power over the ashen was less acute the further they roamed from Kayj. But it didn't explain how quickly he was able to heal me after my throat was slit. Unless he wasn't in Nivis or on Kayj when it happened.

"Is there a way to get to him?" I asked, whispering once more.

She nodded emphatically. "You may be able to use the Itherian corridors."

I narrowed my brows in question.

"Hundreds of years ago, even before King Daimos, the king of this castle enslaved Itherians. They were small, winged creatures that did everything we slaves do today—cooked, cleaned, changed the linens, anything that could be done without engaging with the elves."

"What happened to them?" I asked, allowing a bit of quiet curiosity.

"The tale goes that a young Queen Olienna freed them. She took off the same night their wings were magically repaired, and they disappeared into the night."

Olienna... The seer was a queen of Nivis.

She continued, "They were not to be seen or heard by anyone. For that reason, they moved about the castle through small corridors between the towers and halls. Nearly all the entrances have been destroyed, many of the tiny halls caved in or sealed off. Except a few..."

She paused, looking around as if we were being watched.

I nodded at her to go on.

She continued in a barely audible voice, "Except a few in the north and northeastern towers."

"There's nothing here," I assured her, disappointment sinking in my gut. There were no doors in my chambers. I'd searched for an escape the last few days, and I would have found something if there had been.

She shook her head. "None in here. But there is one that leads from the infirmary to the old queen's chambers. I'm not sure why it exists, but it was rediscovered by the healer slaves only a few years ago. We've no reason to report its existence. If we did, we'd likely be lashed and accused of using it, so it's best kept a secret. No one uses it for fear of that reason."

"But how can I get there?" I cut in, shaking my head. "Even if I faked an injury or a fainting spell, wouldn't the dark king just heal me?"

"Yes, you're right. Which is why you aren't going as you. We switch places. I'll find another collar, and we'll swap. The kitchens say your father gets one meal a day. It should only take a small bribe to get the slave making the delivery that day to take it to the infirmary instead of your father's chambers.

You go there, take the tunnels to the queen's old chambers, and his room should be around the corner and down the hall. There will be guards, but they'll be expecting you. They won't look twice since you'll have this around your neck." She yanked at the iron chain hanging down her chest.

"Why not come directly from the kitchens?" I asked as she shook her head at me.

"Too many eyes. Someone is bound to notice you. And while we generally have each other's backs, some of us are more beaten down than others and any chance of gaining the king's favor may mean the difference between their family spending the winter in the slaves' quarters in the castle grounds or out there, in the Albyrn Mountains."

I studied her face. If I could trust her, this could work. I had to see my father. And maybe there was some way I could help him escape... I could smuggle him into these corridors, and he could hide out there. I tried not to let hope slip inside my heart.

"Why are you helping me?" I asked softly.

Eira pulled her ocean gaze from mine and swept it over the walls of the ornate room.

"I think you are our one chance at changing the fate of the Kingdom of Ice and Gems." Her gaze fell on mine once more. "There are texts in the libraries below that speak of this once being the greatest kingdom in history. You can see the wealth." She gestured to the walls clad with silver and gold, embedded with gems. "What's happening on Kayj won't only destroy our frozen sanctuary—it will destroy the Vael."

"You know about the ashen," I said, "Do you know how many he has?"

Her face crumpled in pain as she said, "Yes, I know about them."

"Did you lose someone to him?"

Her face twisted in fury. "My entire clan was taken. All but myself and my sister. We weren't always slaves."

Horror roiled in my gut. "How does he do it?"

She shook her head. "No one knows. A spell perhaps. And I have no idea how many he has. But that's not what I'm talking about on Kayj."

Dread pitted in my gut. What else could he be doing? What was worse than an army of undead?

"What—" I began as a thunderous knock sounded at the door.

Later, she mouthed before hurrying off.

I PACED my room for the remainder of the day, jumping at any sound of movement outside of my door. The sun made its way across the sky, the white mountain casting a massive shadow against the castle. Eira returned shortly after noon.

She lifted a heavy, iron collar from under the tray she carried. "You'll have to be fast," she whispered. "And this won't sit on your neck quite right. It's meant to be locked in with a hammer and nail, but once it's locked, it's almost impossible to remove."

I glanced at her neck. Worn, calloused skin marred the areas where the iron rubbed, never having been removed. Her eyes found mine, and I quickly looked up.

"So, it would be best to draw as little attention to yourself as possible. Be small. A grain of sand, a flake of snow, a—"

"A pebble," I finished for her.

She nodded and gave me a half grin. "Yes," she said, "a pebble. Are you ready?"

I shook my head. "No. I'm not. But I need to do this."

We hastily swapped garments. The black slave's dress and

headpiece were cold and itchy. I grimaced as I pulled it over my shoulders while she slipped the silk gown over her head.

She fastened the collar around my neck with a small piece of string hidden behind the headpiece. I glanced in the mirror. If you looked close enough, you could see it didn't sit right. I'd have to keep my head down, literally. The weight of it pressed uncomfortably into my collarbone and scratched at my fresh scar. I bristled at the touch.

I turned to Eira, whose loose bleach-blonde hair hung in large waves down her back. She shone in the stunning silk day gown. The iron collar around her neck was an ugly ink splot on an otherwise flawless painting. She took my shoulders in her hands.

"Be quick," she whispered. "As we discussed. Head down. Or it won't just be your father who is entertaining the court tonight." Her hands shook against my shoulders, and she quickly pulled them away.

I gave her a firm nod and slowly slipped from the room.

CHAPTER THIRTY-TWO

My heart grieves to learn of the death of my brother. He'd been so lost since leaving the Death Scholar order. His wife remains missing, though Stynguard patrols continue their search.

— Journal of Father Marcus, dated 71st of Autumn, 048.3E. Aedrialis.

I kept my head down as I quietly closed the door behind me, not daring to look at the two guards standing outside my chambers. Eyes on the floor, I followed the steps down two levels. I passed two doors as I moved through the halls before turning left down a narrow corridor and into the infirmary. Tables laden with ancient medical supplies filled the space. The dark king must have had the healing bone long enough that they didn't need updated supplies. Or perhaps he didn't care.

My eyes caught on the tray of food left next to the fireplace. I picked it up and began running my fingers along the walls of the north side of the infirmary. Eira said it would feel like an invisible divot on the third set of bricks. One... two... there. I felt along the divot and pushed in. *Click.*

A tiny door cracked open. I felt the familiar surge of excitement at finding something old and forgotten from long ago. It was replaced by sudden anxiety as I crawled into the small space, pushing the tray quietly in front of me. The last time I'd been in a small space like this, I'd been in another fortress with Vulcan ushering me forward and Oslo trying to keep me calm. I slowed my breathing thinking of them. I got out then. I'd get out now.

This tunnel was somehow larger. Once in, I only had to crouch down but could stay on my feet as I shuffled through. The creatures who had used this long ago—the Itherians—must have been small. What had happened to them once freed?

I padded along the tiled floor softly. Although the tunnel was dirty from years of disuse, it was finished. My fingers traced lines through the thick layer of dust on the plastered walls. I held the small lit taper to the walls as I walked. In different circumstances, I would have stayed and studied the art. Winged creatures danced and glided across a snowy scenery. They were meant for the sky, the open air. These corridors would have been suffocating.

The tunnel ended abruptly. I quietly unlatched the door from the inside, peeking out as a slit of light shone into the tiny corridor I'd come from. Seeing no one, I stepped into the old queen's chambers, head on a swivel. It appeared to be deserted.

I hurried to the door leading to the hall and stepped into it.

I bowed my head and held the tray neatly in front of me as I walked timidly, yet dutifully down the hall toward the door with a single guard standing outside.

"You're late, muck," he growled as I approached.

I kept my head bowed and dipped my chin in apology. He grunted in reply and swung the door open. My heart hammered in my chest as I stepped inside and set the tray down on a nearby table without looking at the floor where my father lay. I turned to the guard, eyes still pinned to the floor.

"His Excellency wishes him to arrive bathed for this evening's activities," I quietly said, curving my voice to match the Nivis accent as best I could.

The guard swore in response.

"Well, be quick with it, muck. And close the door. I don't want to see the bastard's gray pisser."

I nodded my head, my face flushed with venom as I quietly closed the door. My heart hammered in my chest. I slowly turned around, keeping my eyes away from my father. The stench of old blood, vomit, and urine mingled in a single sickening breath, and I swallowed the nausea that rose. I kept my eyes down and walked to the bath where I drew the water.

I allowed myself four heartbeats. Finally, I turned to face my father, and my heart shattered. Ragged, broken, and bleeding, he lay curled up on one side in the center of the room on an elaborate rug. They hadn't even bothered to lay him on the bed in the corner. And he hadn't the strength to pull himself up onto it. His clothes were shredded and stained with fresh and old, crusty blood. I slowly walked to his side and knelt. I laid my hand on his arm, and he flinched, letting out a soft, broken whimper. Tears welled in my eyes, and I knew in that moment what I would need to do. He was beyond saving.

"Papa, it's all right. It's me," I whispered, little droplets of salty wetness falling on my hands as I pulled him back toward me. "It's Lyvi, Papa."

He turned his swollen, purple face toward me. Tiny slits of brilliant blue peered at me through his puffy black eyelids. My own swelled as tears poured out of them and onto his face.

"Badg... Badger," he croaked. His breath reeked of stale blood and rotting teeth. "I'm sorry, Lyvi," he breathed, "The tea... not what they thought..."

"I know, Papa. It's okay. I know you didn't give me the elixir," I cut him off with choked words.

"So... sorry," he repeated, and my chest caved in.

Tears stung my eyes as I wiped them away.

"Truth hidden... From you... Not what it seems. *You* are not what you seem..." His voice shook through his ragged breathing.

"What do you mean, Papa?" I choked out, snot and tears now covering my face and his.

I tried to lift him up, and my fingers caught the deep slice of skin between his vertebrae. *Oh gods...*

"Mes... Message. The Sea Sp... Spear. White... The moons. The s... the sun," he continued.

My heart sank. He was delirious, his mind crumbling.

"Hurry up, wench," growled the guard from outside.

"N... No... t-time," my father stuttered, "Elp... Elp... is... point—"

My shoulders shook as I sobbed, holding his head in my lap. He could barely speak. *Help is pointless.* Was that what he was trying to tell me? I had seconds, and I needed to get out of here.

"Papa, I've come to say goodbye," I said as I gently tilted the vial of the nyxteria sleeping draft. He choked it down, groaning as it hit his throat. I hummed the soft melody of the flower as his breathing slowed. I quietly pulled the fortissa chain out of my pocket and whispered, "And set you free. I love you."

I took a steadying breath, steeling myself and allowing the memories of the past four nights to fly through my mind in a tortuous replay. I wrapped the fortissa chain around his neck twice and pulled the two ends as hard as I could.

I tore my eyes away and focused on the painting that stretched across the wall. A fresco of the gods, Aelius, Ganmira, and Renova standing over the planet of Vael, Tynan below, arms outstretched in a cloud of darkness. The god of death watched me.

My father's limp body thrashed for what felt like an eternity, trying to escape the chain. I was going to be sick. I would burn for this. A darkness clouded my soul as the seconds ticked by slower than ever.

Suddenly, the thrashing stopped, and his body convulsed for several seconds. Adrenaline rushed through my veins as my heart pumped blood like a burst dam. His body went still. I held tight for a few more seconds, and it jerked once. I loosened my grip, hand sliding to his wrist.

Warm blood stilled beneath his pulseless skin. My vision blurred, and my heart stopped as something inside me shattered.

I killed my father. My *father*. Strangled him with a fortissa chain. A distinct memory hovered like a wraith nearby... My father showing me how to hold the light chain in my hands atop his stallion as a young child, giggling as we bounced along the streets of the capital, getting looks from other lords and ladies. A shake of the head from a priest walking by. My father pinched my side, a raucous laugh escaping my lips and the agrippa jogged in place before taking off at a gallop. The vision commanded my attention, lingering center stage in my consciousness, haunting me.

I fell onto him as sobs shook me, and I broke inside. This had undone me. I deserved whatever hell awaited me from this day forward. The sin I had committed was beyond forgiving.

I would burn.

Burn, burn, burn, burn.

I *deserved* to burn for this.

My hands shook wildly as I gripped his bloody, scorched jacket. Nothing mattered anymore. Not the bones, not the prophecy, not getting out of here alive. Nothing. I didn't care what Dark King Daimos or King Saros did. I wanted to die. I wanted nothing to do with any of it. I wanted to disappear. I wanted to float back on that river of air that carried me through time and space. Where I had no cares or feelings. No memories. No existence. I was as alone as that boy on the ship.

I sat there, quietly crying into his chest for minutes. Distantly, I heard the guard bark something from behind the door.

And then, the strangest sensation washed over me. The humming of the Obscura Bone and the singing and beating of the other two bones in the castle collided together in an enchanting sensation. The most beautiful sound I'd ever heard. And I wasn't quite hearing it. I was *feeling* it. It pulled me out of my head and back into the chamber.

It sent my mind chasing after sunshine. After memories of Bayne's fingertips tracing lines along my arms. Of Drystan's encouraging smile when I'd unlocked the puzzle. Of Evony's laughter after I'd missed the target and nearly skewered the rooster, sending it flying through the barn. Of Isla laughing and dancing with Ronan as they glided across the deck of the *Evecta*. Of Tiberius's soft nicker before I swung onto his back and galloped outside of the walls of the capital. Of Oslo's reassuring grin as he helped me cut up vegetables in the kitchen. Of Aquila's eyes and his subtle nod, which I now knew was his way of saying hello. And finally of Bayne's gaze. The intensity of it. The calm confidence and determination. I let it drift to Enya. And the command she'd given me.

Get up.

I had to go. I had to get up and go. I unwound the chain from his neck, tucking it into my pocket. I hurried to the bath where I dumped the tray of food, turned off the faucet, and toweled off the tears from my face. I took two deep, shuddering breaths and picked up the empty tray.

Face down and eyes locked on the steps in front of me, I moved down the hall without a word. The door closed and locked as I walked away. My heart hammered in my chest as I passed through the queen's abandoned chambers and into the Itherian corridor where I broke into a bent over, shuffled run and ditched the tray. I quietly stepped into the deserted infirmary, sending up a silent prayer of thanks that I hadn't run into anyone yet.

A different guard stood watch outside my chambers and I waited, hands crossed behind me as they shook out of control, and he unlocked the door. I stepped inside, eyes focused on the floor. The door clicked shut, and I hurried to the bathing chamber.

Eira had the water running as I hurled into the toilet, repeatedly. I wept and wretched nonstop until I collapsed on the floor with nothing left in my stomach. I stared at the beautiful wall, tears trickling down my face. Eira didn't say a word, somehow knowing what I'd done. Her fingers sent ripples through my hair. After a few minutes, she coaxed me into the tub while she donned her slave garments.

"In the Kingdom of Ice and Gems, when we lose a loved

one, we light an ice candle so that the stars may find him in the darkness below."

I barely heard her as the screaming in my head returned. A dark evil had crept its way into my heart. Shame and guilt and hatred rippled through my chest. And the words of the dark king echoed like a cursed chorus in my mind.

Daughter of Darkness.

Tynan's Accepted.

CHAPTER THIRTY-THREE

General Oslo Archer, age thirty-eight. Last seen in Stynguard. Wanted for murder of a commanding officer, destruction of ship, and desertion.
   —Wanted Poster. 65th of Autumn, 048.3E. Aedrialis.

Two hours later, I sat unfeeling as Eira wound my hair into a simple twist. Less elegant than previous nights, somehow more reserved, subtle. Suitable for mourning. She dressed me in a velvet ebony gown, so devoid of life and light, a perfect match to the darkness tumbling down inside of me.

The frozen taper stick she brought along was indeed made of ice, carved into an intricate, swirling design with beautiful snowflakes and stars. In the center sat a white wax candle she'd lit after placing it on my windowsill. A flap of wings sounded beyond the window followed by the trill of the snowy white hawk.

I couldn't bring myself to look at it. Nor could I look at the two moons shining in through the window that evening, not deserving to gaze upon our goddesses after the sin I'd committed. My heart was hollow. And I deserved anything coming to me this evening. In fact, I hoped the Tauruk would be set loose on me.

Eira did not speak until we stood, readying for our trip to the throne room. She grasped my shoulders and peered into my eyes which were still on the floor. She gave my shoulders a shake until I dragged my dead gaze up to hers.

"Listen to me, Lyvia of Sultira. You gave your father a gift. *Mercy*. How many more nights could you have endured watching him suffer? How many more nights could *he* have endured without completely losing his mind?"

The cloud of darkness in my mind struck like a viper, a barrage of guilt slicing through me.

"Look at me!" she yelled. "It doesn't matter anymore. They will know that I helped you. I will not see you again after tonight."

Dread slammed into me. I hadn't even thought about what this would do to her. Of course, they would know she helped me. Who else could have?

"I'm sorry, Eira. If I had figured out how to use this damned thing—" I began, holding up my left palm with the onyx bone.

She shook her head vehemently. "Don't do that, Lyvia. Even if you had figured out how to use it, King Daimos would still have held your father captive to control you. You will eventually unleash its power, but you will need to learn how to control it. And that will take time. More time than you had to save him."

I gazed at her, vision blurry from the tears welling in my puffy eyes.

"They say the strongest glaciers cannot be melted by the

sun. Even when the warmest summers blaze, melting the caps of our white mountains, the glaciers simply shine right back at that blazing ball of fire. Be strong, Lyvia. Be a glacier. And don't let him hold me over your head when we walk into that throne room tonight because he will try. We are not friends. I am a slave.

"He wants you to be the Daughter of Darkness, but you are not its daughter. You are its *queen*. Be the Queen of Darkness. And when you inevitably unleash Tynan's power, the power of shadows, and night, and death, do not fear it. Command it."

I blinked tears away at the conviction in her words.

"Thank you, Lyvia of Sultira, Bonder of Bellators, Prophesized One. I can almost *see* the spark of your flame. It was my honor to have known you, *sobraen*." She took my right hand, kissing the top of it.

For the briefest moment, a small bit of warmth bloomed in my chest. I pinched my brows, replaying Nerissa's words that night in Aedrialis. An awareness crept through me, and I could have sworn the bone in my palm reacted, humming encouragingly. Eira dropped my hand and turned swiftly on her heels.

A swath of guards marched us to the throne room. Four more than the usual two that flanked us. They eyed me suspiciously, glancing at my hands. Word of my father's death had gotten out, and they knew the two of us were to blame.

We stepped into the massive throne room, empty, save for Dark King Daimos, the Tauruk, Cyril, and Selvina. Looks of contempt etched the faces of all except the dark king. His yellow eyes locked on my hand as we walked up the aisle. I opened my palm to him, displaying the powerful bone.

He dragged his eerie eyes up to mine, fury now coating his features. "How?" His deep voice was quiet and predatory.

"How, what?" I asked, determined to keep my voice from shaking.

The wrath that erupted shook the entire throne room, leaving the chandelier trembling above us. The guards stepped back. Everyone but Selvina cowered beneath his bellow of fury. I could see Eira from the corner of my eye. Without looking at her, I knew she stood tall, not pulling her gaze from the king's face. I felt a lifeline to her then, a surge of strength and courage that I couldn't explain, and I lifted my chin.

"You know exactly what. And I will not repeat myself," he said, so softly it stiffened my spine.

My mouth clamped shut. He gave a subtle nod to the Tauruk who moved on Eira. I stepped toward her out of instinct.

"I used the Obscura Stone," I said hastily. "You armed me with one of the deadliest weapons known to this world. Did you think I wouldn't use it?"

"Lies," he whispered.

The Tauruk held Eira with her arms pinned behind her. Her defiant, ocean eyes didn't meet mine, refusing to pull them from the dark king. A soft chuckle left his lips.

"Why don't you use it now?" he said mockingly.

The Tauruk gripped Eira's collar and slammed her to the floor, a quiet sound escaping her lips before he began to beat her. I stepped toward her and paused, remembering her words. But I *couldn't*. I couldn't sit here and watch her be tortured and tormented like my father. I couldn't bear any of it any longer. I threw everything into the bone on my hand, squeezing it until the fortissa chain ripped into my palm, *willing* anything to happen. It sat quiet and cold, humming quietly and timidly, as if confused.

My heart hammered in my chest, my fists shaking with frustration and fury. I ran at the Tauruk, throwing everything I had learned from Bayne at him. Barely caught off guard, he dropped his grip on Eira. I caught him with a jab below the horrifying mask, where I thought his neck might be, and barreled into him. He staggered back a step before his gloved fist met with my gut, and the other swung upward beneath my chin. I coughed up blood, spitting it as my head flew back and pain-ridden stars danced behind my eyes.

"Enough," commanded the king.

Guards hauled me up from the ground, and I blinked my eyes open, gut sinking as they landed on Eira, now in the arms of Cyril.

He drew the same dagger, fangs of silver stretching between his left hand and the beautiful golden gem shining in the moonslight coming through the massive windows in the throne room. Cyril pressed it against her neck, above her iron collar. Eira finally looked at me. Unwavering certainty shown in her eyes. She blinked away a single tear before giving me a soft smile.

Eira moved so fast I might have thought her Nerissa. She grabbed Cyril by the wrist and sliced the dagger into her neck so deep and fast it cleaved through her esophagus. A scream ripped from my throat as utter horror roiled in my gut. I slumped in the grip of the guards.

The dark king surveyed me with a look of disdain and waved a hand to a slave in the corner. "Clean up this filth."

His gaze slid to Cyril, annoyance stretching across his features. Cyril returned it with his own look of defiance as he bared his teeth.

"I told you she isn't worthy of it, Your Grace," Cyril said, turning to Dark King Daimos. "She mourns the *dirt*." He gestured to Eira's limp body. "And she cannot use it! You've seen that now. Give it to me. I swear I can wield one just as well." Cyril shot a lethal look at his sister. "It should stay in the royal bloodline. She has nothing to do with the prophecy. Human filth. She's as low as the rest of them. Lower than these." He spat on Eira's body, moon-blue light reflecting off the blood pooling beneath her black dress.

Dark King Daimos surveyed me and cocked his head.

"Very well."

My mouth dropped in shock. Surprise flashed across Cyril's face, followed by cruel greed, the corners of his lips twitching. Selvina was silent but eyed her brother with a look of disregard.

"And this one?" Cyril asked, jerking his head as he stalked toward me. He ripped the bone off my palm, flinching. I could hear the bone humming *not yours, not yours*. His eyes shot to mine, and the corner of my lips twitched. He knew. He could feel the stone pushing him away. He threw me a sneer before turning back to the dark king.

"Do with her what you will," the dark king murmured indifferently.

My stomach twisted. Cyril's eyes snaked up my body.

"Collar her," he commanded without looking back.

My spine locked up, and I jerked, trying to pull out of the guards' arms. Orders were barked, and a tall slave approached with an iron collar. He timidly met my eyes as if in apology. The heavy, cold collar clamped around my neck, iron biting into my collarbones. This time, it *clicked*, locking into place, my sentence dealt.

The sharp permanence of it weighed down my shoulders and sank into my gut, but it somehow steadied me. Grounded me. My heart slowed, and the naked skin on my palm felt suddenly cold. Clarity bloomed in my chest as a new purpose cleared my mind. The slave's eyes slid up to meet mine once more. I smiled at him before he was shoved to the side, and I was marched to Cyril's ship.

———⚬———

GREAT PLUMES of deep purple and gray storm clouds gathered over the island of Kayj during the quick hour-long sail away from the snowy, mountainous landscape of Nivis, now veiled in the dark blues of night. I felt the familiar, ominous presence of the Mortis Shroud before it appeared in the distance, barely visible. It wound and swirled in the air above the water before pausing, as if watching us as we drifted by.

Chained to the back of Cyril's horse, we took the road leading through the slave camps and mines up to a massive, black fortress. The sharp whistle of whips and resounding screams mingled with the moans of dying slaves. Men and women of all races and ages gawked at the sight of a human dressed for court with an iron collar to match their own.

Covered in bruises and soot, several of them placed their thumbs to their lips, murmuring, "Sisters protect you." I did my best to hold my head high and keep up with the horses I walked behind, stumbling through the frigid muck in the soft slippers Eira had slid on my feet.

Torchlit entrances to tunnels dotted the dark hillside where tributes pushed wheelbarrows full of gems and rock, dumping them in large wagons guarded by whip-wielding men in silver suits. My eyes drifted further up the hill, not far from the fortress, where several guards stood watch at another entrance in the hill, without a slave in sight. No one stepped past the invisible line of demarcation drawn around that barren hill. A soft yellow glow snaked from its entrance, eerily similar to the irises of the dark king.

A blood-curdling wail echoed off the black stone of the fortress ahead, sending chills up my spine. I jerked to the left, searching the forested hills, dark and ominous below the ancient storm swirling overhead. Another lurid scream followed in its wake. *Ashen.* My eyes darted through the trees, watching for any sign of bloodless limbs. I looked ahead and caught Cyril watching me atop his gray mare. A sinister grin formed on his lips.

"They're out there, *paedor*," he said, voice laced with threat.

Paedor. The elven word for dirt, filth, I'd learned. I smiled inwardly, laughing at the irony of the name. I'd spent my life in the dirt and filth. And it was perhaps one of my favorite places to be. Memories with Drystan and Father Marcus brushed away a tendril of rising fear.

My legs burned by the time we reached the entrance to the fortress in the middle of the island's hills. Ominous black towers stretched high into the sky, piercing the violent storm clouds above. *This* was where I'd imagined the dark king on his throne. The *Onyx Tower*. Not the castle of ice and beauty we'd left behind in the north.

A thick, sturdy chain hung from my collar, rusty from use. A guard jerked it forward, the iron biting into the back of my neck, and I followed quickly as we entered the black gates. Darkness loomed in the massive entry hall lined with rows of ebony pillars and dimly lit sconces. A chill breeze snaked its way through the labyrinth of aisles.

Cyril murmured something to the guard, who nodded in return. He turned his light brown eyes toward me and once again greedily slid them down the now torn and muddied gown. The thought of what might happen next hovered in the dark. The guard jerked me forward, and I reluctantly followed, climbing a set of narrow stairs.

We passed small windows as the staircase wound higher up the dark tower. The storm crashed outside, allowing a cold sprinkle to snake its way inside the walls. I willed my pounding heart to calm, my mind searching for any strand of hope to hold on to.

My thoughts snagged on Morwyn's words from months prior. *Somewhere in the world, something good is happening.* I breathed in the cool mist, closing my eyes for a moment, pretending I was on the *Evecta*, riding the rolling waves of the Juniper Sea as a spindrift rushed up to meet my face. Bayne's eyes were as bright as the emeralds in the walls of the Crystal Castle. Nerissa's cool gaze drifted to mine where she stood at the helm. The others were there with Drystan and Father Marcus. Aquila swooped down from above, his strong wings blowing a gust of wet air in my direction. The thought of the Ravindras and their bond stirred a foreign feeling in my heart. Without thinking, I leaned into it, throwing everything I had into the strange sensation lingering in my chest. It disappeared as quickly as it had materialized. The dank cold of the staircase returned in an instant, and we continued our march up the tower.

The guard shoved me into a room off the stairwell and, to my horror, chained me to a four-post bed at the center of the chamber before making his exit. My senses tingling, I looked around the room frantically for anything I could use as a weapon. My shackled hands clanked as they tugged on the chain.

A few soft tapers glowed near the door. The walls were lined with the heads of beasts ranging from stags to massive white bears and reptilian-looking wolves I'd never seen before.

A glint of silver caught my eyes as I followed their leering, vengeful faces.

I squinted in the darkness at the chain-like ornaments hanging from the ceiling. Nausea slammed into me as I realized what they were.

Collars.

CHAPTER THIRTY-FOUR

*I'm beginning to worry about Lyvia's ability to locate exca-
vation sites. Luck seems to have nothing to do with it.*

*—Journal of Father Marcus, dated 2nd of Summer,
069.3E. Aedrialis.*

A curse escaped my lips in a breath. I was to become his
plaything, and then, I was going to die. My collar
would join the rest of his trophies on the ceiling.
My heart fluttered out of control in my chest, like a bird
trapped below deck.

I jumped at the sound of the door clicking open, the rings
on my chain clanking against the post of the bed. Cyril stepped
in and slowly latched the lock on the door. He turned to face
me, a look of lustful possessiveness etched across his features.
Some primal part of me sent adrenaline rushing through my
veins.

My fists clenched in an attempt to stop shaking. He stalked

to the corner of the room where he picked up a small grape between his thumb and pointer finger, lips twitching as he eyed the fruit before placing it on the small table. He lifted the lid of a small container of some type of powder and examined its contents, poking the tip of his pinky inside. His eyes slid to my face and neck, as if in consideration, before closing the lid and pouring himself a glass of dark brown liquid. He swirled it before taking a slow sip, eyes dipping to my chest.

"I take my time with the whores of Sultira," he began. "A perk of King Saros's tribute. We only need a few hundred to man the mines. The others are caged in and... well, you know." A sickening grin slid onto his face. "Still, when they don't die immediately or tear each other apart in the process of... changing..."

The word made me pause. *Changing.* The ashen, of course, but something nagged at me. My mind snapped back before I could think about it further.

"No one notices the loss of a few able-bodied females in the herd."

Horror roiled in my gut.

"Humans are useless filth. You will *all* serve us again, someday." He played with the fortissa chain holding the Obscura Bone in place on his left palm. A flicker of discomfort passed over his features before taking a step toward me.

"They all die in the end. Sometimes, we get to have a bit of fun before that happens," he whispered.

My hair stood on end as I attempted to steady my breathing.

"Not what I'd expect from the Prince of Darkness," I said, steeling myself. "But I suppose you aren't one, are you? A prince, I mean."

He stepped forward and brought the back of his hand across my cheek so fast that the gems on the fortissa chain holding the Obscura Bone in place ripped through my skin. A trickle of blood dribbled down my chin. A small voice inside of me whispered, *You deserve this*. He flexed his hand, wincing as the Obscura Bone rubbed against his palm.

"Maybe I'll start our games by taking an eye." His hand drifted to my cheek.

I flinched upon contact. He stepped close, breath laced with alcohol moistening my skin.

"Or maybe a hand," he threatened, as he held up his right arm. "There's no one coming for you, *paedor*. Your friends weren't happy when I slit your throat. You should have seen the look on his face when Talon drew a dark line across your neck. The blood was," he paused, a sinister grin appearing on his face as his eyes flicked to the dagger on his belt. *Talon*.

"Well, he knew there was too much blood for you to stand a chance at surviving. That Lotrennian rat with the ink on his face made a mess of my guards. And the other," he grimaced, voice shaking with pure loathing.

He paused. I kept my gaze on his eyes, not far from the color of my own, a light caramel. I reeled at the likeness.

"Let's just say, as we proceed, know that the pieces of you I send to him will do more than deliver a message. They will destroy him, bit by bit. And I will enjoy every moment of it."

My heart pumped wildly as I succumbed to the fear winding its way into my chest.

"Before I start cutting pieces away, however," his prying eyes drifted to my chest, and lower, "I plan on enjoying my prize."

Without thinking, I jerked my shackled wrists up, ready to slam them into his jaw, but was too close for the maneuver to work. I knew that, but instinct drove the movement. He caught my wrists, grinning wildly.

"Still a little fight in you," he said hoarsely. "We can fix that."

Dread unfurled in my chest as Cyril's forehead collided with my nose. Pain lanced through my face. I staggered back, eyes watering, as he wrestled me to the cold stone ground. He was atop me before I knew what was happening. His hand groped up my mud-stained gown, tearing at the bodice. I kicked and shoved at him, trying to wiggle out from underneath his heaviness. I flinched as I felt wet warmth on my neck, where his lips and tongue slid over the scar he'd left days before.

No. No. No.

Cyril was strong considering he was missing a hand. He gripped my shackles and pinned them over my head as he trespassed over my body with his mouth. The Obscura Bone hummed rapidly in his hand. I could feel its panicky rhythm picking up pace to match that of my heart. My hands flexed, reaching for it, for any lifeline as panic took root. I struggled, forgetting all my training. Sharp teeth sunk into the skin on my breast and I let out a piercing cry. Blood dribbled down my side as I bucked and thrashed beneath him.

He reached his crimson-dripping mouth to mine, and I reeled against the taste of my own blood, snapping at him. He had me pinned beneath his body, knees digging into my thighs and his stumped forearm pressing into my chest while his hand ripped through my dress.

An icy chill ran along my bare back I was sure had nothing to do with the temperature of the room. I yanked at my collar, and his fist met my cheek. He undid his pants, and fear like none I had ever experienced slammed into me. He came at me from behind, hand and stump grappling for my waist and hips. I felt the Obscura Bone slide viciously around my inner thigh, and I grabbed at his hand with mine, forcing my fingers into the various loops of the fortissa chain wrapped around his hand as he tried to force himself on me. The bone hummed wildly as I gripped it in my hands, ripping it free from the fortissa chain with all my strength.

Cyril let out of cry of wrath, pausing his attempted attack. I clenched my fist around the bone as he tried to pry it from my fingers in a rage.

"GIVE IT TO ME!" he bellowed.

I clamped my other hand over it and tucked them both to my chest.

Stars danced behind my eyes as he slammed my face into the bedpost before stalking to the wall of weapons and withdrawing a short sword. He raised it above his head and brought it down across my back, slicing a line down my ribs. I screamed, arching in pain, tightening my grip on the bone.

"You are a waste of my time," he hissed and brought the blade up once more. He shook, his eyes bursting with a lust for murder. In that moment, I knew the blow that would follow would kill me. The Obscura Bone hummed hysterically against my palm, and suddenly, I could feel it in my heart. Instinct raised my hands to shield my face as Cyril swung toward my head, and I threw my entire being into the frantic humming against my palm.

My mind's eye flashed between what I saw in this tower on Kayj and a battlefield of ash. I was met with a tumultuous current of magic, racing up and down my spine, through my veins, and swirling in my head. Time stood still for a moment as Cyril's blade sliced through the air toward my chest and a warrior screamed in battle, her eyes ablaze.

Cyril's rage-filled eyes met mine for a heartbeat, and fear quickly replaced a sudden realization. I pulled myself back into the tower, and as flame ignited in my chest, shock waves radiated from my left palm as clouds of vaporous black reached for him. Terror rippled across his face before they completely devoured him. The darkness disappeared after an instant, and his blade fell to the ground upon a pile of soft black ash where Cyril had stood.

I staggered back, collar catching on the bedpost as I fell to the floor. I stared at my hand, now shaking uncontrollably, where I'd gripped the Obscura Bone.

There, in its place, seared into my palm was an eight-pointed star. It burned, skin blistering and smoking like a fresh brand. Rivers of black ran down my arm and fingers, pooling at the center of the star. I stared as they shifted and danced, slowly disappearing, one by one, until all that remained was the fresh brand on my palm, glowing white and iridescent.

I sat there for several heartbeats, staring at my palm, feeling the magic of the Obscura Bone humming contentedly in my chest. My hands shook as I took in my surroundings and the magnitude of what happened hit me. I killed Cyril.

I didn't just kill him. I *obliterated* him. The rings and jewels from his coat remained, glinting in the large pile of black ash. No bones. No flesh. This was my chance. I had to get out of here. I shifted closer to his remains and caught my reflection in the floor-to-ceiling mirror across the room.

I stared at myself for a moment, the stillness of shock spreading through my being at the sight of my muddy, bloody, half-naked state—collared and chained to the bedpost. But that wasn't what held my attention.

A thin ring of brilliant orange, like dying coals, snaked around my pupils before disappearing into my mild caramel irises. My eyes drifted up to the collars hanging on the ceiling. To my predecessors, who no doubt met a horrifying end to their torment. Rage crept its way into my chest and soon replaced the shame and sadness. I would end this place. All of it.

I snatched Cyril's dagger off the edge of the bed. *Talon*, he'd called it. I vaguely noted the elaborate, foreign script that shimmered on the blade, despite the darkness of the room. The edge of it scraped against my forearms as I tried to break free of my shackles, unsuccessfully. I cursed and looked around, eyes finally landing on Cyril's ashes. Shit. If the jewels survived, maybe iron would as well. Cyril had to have the keys on him. I sifted through his remains, gagging as the black ash coated my hands in a dark layer. All I had to do was dig. This was just like an excavation. Dig.

Relief swept through me as my hands landed on a single key. I sighed as I *clicked* the shackles off my shaking hands. I flexed my wrists, aching and bruised from the bite of the iron. Now for the collar. Movement sounded outside of the door, and I fumbled with the chain tied to the bed. Sweat mingled with blood as it dripped down my neck despite the frigidness in the room. My fingers shook as I worked through the knot, which at last came loose as the chain thumped onto the rug on the floor.

Someone called for Cyril beyond the door. Hands free, I picked up the blade and turned to face them. Knees bent, feet apart, and sword at the ready, I stood prepared to attack as the door to the chambers opened slowly and two guards stepped in. Gasps of breath sounded as their eyes scanned the room and landed on the pile of dark ash next to Cyril's bed and then me. Looks of loathing mixed with awe coated their features, but they didn't step toward me. They took up positions on either side of the door, unease threatening their composure.

I shifted on my feet, ready to attack, feeling the icy burn on my blistering hand, Tynan's power thrumming in my chest mixing with newfound adrenaline. Slow steps padded up the stairs outside the chamber. The dark king entered, stopping just inside. His eyes swept the room, and his mouth tilted up in an insidious grin as they landed on me.

He lifted his hands and softly clapped them together, the bones of power clanking together as he did so. I saw the flash of a gown beyond the door before pulling my attention back to the dark king.

"Bravo, Daughter of Darkness," he applauded, yellow eyes gleaming in the dimly lit room.

My stomach churned at the response to the obliteration of his nephew. My brows pinched. He chuckled, and it was then I realized I'd fallen right into his trap. He'd planned this. He hadn't broken me by using my father. He had to break me by threatening my life, and he knew Cyril would be enough to put me over the edge.

Longing and lust danced in his eyes as they darted between my hands and where Cyril's remains lay.

"It is consuming, is it not? To wield the power of the gods," he said, stepping toward me.

I shifted my stance, angling the blade toward him. The guards stood their ground as he slowly made his way across the room.

"I should have known it would come down to preserving your own life," he said, shaking his head. "It wasn't enough to put your father's life at risk, or even put him through days of torment." A sickening smile slid across his face. "Though, the Tauruk did enjoy his time with him."

Bile rose to my throat.

"No, you needed to feel as if your own life were at risk. Typical for a Sultiran. A human. Selfish to their core."

Nausea slammed into me at the truth in his words. I hadn't

broken when he'd tortured my father. It was only at the necessity of preserving my own life that I gave in to the darkness of the Obscura Bone. Guilt wrapped its claws around my chest, suffocating me with the raw truth.

"Do you know why I cannot wield the Stone of Darkness? The Obscura Stone?" he asked as he circled me like a wraith.

I cross-stepped one foot behind the other as I'd done a hundred times with Bayne, blade following a defensive pattern.

"The Stones of the Bellators can only be wielded by those with magic in their bones. Elves, for instance, all have a natural ability to wield the stones. But the Obscura Stone is different. Picky, even. It will only yield to someone in its predecessor's bloodline."

Bloodline.

My mind whirled at the impossibility of it. He held his palms toward me, and I could feel the song of the deep golden bone, light and airy as it whispered through the chamber like the sound of countless choirs calling to the heavens. The blue bone answered its call with a steady pulse, as if it were the beating heart of this world.

"I've been searching for you for a long time. And the one who yields to the Stone of Darkness inevitably succumbs to it," he said, eyeing me with evil intent. "Enya, the last bearer, nearly destroyed the world."

My head shook. In denial or terror, I wasn't sure.

"But fear not, Daughter of Darkness. I will not let you destroy the world. I will teach you how to wield death. You will be a weapon in the great war to come. The war to reclaim our lands, rid them of the human filth that arrived a millennia ago, and restore the Elven Empire that once was. Our gods will thank us."

He paused a few feet away, eyes wide as he drew his

eyebrows up. His yellow eyes stared at my hands, white with my grip on the hilt.

"Where is the stone?" he demanded, voice shrill with an edge of madness.

His gaze darted quickly around the room.

"Where did you put it, you who—"

He was cut off by a blast that sent rock and stone flying from the window. I staggered back and shielded my face as a familiar brilliant white light coursed through the chamber. The dark king stumbled a few feet away, and I nearly lost my grip on the blade trying to stay upright.

Shouts of alarm sounded from outside the chamber as the guards turned their attention to the hall. Dust hung in the air, and I stood still with shock as the outline of two massive wings shadowed the blinding light. Bayne and Aquila were here.

They came for me. Tears welled in my eyes as I sagged.

Chaos erupted everywhere. Bayne's silhouette appeared in the giant hole that gaped in the stone wall, a torrent of rain filling and soaking the space. He held me in an unblinking gaze for a moment, eyes electrified in the light of the crashing storm outside the tower. A determined fire sparked in my chest at the sight of the captain, and the Obscura power *hummed* in delight as I turned toward the dark king.

I threw my entire being into that feeling, gripping the blade with my right hand and splaying my left fingers wide—star still searing on my palm—and shoved my hand toward the dark king.

He tore his eyes from Bayne, face contorted in rage and madness as it landed on me. His mouth dropped as he gazed upon the blistering star which now emitted vaporous black mist spearing straight toward him. He threw up a shield, and the torrent of magic shuddered against it. The Obscura power pushed, its frustration building. Bayne slammed into him from opposite the room with his own blast of white light, and the dark king bellowed before throwing him back.

The darkness twisted and shoved at the barrier. I could feel its fury racing through my veins as it pushed, weakening the shield. A ravenous smile stretched onto the dark king's face as Bayne threw another blast of white light at him, his teeth bared and yellow eyes hungry.

I threw myself into the power when something careened into me. The tumultuous wave of magic cut off like a taut rope had been snapped as I caught myself on the bed. My eyes scanned the chaos of Cyril's room which had become a battle-field, and my heart gave in as Nerissa flew through the chambers, cutting through guards as she went. Bayne and Dark King Daimos stood against a storm of wind, blasts of white light clashing with blades of ice.

Bayne's body slammed against the wall as the dark king speared his magic through the captain's shield. "You thieving fools!" he laughed as he screamed, "To come *here*, to bring this magic *here*. Oh, how they will reward me!"

Nerissa grunted as she shoved against two guards at the opposite end of the room. The dark king raised his hands above his head, bones like beacons glowing on his palms. I sprinted across the room, arms raised overhead as the golden bone sang to me through the chaos.

Cyril's blade hissed as I sliced with all my remaining strength through the dark king's left forearm. He let out a bellow of rage that shook the tower as his hand bearing the golden bone thumped to the ground. Nerissa's arm wrapped around my waist as I stumbled forward, snatching the severed hand with the golden bone. We sprinted to the far side of the chamber where Bayne was back on his feet throwing a blast of magic at the guards filing into the room.

He tore his eyes from the dark king, and they landed on me.

For the briefest moment, he scanned my broken and bloodied body, eyes lingering on the scar above my collar and torn dress. Rage, hot enough to melt the world, simmered in his pupils before he reached for me and the three of us leaped from the tower and into the storm.

CHAPTER THIRTY-FIVE

Though we've received your letter of recommendation from the Master of Spells, the Elders have rejected your request to partake in the Mystic Magnum. You shall remain a mage.

—*Correspondence to Isla Jasira. Isla's private quarters, Evecta.*

My arms clung to Bayne and Nerissa as we fell through the violent storm for several long heartbeats. A sadness crept through the shock of what they'd done for a moment. At the sacrifice they were willing to make. I fell with them and suddenly felt a whoosh of warm jasmine air and the nauseating sensation of our momentum abruptly slowing before we slammed into a hard, soaked wooden floor.

We lurched forward, sliding until we bumped into the main mast. Nerissa groaned but shot to her feet as Bayne's hands gingerly rolled me to my side and he lifted me in his arms. His gaze held mine for several moments, eyes like a thousand emerald forests, as my fingers drifted to his wet cheek, the rain pelting us from above.

"Hey, Angel," he whispered, "I've got you."

My eyes scanned the soaked sails of the *Evecta* whipping in the stormy wind above Kayj. I didn't understand. This was a decadent dream, I realized, as I gazed back at him. I'd be happy to die and dream in his arms. My eyes drifted shut.

"Stay awake, love," he said, a little louder this time, gently shaking me. *Love.*

I was surely dying and happy to do so if it meant lying in his arms and listening to these words come out of his beautiful mouth. I smiled, a warm wet trickle dribbling down my chin. A cough escaped my lips, my chest sharp with pain.

"Lyv. Stay awake."

The command of a captain, not the croon of a lover. I frowned through slitted eyes as he barked muffled orders. Lyv. He said *Lyv.* Not love. I wilted and let my eyes drift closed, sagging into his warmth.

"Lyvia! Awake! Stay the fuck awake!" he shouted, a panic I hadn't heard before entering his voice.

I groaned as he shook me. "So bossy," I mumbled.

His chest bounced as he let out a shaky laugh. Shouts arose from nearby, and a calloused, warm hand gripped my left hand. Searing pain burned through my palm, shoving my consciousness at me. I screamed and jerked my fist away, tucking it into my chest.

I was not dying. I was not dreaming. I was escaping. *I had escaped.*

"Lyvia, open your hand." Bayne's tone was firm.

My fingers spread wide at the command, and a gasp sounded nearby. I blinked open my eyes which had squeezed shut at the burning in my hand. I gingerly turned my face to his to find his gaze a mix of loving concern and raw rage.

"Bayne," I croaked, voice barely audible.

"I'm here, Lyv," he whispered, voice softening.

He pulled me close, and I wrapped my arms around him, breathing in the familiar pine scent and savoring the hard, warm strength of his body.

I stared over his shoulder in disbelief. We were on board the *Evecta* and sailing through the violent Kayj storm, the persistent cracks of lightning illuminating the world around it. A dark hill peaked through a break in the ominous clouds, and my heart stuttered. We sailed *over* the island. I let go after a few moments, and he took my face in his hands, pulling me into a kiss so gentle I thought I'd melt away. I sighed against his lips.

"Are we flying?" I asked, looking around.

His grin sent a frenzy of birds flapping in my stomach.

"We are flying," he murmured against me. "I have so much to tell you. Are you okay?"

No. I would never be okay.

"How did you find me?"

A look of wonder filled his eyes as they darted between mine, searching.

"You *called* to Aquila. We were sitting a few hundred feet off Kayj when he lost his mind from your beckoning. We don't know how you did it, but he heard you and..." He paused, thoughtful for a moment, and looked up, nodding to another.

"Marian's here to help."

Marian. I thought I'd never see her again. Small wrinkles crinkled at the corner of her warm brown eyes, and she smiled as she signed, "Thought I needed another hand in the kitchens?"

She gestured to the dark king's severed hand that lay on the deck next to us. I coughed out a laugh in response, sending specks of red at her, which were quickly washed away by the torrent of rain, and threw my arms around her. She returned the hug, thin arms tight but gentle around my shoulders.

"Let's get you below deck so I can have a proper look at you. And get this thing," she signed, gesturing to my collar, "off you."

She looked briefly at Bayne, and he gave her a small nod in return.

"Wait!" I rasped, turning to Bayne. "Evony? Is she okay? Did she make it off the tribute ship?" I'd nearly forgotten how I'd gotten here and what led me to my capture.

He smiled at me, warmth entering his eyes. "She's okay. We found her offshore. All we had to do was follow the smoke," he said, grinning widely. "You were spectacular. And..."

Bayne dropped his hands from my face and turned to the stern of the ship where Nerissa stood, freely using her magic as I hadn't seen before. Massive blasts of light erupted from the back of the ship. And behind her...

My knees wobbled in relief as I took in the thin form standing behind her, arms stretched wide, small sparks of light dancing off his palms, and little blasts of wind following Nerissa's light.

"*Drystan*," I sobbed. "You went back for Drystan."

How he stood there—and practiced the lost arts, for that matter—was beyond me, but waves of relief and gratitude rolled over me like the Atrulean Sea we sailed toward.

Bayne swept me off my feet and followed Marian across the deck. Vulcan shouted something at the helm, and I followed his gaze to Isla. Her ebony hair flew wildly in the storm, and her hands shook from the force of the magic rippling from her small form.

Despite the black clouds overhead, a darkness lay over her, a shadow in a lightless cave. I craned my neck as Bayne hurried to the stairs, blinking to determine what it was I saw. Isla glanced up, pulling her focus away from the draining magic. My pulse faltered as two violet eyes met mine across the deck. My spine stiffened.

We hurried below deck. Rain pounded on the wooden ceiling creating a deafening roar. Bayne gently sat me down on a table in Marian's workspace before taking my face in his hands once more.

"I have to go back up. We're not off Kayj yet," he said, pressing his lips to mine. "I won't lose you again." His voice and demeanor returned to the calm confidence I'd grown so used to.

I met his eyes with my own fierceness and gave a firm nod.

I glanced back at Marian who had been watching us closely. She approached and gently opened my left hand, careful not to touch the star searing in its center.

"This is deep, dark magic, Lyvia. Was this from the Obscura Stone? Do you have it?" she signed, watching me carefully.

"It is gone," I said, voice still shaky. "I think it is..." I paused, trying to decide how best to explain what happened. "I think it is a part of me now. It was a bone, not a stone."

Marian's jaw wavered but she quickly recovered and signed, "Bayne and Nerissa should know. Let's get you cleaned up."

She took a giant pair of shears to my bloody, torn gown before dressing and stitching the slice on my back and cuts on my hands and face. Her eyes widened as she got a closer look at the thick, bulging scar across my neck. I flinched as her fingers got close to examine the collar.

Her gaze hardened. "I will need some help with this. Put this on for now. I'll be back."

I slid the oversized shirt on, wincing as I lifted my hands

above my head. I tugged it around the thick iron collar, lifting the chain through the neck hole.

The ship lurched as it continued its flight over Kayj. I sat alone for a few minutes as it steadied and rocked through the wind and rain. It was a different sensation from sailing through the water. Every dip sent butterflies scattering in my stomach. Still, I breathed in the sea-soaked teakwood that made up the room below deck, savoring its scent, feeling more at home than I'd ever imagined.

Thoughts cut through my mind as I waited. Evony was safe. Drystan was here. Aeriden was dead. My father was dead. Darkness ebbed at my vision as memories of those final moments snaked into my mind. Another dip of the ship and some shouting above. I leaped from the table and hurled into a bowl of bloody dressings. I heaved for several moments, the stench of the soiled rags enough to drain my stomach.

A soft tap on the door pulled my mind out of the current well of despair and guilt. I glanced over my shoulder to find a head of sandy gray hair and two deep blue eyes peering at me. *Oslo.*

He surveyed me for a long moment before bending into a bow and softly saying, "My lady."

I limped toward him, not sure at what point I'd injured my leg, and embraced him.

"It appears you have quite the tale to tell," he said softly, raising his eyebrows.

My heart squeezed at the paternal tone in his voice. He stepped aside as Marian approached with a large hammer and chisel. I gaped. There was no way.

I opened my mouth to protest, and Oslo chimed in, "Don't worry. We'll wait until we're safely out of sight of Kayj and we'll have one of them do it." He pointed to the ceiling above deck. While an elf would have the strength and precision to break me out of my collar, it did little to ease my anxiety.

As if the *Evecta* had heard him, the floor beneath us tilted abruptly. Oslo cursed as he caught the sliding table, and Marian hurried to the dishes clanging in the neighboring kitchen. The sudden shift in gravity caused me to stumble, skittering into the wall. I gripped the edge of the door as we continued our descent for several moments.

Marian and Oslo eyed each other warily, lacking confidence in this newfound power of the *Evecta*. We barreled toward what I prayed was the sea for several long seconds, breath held. The little room shook and threw the three of us back as the hull smashed into the sea with a deafening crash. We rocked wildly for several moments, bracing ourselves before the *Evecta* at last settled into an easy sway over the Atrulean waves.

Footsteps hammered down the stairs, and Bayne stepped into the small room, drenched from head to foot. He found me braced against the wall and had me in his arms within an instant. The heat of his body burned through the cold wetness of his clothes.

"You're getting my shirt all wet, Captain," I mumbled, pushing him gently away.

He chuckled, bringing my chin in between his thumb and forefinger, lips inches away.

A soft cough pulled our attention back and I turned, finding Oslo and Marian shifting on their feet.

"Captain," he said, gesturing to the hammer and chisel, "for the iron."

Lightning flashed in Bayne's eyes for a moment as they darted to my collar. He nodded to Oslo. "Thank you. I will handle it."

Taking it as a dismissal, Marian and Oslo moved to exit the room.

"In my quarters," he finished. Picking up the hammer and chisel, he scooped me up, and we made our way to the captain's quarters above deck.

I didn't pull my eyes from his face even as we stepped into the soft light of early morning spring and salty sea air, the thunder of Kayj now miles behind us.

He returned his gaze to mine as we stepped inside the room, and for a moment, I was lost in a sea of green. He set me down on the velvety chair across his desk. From behind the bookshelf, he pulled out a steel sculpture of Renova.

"Let's get this off you," he murmured.

I stilled as he gently pulled my hair to the top of my head.

"Hold this, please. And hold very still."

My hands gripped my knotted hair above my head as he slowly twisted the front of my collar to the back of my neck, wincing as it slid against the long scar.

He angled the spiked shoulder of Renova's armor beneath the three rings that clasped the collar together. Bayne's breath slipped through his lips and the piercing clang of metal on metal sounded before the heavy iron fell to the floor. My hands dropped to the back of my neck, massaging the bruised and chapped area where it had rubbed. I sagged in my chair and let out a sigh.

Bayne picked up the iron collar and chain and chucked them into the sea before returning to kneel before me. "I thought I'd lost you," he whispered, voice shaking. "When he..." A river of wrath swirled in his gaze as it drifted to my neck.

"It doesn't matter what I felt. Compared to what you went through." He gripped my hands, careful not to touch the blistering star on my left.

"You came," I said through a cracking voice, tightening my grip on him. "Thank you. I wasn't sure you'd come."

Bayne held my gaze a while longer, something like grief glimmering in his eyes. "I will always come for you."

He carried something new and raw in his eyes. My heart trembled in its presence, longing so badly to grab hold of it. Something sharp inside of me resisted, the darkness in my soul recoiling at its warmth.

"Do you want to talk? Or just rest?" he asked, searching my eyes as if they held the answer.

I scanned the captain's quarters, noting the luxurious furs draped over the bed behind the half-drawn curtain.

I was free of Kayj, free of the dark king. But how could I be free knowing what I'd left behind? The dark island was a mere smudge in the distance as I peered through the small windows of the captain's quarters. The *Evecta* sailed south, the crack of Kayj's thunder disappearing into the whisper of waves. Yet I could still *hear* them. The wails of the ashen. The sobs of the slaves. The crack of the whip.

I shook my head.

"No. I want to train."

CHAPTER THIRTY-SIX

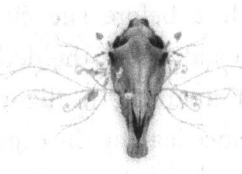

Ro, it's called the Ode to Aurora, but it's for Soulbinding, so you can forget it. And I get the sense Aquila is feeling like a carrier pigeon. He nearly took off my finger when I handed him this note. This is the last he'll get to Sultiran shores. See you soon. —Nis.

—Correspondence from Nerissa Ravindra, 82nd of Autumn, 064.3E. Ronan's private quarters, Mount Telum, Aedrialis.

H ours later, my shirt soaked with a mixture of sweat and spindrift, Nerissa's blade hammered down upon my own. My fingers ached from the reverberation of metal and the slippery hilt flew from my hand.

"Again," she said calmly. "Wider base. Your forearm tilted too early. And this time, breathe from your core." She tapped my abdomen with the flat side of her blade.

"It would be easier if I were using my right hand," I murmured, picking up the blade and widening my base.

"You said you wanted to train," she retorted, bringing the back of her hand to her forehead in silent salute. "You've improved with your right. You're terrible with your left. Again."

I matched her salute before she charged. Parry, block, parry... Shit. My blade slid across the deck to where Isla had stood hours before, commanding the flight of the *Evecta*. I'd yet to see her or Drystan since leaving the captain's quarters. They were both resting now, drained. Drystan had been practicing magic. Had he known all along? Or had his limited time on this ship been enough to teach him? My stomach churned at the idea of him hiding something like this. There would be time to discuss. Time to tell our stories.

"We flew," I said, returning to Nerissa. "The *Evecta* was flying."

The elf's lips twitched. "Obviously."

I pursed mine in response. "How?"

"The Stone Witch likes to trade in favors," she said, planting her feet for another attack. "She owed us."

"And what did you give her in return?" I asked before dodging Nerissa's swing.

"Saros trapped her there long ago. The kryax was merely one of its gatekeepers. We traveled through a network of tunnels in the mountain range to keep hidden, knowing Bayne would meet us in the north. Along the way, we slew a number of others."

My stomach flipped at the casual nature she made the claim.

"So, you freed her from the mountains?"

"No," she responded, adjusting her stance. "Spells still bind her to the Lumerians, but she's no longer trapped in Crown

Peak. In return, when we needed to get to Kayj, she lent us some power."

My brows furrowed as I said, "But Isla—"

I was cut short as the memory of Isla's violet irises shot through my mind's eye. A harrowing sense of violation shuddered through me. The Stone Witch's voice in my mind was enough to churn my stomach. How far did she reach into Isla's to transfer some of her power? I had to talk to Isla...

As if reading my thoughts, Nerissa let her blade fall and shook her head. "Isla is recovering. She will need time. And space."

A twist of guilt speared through my chest, adding to the barrage of fresh wounds. She'd done this for me.

"As is that friend of yours," she continued, raising her scarred brow. "He's quite powerful."

Another dip of my stomach to match the swell of the Atrulean Sea.

"Is he now?" I murmured, glancing toward the horizon.

She grunted her confirmation. "Isla has taken him under her wing. We found him at the university." She paused, tilting her head at me. "You knew you were being taken, and your last words were to save another."

I kept my gaze on the horizon as her eyes bore into me. My good intent in Stynguard was nothing compared to the sin I'd committed since. I turned back to her after a moment and moved into position, my muscles sluggish. She followed suit, striking me on the shoulder, hard enough to sting.

"We should stop. You're too tired for this right now," Nerissa said.

I opened my mouth to protest when she sheathed her blade and plucked my sopping shirt from my shoulder.

"And you're bleeding." She opened her mouth again and

paused, her emerald eyes darting to the crescent-shaped bite on my chest that had broken open.

Her eyes slid to mine, fingers dropping the fabric.

"I hope you made him pay." Fire danced in her gaze for a moment. "If you want to talk about—"

"I do have much to share with you all," I cut in, tearing my gaze away, unwilling to acknowledge that wound. I sheathed my blade before heading below deck.

⸻

NERISSA STOOD behind me as I paused at the bottom of the stairs. A savory scent floated from the kitchens, yet I had no appetite. Muffled talking sounded from behind the door followed by Isla's soft giggle.

I stood there for a few minutes, listening, when Bayne's tall figure emerged from the room and froze at the sight of me. His emerald gaze pinned me to where I stood, and I felt as if my soul reached for him. I slowly stepped forward into the light coming from the kitchen and grasped his hand. He raised his other to my cheek, and my eyes closed against his warm, calloused skin. The talking quieted, and I opened my eyes to find Drystan behind him.

Tired eyes peered at me through clear spectacles. I could feel Bayne's smile as he dropped my hand, and Drystan wrapped his long arms around me. I returned his squeeze, shutting my eyes against his shoulder for several long moments. He released me and turned to the remaining crew gathered around the small table. I'd barely known them, but I had missed them. This crew. This family.

A hush fell over the dimly lit room. I slowly scanned the crew. Isla's amber eyes had once again returned, and she grinned widely at me before standing and pulling me into a tight embrace. Oslo and Marian were by my side a moment later. Vulcan gave me a nod across the room, and I swear I might have spied the upward tug of Nerissa's lips. I cleared my throat as I stepped forward.

"I have some things to say." I took a seat next to Isla and Drystan. "First, thank you."

Warm liquid threatened to pool in my eyes. Isla gripped my hand as I hastily blinked. "Thank you all for coming for me. I didn't think I would leave Kayj alive." My voice broke, and it took me a moment to steady my breathing enough to continue.

"Second, I have some information to share."

I took a deep breath and relayed everything I had learned in Nivis and on Kayj, only leaving out the details of my father's death and the haunting events in Cyril's tower. Isla's hand never left mine, and I could feel Bayne's unblinking gaze as I spoke.

The room fell silent as I finished and heaved a sigh, utterly exhausted from the act of speaking it out loud.

"I'm so sorry about your brother and father, Lyvia," Isla said gently, giving my hand a squeeze before releasing it.

I blinked again, my heart quickening as grief threatened to take hold.

"Bone..." Vulcan muttered.

I glanced at him, grateful for the change of subject, whether he knew I needed it or not.

"Why does it matter?" I asked, steadying my breath.

"Only organic material can be used as amplifiers," Isla began. "The fact that Bellator Stones are actually *bones* changes things dramatically. A mystic can funnel their magic into an inorganic object, such as a stone or a book. The magic is stored there for later use. With the correct spell, it can be unlocked and wielded. That's what we always thought the Bellators did with their magic. It was always unclear whether the magic was theirs to begin with, or they'd found the stones with the magic and were powerful enough to unlock it and wield it."

"Regardless, this," she said, picking up the golden bone, "does more than just hold magic. It will *magnify* the magic of anyone wielding it *and* allow the wielder to tap into the magic imbued within it. Most amplifiers disappear when properly harnessed—they become a part of you. Which would explain why the bone with the Obscura power disappeared. And it would also explain—"

"I'm more concerned with the fact that the dark king still has one of the bones. And what about this second threat on Kayj? The one that Eira mentioned?" Nerissa cut her off, voice clipped.

Isla stilled next to me as she fell silent. Bayne's eyes shot to Nerissa's before falling back to mine.

"How much harm can he do with the Ramadiel power? It's healing power, right?" I asked after a few moments of silence, unsure how things had gotten so tense in the room.

"Any object of power the dark king possesses is a threat. If anyone can find a way to twist healing power into something ugly and dangerous, it's Daimos," Vulcan said from across the table.

We sat in the kitchens for hours that evening debating what else the dark king could be doing on Kayj. I dozed off at some point in my chair and awoke in the captain's quarters some hours later.

———

MY EYES SHOT open through darkened slits, a heavy hood masking my features. The whip was in my hand and a broken and bleeding figure lay sprawled on the floor of the Crystal Castle. I glanced at my hands, covered in hot, wet blood. My father's shaking fingers slowly *pulled from his face. Horror and fear coated his features as he met my eyes. He crawled away from me. I stepped forward, the mask of the Tauruk heavy on my shoulders. I raised my right arm, whip flying high in the air above me...*

Screams filled the dark chamber as I gasped for breath. A man shouted my name. Strong hands gripped my shoulders. I thrashed in the darkness, panic taking over. Cyril was here. He was here, and he was on me. He had me. I kicked and screamed, and the Obscura power blinked an eye open. Hands released my shoulders, and a match sounded.

Bayne knelt on the bed and held a small candle in his steady hand.

"Lyv, it's me. You're safe. You're on the *Evecta* with Bayne and the crew. You're with friends. You're safe."

He repeated the words while keeping a short distance from me. My eyes darted around the room, the panic in my chest slowly subsiding. My hands shook as I panted and shivered. My shirt was drenched.

Pounding sounded at the door to the captain's quarters. Nerissa's voice followed.

My eyes shot back to Bayne, who held my stare unflinching. He slowly repeated those words before setting the taper in its holder on the windowsill. The pounding ensued outside the room. He tore his eyes from mine, looking to the door.

"I'll be right back. You're safe, Lyv."

He stepped from the room, the door open beyond the curtain. Hushed talking followed, and I steadied my breathing, repeating his words in my head. A vicious voice responded in its own tormenting truth.

I was safe. *You don't deserve to be.*

On the *Evecta*. *Which you will undoubtedly destroy.*

With Bayne. *Who has no idea what you've done and will despise you for it.*

With friends. *Friends you will surely lead to death.*

I tugged my knees into my chest, a shiver running over my shoulders. Bayne stepped back into the room.

"I'm sorry," I began, looking at the wet furs on the bed. "I–"

He had my hands in his, kneeling before me before I could finish.

"Do not apologize. You apologize to no one," he said, eyes searching mine for the cause of my panic. He was waiting for me to talk. To tell him about the dream. About what had happened in the last week. I pulled my hands away, shaking my head.

"I'm sorry," I said again. "Bad dream."

"Lyv—"

"I'm fine," I cut him off. "I'm just tired. I'll get some dry clothes and blankets..."

"Nerissa is grabbing them."

"Oh."

His eyes bore into me, searching for a way to ease my pain and distress. I couldn't bring myself to meet them. Not after that dream. Not after what I had *done*. A tiny, weak voice in the back of my mind leaped to my defense. *You had to do it. It was a mercy. You saved him from a fate worse than death. It took immense courage.*

The quiet, barely perceptible song of the golden bone on the small table sounded in reply as if trying to ease my discomfort.

The aching in my heart bit back. *Monster. You deserved every threat Cyril dealt. You killed your own father. He gave you every- thing. You strangled him. You ripped the life from him.*

Nausea slammed into me, and the color drained from my face. Bayne was in front of me with a bucket before I knew what was happening, and I hurled into it for several minutes, dry heaving as I'd barely eaten.

Bayne stepped out for a moment and returned with dry clothes.

"Do you want help?"

I spit into the bucket and wretched once more at its scent. I lifted my shaking hands to the buttons on my shirt and saw Bayne take a step forward out of the corner of my eye. I shot to the back of the bed.

A flash of pain crossed his features. He recovered quickly and nodded. "I'll get Marian."

"No," I said.

He stopped at the curtain, looking back at me with pinched brows.

"No, I'll do it alone."

CHAPTER THIRTY-SEVEN

Death by drowning shall be reserved for the most heinous criminals, so their souls may never ascend to the Beyond.
—From the Execution Protocols at Pyracantha, Lotrennia.

Mumbled talking dragged me from my sleep the next morning. "We need to get this information to the Rising," Oslo said to murmurs of agreement.

I tugged on my boots, braiding my hair as I stepped out to join them.

The crew stood gathered outside the captain's quarters, deep in conversation. I ignored their stares at my puffy face as I joined them. Bayne scanned me, eyes searching for hints of lingering pain. He'd held me all night. Shadows lingered beneath his green eyes that had dimmed since our departure on Kayj. His usually clean-shaven face was covered in rough stubble, heightening his haggard appearance. The guilt gnawed at me. That *I* should be the cause of his worry.

"What is the Rising?" I asked, glancing at Oslo.

"The rebellion has started in Sultira, my lady," he said with tight lips, signing the words as Drystan approached.

"Is that where we're going? To fight?" I asked, a surprising eagerness entering my voice.

Vulcan slid a curious gaze to me.

Bayne nodded. "Yes. That's the plan. Though if you don't want to fight..." he began.

I shook my head vehemently. "No, I want to help. In any way I can."

He nodded once, a look of doubt flashing across his face before disappearing.

"Good. Because they need all the help they can get. Especially after what we saw when flying over Kayj," Oslo said.

I stared at him expectantly.

He returned my gaze. "We passed the ashen camps, my lady. There were..." he paused, turning to Vulcan.

"Thousands of them," Vulcan muttered. "Tens of thousands. More than we could have imagined. That, plus the dark king's own forces... If he attacks Sultira in the middle of a rebellion, the results will be catastrophic."

Dread pitted in my stomach. The thought of thousands of ashen unleashed on the land plus the deadly onslaught of our own forces and those of King Saros...

"Ronan is going to want to see the stone... er... bone," Oslo said.

My head snapped to him, rage roiling in my stomach as I processed Oslo's words. My eyes shot to Bayne.

"*Ronan?* He is not getting near the bone!" I growled, holding my hands up.

They stared at the eight-pointed star on my palm now on display. Remarkably, the blisters had healed completely, and the star took on a glossy, luminous appearance. I ignored their looks, my temper rising rapidly.

"Ronan is leading the Rising, Lyv. That's why he tried to persuade you to go after the others," Bayne countered, "He wants them for the Rising force. We found out shortly after you were taken."

I shook my head at him, cheeks heating at his use of the word *persuade*. "He's a traitor," I said, looking to the others for support.

Nerissa was quiet, eyes pinned on the horizon.

"Ronan came to us after you were taken on the tribute ship. And I nearly shred him to pieces before he came clean," Bayne continued, "He's been orchestrating the Rising from within the walls of Mount Telum for the last few years, in league with Queen Galena. And he gave us the exact location of where to find you once you were taken on the tribute ship."

Ronan helped them find me in Stynguard, where they had *almost* saved me, yet my heart still burned with betrayal.

I spun back to Bayne, "How can you defend him?"

My temper boiled. I realized then what a dilemma my relationship with Bayne posed. I was part of the crew, yet Bayne was *with* me. We hadn't discussed the status of our relationship. We didn't have the time to. But it was obvious to us and to the rest of the crew. That didn't mean I didn't question him. In fact, the others questioned him enough, so why shouldn't I? Had Lida?

"There is a lot we need to debrief on, Lyv. And I'm not saying I trust him entirely either, but he's leading the Rising. He is planning an attack on King Saros and will lead the rebellion forces. Don't you want to support that?"

My chin rose at the authority that had entered his voice.

"I will support that. But I won't support *him*. And he's not getting his hands on this," I said, lifting the golden bone from my chest. I'd fashioned a thick leather lace into a carriage that looped up and around the bone.

"That's not yours to decide," Vulcan cut in, ending the conversation.

———◦—◦———

I COULDN'T HELP but feel the shame of my words and actions above deck hours before. I had stormed off like a child. Vulcan was right though. What had I been thinking?

I found myself at the stern of the ship blocking more of Nerissa's blows. My mind spiraled back into that tunnel of darkness. Every painful slap of the sword, every ache of a sore muscle, every burning breath was a justified sentence. An hour passed, and Bayne stepped up to the mast, watching us parry. I didn't dare look at him.

"Training until you bleed doesn't change what happened, Lyvia," Nerissa said, twirling through the night and crashing into me.

I shoved her off and leaped to my feet before launching my attack.

"Do you hear what I'm saying? It doesn't change anything," she snapped.

By now, I could feel the Obscura roiling in my chest as tight anguish squeezed my heart. I shoved both down deep and focused on my attacker.

"Whatever happened in Nivis... on Kayj, it is *fact*. And it is history. It is not something that can be undone. You acknowledge that, acknowledge that it changed you, and focus on the future. You *cannot* survive by living in the past."

I threw myself into my next maneuver as I said, "It is *not* history. I relive it every moment of every day. And at night..."

The words caught in my throat. Nights were the worst. Every night, it painted my dreams in a tapestry of torment.

"Then they win, Lyvia," she growled, throwing me back. "If you allow it to take you, consume you. They *win*. Don't let it be for nothing. You are stronger than this—"

I was breathless as she caught me on the cheek this time, and I barreled toward her, losing my balance as she dodged around me and slapped the freshly healed slice on my back with her sword. A sharp sting ripped across my back, and the image of Cyril's face clouded my vision.

I faltered and staggered back, dropping my sword and crashing to my knees. I lifted my hands to my face, the same way my father had as they beat him bloody night after night.

Nerissa froze across the deck. Anguish squeezed my chest. Hard arms wrapped around me, and I breathed in sweet pine through my shaky gulps of air.

"*I killed him,*" my confession choked out, barely audible, my body beginning to seize. "I killed him."

My breathing hitched, the words barely leaving my lips. And then I screamed into the night. Screamed and howled as Bayne rocked with me on our knees.

"I killed him with..."

I couldn't say it. I choked on the words while my shoulders shook uncontrollably.

"It's okay, Lyv. You're safe. You're on the *Evecta*," Bayne repeated.

I violently shook him off and finally met his eyes through tunnel vision, shaking my head at him.

"It's NOT okay, Bayne! Nothing about this is okay!" I screamed. "I don't deserve to be," I choked, shaking my head, barely able to take a breath. "I don't deserve to be safe. I deserve to drown for this."

The Juniper waves lapped dangerously against the hull of the *Evecta*, as if luring me into their depths. Bayne's cheek was against mine, arms tight around my shoulders as I shook. No tears came. They bucked against the dam I'd slowly built up over the past year.

⊰——⊱

BAYNE LINGERED at the base of the mast, searching my eyes for any sign of hesitation. He stepped forward and gently planted a kiss on my temple, scarred hands sliding into my hair to cup the back of my head before I pulled away.

The rope ladder scraped beneath my palms as I climbed up to the crow's nest atop the mast. The small space dipped and swooped through the air as the *Evecta* rocked through the waves.

High above the ship, the chatter of those above deck disappeared in the whistle of the wind and water crashing against the hull. Evening light danced on the surface of the waves in the distance.

Days had passed since my confession to Bayne. I'd shared it all. Every horrifying moment, every damning memory bled from my lips. And Bayne simply listened as steady as a rock against the crushing waves. Nightmares continued to chase me through the nights until I felt his warm hands on my shoulders, his voice sounding in the dark.

You are safe. You are on the Evecta. *You are with friends.*

This ship *was* safe, but crowded, the closest thing to privacy being the nest I sat in. I didn't want to talk to anyone. I came here to suffer. To allow the agony of my reality to cave in. To wallow in the despair and suffering that I deserved after my time at the Crystal Castle.

Nerissa had been right. Training was a distraction. And though my body was healing, my mind... My mind was broken. Soul shattered. Endless guilt pounded in my heart like a hammer driving a nail. A darkness had crept upon my soul hours before the Obscura power had even slithered into my being. Two shadows now loomed inside me. One, an ancient and deadly force stripped from an object of power. The other of my own making, derived from the sins I'd committed.

Aquila's screech sounded below the clouds as if he could feel the tunnel of anguish I'd descended into. His gaze weighed on me even from this distance. I swallowed against the strange sensation rippling through my chest whenever I saw the seahawk.

I jumped as a hand slapped over the edge of the crow's nest. Drystan's face peered over the edge, and I scooted to make room. He scrambled up, irritation over his flushed features as he sat beside me.

"Tried to get your attention below," he signed before shoving his spectacles back up his sweaty nose. "But you seem to be ignoring me."

"I come up here to be alone," I responded.

"You aren't the only one who has suffered," he signed, frowning. Pain and scars were written in his gaze. A lump formed in my throat. Of course, I wasn't.

"I'm sorry," I signed, shaking my head. "I've been selfish. I haven't been ready to talk."

Drystan's brows pinched upward. "To anyone but the captain."

"I'm ready to listen," I countered, forcing my lips upward.

Drystan swallowed once before telling me his story. We sat atop the *Evecta*'s crow's nest until the sliver of blazing yellow dipped beneath the pink streak it left across the sea. My thoughts drifted to that bleeding boy on the ship. The strange, horrifying vision I'd seen in that in-between state. *A dream*, I reminded myself.

I let my head fall against Drystan's shoulder and allowed myself a moment of peace as night arrived.

CHAPTER THIRTY-EIGHT

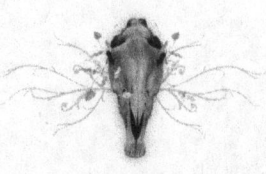

Despite Lady Lyvia Cantor's top marks on her examinations, she will not be allowed to enter the order of the Death Scholars, though I insist you continue allowing her access to your excavations.

— Correspondence from High Priest Helmar to Father Marcus, 5th of Summer, 070.3E. Temple of the Sky, Aedrialis.

A curse escaped my lips as I sliced through a carrot below deck. Marian was good company. She didn't ask questions or pry. She instructed and didn't hesitate to pile on the work. Isla blew into the kitchens a few hours later.

"You," she said, pointing to me. "We need some time together to work on this bone. And your fancy new powers."

She winked at me. We had barely spoken since our retreat from Kayj. Isla had been busy with Drystan, training and

354

teaching him. And there was a part of me that resisted her warmth, her company. There was something about facing her after what I had done that left a tight knot in my stomach. She had tried so hard to teach me about magic all those months ago. And had I listened... Things might have ended up much differently for myself and my father. I forced my lips upward.

"Sorry, Isla, I'm helping Marian," I said, gesturing with my paring knife.

"Go. Your sulking is giving me a headache," Marian signed back. My mouth dropped, ready to protest.

"I can cheer her up!" Isla piped in. "Come, I am teaching you magic today," she said as light danced in her eyes.

A kindling of warmth flared in my chest. The kind that sparked into existence in the presence of a friend. Grief squeezed my heart as I thought of Morwyn. I stared at Isla for a moment before nodding.

Bowls of herbs and smoking incense wafted throughout her small chamber below deck. I breathed deeply, savoring the soothing scents.

"Don't tell Bayne," she murmured, motioning toward the incense. "He'd kill me if he knew I was burning this below deck. It's under control, trust me," she said with a wink. She gave me a warm smile before plopping down on a pillow on the floor, motioning for me to do the same.

"How are you doing?" she asked.

I shrugged, avoiding her eyes.

"It will take time to heal unseen wounds," she said, voice soft.

I glanced at her, not wanting to talk about what happened in Nivis or Kayj the weeks before.

"How are *you*?" I asked instead.

She shifted uncomfortably, now the one avoiding my eyes.

I immediately regretted the question. She was clearly haunted by the experience.

"I'm sorry. Nerissa mentioned—" I began.

"Don't worry about it. I just..." she said, cutting me off. "It was just an... invasive process. I'm not sure I'm ready to talk about it yet."

"Of course," I said, nodding as she met my eyes again. "Thank you for coming for me." I bit the corner of my tongue to stop the rise of tears.

She gave me a soft nod, squeezing my other hand.

"Will you help me?" I asked. "With this?" I turned my hand over in hers, displaying the star.

Her brows pinched together as she nodded. "Talk me through how it all happened."

I started at the beginning, not leaving out a single detail this time. By the time I'd finished, she'd lit more incense and pulled a blanket over us.

"Magic is a give and take, as I've said before. Threads of energy and power exist in the universe, connecting everything, living or otherwise. A tug on one thread has a ripple effect to anything it touches. Some of those threads are stronger, tighter, their strands already woven together, like beings who are compatible for soulbinding. Others, we push and pull, weaving their purpose, the end result yielding to the intention of the mage or mystic. There were once mystics of such power, they could actually *see* those threads. We called them Elders.

"These threads flow within us, and because of this, magic has a close connection to our emotions and mental state. For example, if I'm feeling scared or angry, the magic I command will respond accordingly. My panic will spiral into the wind, picking up its pace, or my anger will harden the next blow. It is both a hindrance and an advantage to those who wield it. If left unchecked, your emotions can override your intent and can have devastating effects. That's why your first lesson will be to control your emotions."

I hesitated before I murmured, "But the only way I was even able to harness the power was because my life was threatened. I have no idea if I'll be able to summon it again without finding myself in a similar situation." Or if I wanted to, I silently added.

"We'll work on that. We're also going to work on basics. If you can harness the Obscura power, you'll be able to access the basic arts. Wind and water whispering and we'll move to spell work. And there's tree singing, but I don't know of any humans who have ever mastered that. It's kind of an elf thing."

"What about fire?" I asked.

She opened her mouth for a moment before clamping it shut. "The power to manipulate fire is limited. Most mages and mystics have no power over fire." Before I could ask more, she launched into a lecture on how and what could be done with wind and water. The scholar in me straightened up, and I devoured the information she spewed. I took mental notes and practiced, repeating everything she said, without success.

"The effect of any magic is magnified with the presence of an amplifier," she continued. "Amplifiers come from organic material that *is* or once *was* living. It's that essence of life that amplifies the magic of the user. Your priests use them, whether they know it or not."

I thought about that for a moment. "The coral they wear on their belts and around their waists..."

"That's what Drystan thinks," she said, nodding in agreement.

"Drystan seems to have picked this up rather quickly," I murmured, eyeing my hands with disappointment. "How is it he can cast a spell without speaking?"

"He has a remarkable connection to the threads." She nodded. "He simply *thinks* the word, and the forces respond."

"He has always been gifted," I murmured. My relationship with Drystan always held a competitive edge, and while I loved him, the idea of him besting me at anything made my molars sore. "And your amplifier is the driftwood you keep around your neck?" I asked, pulling our attention back to the business at hand.

She smiled softly, picking up the wood carved like an eagle and staring at it. Sad memories danced in her eyes. "No. This is not an amplifier," she said, shaking her head. "My sister made this for me before our village was attacked."

My hand clasped around hers in a tight squeeze. "It looks like Aquila," I said.

Her lips tugged up. "I've always thought it led me to him. To them," she murmured, glancing at the ceiling as if she could see above deck.

"Mine are more subtle," she continued, squeezing back before tucking her hair behind her ears. The small pink and white rings glittered down the side of her pointed ear. I examined them closer, noting they were small carved shells.

"My mother would collect seashells with my sisters and me as children. When I took up the study, I needed something subtle and small I could use as amplifiers. No one expects much of these. And with their size, I can go through one by one without drawing attention."

"How do you make them?" I asked.

"A spell. One that I will teach you."

She pulled my hand out and examined my palm. "The Obscura power is part of you now. There's a lot we don't know about the Bellators." Her voice quieted, taking on an uneasy tone. "But this power is unlike anything we've seen in our lifetime. It is... godlike. And what the dark king said about bloodline," she continued, shaking her head, "It's impossible. Humans and elves cannot reproduce. I hope that gives you a little comfort, knowing you couldn't be descended from Enya, the Betrayer. There must be another explanation."

Betrayer. Something felt wrong about that. I scratched at the scar across my neck, the taught skin still numb and tingly. I'd seen her again in that dreamlike state before Nivis, but it wasn't a dream. It was different, more real and unnerving than the other messages from her. I closed my eyes, letting the memory of that last encounter replay in my mind.

"Isla, I don't think she betrayed the Bellators," I said as my eyes shot open. "When I saw her on that last battlefield, the world *was* shattered... I could see the outline of Sultira as it exists *today*. Saros tried to take the bone from her when a blast shook the world, but the Vael was *already* shattered..."

"I don't know, Lyvia," Isla murmured. "You have obviously always had some connection to this bone of power. Any connection to it will imply some connection to her since she wielded it last. If she's truly contacting you in some way, through visions... I'm not a seer, but you must be careful. You could be seeing *exactly* what she wants you to see."

I frowned. She wasn't wrong. And the power was dangerous regardless of what message she was trying to send me. Did it even matter in the end?

"But Lyvia," she continued with a serious calm settling over her eyes, "I think it's important you don't let this happen again. These bones may have been made to contain the power within them. It might be too much for any one being to hold. There is a reason there were eight Bellators with eight powers. There's no telling what would happen if you harnessed both powers. The golden bone is meant for someone else."

I pulled my hand away. "Not Ronan," I said, icy bitterness entering my voice.

She sighed, dropping my hand. "Be careful with that rage, Lyvia. You'll level more than just kingdoms with what storms inside you."

I bristled and opened my mouth to respond when she cut in. "The number of women Ronan has seduced to get something he wants surpasses what you would imagine."

My cheeks heated.

"You aren't the only one who has fallen for those steamy eyes and lush curls," she said, scratching at the ring in her nose.

I glanced back at her, raising my eyebrows in unspoken question.

She shook her head, her own loose curls bouncing around her face, and pointed at the ceiling to the upper deck.

I leaned forward and mouthed, *Nerissa?*

A mischievous nod and a wink. "I can't blame her. He's gorgeous. And he is *charming* when he wants to be. I certainly would *not* turn down a friends-with-perks situation, should the occasion arise," she mused, eyes drifting away from me as if imagining just that.

I cleared my throat, pulling her attention back to our small room.

"Ronan is a friend to me. He's been a great friend to me, actually. Almost like a brother. But not *too much* like a brother, if you know what I mean."

She winked and I coughed a laugh.

"I heard what happened," she continued.

I looked away as heat rushed to my face.

"Don't be embarrassed. I don't blame you at all for feeling betrayed and not wanting to trust him. I wouldn't either. I *don't* trust him, not entirely. But Bayne is right. If we want to help the Rising, we help him."

"Whether that's giving him the bone or not. We should be

there, with him. He's still a part of this crew. Though I think it was a miracle Bayne didn't tear him apart when he found him." She shook her head, rolling her eyes.

Then she turned to me, a wicked girlish grin appearing on her face. "Speaking of *Bayne*..." She waggled her eyebrows and leaned in close.

I rolled my eyes in response.

"Oh, come on, Lyvia! I haven't seen him so enamored with someone in years. Even with Lida."

I blinked. "What?"

She shrugged. "I mean, sure they loved each other for a while. But before Lida was taken, they were on rocky ground. She was *obsessed* with getting him to retake the throne of Lotrennia, and you know he wants nothing to do with it. I'm not even sure they were on speaking terms when everything went down in the north."

Her words sank in. *Taking back the throne.* Bayne had left that out of his story. Was he in line for the throne? A flash of Bayne, resplendent in golden armor and a jeweled crown on his head danced behind my eyes. I could see it clearly. His integrity, loyalty, strength... Power. He would make a magnificent king. I pulled myself back into Isla's small room.

"I think that's why he felt so guilty about it. They'd fought hard in the months leading to her capture. I think if she hadn't been taken, things would have ended between them. But seriously. I want to know *everything*."

She stressed the last word, and warmth bloomed in my chest as my face reddened. I'd never had anyone to share things like this with, and I was surprised at the happiness it brought. I heaved a sigh, and grinning, I started with our nights in the mountains and winter months with Bear and his family.

"Someday," she said after she pried out the details of our

escapades on the Lake of Light, "I'm taking you to the Living Library in Lotrennia. And there, I will show you all six volumes of the *Sensua*. The Book of Bodies." She raised her eyebrows. "We don't lack imagination when it comes to sex positions." She winked.

My cheeks reddened further, and I wasn't sure how I could be more embarrassed after everything I'd divulged.

"Then you can show Bayne the Slippery Serpent."

I choked on a laugh, imagination whirring. We stayed in her room well into the evening, laughing and talking. Hours after sunset, we heard a knock on the door. Bayne stuck his head in.

"Everything okay in here?" he asked, cautiously meeting my eyes.

I returned his gaze with a wide grin and could see him visibly relax. I turned back to Isla, grateful for her time, her friendship. *This* was exactly what I needed. To remember where I was, and who I was with. *You're with friends*, Bayne had tried to tell me.

"Yes, nosy, we're getting much accomplished," Isla said, straightening up.

"Oh, yeah?" Bayne asked, raising his eyebrows, humor dancing in his eyes. "So, you're a full-blown mage now?"

"We're working on all of that," Isla said, shooting me a glance. "And yes, we are getting plenty of important work done. Lyvia will be a master in no time." Isla winked at me, and I knew exactly what mastery she referred to.

Bayne glanced at me, and heat rose in my cheeks once again.

"But we'd make better progress if you brought out some of that wine you've been hiding on us," she continued in playful accusation.

He stepped back, placing a hand to his heart, "I'd never!"

I tsked with my tongue. His eyes flashed to mine.

"Bring us the wine!" I cheered, joining in Isla's fit of laughter.

His eyes sparkled with some mixture of joy and relief. He opened his mouth and shut it, nodding his head.

"As you wish, my ladies," he crooned, bowing low before closing the door.

Isla snorted and rolled her eyes.

I STAYED in Isla's room well into the night, my heart feeling free for the first time in weeks. A couple hours before dawn, I stumbled a little drunkenly from her room, making my way to the captain's quarters. My hand lifted to grasp the handle, and it turned on its own. I blinked, trying to focus my eyes as the world tilted. I blinked again and now the door was opening on its own. Magic. I was doing magic!

"*Magficinet!*" I exclaimed and furrowed my eyebrows, feeling a slight headache coming on. "Mag*cifi*net," I mumbled, speech blurred.

I looked up again, and Bayne had also magically appeared in the doorway.

"Oh my," he said, looking me up and down.

"Bay... Bay!" I cried, throwing my arms around his neck. Gods, I was so happy to see him!

"Oh, gods, please don't call me that. How much wine did you two drink? I only brought a bottle down..." He eyed me before leveling an incredulous look.

"Did you find the ridecus?"

"No, *you're* ridiculous!" I stammered back at him, slapping him on the chest.

He shook his head and closed his eyes, pinching the space above his nose.

"Let's get you some tea. Or water."

"I don't need tea or water. I need *you*," I said huskily, heat appearing out of nowhere and racing to my lower abdomen. I threw myself at him, lips and tongue sliding over his sweet and salty neck. Burning Aelius, I needed him.

He let out a low growl of approval under my lips and I smiled, teeth scraping against his skin. His hands grasped my shoulders, and he gently pushed me back.

"Tea. *And* water. And then bed," he said gently, rubbing my back.

"You don't want to see what you do to me?" I breathed, melting into the heat of him, my fingers drifting to the laces on my pants. A steady throbbing had begun between my legs.

Bayne caught my wrist with a sharp inhale. His lips found my ear through my hair as he whispered, "Though you, Lyvia dear, are more intoxicating than a *sea* of ridecus, I will not bed you while you're this drunk. Water."

He pulled away at the last command and turned me toward the kitchen.

CHAPTER THIRTY-NINE

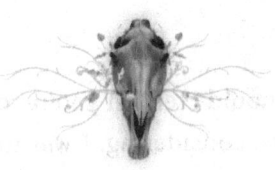

Vulcan Vetiver, son of Ghyslaine, Lady of Tomorrow. Father unknown. Released by payment.
— Signed release of Vulcan Vetiver. Hall of Records at the Living Library, level 6. Lotrennia.

Ablazing headache woke me the next morning. Groaning, I rolled over, reaching for Bayne, who wasn't there. I tucked my knees to my chest, curling into myself and cursing Isla for convincing me to hunt down the ridecus. My leather leggings tugged uncomfortably around my waist, and I loosened the ties. Pants still on.

Bayne. Ever the gentlemen. Had my head not pounded relentlessly, I might have felt a flicker of embarrassment at the brief memories that now replayed in my mind. A sloppy tug on his pants, kneeling before him as he gently lifted me to my feet, throwing myself on the kitchen table, and...

I groaned, shutting out the hazy images. A soft knock sounded on the door and Bayne stepped in.

"Hey, Angel," he said quietly. "Heads up. Nissa's on her way to start training."

I looked up too quickly, pain filling the space between my eyes.

"*What?* No."

He chuckled. "Should I tell her you're too hungover?"

I closed my eyes, considering. I *was* too hungover. But I'd felt more alive these days training with her. And with what was coming...

I groaned again and his strong hands rubbed my back as he leaned in and planted a kiss on my forehead. "Tea," he said, handing me a hot mug.

I gingerly sat up and took a sip.

"Last night," I began, a soft shade of pink embarrassment appearing on my cheeks.

His chuckle danced along my skin as he sat down on the bed, leaning in close. "As much as I would have loved to ravish you," he purred, "I would rather our first night back together be something you remember. And choose to do without the influence of something like *ridecus*." He raised his dark brows higher.

My toes curled in response to the way his tongue slipped over his lower lip, making me briefly forget the pounding in my head. He lifted his hand, fingers brushing a stray strand of hair from my face as his eyes simmered.

Nerissa strolled in with the salty ocean breeze and made an exasperating sound as she took in the two of us on Bayne's bed.

"Two minutes. At the bow."

I nodded as she swept out of the room. Bayne gripped my

chin as he lowered his lips down to mine in a soft kiss. He held my gaze a moment longer, lips a breath away.

"What is it?"

"You are so much stronger than you've been led to believe," he murmured with a slight shake of his head. "Movement will be good," he whispered, pulling away.

———

I MADE my way to the front of the ship and stopped short when I found Vulcan standing at the bow. He turned, the dark ink of his fern tattoo shifting with his grimace as he took in the sight of me.

"You look like hell."

"Good morning to you, too," I growled back, not in the mood for his irritability. I reached for the short sword I'd been training with.

He shook his head as he quickly tied his blonde hair back into a knot.

"Put this on," he said, motioning to a leather harness fitted with two crossing scabbards.

I'd seen him and the others wear a similar one when wielding two short swords. I looped the leather around my shoulders and waist as he stepped over and tightened it snuggly.

"Your footwork with a single sword is good. Today, we add another. Put that on, too." He pointed to a bow and quiver of arrows.

"All of this?" I asked.

"Yes. We're running out of time. We'll be in Sultira by the end of the day, and once we've made landfall, there's no telling how quickly Saros's forces will retaliate against the Rising."

I pulled on the bow and arrows and attempted to sheath the two short swords, awkwardly clanking them against each other. I repeated the move, sheathing, unsheathing, and drawing my arrows over and over again until I got it down. Vulcan then drilled me on two-blade attacks.

"Do you really think this is necessary? I am just now feeling like I can use one blade with either hand," I said as he attacked. I caught one blade between the two of mine and dodged the second, stepping around the mast and tripping over my own feet.

Vulcan growled in annoyance, his patience worse than Nerissa's.

"*Yes*, it's necessary," he hissed. "If you're part of this crew, you *live*. And if you're going to live, you learn to be lethal."

He repeated the same move, yielding the same result.

"Fuck," I growled.

"Your balance is shit with two swords," he said as I stood up.

"I know," I snapped back at him. "And not helpful."

I eyed him grumpily. He sighed, dropping his sword and gazing up at the bowsprit.

"Okay. We're trying something different. Take these off," he said, gesturing to the weapons and harness. "And those," he said, pointing to my boots.

"These?" I asked, confused.

He leveled a stare at me. "Do you want my help or not?"

I rolled my eyes and began removing my weapons. I wasn't sure I *did* want his help. He was more than a pain in my ass. Vulcan stepped to the front of the ship, facing the bowsprit.

"Precision is vital in wielding any blade, especially two. Precision is impossible without balance. We're nearing Odessa, but, when possible, you will meet me here every morning, an hour before sunrise. Follow my lead."

Vulcan began a series of slow, torturous balancing movements made impossible with the rocking of the *Evecta*. The only words he spoke were basic instructions, and then we would keep that pose in silence for minutes at a time. My muscles *burned*. Vulcan met my eyes with a scowl every moment I opened my mouth to protest. Right. Silence.

An hour later, we stood on one leg with the other pointed straight behind us and arms out to the side. My quad shook from the strain on the tiny muscles needed to balance, and a drip of sweat slid down my nose. I watched it splat and absorb quickly, the dry wooden deck thirsty for the moisture.

Vulcan stepped down and reached his hands over his head before slowly bringing them to his sides. He sighed. I eyed him from behind, feeling a change in his countenance.

"We're done for today. Don't forget. An hour before sunrise."

I opened my mouth to ask what the hell we just did, but as I let out a breath, a weight lifted.

―――※―――

ISLA FOUND ME SOON AFTER, and we set to work on basic commands with wind and water before attempting to tap into the Obscura power. I caught her pinching her nose and rubbing her eyes on several occasions, clearly regretting the ridecus we'd finished the night before.

"You need to call to it like a lover. *Coax* it out," she said to me after my multiple failed attempts to obliterate the jerky that sat before me.

Every time I reached for the power, it lazily swatted my hand away like a fly.

"I'm trying," I said, irritation flaring. "It's like it's hungover. It's tired."

"Impossible. Magic doesn't work like that. It is not sentient. *You* are hungover, Lyvia."

"And who is to blame for that?" I snapped back.

"I'm only trying to help," she said and sighed. "This is giving me a headache. We'll try this again after we've made landfall."

I cracked my neck as she walked away and chewed on a chunk of the stupid jerky. The Obscura power *hummed* in agreement like it wasn't worth its time. *Not sentient*, I reminded myself.

I meandered above deck to find Bayne training with Nerissa. They mirrored each other with such focus and intensity, their movements a perfect action and reaction to the other's.

Aquila sat perched on a beam nearby. I didn't meet the hawk's gaze, which he'd rarely taken off me since boarding the *Evecta* during my escape. A connection had formed between us on Kayj, and it was more disarming than the star that glowed on my palm. Oslo's sudden appearance shook me from my reverie as he leaned forward to watch the two elves dancing across the deck.

"They are amazing."

I saw him nod in agreement out of the corner of my eye.

"Aye, my lady. And you've come a long way yourself if I do say so."

I smiled at him. "Maybe. But I'm not ready for war," I said quietly.

"No one is ever truly ready for it. Even after surviving it for years, everyone faces doubts. But it helps to have men and women like them on your side," he said, nodding to the swirl of blades.

"I know you didn't ask for any of this, Lyvia," he began

after a few minutes. "Your entire world has been tipped upside down. And your brother and father..."

The burning sensation of forming tears began, and I hastily shoved the emotion down.

"I never knew your father, but I knew of him. And though he was close with King Saros, the things that I heard of him were honorable. He was a good man. I am so sorry that the events in the past months led to his death. And that of your brother's."

Oslo shifted next to me, his soft eyes landing on my face. I glanced over, and his eyebrows pinched up in a look of sincerity. I pulled my gaze down, nodding my head in thanks. He squeezed my shoulder before turning back.

BAYNE PEELED off his sopping shirt two hours later, and I felt myself stir as he shook his head, dark hair spraying the deck with sweat. He took a long swig of water and glanced up to find me gawking at him. He grinned mischievously before giving me a playful wink. Oslo chuckled, and I bristled at being caught. I gave him a soft punch on the shoulder before heading back to the captain's quarters to change.

The image of shirtless Bayne chased away any thoughts I had about our arrival in Sultira and the impending battle I clearly wasn't prepared for. Either the ridecus or the time spent with Isla had unlocked a part of me that I'd shut tight since Nivis. I paused, pulling a fresh shirt over my head, and eyed Bayne's spare shirt slung over the chair behind his desk. Trading his for mine, I draped the oversized shirt over my shoulders and skipped the pants altogether. I hopped on the beautifully carved walnut desk with seconds to spare before he swung the door open.

His eyes found mine and quickly darkened as he took in the scene. Closing the door, he slowly walked to his desk, eyes devouring me step by step. Heat swelled in my midsection, and it was all I could do not to leap off the desk and pin him to the floor. I scooted to the edge of the desk as he drew closer, legs spreading. A soft sound escaped his lips that turned me into a puddle.

He stepped between my legs, and I could feel wet heat radiating off his bare, glistening chest, the black ink a mirage of swirls and sweat. I locked eyes with him as my hands slipped through his soaked hair. His lips pressed against mine with a crushing passion, and a moan caught in my throat. The Obscura power roiled in response, pleased with my break in control, and I shoved it down, disarmed at its presence during such an intimate moment.

Bayne gripped my hip with one hand as his other slid slowly along my inner thigh, tracing a long line from my knee to the space in the center gathering heat. His tongue danced lazily along my own as his fingers continued their slow teasing. My blood sang in response, and my control began to slip. As if sensing my shift, he moved to his knees as Aquila let out a piercing shriek.

Bayne spun across the captain's quarters to the door where Vulcan's voice sounded from outside.

"Escort ships from Odessa," he called.

Bayne ground his teeth as his eyes, still bright with lust, roved over me.

"We'll be on Sultira shores within the hour," he murmured, stalking back to where I sat.

"And while it will take all of my self-control to walk away from this," he purred, stepping back between my legs and sliding his hands along my hips, "I'll never rush my time with you."

It took everything in me not to self-combust at his words. My blood thrummed in my veins, and his nostrils flared. I swallowed, willing myself to calm down as he planted a soft kiss beneath my ear before stepping outside.

CHAPTER FORTY

Nissy, How could I possibly forget about it? I've seen your face in the dawn of every day since. Soulbinding be damned. I'd bind my breath to you. —Ro

—Correspondence from Ronan Merik to Nerissa Ravindra, 37th of Winter, 064.3E. Nerissa's private quarters, Evecta.

Massive white cliffs jutted out from the sea, painting the horizon in azure blue and white stripes. The northern region of Odessa lay before us as the *Evecta* wound its way around the corner of the cliff into a small bay.

Unmarked civilian archers stood guard atop the cliffs as we passed. The bay, typically under royal guard, was filled with anchored ships flying various flags. Stolen Sultiran naval ships sat docked without the emblazoned flag of the king. I scanned the small fleet for the blue shield and spear flag that marked

Lord Pavel's ships, not spotting any that belonged to my father's friend. A group of buildings made up the small port town and behind it, on miles of sprawling fields sat several hundred mismatched tents. Men stood in various groups scattered across the makeshift camp.

I tugged on my gloves, adjusting the leather to fit more snuggly on my fingers. Nerissa warned me not to show the eight-pointed star on my palm.

The Obscura rumbled in my chest as we stepped off the *Evecta* and onto Sultiran shores. Marian remained behind, and I walked side by side with Bayne, whose pointed ears were on full display in the spring sunlight along with the rest of the elves that strode behind us with Drystan and Oslo. The golden bone bounced softly on my chest. It had taken on a quiet, easy song since our escape from Kayj, and I'd become used to its presence, despite Isla's warning.

We walked down the center aisle of the camp to the base of operations. Men and women paused in their tasks as we swept through the tents, gawking or grimacing at the sight of four elves and three humans strolling down the center of the Rising. Awe and whispers of prayer spread throughout the camp. *Brother defend us, Sisters protect us.*

Bayne's composure didn't falter. In fact, as I glanced sidelong at him, a military leader had taken the place of the rogue captain. Here was the king of Lotrennia, despite his rough leather vest with the numerous hidden daggers and the snug pants. Militant professionalism replaced his casual swagger as he strode through the camp. I had no doubt this army would be his, if he wanted it.

I scanned the gathering crowd looking for any familiar faces. My heart leapt as my eyes snagged on Vander, watching our group from a distance. His mouth parted as his gray-green eyes landed on me. I caught his gaze and smiled. He glanced briefly at my companions and gave me a soft nod in response.

My thoughts flew to Aeriden, my mind conjuring the image of his vacant face staring up from the ice chest in the Crystal Castle. My heart clenched, and I sucked in a breath. Bayne's pace slowed next to me, sensing my shift. I took a shuddering breath and pulled my eyes from Vander to the large black tent where a curtain door swung open.

A head of light bouncing curls and penetrating blue eyes peered out as Ronan lifted the flap. With an arrogant smile plastered on his face, he greeted Bayne like old friends. I bristled, not bothering to hide my response. Ronan was dressed down in plain training leathers. Gone were the frills and uniform of the queensguard and the colors of the capital. A large, half-healed scar stretched across his chin and down his neck. His gaze slid to mine, and I held it with cool resolve. His smile disappeared, and he glanced at my neck, examining the thick scar that stretched across it. My gloves stretched over my knuckles in my clenched fists. I felt exposed.

Ronan nodded to the crew behind me, lips tightening as his gaze found Nerissa. "Nis—" he began.

"Don't," she said, cutting him off. "We are here to help the Rising. And that is the only reason."

He caught the involuntary tug of my lips and pursed his own. Turning to Bayne he said, "I'll have my men find your crew some tents while we share our plans. We have much to discuss."

Your crew. Not ours, as if he truly was no longer a part of the *Evecta*. He motioned to a few soldiers who stepped forward, eyes pinned to my neck. Ronan waited for Bayne to follow.

"The crew will join us in the briefing," Bayne said, all captain now. Ronan held his stare for several heartbeats.

The air outside tensed as the guards shifted awkwardly on their feet.

Ronan nodded once and strode into the black tent. My eyes took a moment to adjust to the dimness inside. Maps lay strewn across several tables. Two small groups sat near the front, eyes wide as we entered. They darted to the ears of my companions, then to my scar and Oslo's stubbed arm, now fitted with a short blade.

After quick introductions, the leaders of the groups began debating the most effective strategy for dethroning Saros. The rest of us sat at a side table with three priests and two women capable of wielding the lost arts—wind whisperers, a healer, and a water witch. Drystan and Isla were deep in conversation with the wind whisperers as Vienah, a stunning young water witch, sidled up next to me. She was petite with strawberry blonde hair and soft brown eyes.

"And do you practice the lost arts as well?" Vienah asked as she replaced a dying taper.

"Me?" I stuttered, glancing quickly at Nerissa. "No. I mean I've tried, but no. I have no power."

Nerissa's clenched jaw relaxed.

Vienah followed my gaze to the warrior and asked, "And you?"

"A bit of wind whispering," Nerissa answered. "And water, like yourself."

My brows furrowed as she responded. That wasn't right. Bayne and Nerissa had something else. I opened my mouth when Isla cut me a glare so deadly I thought I might wither. I blinked, looking up to find Ronan's gaze pinned on me from a table over. His eyes widened, as if urging me to do the same.

I answered him with a sneer of my own, one I'd gathered from being forced to spend so much time with Vulcan. The odious elf stood next to Bayne peering over his shoulder.

"You aren't ready for this type of attack, Ro," Bayne said. "You said the other Rising camps are west of the Lumerians. Why wouldn't you wait for them? If these are all your numbers," he said, motioning to the camp outside the tent, "you'll last a day against Sultiran forces. Maybe two. Why rush this?"

Ronan stood at the front of the table, both hands placed on the map in front of him. He raised his eyes to the other Rising commanders across the table.

"We need to move on Saros by the end of spring. It's nonnegotiable," he stated, straightening and running a hand through curls. His gaze was hard.

Bayne narrowed his eyes at him. *Ronan wasn't telling us everything.*

Aelius's rays blinded me for a moment as afternoon light flooded the tent. The curtain door flapped shut taking the sun with it. I blinked against the darkness, the lit tapers doing little to illuminate the three dark figures that had abruptly entered the tent. The woody scent of enderleaf smoke filled my nostrils.

Bayne froze.

Dark eyes sparked from the front of the tent as the man in the center took a long drag of his smoke, the tip burning bright orange.

Unsure of when it happened, my companions had formed a protective hexagon around me. Isla was suddenly by my side, and Nerissa took a step forward, a soft snarl escaping her lips.

Weapons clinked as the man strode through the tent, flanked by two others. A strange sort of awareness swept through me, senses on high alert.

The rings on his fingers clicked as he pulled a black leather hat off his head, revealing dark auburn shoulder-length hair, half of it tied tightly behind his head, braids lined with silver beads tucked behind rounded ears. His short, cropped beard was neatly trimmed, despite his rough appearance. My breath hitched. Had the promise of death not lingered in his gaze, I would have been awestruck by his beauty. He was handsome. Striking, even.

His dark eyes followed as my gaze slid from the curved blade that hung on his belt to the two curious white daggers sheathed on either side of his vest. A scar cut through the side of his lower lip, whitening as the corners of his mouth tilted. Above his black fighting leathers, his ocean blue coat was adorned with an array of mismatched talismans, gems, and bones.

Dark, inked designs inched up his neck in the bit of skin that showed at his collar and chest, where they met with a grisly scar. My heart picked up the steady beat of the hunted as he approached.

Stretching his arms to the side, he sketched a mock bow to Bayne, finally dragging the murder in his eyes away from me.

"Captain," he murmured through the rolled smoke in his lips.

Bayne ignored the greeting and turned to Ronan, eyes wide with fiery wrath. "You would call on the Lords of Marisarma?"

Marisarma. My pulse quickened, its beat hasty with fear as if chanting, *pirate, pirate.* Ronan lifted a chin and met Bayne with his own look of steel. He slid his azure eyes to the pirate, whose lips curled into a terrifying smile.

"Lord Kellan Astraeus," Ronan said, offering the pirate a curt nod, "the Marisarma fleet is most welcome here."

Silence stretched across the room. The Obscura power bucked beneath a thick layer of fear that coated my entire being.

Lord Astraeus. He appeared so much younger than he

should have for the record he kept. For the distrust he instilled in the crew.

"Commander," Lord Astraeus crooned, stepping past Bayne and plunking down in a chair. His eyes shot back to mine, narrowing in on the bone hidden beneath my shirt. The grip on my goblet of dark wine tightened.

"I've agreed to reopen the Votruvian trade winds, Bayne. And now that you've all joined us," Ronan paused, motioning toward Bayne and the rest of the crew, "I believe we have what it takes to win this war *and* the next."

Tension hung in the air at the silence that followed. Bayne's posture went deathly still as Ronan's eyes drifted to me, scanning every curve and pocket on my body as if searching for the Bones of the Bellators. I found myself adjusting my stance to a defensive position.

"Don't worry, Princeling," Lord Astraeus quietly drawled, turning back to Bayne and scraping his boots against the wood of the main table as he reclined and crossed one foot over the other. "I'm here for one thing."

Dark eyes slid back to mine, narrowing. A threat. The snarl that ripped through Bayne's lips was like a canon in the quiet of night. Before I could blink, his dagger was at Astraeus's throat, but he stilled.

Bayne was fast. But as if he knew it was coming, Astraeus had his own already poised at Bayne's groin. The pirate lord's lips tilted upward, flashing the whites of his teeth. The room froze, but my veins pulsed with power at his threat.

Darkness gathered as the Obscura roiled within me, humming encouragingly. It beckoned. *Release me*, it purred, *you are not afraid of the dark.* I swallowed against the pressure in my palms, willing myself to calm.

"Sisters protect us," a voice whispered into the silence.

Bayne and Astraeus tore their gaze from each other to me. I

blinked, feeling the heavy stares of the people in the room. Bayne's brows pinched in a hint of concern.

"It appears you found the prophesized one after all," Lord Astraeus said coolly, releasing his dagger. The pirate's eyes darted between mine as sharp intakes of breath sounded all around.

"Twin eclipse, indeed," Ronan muttered, his words a whisper in disbelief.

Isla's hand wrapped around my shaking goblet. I glanced down at the dark wine and was met with my reflection. Two large pupils stared back, with a blazing rim of sunset orange, as brilliant as any fire. The Obscura spun excitedly in my center as I registered the sight. Taking a few slow, deep breaths, I willed it to cool. The fire died slowly, and my irises returned to their natural caramel hue.

Astraeus grinned and turned back to the table. "Shall we begin?"

CHAPTER FORTY-ONE

Loyalty means nothing to the Lords of Marisarma or their
spies. Find them. Convince them. I'll pay steeply.
  —Correspondence from Queen Antares to Anonymous.
Date unknown.

"Cantor. A word," Ronan called, as he rushed
forward.

Bayne paused in the doorway of the tent,
looking back at me as our group exited. Ronan's unexpected
ally triggered something with the crew, and the willingness to
launch headfirst into this rebellion was staunched with hesitation at the arrival of Lord Astraeus.

I waited for a nod of encouragement but was only met with
calm certainty. Right. I didn't need Bayne's permission. He
held my stare for a few heartbeats before stepping out of the
tent. Isla gave my hand a squeeze on the way out as the rest of
them followed. Ronan had dismissed the others, the Maris-

arma pirates exiting with menacing glares, leaving us alone for the first time in months.

I turned to face Ronan.

"Lyvia," he began, voice soft and calm, "I'm glad you are all right." A cloud of betrayal blew into my chest as memories of the past weeks flashed through my mind.

"All right?" I asked, voice barely audible. *"All right?"*

The darkness bucked. *Use me, use me.* I shushed it in my chest or out loud. I wasn't sure as Ronan blinked in confusion. I was frustrated at its interruptions. The song of the bone that hung around my neck had grown eerily quiet.

"I am not all right. I—" I began and paused. "No. I don't have to talk to you about anything that has happened. *You.* You are a bastard!" I said, stepping forward and jabbing a finger in his chest. His arms flew up in defense.

"Lyvia, everything I did, including lying to you—"

"And stealing from me!" My voice had risen to a yell. He held up his hands, shushing me.

"And stealing from you... was for the Rising. To remove Saros from the throne and stop the dark king. You *have* to know this."

"And using me!"

He stepped back, dropping his hands to his sides in defeat.

"Yes! Lyvia, *everyone* will use you now that you're in possession of two of the Stones of the Bellators. You will either be used or you will be dead. That is your reality now. Be grateful you've made it to my camp and aren't stuck in Saros's dungeons or on Kayj."

"I'VE BEEN TO BOTH!" I screamed at him. "And I'm only out thanks to the crew of the *Evecta*. *They* are my family. They have my loyalty. Not you."

"You would abandon your own family so soon? What about those here in Sultira?" he said, voice laced with accusation. "You would abandon them to the fate King Saros bestows on them? To become monsters or slaves? Not even given the liberty to die with honor?"

His words sliced through me like a blade. I didn't respond, letting the guilt that rode his words slam into me.

"Cantor—" he said, reaching for my hand. I jerked it away.

"Don't call me that," I spat at him. "I'm not a Cantor." My voice broke at the end, the truth of it shattering a tiny piece of my soul.

His face softened on the edge of pity. "Listen to me. People know you have the stones. You have two of the most powerful possessions known to the realm of Vael. I know you have one on you now after that little show." His eyes scanned mine, searching.

"Others will come for you. For the stones. Help me. *Help us.* We need them. They are our only hope at restoring Sultira and defeating Saros *and* the dark king. I saw you in Rivaner. You leaped aboard the tribute ship to save others. I know you want to save the rest of them. This is how," he said, gesturing to the camp surrounding us.

He was right, of course. I would help. I *wanted* to help. I was just so damn tired of being used and betrayed. And every shadowed memory from the last six months continued to lurk in my mind, quietly darkening my thoughts.

Ronan's eyes pierced my gaze, and my molars scraped against each other. He didn't deserve to be so handsome. Or charming. It irritated the hell out of me.

"I'll think about it," I said before turning to exit the tent.

"One other thing, Lyvia," Ronan called after me.

I paused in the doorway, refusing to look back.

"Let the others know I've written to Queen Antares, calling for aid."

Coward.

384

Coward to leave it to me to deliver that message. I stepped into the low, evening light to find Bayne in quiet discussions with Vulcan and Oslo. He looked up as I exited, and I gave him a curt nod, joining Nerissa and Isla who were heading down a row of tents.

"He's an ass," Nerissa said.

"Fucking ass," I agreed, falling in step with her.

Isla remained silent as we made our way to the western edge of the camp. We passed rows upon rows of mismatched tents. The men and women mulling about camp ranged from the dark-skinned farmers of the southwestern region of Sultira to the light-skinned miners hailing from the northern Lumerian mountains. While few of them appeared to be trained in battle, they all carried the same heaviness to their shoulders. They'd all lost someone at the hands of King Saros.

<hr />

THE SIX OF us returned to the *Evecta* shortly after to debrief with Marian. We agreed the crew would stay and fight so long as the pirates maintained their distance. Bayne and Nerissa kept their cool resolve as we discussed Ronan's plea to Queen Antares, but I could tell they were on edge.

We'd split up, leaving half of us on board to guard the ship and keep it ready for retreat if needed while the others stayed in Ronan's camp. We also agreed that the second bone of the Bellators should be passed between us. I had a big enough target on my back as it was, given I couldn't separate myself from the Obscura power. I passed it to Nerissa as Isla, Oslo, Bayne, and I exited the ship and made our way back to the camp later that evening settling into the three tents Ronan had procured for us.

Bayne wrapped a fur around me, tucking me close as he

doused the taper in our tent with a pinch. His fingers tugged on the leather tie at the bottom of my braid, loosening my hair. He buried his face in it, taking a long inhale. Heat rushed to my midsection as he let out a hot sigh. He combed it gently in his fingers as he pushed himself to his elbows. I closed my eyes, fully relaxing in the small, cozy quarters.

I blinked my eyes open to find him staring at me, brows pinched with concern.

"What's wrong?" I asked, pushing up to my elbows.

"Stynguard," he murmured.

I frowned, a question forming on my lips.

"I thought you were dead. I lost all control. I didn't hear Vulcan or Nerissa. I stopped working as a team. All I saw was red," he said, voice quiet and eyes dark. "I ignored the decades of training and the loyalty in my heart. It nearly got them both killed."

Even in the dark of the tent, I could see the guilt strewn across his features.

"I stopped being their captain." He shook his head.

I reached out and cupped his face in my hand, brushing my thumb along the scar on his temple.

"You will never stop being their captain," I said, crushed at seeing him so vulnerable. "This is just something you learn from. Right?"

He gave me a smile that didn't quite reach his eyes. "The thing is, I would do it again. I wouldn't hesitate. I... You are..." he began.

I'd never seen him at such a loss for words. I stared into his eyes, lost in a sea of green, wondering what he saw looking back at the dullness in my own.

As if reading my thoughts, he said, "Home. Being with you is like being home. Lyv..." His hand cupped the side of my face, before sliding smoothly into my hair.

"I have had decades in this world to know what it is I feel. And while the Vael has yet to make its full rotation around the sun since I've known you, you *ignite* me. I've burned brighter these past months than I have my entire existence. Those three simple words have danced at the edge of my mind since the moment I laid eyes on you, yet they pale in comparison to the sea of devotion and need that moves in me. I need you to know you *have* me, Lyv. My heart, my soul. My blades, my power. Every bit of me is yours. I love you."

Something deep inside me stirred as I processed his words, as if my soul, the very essence of my being inched closer to his.

"And if you're not ready for something like that," he began, shaking his head, "I understand. It's a big thing to hear, and I know we haven't known each other for long..." He was backpedaling.

Oh gods, don't walk it back now. He didn't know.

"Bayne," I cut him off with a soft chuckle, "I have been yours since the moment we pulled you aboard the *Evecta*. I didn't know it then. You..." I shook my head. "My heart has been yours since that moment. You *see* me. I sometimes think you know me better than I know myself. And I love you, too."

His green eyes sparkled with a joy that was a mirror to my own. We held each other for several moments as he slowly tugged his fingers through my hair, brushing them away from my face before planting a kiss on my forehead.

"Sleep, Angel," he said quietly.

I brought his hand to my chest where I felt the aching emptiness of the musical bone that normally sang softly. His face nestled into the hair against my neck as he inhaled deeply.

"Why do you call me that?" I breathed into the dark, my voice shaking. I was the furthest thing from an angel, as literal darkness swirled in my veins. Images of my father's face, eyes wide with shock as I twisted... No.

No, no, shut it out. Not now. My stomach churned, bile rising to my throat, and I pinched my eyes closed, shoving at the memory.

"Look at me, Lyvia." He cupped my face in his hands.

I stirred at his closeness.

"Nothing you've done, or could do, would ever change how I feel about you."

His gaze pierced my soul as his words settled in me. It didn't change the guilt that continued to devour me, but this closeness, the look in his eyes... I could forget about it for a short while. Heat swirled in my veins as his lips drifted closer.

"You didn't answer my question, Captain," I said, inching closer and sliding my thigh between his legs. It earned me a soft growl that sent my spine tingling with anticipation.

He adjusted himself so his hips sat comfortably between my legs.

"I thought I was dead when I left Kayj," he murmured against my skin, planting a soft kiss on my temple. "One moment, I was swallowing sea water, sinking beneath the waves." Another kiss to the space below my jaw, above my scar. "I saw darkness, Lyv." Ever so gently, his tongue slid over my scar.

I tensed for a brief second as he moved past it, sucking softly on my neck below. My heart began a quiet gallop in my chest as need pulsed through me.

"And moments later, I was home. Aboard the *Evecta*, staring up at an *angel*, like you had flown down to save me." He paused to look at me, his hand sliding a strand of hair from my face. "You've been to hell and back. What else could do that but an angel?"

His lips traveled down my chest, pausing over the crescent-shaped scar that Cyril had given me. The shudder of a growl escaped his lips. "I wish I could have ended him for you. We should have gotten there sooner," he said in soft regret.

I looked up at him, holding his gaze from under those dark, thick lashes.

"We cannot change the past. It is fact," I said quietly, repeating Nerissa's words to him. "And you *did* save me. I would still be on Kayj if you hadn't come. And I *want* to forget it. Help me forget. The future is what I want now." I shifted my hips under him, unable to keep still at this proximity.

His eyes drifted to my lips and down the trail of kissed, bare skin.

"And what kind of future do you have in mind?" he purred, his voice dangerously delicious.

My tongue slid over my lips. "One with you in it."

"Anything else besides my presence?" he asked, eyes darkening further.

I bit my lip as my heart began to beat between my legs. From the look in his eyes, he might have been able to hear it.

"I need you, Bayne. All of you."

My fingers crashed through his thick hair, snapping the tether in myself and pulling his face to mine. His kiss crushed against my mouth, desperate and searching. I slid my hand down his chest, fingers bouncing over the hidden scar and the ridges of rows of corded muscle until they reached the hard length of him ready to burst through his leathers.

I squeezed gently, earning a moan of approval, before tugging loose the laces, freeing him as his fingers found their way from my breast to between my legs. He groaned as they met the warm wetness that had pooled between us, sliding a finger in and rubbing his thumb against the small bundle of nerves at the top. My hips moved in response, my core desperate for more friction.

"Fuck," he muttered into my hair.

I gripped the sides of his pants and edged them down, enough to completely free him before guiding him into me. He plunged in to the hilt. I moaned quietly, savoring the stretch as he filled me completely. He moved slowly at first, cautious even, treating me delicately as if broken. I bristled at the idea of him thinking me weak. I reached behind, pulling him close and moving faster with my hips as I found his mouth again.

My kiss was a bruising passion, spurring him faster. The pounding in my core deepened, and the maddening pulsing between my legs thundered until I broke, fire dancing in my vision as I was sent over the edge. Bayne slowed, lifting his head and brushing his nose against mine.

"Why did you stop?" I asked in a mumbled whimper. My gaze found his, and the adoration in his eyes set me ablaze once more.

"I needed to look at you," he said simply, eyes drifting again to my lips.

My breath hitched, and need suddenly returned to my center. My eyes grew heavy with lust as I pushed my hands against his chest, flipping us over. Our hands interlaced as I leaned forward, breasts tickling his chest.

"*Don't* stop," I breathed into his lips.

This time, he unleashed himself. I was back on the ground, face down, my hips in the air. He plunged deeper, and his fingers found their way to the front of me. I gasped, biting my tongue to keep from crying out as I crashed into completion after a minute of his mind-tingling fullness and the rapid circles his fingers made at the apex of my thighs. Seconds later, his body racked against mine as he crashed into me. He slumped over my back, sweat dripping and rolling off my side.

We collapsed to the ground, his hand finding mine and lacing his fingers through. A light, tickling breeze drifted in through the gaps of our tent, and I took a deep breath of the cool spring air. *I could stay here forever*, I thought, as my eyes drifted closed. Bayne's heartbeat thudded against my back as we lay in silent bliss.

Footsteps sounded outside the quiet of our camp, and Bayne was on his feet in a crouch, pants on in seconds before he stepped from our small tent.

I tugged my pants back on, hastily lacing up the front of my shirt when the arguing started. Stepping from our small tent, I found Ronan inches from Bayne's face.

His blue eyes shot to mine and widened for a moment. They darted between me and Bayne to the small tent behind us. His jaw clenched before his lips curled into a half smile that didn't quite meet his eyes. He raised his eyebrows at me.

"A thing for the pointed ears, huh?" he grunted.

A prickle of embarrassment sent heat to my cheeks. My relationship with Bayne was no secret, but Ronan hadn't known. And the last time I'd really seen Ronan we were... Well, we weren't exactly just friends. Anger quickly mottled out the embarrassment.

"A thing for honesty," I retorted, stepping up to them.

His eyes widened, and this time he did nothing to hide his reaction.

"*Honesty*?" he scoffed, glancing quickly at Bayne.

"Careful," Bayne said, lethally quiet.

Ronan surveyed me with a hard look, the smile disappearing. "So, he's told you everything then? You think you know everything about Captain Ravindra?"

Unease crept its way into my gut as I thought about my last conversation with Isla. The throne of Lotrennia. No. Ronan was right. I *didn't* know everything there was to know about Bayne. He still held secrets. I bristled at the thought. But had I even had enough time to think about this yet? Shame crept into my chest at how easily I felt myself giving my heart away. Because

I knew in these last few days, he had my heart. I had fallen so deeply for him that I was already making excuses for him.

Oslo and Isla were out of their tents now. Oslo's hand was at his side, resting easily upon the hilt of his other sword. Isla watched us intently.

"Ronan," she cut in.

His eyes whipped to hers. "Isla. Seriously," he said, waving his hand between me and Bayne.

"It's none of your business," I snapped before our relationship became a topic of conversation for this midnight meeting.

Ronan pinched the space between his eyes with one hand, closing them briefly. He huffed a laugh, letting his hand drop. Nodding, eyes filled with derision, he said, "You're right, Lyvia. It's not any of my business who you choose to fuck. But it is my business if it puts the outcome of this war at risk."

The mockery eased and seriousness entered his voice. "I need to know you can wield the stones, Lyvia. I need to see it."

"Why?" I asked, stepping forward.

"*Why?* Because it might be the difference between winning this war and saving *our* people!" His voice had risen, control snapping. *Our* people. He was right, of course. I was human. This was our land. And it was our people at stake during this rebellion, not the elves, even if they were here to help. Bayne moved between us faster than I could process, and his face was in Ronan's within a second.

"Bayne," I said quietly. "It's fine."

Ronan rippled with fury. He quelled it, taking a breath. "The fate of Sultira rests with the power of the Bellators," he said, his stare as hard as the black armor he'd left behind. "The responsibility is heavy, Lyvia."

CHAPTER FORTY-TWO

Only one prisoner managed to escape. Though we are still unsure where Belgar Greenfoot fled, two sentries claimed they saw a ship offshore before it vanished.

— Prisoner Records dated 2nd of Winter, 045.3E. Demon's Door.

The next morning, I set out to find Vander after an hour of what Vulcan deemed *centering exercises* aboard the *Evecta* and two hours of training with Isla and Drystan. I wandered through the south side of the camp, eventually finding him sparring with an older gentleman. His height gave him great advantage with the sword, an easy extension of his arm.

I smiled, leaning up against the makeshift fence. An ache, deep in my chest grew as he danced across the space in a flurry of blades. Distant memories of him and Aeriden training at the manor brushed against my mind. That ache deepened to a stinging pain, my smile fading.

He sheathed his sword after spotting me at the fence. A broad smile spread across his face as he strode to where I stood. I forced a smile and reached out as he wrapped me in a sweaty hug.

"Lyvia," he said, voice rumbling into my chest, "I can't believe you are here. Where's Aeriden? Did you find him after the lake?" He pulled away, eyes scanning the camp as if Aeriden might walk up any moment.

I quickly looked away, blood draining from my face. He gripped my shoulders and hunched down to me.

"Oh, Lyvi," he said, voice softening. "What happened?"

AN HOUR LATER, we sat outside his tent, sipping on ale after I'd told my story. *Most* of it, at least. We toasted to Aeriden before getting lost in stories from our youth. I sat back on the heels of my hands, warmth swelling in my chest as laughter bubbled out.

"And he had the fucking nerve to shove me off that branch! I thought your dad was going to butcher us," he laughed, shaking his head. "Weird to think he's gone. I thought he'd outlive all of us," he murmured.

I nodded, eyes locking on my mug.

"Thank you, Van. I needed this," I said. "They would have liked this more than a grand funeral."

His gray-green eyes slid to mine. "They hated funerals," he agreed. "Look, I know you have your own crew now and your... own way of defending yourself." He stopped and side-eyed me. "But you tell me if you need my help, yeah? I'll always be here for you." His elbow nudged me in the side.

My lips tugged up. Van had always been like another brother. He returned my smile for a moment before argued shouts reached our ears. He popped to his feet, offering a hand as I followed his gaze to the commotion.

A crowd gathered around a large man bellowing at the guards manning the food tent.

"Rations are divided after you check in with one of the officers, *lake rat*," spat one of the men.

"I have men waiting to speak with them, but it seems your officers are too busy treating with *pirates* to greet their newest recruits. We've been riding for *four weeks* to get here on time. My people need food and water, *now*," the large man roared at them, straightening and blocking the sun from the group with his shadow.

My heart leaped into my chest at the sound of his voice, and I darted through the crowd, earning grumbles of irritation along the way.

"Bear!" I shouted over the noise.

He paused, his head whipping around to scan the crowd.

"Bear! Here!" I cried, pushing my way through the throng of people.

He turned, eyes finally finding mine as his face lit up. "Lyvia!" he called back.

The crowd parted for the giant man, and he scooped me up in a back-cracking embrace.

"Oh gods, it's good to see you," he said as he squeezed. He pulled away, large hands grasping my shoulders. His eyes scanned my face and drifted to the large scar on my neck.

"What you did," he began, shaking his head, small buds of silver growing in the corner of his eyes, "Evony..." The wide column of his throat worked as if he couldn't finish the thought.

"She's okay? Bayne said she got out?" I asked, unable to keep the worry from my voice.

He nodded quickly. "Yes. She got out because of you." He dropped to his knees, my hands dwarfed in his. "She swam to shore, and we found her in the woods not three hours later. Battered and bruised but otherwise fine. I can never repay you for what you did." He shuddered.

"I would do it again. I just wish... Bear, I'm so sorry about Morwyn," I said, forcing the words through the vice that wrapped around my chest anytime I thought of her.

His eyes hardened, the pain and grief of his loss tightening the broad features of his face into a portrait of anguish. I squeezed his hands, meeting his gaze with my own fire. We'd avenge Morwyn. His eyes fluttered for a moment, acknowledging this unspoken promise.

"Where is Evony now?" I finally asked, looking around.

"Somewhere safe," he murmured, sliding his eyes to the Lumerians.

I nodded, now noticing the gathered crowd watching us and Vander still standing behind me. After quick introductions, I marched straight to Ronan's tent to demand he speak with Bear to get rations for the fighters from Rivaner.

I helped get Bear and the others settled in the southwest portion of the camp, not far from the foothills of the Lumerian Mountain range that stretched almost to the cliffs. A soft nicker sounded, and I spied the sorrel coat of Anchor carrying a load of supplies. I gave his shoulder a pat as I unloaded the packs from his back, earning a relieved sigh from the tall horse.

"Bayne is going to be happy to see you, buddy," I whispered to him.

"Where is he anyways?" Bear asked. "Does he know the godsdamned *Hydra* ship is here? The Marisarma are filth."

My stomach twisted. "He knows," I grumbled. "He's with

their leader getting briefed by Ronan and the other commanders for the offensive attack. They should be done soon."

Bear had brought over one hundred people with him from Rivaner. Mostly men, but some women had joined. They'd trained on their way here, but most of them hadn't much experience fighting, let alone facing the battlefield. I made a mental note to get Nerissa out here as soon as possible.

Bayne found us soon after and was followed by the rest of the crew in small groups. Bear greeted them like old friends. We gathered around a fire and exchanged stories for hours that evening.

Oslo's eyes sparkled in anticipation as Bear pulled out a menacing-looking contraption he'd made for his arm. A metal ball covered in razor-sharp spikes connected to the base of the attachment. Oslo buckled the leather straps into place. He stepped back and swung, the ball flying from the base on a thick fortissa chain, before retracting. The weathered soldier was giddy with excitement as he showered Bear with his thanks. He'd been sparring with the blade attachment, but he'd lost significant range of motion with the loss of his hand and arm. He replaced the blade and began training immediately.

A MONTH PASSED IN A BLUR. Three more camps for the Rising were settled in classified parts of Sultira. Ours was the biggest, still only three thousand strong. Yet the camp had grown to the size where new buildings had been erected in addition to those that had been taken over in the small town.

The camp buzzed in constant preparation for our attack on Aedrialis while we waited for any remaining Sultirans to make their way to the Rising's base and anyone else who might come to our aid. Ronan had heard nothing from Queen Antares or the elves of Lotrennia.

We kept to the southern part of camp, and I only caught the occasional glimpse of the famed Marisarma pirates. Bayne and Vulcan kept close, and I didn't mind, given Lord Astraeus seemed to have eyes everywhere, often leering in the dark shadows of the camp. I caught the flash of his blue coat on occasion, and more than once, his dark eyes found mine in the distance. Young. He seemed so much younger than I'd expected. Maybe only a few years my senior. Though his unnerving glare sent shivers down my spine, I had a difficult time looking away.

Despite spending hours onboard the *Evecta* training my powers with Isla, I had yet to manifest the Obscura. I could always feel it there. But to release it... To risk letting it out...

What had happened in Cyril's room in the tower on Kayj left a pit in my stomach. Not only did I have no idea how I did it, but I *knew* I lacked control. It was agreed that I would only be asked to use the power in battle as a last resort—if I *could* even wield it again. The mysterious songlike golden bone remained quiet, even as Bayne, Nerissa, and Isla all attempted to unlock its power.

Vulcan took over my training with twin blades after our centering exercises. By the end of sixty minutes, my muscles quivered with fatigue, but my mind felt free. It somehow quieted that small voice in the back of my head that continued to beat me down. My skill with the short swords improved greatly, and though he still wasn't overly friendly, Vulcan was a far cry from the terrifying enemy I thought he was all those months ago.

Despite being ready to collapse after hours of training, my insatiable appetite for Bayne always won out over the exhaustion in my bones. Gods, I couldn't keep myself off him. There was something freeing about him openly accepting me, *claiming* me in front of the rest of the crew and the others who had joined the Rising. I was his, and he was mine. We mirrored each other's movements in the most natural way. The subtle brush of his fingers against mine, the soft touch of his hand against my back. I found him fitting into my life like a piece of a puzzle.

Aquila was surprisingly absent during our time in the camp. I caught only brief glimpses of him near the *Evecta* before he flew off toward the Lumerians.

It was probably fine he steered clear of camp. Most of the men and women who came to fight were half-starved by the time they arrived, and I wouldn't put it past them to shoot down a large seahawk for a feast. I felt his presence more and more. I knew he was gone, away from the camp because I could *feel* when he returned. I mentioned it to Bayne briefly one night after he took me over the edge, laying sweaty in our furs on the *Evecta*. His brows pinched together, considering.

"Something happened between you two on Kayj. The powers of the Bellators are mysterious. Maybe unlocking the Obscura allowed you to connect with another being. Though, Aquila's not a caeluma. There's a lot we don't know." His fingers brushed along my arm.

I shivered at the sensation, snuggling into him tighter.

Ronan kept his distance from the crew, only speaking with us during attack briefs. I strode from his center of command late one afternoon when he snagged my arm. Bayne turned on him with full force.

"Easy, Cap," he said, eyebrows and hands shooting up. "Just looking for a word with Lyvia." His eyes shot to mine before leveling a hard look at Bayne, whose shoulders tensed. "Or do you decide who she gets to talk to?" he challenged.

Bayne's jaw clenched, the tips of his teeth shining between his lips.

I rolled my eyes before gently touching Bayne's shoulder. I knew he was just looking out for me, and with the loss of so many I loved, I loved him even more for it.

"It's fine. I'll meet you in ten for training," I said, giving it a squeeze.

His finger and thumb gripped my chin before he planted a luxurious kiss on my lips, tongue slipping inside for the briefest moment. It took everything in me not to slide my fingers in his hair and wrap my legs around his waist. Ronan let out an exasperated sigh before clearing his throat. Bayne dragged his gaze from mine before walking off without another look at Ronan.

"What can I do for you, Commander?" I asked, allowing some sarcasm to slip through.

He rolled his eyes and turned. "Follow me."

I followed, noting the way the men and women in the camp eyed him with respect. The smallest twinge of guilt crept in at the sight of a man who removed his hat, offering a deep bow.

"Brother bless you, Commander. We owe you everything," he said.

Ronan returned his gaze with a nod and a smile as we kept walking.

"What was that about?" I asked.

"These men and women have lost everything to the tribute. We tried to get warnings out to most of them, but the ships were moving faster. I'm not sure what the dark king has planned," he paused, looking at me expectantly, "but he needs bodies for it."

"Other than taking over the world and ridding it of

400

humankind?" I murmured, as if the implications of that question weren't mind-rattling.

He led me through the camp to his own quarters, where he
plopped down and offered me a chair in the spacious tent.

"I know you don't trust me," he began, turning his
sapphire eyes toward me.

"Understatement of the year," I cut in. It was more than
not trusting him. I'd found a friend in him. He was a lifeline
after I discovered Enya's burial chamber, and my life changed
forever.

My chest ached as I thought about those first few days on
the *Evecta*. His presence had been so reassuring. Maybe it was
his charm or the simple fact I'd seen his face at the palace so
many times, but he'd gained my friendship, my trust. And then
he threw it right in my face as soon as I let my guard down. Even
if it was all for the good of Sultira, it didn't change the hurt.

As if reading my thoughts, he leaned forward and grabbed
my hands in his. I shot him a look as I tried to tug them back.

"I'm sorry," he pleaded, pausing as his throat bobbed. "I'm
sorry I lied. I'm sorry I used you to get the journal. I'm even
more sorry I lost you as a friend."

He had an infuriatingly firm grip on my wrists. Even worse,
his eyes held mine, and he looked genuine. And guilt-ridden.
Good.

"You tricked me," I said after watching him for a few
moments. I ground my teeth as insufferable tears threatened to
form.

He blinked and let go of my wrist. I swallowed, snuffing
out the surge of emotion bubbling up in my chest.

"A lot has happened since Westwyn. I didn't ask for any of
it," I said, voice cracking at the end.

His face softened as his eyebrows tilted up. "I know. Lyvia,

I'm sorry. Nothing is more important than this war, though. And I had to take whatever chance I could at gaining the upper hand in this. My—"

He paused mid-sentence as if catching himself before saying something he shouldn't. My brows shot up as I huffed a sarcastic laugh.

"More lies," I whispered, shaking my head.

He stood and began pacing the space of his tent.

"I should go," I started and he held his hands up, taking a knee before me.

"Wait. Just wait." He sighed, looking down before meeting my gaze again. "I will tell you everything. But you must understand some of this cannot be uttered outside of this tent. And," he paused, searching my face for something, "you might not like everything you hear."

I grimaced, feeling uncertainty squeeze my chest. "Tell me everything."

CHAPTER FORTY-THREE

A new student will study with our team of Death Scholars as an apprentice, though they won't be permitted to join the order. Surprisingly, it is a young woman. Headstrong and stubborn, I'm finding. Unsurprisingly, High Priest Helmar gave me no say in the matter.

—Journal of Father Marcus dated 6th of Autumn, 066.3E. Aedrialis.

Anger squashed the growing nausea that had consumed me by the time I left Ronan's tent. I stalked through the camp toward the designated sparring area, ignoring the stares of the people I passed and the quiet whispers of prayers. Most of these people had no knowledge of higher powers before now.

Witch, some muttered before bringing their thumb to their lips in a call for protection. *Elf-fucker* was another one often followed by a rude hand gesture or even a wad of spit.

I didn't care about either as the humming of the Obscura power, fueled by my rage, drowned out every other sound as I stormed across camp.

Bayne was deep in conversation with Vander as I approached. He turned to face me, eyes bright with relief and a hint of lust as he took in my figure.

"You're late," he purred, grinning part-way and pausing. A brief scan of my face told him enough of my mood that his features quickly turned.

"What's wrong? What did he do?" he asked, tension growing in his shoulders as he strode toward me.

I hopped the small fence around the sparring ring and practically sprained my wrist as I shoved my hand against his chest.

"You!" I seethed at him. The hurt of what Ronan shared had cut deep. His eyes flashed in surprise, replaced quickly with a dark, quiet rage.

"Lyv, tell me what he said," he said in a lethally soft voice.

"You're just as bad as him!" I cried, my face crumpling as my chest constricted.

He glanced around, reaching for my shoulders as I ducked away.

"We should talk somewhere else. Come on, let's at least get on the *Evecta*." His tone had taken on that of the captain, and it only fueled the fury building in my chest.

"Why's that, *Captain*?" He flinched at the word. "Wouldn't want someone overhearing what he shared with me? Big secret?" I asked, not caring who overheard us.

Bayne's eyebrows narrowed, and I felt a distant tension I couldn't place.

He leveled a serious look at me before softening his features.

"Please, Lyv," he said quietly, releasing my arm. A pleading entered his voice that softened the fury in my chest enough that I nodded.

We walked in an uncomfortable silence to the docks. Vulcan eyed us from the stern of the ship, nodding his greeting. I didn't keep the look of distrust from my face as his eyes met mine. They all fucking *knew*.

We barely stepped on deck before I unleashed myself upon Bayne.

"*You* are a fucking *Bellator*!" I bellowed at him.

It took everything in my being not to pound my hands on his chest as the Obscura's relentless humming buzzed through my veins.

"You! And Nerissa!" I shouted in accusation.

The look on his face confirmed the obvious, devastating truth. That he and Nerissa wielded the powers of the Bellators, the power of the gods. They'd kept this vital information from me since the beginning, letting me stumble my way to the Obscura Bone, lost and unsure of my role in all of this.

I was mildly aware of others on the deck, and I felt that same foreign, growing sense of anxiety coming closer.

"You both wield the power of the sun! *Soleia*. I was fucking blind to it this entire time because I was falling *in love* with you. Did you think to tell me? Were you ever going to tell me?! How about the fact that you all think it was Enya's power..."

I paused and swept my arms out, gesturing to the rest of the crew now gathered on the deck, "*My power* that brought on the downfall of the others? My power that caused the world to shatter during the War of Ruin? Is that why you stayed so close? Because you knew I was drawn to this power of destruction and someone needed to keep an eye on me? Someone needed to stop me from using this power? *Were you going to kill me?*"

Ronan's words echoed in my mind. The suggestion that

someone needed to stay close to me, in case the darkness chose me. I was a liability on my own. Pain and regret stretched across Bayne's features that, had I not been seething with fury, might crack me open with the need to ease it. He reached for my hand, which I quickly whipped away. The foreign sense of anxiety morphed into concern. I resisted it, trying to put up a wall but it only grew stronger.

"Would you have let me go, Bayne?" I asked, voice barely a whisper. "When you found me in Westwyn, after Ronan. Or at the Lake of Light? When you said you would come with me to find Aeriden, were you ever planning on letting me leave without you? Would you have gone north without me?"

Bayne opened his mouth to say something before clamping it shut, swallowing the words about to form. No. He never intended on letting me leave. Giving me a real choice. He'd played me.

"Do you love me?" I asked at last, voice shattering. "Or did you just take a page from Ronan's book and realize I was that easy to fool? That I'd spread my legs for you and then I'd fucking *fall* for you because I'm a young, naive *human*?"

My chest threatened to cave in as the truth hit me. Of course, that was what happened. I'd laid out his plan for him. Whoever could get to me first. The pity on Ronan's face as he told me about Bayne and Nerissa was like a blow to my already cracking heart. A single tear formed, quickly whipped away by the wind off the Juniper Sea. Bayne's face crumpled.

"Lyv—" Bayne faltered.

Aquila shrieked before sending a gust of air across the deck as he landed on the railing. I needed to get out of here. I needed to be somewhere else. Now. Turning on my heel, I hurried off the ship. Bayne called after me, but footsteps and shuffling sounded among arguing voices. Someone was trying to stop him. Good.

I made it no more than five steps across the dock before hearing the powerful beats of Aquila's wings behind me. I whirled to face him where he hovered, wings blocking the sun. A pleading sense of desperation and guilt slammed into my being as I realized it was *him* I'd been feeling.

I could feel Aquila's emotions. I brushed aside the implications of what that meant as I hurled my own back at him. I let the pain, the betrayal, the embarrassment, and the cracking of my heart slam through me into him. The bird faltered mid-air before catching himself, eyes widening.

"Stay. The. Fuck. *Away*," I seethed and stalked off toward the camp, not sure where I was going. The Obscura power roiled in my veins, its hum deafening in my ears. As much as I longed to take out this rage in the sparring ring, I knew enough by now that in doing so I'd let slip the chain I had tethered to my power. *My power*, I repeated in my head. Despite what the others thought about Enya and the demise of the Bellators, this was *my* power, and I got to decide what to do with it.

As it was my turn to carry it, the soft golden bone bounced on my chest as I strode through the camp. Despite the humming of the Obscura and the pounding in my ears, the bone had picked up a soft tune that somehow cut through the noise.

I found myself in the westernmost corral where Anchor was being kept. He whinnied at my approach, and eyed me apprehensively, as if he could sense the danger in my veins. I took a shuddering breath and closed my eyes, willing the power to settle before I approached him with my fist out. He slowly touched his nose to it, eyes wide and ears forward, as he blew a loud snort onto my knuckles.

"It's okay, bud. It's just me," I said quietly. I led him into a small space under the trees in a grassy grove just off the camp. I spent the next hour tending to him, working through the tangles in his mane and tail before moving to his coat. I spent a fair amount of time on his hooves, noticing a crack that split up the center.

The tension in my shoulders eased as the Obscura power calmed. I found myself relaxing into the rhythm of the golden bone and the steady brush strokes I ran along Anchor's back. I could see clearly for the first time in months. It all made sense.

I'd never analyzed Bayne or Nerissa's powers. They weren't only hiding because they feared Antares might think they were after the crown. They were hiding because they were the last of the Bellators. Or the first? I didn't know enough about the higher powers to understand that what I'd witnessed in the Pool of Kryax and on Kayj was more than the power of ordinary mages or mystics.

And who all knew? Isla certainly. My stomach knotted at the thought of her hiding this from me. They all knew. And what was I? Some kind of experiment? They'd gotten their hands on me as soon as they learned I found the Obscura Bone. They'd sprung me from that cell under Mount Telum hours after I was taken. They'd gotten me back from the dark king. And not only had I manifested the Obscura power, but I'd stolen another one of the bones of power for them.

My nose crinkled at the rotting scent of muck I picked out from Anchor's hooves as I sorted through the math. I had two Bellator powers on me at this moment. A third sat on Dark King Daimos's palm. Was the fourth split between Nerissa and Bayne? Were they there, over a thousand years ago during the fall of the Bellators and the War of Ruin? Did they find the Soleia bone or somehow inherit this power?

Questions flooded my brain. I'd always been able to think better around horses. Memories of scanning pages of skeletal anatomy while lounging with Tiberius near the walls of Aedrialis edged into my mind. I smiled at the thought. My heart still ached for Tiberius. What I would give to jump on his broad back and fly along these cliffs... I turned my attention back to the horse in front of me as I began tugging out the tangles of burrs in his tail.

That left four more Bellator Bones. The crew of the *Evecta* knew so much more than they let on. My heart stuttered at the stab of betrayal. I felt more alone now than I had in the halls of the Crystal Castle.

It was nightfall by the time I led Anchor back to his paddock and tossed him a flake of hay before heading to my tent. Shit. *Our* tent.

Oslo and Vulcan's tent flaps were closed, having already settled in. Embers sat dying in the small fire in the center. Oslo poked his head out at the sound of my approach. He gave me a soft, sad smile and opened his mouth to say something, but I ducked inside.

Blessedly, I found it empty as I lifted the flap. Bayne must have decided I needed the space tonight. He wasn't dumb. I'd give him that. Air thumped overhead and I knew Aquila was off to somehow communicate I'd made it back to my tent. I grumbled at the thought of being babysat by a giant bird.

I stripped my clothes off, then quickly put them back on, surprised at how chilly the night was without Bayne's warmth. He was always so warm. Always had such a knack for keeping those fires alive during our nights in the Lumerians...

A small part of me yearned for his closeness and ached at the empty space beside me. Annoyed, I pulled the furs tighter and willed myself to fall asleep. I tossed and turned most of the night, the Obscura power seemingly at odds with the musical bone on my chest.

Darkness swirled in my veins, raging off the fury that still burned in my chest, while the bone on my chest sensed my pain, filling me with a soft, sad lullaby. I finally drifted into a fitful sleep, waking occasionally to unseasonable flashes of heat lightning in the sky. Nightmares chased me through the night until I was blessedly interrupted by the tall, blue-eyed elf.

Enya was alive and well, dressed in long drapes of green silk that gathered at her waist with a thin chain. The Obscura Bone sat in an elaborate necklace on her chest, the deep onyx sucking the light from the nearby sconces in the ornate room where she stood. She smiled sadly at me as if she knew what I had discovered, but there was no pity in her eyes.

A man entered the room. Hair as dark as the onyx stone tucked behind rounded ears, eyes as piercing blue as the sea beyond her window. He knelt before her, his black armor clanking on the stone floor. She pulled her gaze from mine to the man. She handed him an intricate scroll case, bedecked in jewels and etchings of snowflakes.

The familiar-looking face paused, staring up at Enya with grief in his eyes.

"The sacrifices of your house will never be forgotten, friend. Your final assignment," she said, bidding him to rise as he took the scroll case. "You'll need a mage's help. And this," she paused, slicing a blade across her hand and letting the blood drip into a small vial.

"You're sure?" he asked, a waver in his voice.

"The end is near," Enya replied, handing him the vial and gripping his fingers. Her head jerked to the side suddenly, eyes widening as she screamed to both of us.

"He is coming."

CHAPTER FORTY-FOUR

Tauruk gleaned the location of the Natara line, yet a different stone was yielded. The clan was purged. Two were chosen to remain enslaved at the Crystal Castle.
—Correspondence to Lady Selvina. Date unknown. Nivis.

Chaos erupted in the camp. My heart hammered in my chest as the sound of gut-wrenching slaughter ripped through the darkness, pulling me from sleep. Screams from every direction filled my ears as I tightened the laces on my boots with shaky fingers and began arming myself to the teeth.

I reached for the flap of my tent as Vulcan ripped it open.

"Sultiran forces," he said quietly.

"From the south?" I asked as Oslo crept out to meet us.

"Everywhere," Vulcan replied.

I took a heartbeat to crane my neck and look around. Little pyres lit up the night, strewn across the camp for miles. *Every-*

where. They'd arrived earlier than our intel had indicated, which meant Queen Galena had been betrayed. Rising soldiers were being slaughtered in their sleep.

"Oslo, get back to the *Evecta*. Take out as many as you can on the way. Lyvia, you're with me," Vulcan ordered as we crept our way through the camp.

Oslo nodded ahead of me, turning as he hurried down a dark path. Worry crept into my chest at the thought of him on his own. Moments later, I caught the rattle of his new weapon releasing followed by a sickening crunch and scream of pain.

We ran along a line of seemingly abandoned tents whose occupants must have woken from the sound of battle. I leaped over a dying fire as two soldiers, clad in black Sultiran armor, hurled toward us. Vulcan whirled around, his two blades in hand, slicing through the first. I ducked into a roll, dodging the longsword of the second which came crashing down into the embers. I unsheathed Cyril's dagger, *Talon*, at my thigh before getting to my knees where I slammed it into his groin.

A scream ripped through the night before I pulled it free and shoved it into the gap in his armor between his jaw and neck, silencing him. I ripped it free, sheathing it before turning to follow Vulcan, ten steps ahead of me. He aimed toward that little outcropping of trees at the edge of camp. What time was it? Our moons, Ganmira and Renova, were nowhere to be seen in the sky this evening. Darkness enveloped the camp interrupted by menacing pyres.

Vulcan pointed to the tall oaks in the center. Order understood. We climbed. I fumbled for footing in the darkness. I made it to the first branch and glanced over to the tree Vulcan ascended. Movement at the top caught my eye. Of course, he'd made it to the top. A pinch of envy flared as I thought about the advantage the elves had over us. No wonder Ronan called Lotrennia for aid. My mind drifted to our last conversation as I pushed myself up to the next branch.

Bayne. Fucking *Bayne*. The aching stab of betrayal was at complete odds with the worry and longing in my heart for him. He would be fine. He *had* to be fine. What in Tynan's hell was wrong with me? Gods, I was so mad... but facing this battle... facing *anything* without him was somehow unthinkable.

I swung my legs over two thin branches. These would have to do. I shimmied myself further out, straddling the two branches until I could get a better view.

Vulcan was smart. With it being late spring, the leaves on these oaks were only small buds and we could see across the entire camp with the light of the fires. My breath caught as I scanned where the ships would be in the distance. Small flames spread across a large space. They were going for our fleet. Fuck. A twinge of panic for the others on the *Evecta* sent my heart stuttering. They would be okay. They had to be. I could feel Vulcan's glare across the trees, waiting to shush me, but I kept my mouth shut.

Cries of slaughter turned to sounds of battle, and my heart eased. Swords clashed among the screams. Enough of us were awake now to at least fight back. What were we *doing* up here? We should be below helping. I glanced at the tree Vulcan crouched in, about to open my mouth when the sound of hooves drew my attention to the ridge jutting down from the last of the foothills.

My heart sank. This was the first round. If there was a second force waiting beyond the ridge, on *horseback*, they would annihilate us. I shifted on my branch, nocking an arrow. This was why we were here. Vulcan knew there would be a second attack. We could assist from above for a short time, but this was to relay information.

I nearly toppled off my branch as Vulcan lithely swung over

from the neighboring tree, landing quieter than should be possible. I hissed as I caught my breath.

"Call Aquila," he whispered in my ear, his voice barely audible.

"I don't know how," I breathed back at him.

"You do. We need him here so he can relay a warning to the others. We have minutes, if that."

He was gone before I could argue further. Fuck. I didn't know how I'd done it in the tower on Kayj. I tried clearing my mind, but the wild mix of my own anxiety and anticipation for battle combined with the rapid humming of the Obscura power, not to mention the bone that sat heavy on my chest with its near-constant quiet song, my mind was far from clear.

I blew a few short breaths out as I pictured myself back in the tower, retracing the steps of my memories from the point of my arrival to the moment Bayne blasted through the wall. Fucking *Soleia* power. No... not now. There would be time to dwell on that later. The ship... the mines... the slaves... the ashen... the walk up the steps to the fortress... the climb to the tow—

Yes. That was it. The climb up the tower when, out of nowhere, I'd felt at peace. My mind had drifted to the crew, my family on the *Evecta*. The bond between brother, sister, and hawk.

Sitting completely still on the branches while my legs dangled, I let the memories of the three of them drift through my mind. Everything I'd felt for Bayne, every nudge of emotion Aquila sent my way... I focused on the feeling, and a sudden sensation emerged in my chest. I hurtled myself into it, willing a connection to form and felt a small tug in response. I blinked my eyes open. Was that it? It would have to do for now.

The flames spread across the camp, lighting up the sprawling field between us and the port town in the distance.

The fighting was disorganized. Not at all what I had envisioned when preparing myself for the inevitable battle. Screams echoed through the night, one so terror-filled it stood out from the rest.

I whipped my head to the side, toward a set of tents near cinders. A soldier, clad in black, dragged a woman by her hair away from the fight and the ensuing panic, toward our sheltered enclave of trees. My stomach turned as she grappled against his steel armor, pounding with her fists as she screamed. The soldier delivered a swift, crunching blow across her face as they neared our small outcropping.

As I nocked my arrow, taking aim, I slid my eyes to where I knew Vulcan waited and watched. The light from the torched camp cast shadows among the trees. I caught his eye and the slight shake of his head. He wanted us to stay hidden. Releasing this arrow would give away our position and we needed Aquila to spot us first.

The soldier pulled the woman into the darkness of the trees. The aim of my arrow followed him to the spot directly under Vulcan's tree, where he threw the woman against the trunk and ripped at her shirt. Was it a soldier, or was it Cyril? He clawed at me, recent panic igniting my senses. Darkness responded. I was not in his tower. Cyril was dead. This soldier would be too.

Vulcan's feet left the tree next to mine as he cleared the space, no doubt to stop me, and I let the taut string of my bow slip from my fingers. My arrow sliced through the back of the soldier's neck, spattering blood across the young woman's face. She screamed, staring directly at the arrowpoint now lodged in his throat. She barely looked around before hopping to her feet and sprinting back into the throng of battle while she pulled a dagger from her boot.

Vulcan landed beside me as pride bloomed in my chest at

the sight of her launching back into the fight. He opened his mouth and paused, cocking his head as if listening for something. I focused, but all I could hear was the ensuing battle and cracks of fire.

Moments later, the steady beat of Aquila's wings whooshed above the treetops. I couldn't see him from my vantage point, but I knew he was there with the sudden foreign sense of relief that swelled in my chest. It quickly morphed into apprehension. He'd spotted the second wave of soldiers beyond the ridge. Another whoosh told me he was headed back to the ship to communicate the danger.

Vulcan dropped to the ground, ripping the arrow from the dead soldier's throat an instant later. He was back on my branch within seconds. I would never get used to their speed.

"You should have waited for me. I wouldn't have let it happen," he hissed before leaping across the gap to his own branch.

I sat quietly for what must have been only a couple minutes but felt like a lifetime. How long were we going to sit up here? My mind whirred as quickly as the darkness in my veins. Only in the worst possible case could I use it tonight. As soon as it was unleashed, a target would be on my back. Same would go for Bayne and Nerissa, I suddenly realized.

The secrecy of the entire thing now had me better understanding the lie. *Lie* wasn't entirely accurate. The *omission* of information. Big fucking omission. They both held the power of the sun. That much was true. And if Saros and the dark king were after the Obscura power, they had to be after the others. Bayne and Nerissa had been running their entire lives. Though it still didn't justify keeping me in the dark.

Soft, heavy hoofbeats pulled my attention to the left as two agrippa riders made their way to our little group of trees. I kept my arrow nocked, ready to release, this time waiting for

Vulcan's signal. They would see the dead soldier but would have to get close enough to determine an arrow from above did the damage, if they cared to look.

The two men on horseback slowed their mounts, stopping several feet from the trunk of the tree I perched upon. An idea took root in my mind as the two remarked on the ensuing battle, too quiet for me to hear. I glanced at Vulcan, who I could barely see in the trees and signed my plan.

I waited to see if he'd seen me.

The softest jostle onto my tree told me he had. He took up a position to my left, with better aim at the two riders, who still sat leisurely upon their agrippa, watching the battle as if it weren't actually people, people of Sultira, dying out there.

The Rising didn't have agrippa in the herd of horses at their disposal. These were weapons in and of themselves and too valuable to pass up. As quietly as humanly possible, I slid the arrow back into my quiver and inched my way down the tree, pausing at the last branch before the five-foot drop to the ground.

I waited, needing to be sure Vulcan was ready, and took a steadying breath. He would be. I dropped to the ground, my boots thudding against the dirt and scraping on an exposed root. The riders turned in their seats toward me as two arrows took them both in the neck.

The agrippa danced with their giant hooves as one of the soldiers slid off the side of his mount, clanking to the ground. The other doubled over the front of his horse, the protruding arrow scraping against the neck of his mount. I spoke softly to the two massive horses as I snatched their reins.

Vulcan appeared by my side, pulling the dead soldier off the mount. We stripped them of their weapons before we leaped atop the two massive agrippa and raced into the burning camp.

CHAPTER FORTY-FIVE

He found us. Send aid to Elpis Point. I'm begging you.
—Correspondence from White Bear to Black Horse. 29th
of Autumn, 048.3E.

D eath was *everywhere*. My eyes stung, water leaking
out the sides, as my horse stormed through the
smoke and flames without hesitation. Screams
echoed through the night. People lay dying. Riderless horses
darted through the tents, frantically looking for an escape from
the flames. People burned. The endless clang of swords and
screams only added to the intense wave of sensations as we
launched into battle.

I nocked an arrow, drawing my bow as we raced through
the camp, trusting the agrippa to keep away from swinging
longswords. I released it, satisfaction blooming in my chest as
it found its target under the arm of a soldier mere feet away. I
nocked again, letting the horse lead us through the camp,

before firing at a second soldier. Vulcan was ahead of me, somewhere, doing the same. Screams of terror at the sight of the agrippa were replaced with looks of relief at the lack of a black armored rider as we galloped past.

On and on we went until my hand only gripped air when I reached for another arrow. I was out. And I didn't have a longsword on me, only the two short swords strapped to my back and Talon. The short swords wouldn't be particularly effective on a horse this large.

I leaned into the neck of the massive horse and urged him toward a general, given his markings. He cut down two men from the Rising ahead of us and did a double-take when he eyed one of his own steeds charging toward him. Agrippa had no allegiance to color on the battlefield.

I tightened my grip, lacing my fingers through his reins and mane, and screamed, "Impetum!"

The general's eyes widened as he stumbled back, reaching for his long sword too late as the agrippa pounded down the short distance, attacking the man where he stood. The sickening sound of bone cracking beneath crushed armor filled my ears as I let the warhorse do his job.

My head whipped around, scanning the madness as I searched for our next target when a blast of wind ripped across the battlefield. My heart dipped. Isla. And *Drystan*. I had the hardest time imagining my dear friend in the heat of battle, yet I somehow knew he commanded the wind that blew through the camp.

Brilliant white light followed a moment later as a second wall of wind surged through the battlefield. *Bayne and Nerissa.* I needed to get to them.

I kept my seat as my horse staggered, grappling with his reins and mane, trying to maintain my grip when a soldier in black barreled into us on his own steed. My mount lost his footing, and we flew backward through the air until we landed on our sides with a hard crunch.

Pain raced down my left leg, trapped under the massive horse before he shot to his feet and took off. The rider in black surveyed me for a heartbeat beneath his helmet. *Shit.* I didn't stand a chance if I didn't get the fuck up. I scrambled backward against the ground, hitting something soft and wet. Bile rose in my throat as my hand slipped into the caved-in chest of a fallen fighter.

The soldier slid off his mount and stalked toward me with his blade out, tilting his head to the side and back as if surveying his cornered prey. The Obscura rumbled through my veins, but I couldn't do anything. I couldn't reach for the power or even my swords. The deafening screams of the valley and cracks of fire had somehow locked me into place after flying off the agrippa.

I must have hit my head. It pounded. The darkness in my veins matched the frantic beat of my heart, willing me to release it as the image of Cyril with his blade raised flashed behind my eyes. Shock had frozen me in place, the Obscura power now locked behind a wall of ice. My entire being, even the blood in my veins, stilled.

The soldier's spreading smile faltered as he lifted the blade and stumbled forward. He pulled his eyes from me, reaching around his back where a thick axe protruded from the back of his armor. The move was enough to snap me out of my shock, and I ripped the dagger from the sheath in my boot and charged the soldier, plunging it into the soft flesh under his chin.

He stilled, eyes wide in shock, as he dropped his sword and grabbed for my wrist before slumping to the ground. Blood coated my hands and poured down my wrist as I ripped Talon free and staggered back.

A large form barreled toward me and I turned, dagger in one hand while reaching for my blade, when a wave of relief hit me. Bear closed the gap between us and ripped the axe from the man's back.

"Bear!" I screamed, reaching for him.

He grabbed my shoulder with a tight squeeze.

"There's a calvary waiting at the south end of the valley!" I shouted through the ensuing sounds of battle.

"They know!" he shouted back.

I still didn't understand how Aquila communicated with Bayne and Nerissa, but the message clearly got across.

I squinted through the smoke. Fifty yards back, Rising fighters lined up in cavalry defense formations. Long rows of men squatted with their shields upright and spears out. A second row of fighters positioned their shields above the heads of the first and their spears at horse neck level. Nausea churned at the thought of the impending bloodbath.

"Where are—" I began.

Bear shook his head vehemently. "No. Stay on this side of the camp, Lyvia," he implored.

I wasn't sure I understood. I needed to go to them. I needed to go to *him*. I didn't have time to think it through as the hoard of agrippa ripped through the line behind me. Screams of men and horses mingled with the moans of those dying around us. Horseless soldiers stormed toward us. I glanced at Bear, nodding briefly before stepping over the soldier we slew, reaching both hands behind my head and drawing two blades.

The two of us sliced through the oncoming forces. A sword caught me in the arm, tearing through my fighting leathers. My breath caught at the searing pain now radiating from my shoulder to my elbow, the gash leaking an alarming amount of blood. Another soldier was on me as soon as my own blade ripped across his face. I spun through the camp, slicing and stabbing, ducking and rolling through the onslaught. I lost Bear after my fourth kill, hands slick with blood that could have been my own.

Several more blasts of brilliant white light and air as hard as a brick ripped across the camp, sending soldiers and Rising fighters staggering into each other's grips. Though my heart lurched, I kept my eyes on the enemy, refusing to lose focus. I couldn't make my way to Bayne until the fighting was over. A sudden gut-wrenching wave of dread passed over me as I began to think of the end. We all might die today.

The brilliant mid-morning sun cast a contrary spring hue across the valley, illuminating the smoke in swaths of orange, brightening the blood. Bodies piled on the ground. I made my way to the northern part of the camp where the valley swung upward and could see down into the port town and distant shipyard below. At least twelve ships were up in flames, if not charred. Almost a third of our fleet. If Saros decided to send his naval forces, we'd have no hope of escaping. The rest of Lord Astraeus's fleet hadn't arrived yet, and the small navy we had acquired in the last few weeks was barely enough to carry half our forces to sea if needed.

I retreated up the hillside, savoring a moment's reprieve after hours of fighting. Every inch of my being ached. My soaked feet had been stepped on by armored boots after sloshing through the mix of mud and blood all morning. My head pounded relentlessly after a few too many blows to the face. Water. I needed water. Blood continued its trickle down the gash in my arm, and the taste of it lingered on my lips.

I stumbled up the side of the hill, craning my neck to get a better view of the camp. The scene below was a stain of reds, browns, and blacks among an otherwise beautiful valley of spring greens dotted with violet and yellow. The Rising forces were dwindling, but so were King Saros's men. I scanned the valley and foothills for signs of additional forces. A small glimmer of hope bloomed in my chest. Maybe we would survive this. We *had* to.

A flash of blue caught my eye in the fray below. Lord Astraeus spun through the enemy, sending a volley of daggers into the necks of five soldiers in black before slicing through a sixth with his curved blade, braids flying through the air. The pirate lord looked up the ridge to where I stood and flashed me a wink. I blinked, and he was gone, blue coat lost in the sea of madness.

A soldier in black spied me at the edge of the battle and locked a target on me. I drew my swords and planted my feet as I took a steadying breath. The quick moment of reprieve at the edge of the valley backfired. My arms slogged as if through mud as I caught the soldier's blade between mine. I shoved to the left and ducked.

I was outmatched in both speed and endurance. He spun on his heel as his armored boot crashed into my side. I let out a yelp as I hit the ground, scrambling to get my feet under me. I'd lost my blades. Shit. I shouldn't have stopped. I'd been fighting for hours, the adrenaline fueling me as I met blade with blade and got lost in the madness of battle. The minute of reprieve allowed my body and mind to finally connect, coming to the devastating conclusion that I was utterly spent.

I scrambled back as the soldier stepped toward me, mustering any remaining strength to summon the Obscura power that hummed impatiently in my veins when the soldier stopped mid-step, a blank look passing over his features. A flash of blue and the soldier's head craned at an unnatural angle to the side and he toppled over.

Lord Astraeus flashed me a smile, his white teeth stark against the stripes of fresh blood sprayed across his face and the dark lines of paint stretching from his forehead. I gaped at him, eyeing the curved blade in his hand. The hairs on my neck rose as he stalked toward me. I found my footing and retreated a few steps back, palming Talon.

"Easy, *Bonscath*," he purred, chuckling. He *laughed*. The deep sound danced on the edge on madness. He clearly enjoyed this fight more than any sane person should. The battle inched closer to the northern edge, and two Sultiran soldiers broke free, heading our way.

I opened my mouth to respond, instead eyeing the soldiers and making the split decision to hurtle Talon at the first, catching him in the face. Lord Astraeus whipped around, cutting down the second.

Two massive flashes of white light came from the center of camp. I blinked, shielding my eyes before craning my neck to try to spot Bayne, but it was impossible with hundreds of people still fighting.

Eyes back on Lord Astraeus, I made to pick up my blades when out of nowhere, a terrible rip sounded from above and reverberated through the camp, rattling my bones. The ground shuddered suddenly, as if the world had split in two.

"Saros's shield is down!" Lord Astraeus called, eyes scanning the Juniper waves in the distance.

I followed his gaze before I froze. Every fiber in my being went taut as the spine-tingling croak of the Stone Witch sounded in my head in the most unnerving violation.

CHAPTER FORTY-SIX

The mare in question is dead. A foal survived. Sire unknown.

—Correspondence from Sea Spear to Black Horse from the
Atrulean Sea, dated 42ⁿᵈ of Autumn, 048.3E.

Death Digger, heed my words unspoken. The lying king's shield has now broken.

The stone on stone grinding of her voice made my hair stand on end. I was vaguely aware of Lord Astraeus inching closer from a few feet away. The shock of hearing someone in my head. Of someone *forcing* their way into my mind paralyzed me.

Girl, turn your eyes to the north. The other sends his not dead forth.

Not dead. *No.* The ashen were on Sultiran shores. They were *here.* I shook my head, trying to clear it, and as I looked up, Lord Astraeus stood in front of me with his dark eyes wide.

"What the fuck?" he asked.

I had no time to register whether this man was an enemy or not. For now, he was human, and he was alive, which meant he was on my side whether he knew it or not.

"Ashen to the north," I croaked. I had to call for Aquila.

Lord Astraeus shoved Talon's hilt back into my hand as he swore and spun around, shouting to anyone who would listen. I reached out with my senses, throwing myself into the bond with Aquila. I turned to the north, scanning the horizon. Trees dotted the gradual slope of the foothills filling out into a thick forest in the distant north.

Astraeus had disappeared, and the foreign sense of concern and question floated from Aquila before I heard the heavy beat of his wings.

"Ashen from the north! I have no idea how far out... Stone Witch!" I called as he approached from the direction of the bay, hoping he didn't need further explanation.

A feeling of alarm and urgency was the only response I got before he banked and flew over the camp. I took a breath and scanned the battle below. We needed to turn our attention north. *Fuck.*

It didn't matter whose side you were on. All of us would be slaughtered if we were taken unaware. There was no way we would be able to set up a defensive position with our armies completely scattered. I couldn't even spot the commanding officers of the Sultiran forces. It was utter chaos below.

My mind whirled, searching for any possible solution, coming to one terrifying conclusion. It was time. The darkness whirred excitedly in my veins as the thought crossed my mind.

Unease crept over me as I reached out with my senses. This time, instead of searching for the warm, sun-kissed feeling that Aquila brought, I snaked them out toward the cold, sharpness left in my mind after the Stone Witch's intrusion.

Can you hear me? I said into the dark cave my mind had reached.

A nauseating cackle resounded in my ears, flipping my stomach.

You've changed, I see. Dark and clouded, you seem to be.

Please, I implored, ignoring her insufferable rhymes, *I need your help. We can't stop them on our own. We will all die.* I didn't bother hiding the panic in my mind's voice.

Release the shadows and the death. Remember how it felt when you heard his last breath?

My stomach plummeted. How did she know?

I can't control it. I have no idea what I'm doing. Please, I begged. We would all die. *I'll make a deal with you*, I added.

What is it that sings on your chest? A song never sung this far west.

My blood stilled. No. I couldn't give this power to her... I'd have to find another way...

Its power is that of the seasons. Undo it for us, undo his treasons.

Say yes and I will tell you how. I'll send a sign from Aelius's brow.

I glanced to where Lord Astraeus gathered a small force of Rising soldiers and pirates, spotting Ronan in the distance. So few. There were so few of us left. I had to do something.

Fine, I reluctantly said, unsure of exactly what I agreed to. *I will undo it.*

A cackle ripped through my mind's ear and my chest caved inward.

The darkness escaped once before. Did he use a key or break down the door?

My brows furrowed as I turned over her words. I sent my thoughts traveling down the tunnel to ask what in Tynan's hell that meant when a thick door slammed against my mind. Connection severed.

Ronan limped toward me. I was relieved at the sight of him, despite our turbulent history.

"How far out?" he asked, breathless.

Ronan looked like hell. The commanding officer, the breathtaking queensguard, every remnant of the swaggering flirt had been swept away in the hours of battle. He stood before me, ragged and bloody, but still standing. And he still carried an air of command I seemed inclined to obey. I glanced down and spied a makeshift tourniquet wrapped around his thigh. He surveyed me as well and looked up, awaiting my response.

"I have no idea. The Stone Witch was in my head," I murmured, still rattled by the invasion.

"The Sultiran army won't hear us. They've come to annihilate us. I sent in men to see if they would entertain a peaceful surrender but—" He shook his head, guilt etched across his face.

Surrender? The shock of it hit me like a brick. He must have read it on my face because his eyes softened.

"We will be lucky if an eighth of our forces survive this," he said, looking back over the miles of cinders and bodies that made up our camp.

"We can't surrender... We—" I began, shaking my head. Was all of this for nothing? So much death. So much life wasted. We had three people here with the power of the Bellators... As if reading my mind, his gaze softened.

"It's not your fault. We weren't prepared. We were betrayed..." he said, scanning the open fields before us. His eyebrows creased in worry that I knew had nothing to do with the approaching ashen.

"If we'd had more time..." he said, voice breaking.

I didn't need him to finish. Guilt slammed into me. If we'd had more time, I could have honed my powers. I could have gained enough control to obliterate the entire fucking army. Instead, I'd pouted after my escape from Kayj and threw myself into my nights with Bayne, losing myself in his love and his ecstasy and comfort, willing myself to forget what had happened.

My chest burned as air struggled to escape my lips. Ronan gripped my shoulder, and I vaguely heard my name being called. My vision became foggy at the edges, and I started to feel the world tilt on its side.

I was on the ground, the blood from my fingers smearing in the dewy grass. I *sat* as the real soldiers on the field continued a relentless fight to the death. What was I doing here? My hands were caked in dry and wet blood. The scum under my fingernails took me back to the day I'd examined Enya's remains, entranced with the notion of a female warrior. And now I was here. A would-be warrior sitting on her ass at the edge of battle, feeling sorry for herself. With Enya's own power roiling beneath her veins. Enough. *Enough.* If we were all to die anyway, I might as well take out as many of those bloodless abominations as possible.

Ronan knelt next to me when I shook my head, clearing away the fog, and shot to my feet. I strode from the ensuing battle and turned north.

"Lyvia, stop. LYVIA!"

I stopped. Not because of Ronan's plea, but because of the slight tremors that now reverberated across the valley. I dipped into a crouch out of instinct, bending my knees to keep balance.

Ronan swore, turning toward the gathering Rising forces and barking orders. The ashen were here. I shaded my eyes from the blinding rays of the sun above and squinted, watching the forest to the north.

The tremors grew in intensity. My knees wobbled as over a

thousand ashen broke through the tree line and hurtled down the valley toward us, their mouths open in spine-stiffening shrieks that echoed across the open space. My heart dropped straight through my gut, and it took everything in me not to give in to the instinct to turn and run. The hoard of ashen sprinted in a giant line that stretched from the diminishing slopes of the foothills to the cliffs the valley rested on.

I took a steadying breath, replaying the Stone Witch's riddle. *The darkness escaped once before. Did he use a key or break down a door?* Daimos had broken me. A part of my soul had cracked open, broken and raw after what he'd done to Aeriden and my father. After what I had done to my father. Allowing a darkness of its own making to slip in before the Obscura power latched itself to me.

That feeling. That dark, broken part of me was what I needed. I planted my feet as a massive shadow fell over the valley, blanketing the battlefield in darkness. I stole a look upward and gasped as our sacred moons, Ganmira and Renova, inched toward each other at unnatural speed. They paused as they crossed directly in front of Aelius, eclipsing the brilliant sun. The Sending had arrived. *Tynan's time.* A singular burning outline blazed in the center of the sky, and the power of the Bellators beat in response.

Nerissa's recitation of Olienna's prophecy sounded in my mind. *The Sisters shield us from the Brother...*

A quiet awareness swept over me despite the roar of battle behind and the thunder of ashen ahead. My heartbeat slowed, and I reached for that broken part inside of me. I turned back to face the oncoming wave of ashen before allowing all the emotions that had culminated in the last seven months to collide in a ground-shattering force. The pain, the wrath, the guilt, the betrayal, the loss... the love.

I let it swell in my chest, holding it there until I felt like I would burst before I released it all, letting out a wild scream and breaking the dam I'd built brick by brick over the past year, allowing me to shove it down as needed. It crashed through like a tsunami, washing away everything in its path. The Obscura power beat with elation before ripping free from my palms.

Lightning-quick daggers of black smoke and mist shot across the valley, slamming into their targets. I dragged it across the front line of the ashen, exterminating them tens at a time. The power was a relentless torrent, flooding everything nearby.

Every sense focused on the stampeding army of the undead. My legs shook as I steadied myself against the relentless tremors as the ashen grew closer and closer. I was vaguely aware of the gathering forces behind me and Ronan's shouts. Time disappeared as I released the shadows upon the threat that kept coming. My vision blurred and I gazed through a long tunnel.

The power consumed my entire being, drowning out all sounds and feeding off the build-up of emotions. The strangest sensation swept over me as I drifted in and out of my body, not at all in control. A spike of fear flared at the thought, and the Obscura power seized it, sucking it up and turning it into another massive blast of darkness.

At a certain point, I became aware of another presence. Worry and a hint of panic stole into my chest, and the Obscura power reached for it, ready to fuel another blast but recoiled as it touched, unable to feast on the foreign emotion. The neighboring presence became persistent, knocking on my consciousness. A blast of radiant white light pushed its way into my limited line of sight, melting the icy darkness like a warm blanket.

I blinked and heaved a breath, exhaustion hitting me like a

stone wall. I wavered as the Obscura power continued to pour from my palms. My eyes strained as I pulled them to the left, searching for the source of the light and that persistent knocking.

Bayne locked me in a piercing gaze as his soul reached for mine. He stood twenty feet away, his power like a wave of white seawater. It smothered the snaking darkness as he threw his consciousness at me. An overwhelming wave of love, concern, regret, anxiety, and fear slammed into me, and I clenched my fists, fingernails ripping into my palms, cutting off the Obscura power. The darkness grumbled as it coiled back inside me, but I sensed the exhaustion of its release as it settled.

My shoulders sagged, and I pulled my gaze from Bayne, who sprinted to my side as my knees hit the ground. No, not the ground. I glanced down. I knelt in feet of ash. As if a snow spinner had passed over the valley and dumped tons of ash and cinder on the ground instead of fluffy white flakes.

What the fuck? My fingers grazed the top layer, and I turned to Bayne as he pulled me into his arms. His eyebrows creased, and he tensed as I scanned the valley ahead.

Miles of black stretched from where I knelt to the forest, not an ashen in sight. My heart ripped from my chest as I turned. A gathering of Rising soldiers stood at the edge of the field of ash. Many gaped, others raised weapons, unbridled *fear* strewn across their faces. My eyes drifted over the valley of black, and a whimper escaped my lips. Empty black suits of armor lay strewn about the ash behind me in addition to an array of mismatched swords, axe heads, and various items of iron and steel. My eyes snagged on a metal ball, covered in sharp spikes. *Oslo.*

Nausea slammed into me, and I hurled, Bayne's grip tightening around my shoulders. He nodded to someone, and I heard Isla and Marian's voices approaching. A buzzing filled my ears as the gravity of what I had done hit me. I killed Oslo. How many of our own did I kill? *Who else?* The questions fueled the sickness that rose, and I heaved again, retching into the dark ground. I glanced at the sky, where the sun hung to the west. Hours had passed.

I shook as shouts sounded in the distance. Bayne tensed and swore as his arms left my shoulders, and he stepped away. The shouting turned to screams. How long was this going to last? I was vaguely aware of Marian at my side, taking my face in her hands, but I couldn't bring myself to look her in the eye. She loved Oslo. She signed at me, and I pulled my face away. I couldn't.

The stony voice filled my head again, and I didn't feel my body react. It was as if any sense of self-preservation had disappeared with the destruction of my soul.

They come for you in cloaks of white. You must rise and face the fight.

I will send water for your bloom, but you must free us from this tomb.

I didn't have the energy in me to try to figure out what the fuck that meant. Another riddle, another bargain. The kingsguards were coming for me. *Good*, I thought. I deserved to die at their hands.

Ha! She cackled. *They will not kill you, Death Digger. Your power will be theirs. Its destruction, bigger.*

A small fire lit in my chest at the last words, and I pulled myself back to the ash, glancing up at Marian.

"We must go. Another force of Sultiran soldiers just showed up. There's kingsguards with them..." Marian signed, her hands frantic.

I whipped my head back. The Sultirans ripped through the devastated camp with calm efficiency. There were so few

Rising fighters left on the field. My stomach twisted at the odds. The white cloaks broke off from the unit and swept to the west side of camp, avoiding the fight riding straight toward the field of ash. For me.

"Marian, go. You have to go. Get back to the *Evecta*. I'll be right behind you," I said as I stood. My voice was hoarse and raspy as if I'd been screaming.

She looked at me and raised her hands, about to protest as her eyes caught on Oslo's weapon in the ash. Her face paled, and she let out a heartbreaking cry. The first sound I'd ever heard escape her lips. She tore her eyes from the ash and stared at me, shock and grief morphing to fear and rage.

"I'm so sorry. I didn't..." I began, shaking my head. "You need to go. We all need to get out of here. Go!"

I didn't wait for her response as I turned west, facing the kingsguards and their agrippa that tore down the slopes of the foothills. I reached a tendril of consciousness down to where the Obscura calmly dozed in my chest. I wouldn't be able to wield again today. And if truth be told, I didn't want to. I wanted nothing to do with it. But it was my only play. I reached out, throwing some emotion at it, and it grumbled in response. Fuck. *Fuck.* Fear slammed into me, and I reached behind, hands grasping the air and coming up empty. Where were my blades? I glanced around. There was no time.

Sounds of battle crashed on the cindering camp. Blasts of light met with countering walls of wind as battle magic waged. The group of kingsguards sped toward me in the distance and an overwhelming sense of self-preservation hurled into me. I turned on my heel and ran as fast as I could toward the coast. As if fueled by the chase, the thundering of their hooves picked up speed. My heart fluttered in my chest as I sprinted across the ash-ridden valley, slipping and falling into the soft powder, scrambling to my feet.

The thundering intensified, and I could feel the ground shake beneath my feet as I prepared to be cut down. Hooves beat wildly behind me and ash flew up to my left. They were going to surround me. The massive black legs slowed, and I stole a glance up at the riderless agrippa. Not just riderless. *Tackless.*

I choked out a sob as realization hit me. I stretched up a hand, grasping the base of Tiberius's mane at his withers, and slammed my feet against the ground as hard as I could, kicking my legs up into the air with the momentum of his gait. I clenched my calves around him, bouncing rapidly as his speed picked up until I finally found my seat on his bare back. I squeezed his body with my legs, spurring him forward. Shouts erupted from behind as the kingsguards closed in, flanking us.

We neared the edge of the northern cliff that wrapped around the bay. We would be over its edge in seconds if we didn't change course. I stole a glance to either side where the kingsguards maneuvered their mounts to keep us locked in. Their hands twitched on the reins as they slowed their agrippa to avoid toppling off the cliff. Ti hesitated as the distance between us and the edge of the cliff closed. My heart leaped into my chest, and I felt Tiberius balk before the two of us hurtled over its edge.

CHAPTER FORTY-SEVEN

Black Horse is dead. Nyxteria is gone. Cease communication until you hear from me.

—Correspondence from White Hawk to Sea Spear. 10th of Spring, 071.3E.

"LYV!"

An overwhelming sense of panic reached me as Bayne's scream diminished and we fell away from the top of the cliff. Time stopped as a gut-wrenching cry ripped from Tiberius's throat, and we dropped from the cliffside. My scream lodged in my throat as wind whipped through my hair. There was no gut-sinking sensation of a long drop, only a tornado of wind pummeling us from every direction. My heart broke at the thought of Tiberius's body crumpling as it crashed into the waves below.

Bayne's last word echoed in my ears. The frantic call of someone losing their love. I could hear it in his voice, and I could sense it in the strange connection that had formed after the twin eclipse. Was it more than Bellator powers connecting us? Was there something higher at work, pulling me toward him? My heart cracked thinking of the love I'd lost and my anger toward him in our last moments together on the *Evecta*. I loved him. And I would forgive him. I knew I would have.

I held onto the sound of his voice as we continued to fall.

Lyv. Lyv. Lyv.

The sound of my name on his lips sent my heart beating strongly in my chest. I could peacefully pass hearing it reverberate in my ears.

Lyv. Lyv. Lyv.

It stuttered suddenly, a different sensation blooming. Not one of panic and loss, but one of command and determination.

Not Lyv.

Live.

Not my name from a lover, but a command from my captain. Or maybe both. My mind whirred in response, and memories flashed behind my eyes, as if searching for any possible solution to prevent our inevitable demise as we neared the crashing waves of the Juniper Sea.

From the visions of Enya to the cryptic messages left behind by Father Marcus. It snagged on the bones. I was the Death Digger. And in an instant, I knew the reason I had been able to find those excavation sites. I had always been drawn to death. I *was* death, Tynan's own darkness, the Obscura power swimming in my veins. I commanded it. And today was not the day it would take me.

My mind's eye flashed to Enya's burial chamber. The octahedron with the strange constellations and skulls... And a winged horse.

Wings. As if in response to the revelation, the golden bone that lay hidden on my chest filled my ears with its song. We continued to fall, headfirst toward the sea, and I could now see the waves racing toward shore. They were wild. More unruly than I'd ever seen them. Desperation held on to the image of the dead horse, willing the possibility of it to life. I grabbed hold of the song emanating from the bone, matching the pitch and tune with my mind's voice.

Air escaped my lungs in a sharp tug as shimmering golden light surrounded us. Dark shadows erupted from both sides, blocking my view as Tiberius let out a piercing scream and snorted. The sea raced up to meet us as the massive black wings beat wildly, sending tremendous bursts of air blasting against the tide. White water sprayed in a spinning array of mist.

I hugged my legs and arms around him as we lurched upward, the maneuver twisting my stomach, and we launched into the sky.

Flying. We were *flying*.

Tiberius leveled out twenty feet above sea level, and I felt a wave of shock. Not my own. Not Bayne's. Not Aquila's. I placed my hand on his neck. I could *feel* Ti. And then my view was *different*. I was seeing farther, more of the horizon as if looking through the eyes of... I blinked, snapping back into my own head, my own vision. A blossoming sense of attachment washed over me, and Tiberius whinnied in response. He could feel it too. And I knew in my heart what he was. What we'd created together with the golden Bellator bone. I had found my caeluma.

My eyes scanned the beautiful, enormous black velvet wings that beat steadily at my sides, and a laugh escaped my lips. I tore my gaze from the wings and looked to the sea we soared over.

My heart leaped at the sight of the gold and white ships sailing, albeit wildly, over the treacherous waves toward the bay. Lotrennia had come. Relief swelled in my chest, and I called for Aquila, reaching out with the tether of whatever connected me to Bayne. I felt a tug of shock and awe in response.

I leaned to the right, hoping Tiberius would understand the cue. He banked to the right and leveled out immediately as I nearly toppled off.

We soared over the crystalline waters, the wind ripping tears from my eyes. We needed to get to land before my adrenaline ran out and the magnitude of what just happened hit me. I eyed the ships below. It would be best to avoid those.

The shipyard appeared ahead of us, and my heart sank at the wreckage that floated near the shores. Half of our fleet was gone. I sighed in relief as I spied the sails of the *Evecta*, the ship untouched. Isla must have held her shield over the ship the entire time. I shook my head imagining the strength it would have taken.

Movement to the north of the docks caught my eye as Vienah, the young water witch, worked tirelessly, still putting out the fires on a ship that just might be salvageable. Water from the bay sprayed the ships in little streams, dousing the fires and leaving damp, charred wood behind. My eye caught on the large *M* rippling in the breeze. The *Hydra*, Lord Astraeus's massive Marisarma ship, rocked in pristine shape.

The shoreline came up faster than expected. I could feel Tiberius's shock as we sped over the ships, barely missing their sails as we'd lost altitude with our approach. Ti wavered and banked to the side, nearly crashing into one of the few buildings still standing in the port town.

The last remaining soldiers and Rising fighters looked to the skies, staggering as we shot overhead. *Shit.* We weren't going to be able land here.

"Higher, buddy!" I called into the air.

Tiberius let out a snort laced with derision. He climbed higher, but I could tell his wings wavered. We soared past the town, and I caught a glimpse of Aquila coming into view before a sense of unbridled elation hit me. He swooped in behind us and banked to the other side as he flew alongside.

We flew over the remains of the Rising camp where only a handful of Sultiran soldiers engaged with the last of our fighters, and my gut sank. Cinders, ash, and bodies. It was all that remained of the miles of camp. Healers marked with white sashes knelt among the dying, easing their pain or calling for makeshift stretchers.

A clearing opened before the cluster of trees Vulcan and I sat in only hours before. I focused on it, hoping Ti would somehow interpret my meaning, and he tilted down, angling for the open space. I felt a push of hesitation from Aquila. Whipping my head to him, he eyed me warily as Tiberius's hooves slammed into the ground, and he thundered down the short stretch into a gallop.

The crash was jarring, and I clenched my legs and arms around him. I lost my balance and instinctively grabbed a wing to steady myself. Tiberius threw up a buck, tossing me into the air. I landed hard on the grassy ground, tucking my knees and rolling a few feet to avoid injury.

Amusement rippled off Aquila, and I flipped him the middle finger. This could easily get old. I gingerly got to my feet as Bayne raced up the hill to where I knelt.

He looked haggard. More haggard than when we'd pulled him out of the sea after Kayj. His eyes, while soft with relief, were dull and tired. Blood covered every inch of him as I scanned him for any signs of serious injury. A long gash starting at his neck stretched down the left side of him, leaving his leathers torn and bloody. He slowed and stopped a few feet away from me. Apprehension crossed his features, and I swear I could feel a little sliver of it come my way.

"Bayne," I croaked out, my voice broken and ragged.

He crossed the distance between us in seconds and had me in his arms. I melted against him, grabbing at his vest, crunchy with dried blood and mud. I held his head against mine, as his fingers laced in my bloody, sweaty hair. He pulled back, meeting my gaze and taking my hands in his.

"I'm sorry, Lyvia. I'm so sorry I didn't tell you. I—" he hesitated, voice wavering. Pain and regret rippled across his features. "I told you once I would do anything to save my people. And I think..." he paused, his throat bobbing. "I was scared. I feared what you could do. I'm so sorry. There's so much I need to tell you."

The forgotten blow of betrayal flooded back into my veins. I dropped his hands and pulled away, hurt replacing the relief I felt moments ago. But I needed him. Gods, I needed him so much. He held me in an unblinking gaze, and my mind drifted to the thoughts I'd had as I crashed toward the Juniper waves. Forgiveness would come... I loved him. We were alive.

I held his gaze, locking on to this strange, foreign connection and allowed the emotions to rip from my chest into his. Pain. Betrayal. Shock. Desperation. Fear. Love. *All of it*. He staggered back, gasping and blinking rapidly.

"No. More. Lies," I said, voice lethally quiet as I let the weight of his dishonesty slam him in the chest. "Ever."

Tiny tears welled in the corner of his eyes as he shook his head. "Never. Never again." His voice broke and he reached a hesitant hand toward me.

I kept my gaze hard but found myself reaching for him. I stared over his shoulder, scanning the valley for the rest of our friends. "The others?"

He stepped closer, pulling me into him. "The rest of the

crew is alive," he said, eyes heavy. "But the Rising..." He turned, eyes sweeping over the devastation that lay behind us.

My heart cracked at the sight. At the miles of ash that blanketed the fields between the camp and the forest. Guilt racked at my senses, and a wave of anguish crashed into me. The *rest* of the crew. I killed Oslo.

Bayne gripped my shoulders. "Look at me, Lyv," he whispered as his eyes pierced my soul.

"Look at me," he repeated, this time the authority of the captain voicing the command.

I dragged my gaze from the wreckage to his face. Tears wet my cheeks, and he took my face in his hands.

"You saved us, Lyv. Ronan thinks there are nearly six hundred Rising fighters left. If you hadn't harnessed the Obscura, *all* of us would be dead. That's six hundred lives."

"Yes, but—" I began as my voice cracked, thinking of the space that had obliterated both sides of the army.

He shook his head vehemently. "There is no use dwelling on it. You saved us. We would be dead if you hadn't."

"I'm... I'm so dark, Bayne. The power... What if... What if the reason it chose me is because my soul is dark. I killed Oslo. I killed my own—" I couldn't finish the sentence, let alone look at Bayne. I repulsed myself.

"Lyv," he said, taking my hands in his. He knelt before me, gazing at me with profound love.

I could *feel* it. It crashed into me with such force that I staggered back. It was like the scent of pine and a sea breeze as it brushed against my soul.

"Stars are lost in the light of day, Lyv," he said, taking my face in his hands. "You *need* the darkness to see them."

I blinked away the tears blurring my vision. His perfect lips tilted into a full grin, the white of his teeth stark against the blood and grime covering his face. He stared over my shoulder.

I felt Tiberius before I turned and took in his magnificence. Massive velvet wings tucked tightly into his sides as he clomped toward us. He'd grown in that moment we plummeted to the waves, now standing a few hands taller. His hooves left dinner plate sized prints in the mud.

"And it appears my angel has found her wings." He gave Ti a pat on the shoulder.

My eyes drifted to the outcropping of nearby trees, and I let out a gasp. Bayne followed my gaze, and I felt a wave of shock shudder against my own emotions.

The tiny buds of spring that had only just begun poking out of the branches were now stretched into broad, wide leaves that covered the trees in a shade of deep green. I blinked as something else drifted from Bayne. His power. Soleia. And something more. *Life.* I looked at him.

My love. Light *and* life.

CHAPTER FORTY-EIGHT

Gold is gone, and he has corrupted the Blue. Stay far away from the Land of Light and Life.

—Correspondence from White Hawk to Sea Spear. 53rd of Spring. 071.3E.

The elves silently moved through the birch white room with an ethereal grace. Long drapes of white silk replaced the usual leather pants and strips that covered their chests. The curved, wooden walls of the Gilded Fortress were as much alive as the trees that surrounded the green and gold palace.

They finished twisting my hair up in an elaborate knot of braids and curls, several little tendrils framing my face. I was dressed in sleeveless, black fabric that hugged every corner of my body with accents of golden leaves that snaked and twined around every curve. Elven royalty apparently couldn't envision me in anything but black, as I thought back to my time in the Crystal Castle. I shut out the memories that crept up.

"Black, to honor Tiberius," the queen's words echoed in my ears.

Golden thread, dotted with obsidian beads and amber sea glass, draped across my chest and over my shoulders, fastening in the back where a long, braided thread, weighted with an onyx stone dangled down my bare back. It stopped inches from where the fabric continued above my rear. I stared at myself in the mirror as one of them placed a delicate, golden tiara atop my head.

IT HAD BEEN three weeks since we'd arrived in Lotrennia. After getting wind of my show of power at the Rising's camp, King Saros had sent a third force of Sultiran soldiers. The kings-guards that rode us off the cliff had promptly returned to Aedrialis with the news. Queen Antares had sent only three-thousand elves to our aid, thinking it enough after Ronan had shared the Rising's initial numbers with her.

King Saros's force arrived not a day later with three times that. Ronan made the decision to withdraw, and the remaining six hundred Rising fighters boarded the last of our fleet, cramming into the white and gold Lotrennian ships before sailing across the Juniper Sea to take refuge in Lotrennia. By some miracle, Lord Pavel's fleet hadn't arrived to intercept us.

Bear had remained behind in Sultira. He couldn't leave Ezrich and Evony, and we couldn't wait for him, not without engaging in another battle we weren't prepared for.

With several mages on board, the trip should have only taken a week, but the sea had become violent, unexpectedly sinking several ships. Likely a result of the unprecedented twin eclipse that had occurred the day the ashen arrived in Sultira. No one could explain the arrival of the Sending two years early.

A calm sadness washed over me as the shores of Sultira sank out of view, but I knew we would return soon. My mind drifted to the promise I made to Ronan in those last hours before we left our home. The secret I agreed to keep. The only reason he agreed to board the *Evecta* with the rest of us.

It was a relief to be with the crew again on board the *Evecta*. Tiberius handled the journey well, taking every opportunity to shoot into the sky. Only the fearless agrippa could *thrive* on board a ship. I smiled to myself.

The crew had grown unusually quiet as we neared Lotrennian shores. Bayne hurled information at me the first night back on the *Evecta*. I'd felt his unrelenting guilt and grief ever since this connection had been unveiled, yet it didn't stop the bud of resentment and hurt that loomed in my chest from his betrayal. I had yet to fully forgive him.

He and Nerissa descended from an original Bellator: Kyson, the wielder of the sun power, Soleia. And as far as they knew, the Bellator powers could be wielded by powerful mystics, the way the dark king had wielded the two bones on his palms, or they could be *harnessed*.

Harnessing was always presumed to be genetic, but it didn't explain why I now had the power of two Bellators swirling in my veins. My fingers closed over the matching eight-pointed star on my right palm. The one that had shown up after the appearance of Tiberius's wings.

The powers mixed hesitantly in my veins, as if unsure of the other's presence. Everything Isla had taught me about the give and take made more sense now. The powers needed access to me, all of me, to manifest. Even the raw, ugliness of my soul that was tainted with death, with murder. Stained and shadowed and dark.

We stood at the stern of the *Evecta* as we approached the Queendom of Lotrennia. The land was like one giant emerald jutting out from a sea of sapphire. I'd never seen so much green in my life. Ferns of every size draped the coast, lost in a sea of deep green forest that stretched up into a sizable mountain range. A growing sense of unease twisted in my stomach as the features of eight massive stone sculptures became clear. Well, seven.

Seven sculpted Bellators stood hundreds of feet high in the air, arms raised in various formations, their harnessed powers etched in shields held against their chests. Kyson Ravindra, Bayne and Nerissa's ancestor, stood in the center. The twins had shared power since birth. And it explained not only Queen Antares's desire to extend the family bloodline, but also the unease the crew had with the approaching land.

Bayne and Nerissa's power was unexpected and had been hidden for most of their lives. The physical marking, a luminous eight-pointed star, twin to my own, sat camouflaged on their chests beneath black ink. The brilliant display of power at the Battle of Odessa was like a beacon to any being who could track power and explained the timeliness of the queen's ships.

My right palm tingled as I glanced at the statue standing next to the sun wielder. His shield depicted the shapes of two crescent moons. The symbol of change and transformation. The power of the seasons. The power I'd used to change Tiberius. *Transcindiel*.

And to his left... My stomach dipped. Where a tall, beautiful elf once stood was open air above a mound of demolished stone. Enya, the Betrayer. The one who was thought to have brought the destruction that split the continents in two and destroyed hundreds of thousands in the War of Ruin.

It was why Bayne and Nerissa and the entire crew had been hunting for the Obscura power. They'd intended to destroy it and anyone who might wield it. And now? Bayne loved me. There was no hiding his feelings now that the door to his emotions was open. I could feel what he was feeling, and he could feel me.

We weren't sure what it meant or if there was some unknown bond between Bellators, since I could feel Aquila and Tiberius too. Soulbinding between humans and elves was impossible, just like reproducing. And if it did have something to do with the Bellators... Nerissa remained completely blocked from me, which was okay. I worried if I *did* get a peek behind that curtain, I might find a beast waiting to tear me to bits.

We passed under the arc of crossed Bellator swords hundreds of feet above us and into an enormous turquoise lagoon where a party of elves greeted us at the docks, lined by hundreds of warriors on the shore. Nerissa stiffened next to me, and I didn't need to look at Bayne to feel the anger and anxiety rippling from him.

Queen Antares loomed at the center of the greeting party clothed in a resplendent white and gold gown with sparkling thread draped across her body, crisscrossing against her chest. A golden crown entwined with living white flowers and twisting greens sat upon her blonde curls and her blue eyes sparkled as they landed on me. The power in my veins rippled in response to my growing sense of apprehension as we stepped off the *Evecta* and into the land of the elves. The land of light and life.

I FLINCHED as the elf's fingers brushed against the scar on my neck as she fastened my earrings, moving a strand of hair out of the way. She hastily pulled her hand away, mumbling her apologies.

"I've got it," I said, picking up the earring and securing it. My eyes drifted to the ceiling-to-floor mirror that stood before me and blended perfectly into the wall of white, twining wood.

I took in my appearance, unable to help a tiny sliver of admiration escape my chest, despite the growing sense of self-hatred that continued to eat at me. Bayne's response hit me in an instant. *Anticipation. Longing.*

I held my gaze for a moment longer, mind drifting through the events of the last eight months. So much change. I barely recognized myself. My eyes scanned the bare skin between my breasts and on my hips, down to the slit in my dress. It snagged on the crescent-shaped scar on my breast that the elf had attempted to cover up using skin-colored paint before I shooed her off.

Some change was... unwanted. I took in the various scars now on display. The slice on my throat, always prominently displayed, shouting to the world I shouldn't be alive. Didn't deserve to be.

But some of the change was good, I noted, as my eyes slid over the toned muscles that rounded beneath my skin. My gaze rose to my eyes, and I caught a glimpse of strength in my reflection. A resiliency I could work on appreciating.

I shook my head, clearing it as I made my way down the winding staircase constructed from living, massive trees, twisting and hugging around the palace. I stepped into an open space where hundreds of silver-white trees stretched high into the air, their long, curling branches arching over the space ahead of me and entwining with those opposite the ballroom. Bits of light hung suspended in the air above a floor filled with elves dressed in similarly risqué gowns, more skin showing than I was used to seeing in a setting so formal.

I stood at the top of the natural staircase, looking down at the court. Queen Antares sat upon a throne of pure life.

Living flowers and vines of green and white twisted and twined up in the center of the dais where she sat ready to make her welcome to the refugees of Sultira. This place was pure light. Light and life everywhere. Not a scratch of darkness or death.

My eyes scanned the room, searching for the source of mixed emotions coming my way. *Anticipation, unease.* I spied the others in a corner off to the side. Nerissa and Isla were in stunning gowns of their own. Forest green silk hugged Nerissa's muscled body, the loose skirts rippling as she turned toward me. Her gaze softened as it landed on me. Sparkles of light danced off the strips of brilliant red fabric that stretched across Isla's petite curves, matching her lips perfectly, as she winked and raised a glass to me.

I grinned as I noted Vander, his arm tied up in a sling, shattered from battle, chatting with Vulcan and Drystan nearby. Off to the side, Ronan lounged against the wall in a dark blue formal jacket and pants and threw me a wink. Our conversation in the camp at Odessa had been... enlightening. Even without a bond in place, I could feel the angst and unease coming from the queensguard. The need to get back.

Marian remained onboard the *Evecta*, uneasy with our current residence and unable to stand my presence. I didn't blame her. I could barely stand it myself.

I continued searching for the one I knew I couldn't be without. Feeling his presence before seeing him, I turned to find Bayne standing next to me, eyes full of admiration. He was resplendent, regal, even, in the darkest green formal jacket and snug matching pants with black charcoal trim. His eyes narrowed in on me before he pulled me into a kiss so deep, I thought I'd drown in it.

Music began. Taking the arm he offered, he led me down the steps where the crowd parted and swept me into strong arms with a confidence in his step that made me feel as delicate as a flower. But I wasn't delicate. I was never delicate.

We twirled across the dance floor, others joining in the celebration as bodies whirled to the music around us until the entire ballroom had transformed into a sea of relentless movement.

Something lingered on the edge of my consciousness as my mind drifted back to the immense change that had occurred over the past year. The Transcindiel power sang in response as my mind spun, distracted from the beautiful array of people and colors twisting around us. I stopped mid-stride, a thought crashing into my mind like a bucket of cold water.

"Lyv?" Bayne asked as he stopped, brows pinched in concern.

My lips were numb with shock as I stood silently in the center of the ballroom, replaying every word Dark King Daimos had said to me.

And I can change... almost anything, Daughter of Darkness. Even people...

"I—" I began, looking at him.

A wave of curiosity and concern rippled to me. His hands slid to my shoulders.

"I can save them, Bayne," I breathed, and it felt as though time itself had stopped. He narrowed his eyes in confusion.

"I can save the ashen," I said, voice barely audible. The revelation sent a spike of thrill and elation that flew through my veins and sunk into my bones. The Transcindiel power sang in response, and I knew I was right. Dark King Daimos had used the bone to create them, to *change* them. If it was used to create them, surely, I could undo it. The elation was suddenly shrouded by a dark shadow as the gravity of my display of power on the fields of Odessa sank in.

We thought they couldn't be saved. I had slaughtered *thou-*

sands of them. A deep weight settled in my chest, the truth in their deaths utterly soul-shattering. I blinked through the tunnel vision that revealed the arrival of my panic. I took a steadying breath as darkness enveloped my soul and another, shameful thought crossed my mind. I could save *her*. And the notion of losing Bayne to the one he had loved might rip my selfish soul in half. Lida was alive. I somehow knew she wasn't in that ashen hoard in Odessa.

I could see Bayne understood the moment I did, and I whipped my mental curtain up before any more of my feelings could betray me. He gaped at me, speechless.

We stood for a moment, lost in each other's gaze, unnoticed by the spinning pairs moving to the music around us. Bayne could read me like a book, even if he couldn't feel my emotions.

As if it could stitch my soul that was tearing down the middle, his bright, fierce gaze pierced the darkness and shame. He gripped my chin, forcing me not to look away before his lips found mine. I let go of the pain, allowing myself to sink into the crushing kiss, lost in a sea of light while our souls shared this one tender moment.

Before it all changed.

CHAPTER FORTY-NINE
KING SAROS

The constellations can no longer be trusted.
—From A Historic Recounting of the Great Purification,
Chapter 89. Mount Telum, Aedrialis.

General Calvus sat before me in the Grand Council room, afraid to meet my eyes as he finished his briefing of the Battle of Odessa. I could barely control the fury after word had gotten out about Lyvia's escape and the news of Lotrennian ships. Fucking Antares. The nerve of the elf queen to sail to my shores and offer safe harbor to a doomed rebellion was inconceivable. She would hear about this. My eyes slid to the golden glow that pulsed in Aelius's orb, suspended in the center of the ornate table in the Grand Council room.

And Lyvia Cantor. My blood boiled as I replayed every conversation with the horse lord about his daughter. Had he known sooner? He wasn't a stupid man. But I'd *trusted* him. Trusted all his forbearers in the years since the Great Purification. Despite the question of his loyalty, his disappearance was disarming.

I hadn't thought twice about the young orphan he'd brought home from the north after his wife had died. Aeriden needed a sibling, and he was desperate to fill that hole that Lady Cantor had left. Lyvia had always been quirky and quiet. I had no problem approving his request to let her enter the Death Scholar order, and when she began locating the dig sites with such efficiency, High Priest Helmar created an elixir to heighten her senses. *Helmar*. He would take time to mend...

Our plans to squash the rebellion, or the *Rising* as that boy Sir Ronan had called it, were nearly successful. We'd taken out 80 percent of their forces, destroying almost all their ships. And a Rising for what? These people had no idea of the true threat. Our *real* enemy...

Images of the Messenger still haunted my dreams all these years later. The liquid silver of his eyes... We didn't have the time for this. Monthly tribute ships were the least of our problems. The *ashen* as they were called. And it was good to see the weapons in action, I supposed. A simple way to arm us against the inevitable retribution we faced. They would return. And when they did, Sultira would be ready.

Daimos only sent them to Sultiran shores because of the girl. He'd wanted to test her power, and sure enough, she put on a show. The Bellators had returned. Unease settled in my gut at the memory of their fall. Enya's fall...

General Calvus cleared his throat. I glanced up and caught the raised eyebrows of my young wife, looking at me expectantly. *Pay attention*, I could almost hear her say. Galena was different. Her stunning blue eyes had darkened, even those soft light curls seemed limp these days. She had taken the betrayal of her queensguard rather hard. She had been ill and barely left her quarters these past couple of months. Sir Ronan was supposed to be leading the hunt for the stones of power, a spy on the elf captain's ship. Justice would be swift for him. For all of them.

I nodded to General Calvus, dismissing him, before gesturing to the lowly Sky Scholar who had been monitoring the unnatural movements of our moons.

"Clear the room," I said to the others.

Galena eyed me, expecting me to allow her to stay.

"Everyone out." I shot her an apologetic smile.

Her eyes flicked briefly to the scepter leaning against my chair as she nodded, kissing the ring on my finger before exiting with the rest.

"What do you have for me?" I said, masking the anxiety in my voice with harsh malice.

The Sky Scholar wore the deep blue robes of his order and square spectacles. He could barely meet my eyes without cowering. He stepped forward and unrolled a large scroll with ancient markings on it from Enya's burial chamber.

Thankfully, Father Marcus hadn't recognized it for what it was, or he might have tried to hide it away, like the rest of them. The old man had lost his mind while studying the Obscura Stone before it was taken by Nivis. Rage thundered in my chest at the thought of it. We'd come so close to harnessing its powers, and it slipped through our fingers. Daimos played me.

I drew my attention back to the ancient scroll that lay before me as the scholar unrolled another that he'd marked up himself.

"Your Grace, I've been tracking the movements, like you

asked since last year when you procured this text," he began, motioning to the first scroll. "And your assumptions are correct. The movements of our moons, Renova and Ganmira, have shifted. Had you not asked me to look at the measurements using the Driadalis Scale, I wouldn't have spotted it. I've recorded the changes here." He motioned to the diagrams of celestial movements.

"There is a clear pattern. And it matches these movements exactly," he said, pointing to the ancient scroll. "And after the unprecedented twin eclipse two months ago..." he began, raising his eyebrows at me, "the early arrival of the Sending..." his voice wavered with excitement as growing apprehension settled in my gut.

"Continue, Father," I snapped, not bothering to keep the irritation from my voice. The Sky Scholar wilted as I narrowed my eyes on him.

"Yes, Your Grace, apologies. It's just," he said, clearing his throat, "nothing like this has ever been seen before and..." He paused, looking at me again before composing himself.

"We were able to trace a *magnetic* pull from the unnatural pattern of the twin eclipse to a location in the Lumerian Mountain range. It's baffling. I can't begin to understand what could have possibly influenced the two—"

"Where in the mountain range?" I cut him off, voice sharp.

He balked and picked up the additional scrolls he'd brought along, rifling through the papers.

"Um... The northern range. Not far from the port city of Odessa. Less than twenty miles away."

He unrolled a map and pointed a shaky finger to a spot near Odessa. The implications of the location sat in my gut like lead as rage sluiced through my veins.

Dismissing the Sky Scholar, I stood and called for General Calvus. I knew what I needed to do, and it didn't matter now how much strength it would take, even with my shield down. Her leash had been loosened, it would seem. And she had hidden it in plain sight. Under my nose for hundreds of years.

The three remaining fingers on my left hand skimmed over the map of the Lumerians. It was time to cut the head off the snake.

ACKNOWLEDGMENTS

Thank you to my husband, Michael. This book would not have been possible without you. You are my biggest cheerleader. Thank you for your endless encouragement. For the countless hours and weekends you spent with the girls to give me time to write. For being the first person to read this book and giving it 7/10 stars even when it needed so much work. Thank you for making it easy to write about falling in love. I love you mostest.

Julia. Thank you for your endless support. For reading this book three times before it was published. For cheering me on louder than anyone and for seeing it through all phases and giving me so much encouragement.

Jenna. Thank you for the snap chats, text messages, Marco Polos and coffee dates listening to me babble about this book. Thank you for reading and your amazing feedback, love and support.

Kate. Your friendship is one of the best things to have come out of 2024. I'm so grateful for you, your friendship, your pep talks and your incredible advice on both writing and motherhood.

My beta readers (Angela, Emily N., Abbe, Sara, Jenna, Julia, Tiff, & Kate). This book would not be what it is today without your feedback, encouragement and ideas. Thank you for taking the time to read the early drafts and help me work through the sticky parts. I will be forever grateful.

My street team (Callie, Ana, Julia, Wanda, Natalie, Caroline, Kate and Elora). Thank you for taking a chance on this book and all the incredible support you've provided in just a few months. I'm grateful to have connected with every one of you.

My PA, Emily. I'm incredibly grateful to have found you when I did. Your advice, support and friendship have meant so much to me. Not sure how I would have handled this launch without you.

My editors. Thank you, Jen, for your detailed review and the countless encouraging comments. Thank you, Alex, for challenging me to make Lyv even more relatable.

Rena, my talented cover artist. Thank you for making the most stunning cover for *Bones of the Bellators*. I could not have imagined a more perfect cover for this book, and I'm so incredibly grateful I've gotten to know you.

Esther. Thank you for bringing my characters to life. Lyv, Bayne, Ronan, Nerissa and Isla will forever live in my head in the way you created them.

Adam. Thank you for teaching me it's cool to be a nerd. For teaching me how to fight with a lightsaber and sharing your love of Star Wars.

Aaron. Thank you for taking me to see the Lord of the Rings in theaters 24 years ago and for joining me in Hobbiton 15 years later. I will never forget that trip.

Mom and Dad. Thank you for indulging in my love of horses and archaeology, encouraging me to follow my dreams and pursue my passions. There is no doubt in my mind that this book would not have been written if you hadn't raised me the way you did—instilling values like hard work, tenacity, and doing what you love. Thank you for reading me Harry Potter and teaching me to believe in magic.

C & V. Thank you for inspiring me to be better in every way. Everything I do is for you.

Lastly, thank you, reader, for diving into this world with me. I hope you enjoyed reading this book as much as I enjoyed writing it. And I hope you're ready for more adventures in the Realm of Vael.

ABOUT THE AUTHOR

A.M. Kay grew up in the Midwest where she spent countless hours on horseback, daydreaming about epic fantasy battles and studying archaeology. She has always had a profound love for reading and all things fantasy. She found her passion for writing in 2023 and believes it's never too late to chase your dreams. Her debut novel, *Bones of the Bellators*, is the first installment of the four-book series, The Nyxteria.

instagram.com/authoramkay

tiktok.com/@a.m..kay

threads.net/@authoramkay

TRIGGER WARNINGS

- Explicit language.
- On and off-page violence and killing of humans and other creatures, including animals.
- Depictions of battle and torture.
- Sexually explicit scenes (open door romance).
- Attempted sexual assault.
- Brief mention of childbirth.